MW01273081

Dudes and Savages
The Resonance of Yellowstone

There are in our existence spots of time,
That with distinct pre-eminence retain
A renovating virtue, whence...
                              our minds
Are nourished and invisibly repaired....

William Wordsworth, *The Prelude*

Richard Bevis

Memorials and Reconstructions II

Order this book online at www.trafford.com
or email orders@trafford.com

Most Trafford titles are also available at major online book retailers.

Front cover photo: "Remembrance: Bears and Dudes in Snow." Mixed media by Vivian Bevis.

Interior Illustrations: "Photographs by Richard Bevis, J. Edwin King,
and an anonymous savage or savages."

Printed in the United States of America.

ISBN: 978-1-4269-7399-4 (sc)
ISBN: 978-1-4269-7400-7 (hc)
ISBN: 978-1-4269-7401-4 (e)

Library of Congress Control Number: 2011911165

Trafford rev. 09/23/2011

 www.trafford.com

North America & international
toll-free: 1 888 232 4444 (USA & Canada)
phone: 250 383 6864 ♦ fax: 812 355 4082

Contents

For Peter, Lou, Will, Clay, and the savages of 1957

In Memoriam

Owl, Ray, Hole, and Woo

Author's Note

Any reader is entitled to ask any author what species of beast he has produced. Some friends who read early drafts of this book saw it as a novel. Though I can understand their reaction, that is not what I was trying to write. This is mainly a recreation of a particular summer in Yellowstone, using some fictional devices: chiefly the adoption of a third-person point of view, some liberties taken with dialogue and unvoiced thoughts, and the addition of a few characters who really should have been there. It is also a documentary about Yellowstone a half-century ago, with a chapter of history for context. A fictionalized memoir with historical-documentary pretensions, then: not a well-established type. Over the years it grew from letters and notes to a short story to various attempts to reconstruct the whole thing, of which this is absolutely the last. Perhaps it is also a screenplay looking for a producer. I doubt it, but stranger things have happened. (How's this for an opening shot? The viewer is in a jet or a helicopter, rising over waves of forested hills toward bare mountain uplands; finally we cross a pass and there before us spreads…Yellowstone Lake. Da-dah!)

I have added two chapters after the main narrative: a short story (#11) and an account of a return to the Park in memoir form (#12). Each provides a glimpse of the protagonist some years after the principal action, while #12 gives updates on other characters as well. The reader may take these chapters either as serial, consecutive disclosures, or as alternative scenarios for Mason, as the reader pleases.

Richard Bevis
Vancouver, 2011

A moose emerges on the bank after swimming the Gibbon River.

A savage checks the battery water as a dude checks the savage.

Looking east from Thumb's thermal field across
Yellowstone Lake to the Absarokas.

Gardiner, Montana, as it was.
The park's entrance monument is to the left.

Under arrest?
No. On our turf: the rangers need a lube job.

The savage versus the chamois wringer.

Three off-duty savages with wheels.

The bears meet the dudes in the snow.

Dudes and savages in the lanes during double shift,
when there is leisure to stand around.

The crew at the station.

One: Points of Departure

1 Genesis

For some it began on a hot June afternoon down in the Piedmont tobacco country. Sunbeams filtered through the shiny drooping needles of southern pines or slanted over their tops to light an old stone dormitory with a golden glow. A blue station wagon was parked in deep shade by its back stairs, upon which two students toiled like ants, scurrying in and out, up and down with suitcases, sleeping bags, cameras, a rifle, a fishing pole, a few books. The slumbrous murmur of insect life droned a background punctuated by distant cries from a few remaining idlers down in the brightness of the nearly-empty parking lot where - beyond the tracery of black tree trunks - a single red frisbee arced in the glare.

When the packers finished, sweating lavishly, there was no one around to say goodbye to - classes being over - so Mason backed the car out, stopped long enough for Cal to get in, and pulled out onto the campus circuit road. They drove past fraternity houses and tennis courts, up the hill by Freshman Field and down the far side, so that the Gothic towers of Debrew rose and then fell in the rearview mirror. After the bright new red, white and blue Interstate System marker, a stretch of smooth blacktop led down between red-clay embankments topped by dense stands of pine to the broad concrete sundazzle of the western highway. Squinting into all that brilliance, they fiddled with the new radio and speculated about what the summer might hold.

Mason, tanning his left forearm on the hot sill of the open window, reflected that what was finally getting under way had begun on a chilly morning the previous winter in the Placement Office. Rain beat against the panes and sluiced along the lead tracery of ogive windows tucked under the eaves of a drafty stone building named for a dubious benefactor. Nanny, the spinster placement secretary, flourished applications for jobs in Yellowstone Park, and enthused about a world beyond the dripping evergreens and the mists that drifted through them.

"Really, I don't see what's holding you back. I *know* it's not much money, but I've sent *dozens* of boys out there and they've all come back swearing by it, Mason."

"At it?"

"By it, I said." She tapped the forms into alignment and handed him a pen. Her glasses, suspended from her neck by a fine silver chain, rested on the long slope of her bosom. Mason thought both of a mother hen and the *alma mater* of collegiate myth, "stern yet tender."

"Eight or nine hours a day, six days a week, $115 a month," he recited in theatrical horror: temporizing, pen in hand, still unsure. "It's un-American, Nanny."

"I tell you, you'll *love* it out there. There's no other summer job like it."

"I can believe *that.*"

Nanny sighed stagily. "Virg, can *you* do anything with him? All he can think of is the *money.*"

"What's so un-American about exploitation, Mace?" Virg peered up through thick glasses, grinning genially but a double agent: fraternity brother *and* Park veteran, one of Nanny's agents. "Seriously, Mace, it's great country, you'll never forget it. Travel, girls, a little money: no reasonable man could ask for more. Wages are just compensation, you know, and who needs a lot of compensation with a set-up like that?"

Virg removed his fogged-up glasses to wipe them, Nanny beamed at his eloquence, and Mason, gripped by a sense of inevitability, shook his head and signed. "You silver-tongued devil." That was when he felt it begin, and he shivered in the damp chill. "My dad will have a fit."

Even as he spoke Mason knew *that* was wrong: successful Boston lawyers do not have fits. But Mr. Dixon believed that his son should be doing a summer internship at Copley, Dixon, and he found ways to make his disapproval known. A self-made southerner who had married into a good Beacon Street family and law firm, he had a keen sense of the value of time and the hazards of drifting. Mason's return to the south whence he had extricated himself displeased him. The boy should have gone to Harvard; he was wasted at Debrew, and probably playing around. Almost the only playful act of Mr. Dixon's life had been the naming of his son. That name, together with his Bahstan accent and gangling frame, ensured that he would stick out at Debrew.

"How did you get involved in this project, Cal?"

"Oh, Virg talked me into it." Cal flashed his sharp-edged smile. "How 'bout you?"

"The same. And what is it...three others that we know of? If it doesn't work out he'll be facing a lynch mob."

Cal laughed silently for a moment, head thrown back, then turned toward his window. He came at Debrew from a sharply different angle: small-town, middle-class South Carolina. From where *his* father stood - a drugstore - Debrew looked like a very good choice, an accomplishment. Mr. Davis knew, and everyone said, that Cal would make his way. He was hard where he needed to be, formidably bright, a Physics major, and something about him said Don't Tread on Me. If he had a fault it was that he drove himself too hard and seldom relaxed - like my father, Mason thought. Mr. Davis believed that a low-key summer in Yellowstone, away from books and science labs, was no more than he had earned. Cal leaned his head against the humming window and let his body unwind in the hot sunshine.

*

For others, the points of departure were vastly different. Four Angelinos painted *Yellowstone or Bust* on the trunk of a recently-purchased junk heap and tried to figure out how to remedy its most serious defects. Up in Vancouver, a budding journalist boarded Canadian Pacific's Transcontinental: the first leg of a trip to report on Yellowstone Park for a kindly editor. A farm boy hung around the freight yard in Sioux City, uneasily waiting for darkness so that he could start riding the rails west. At the Memphis train station, Beatty was saying goodbye to his parents on the platform where the St. Louis train was about to depart, while Pris (voted "Most Likely to" by the yearbook staff, but the faculty advisor nixed it) said a passionate farewell to her disgruntled boyfriend at the Tempe bus depot. And in Oklahoma - or maybe California - a swarthy young man of Cherokee blood climbed onto a train and waved to his family, standing in the sun on the dusty platform and shading their dark eyes.

2 Exodus

The low sun was blinding by the time Mason took the Catawba exit to rendezvous with the rest of the party. The Vines lived a few blocks from downtown, in a brick bungalow with picture windows, a manicured lawn and two concrete strips for a driveway. They parked behind Virg's natty green-and-white Ford coupe. Mrs. Vine, all plumpness and hospitality, almost filled the doorway as she cried a welcome, but Mason caught a glimpse of something more interesting behind her. "Who's the blonde talent?" he asked.

"That's Cleve's sister Polly," said Cal. "Still in high school. A nifty girl with a classy chassis: you'll like her."

"I don't doubt it." They opened the screen door and went in, Cal introducing Mason to Mrs. Vine, who returned to the kitchen. In the living room were familiar faces: Virgil Vine (usually "Butterball" but currently "our leader"), Cleve Clifford, aka "Polly's brother," Peter Trueblood, and Marsh - all fraternity brothers. They stood on deep pile carpets in a shallow arc facing Polly, perhaps a bit overdressed for the occasion in frilly black blouse and sheath skirt, Mason thought, but certainly no disappointment at close range. Her blue eyes shone with excitement at being surrounded by *college men*, all of whom except her brother were rocking on the balls of their feet as they jockeyed for position. When the newcomers arrived, the inside track seemed to belong to the rugged, handsome Trueblood, a man of few but telling words, while Virg, always diffident around pretty girls, and the sallow, sardonic Marsh, also ran. Cal, as short and thickly bespectacled as Virg but lean and smooth, presumed on prior acquaintance to claim a brotherly hug from the princess. Cleve looked on with amused protectiveness. "Dinner!" trilled Mrs. Vine.

As they ate fried chicken and potato salad from paper plates and drank iced tea, the conversation turned to arrangements for riding west. When Peter announced that he had agreed to ride with Virg, Mason stopped eating, wiped his mouth and quietly asked Cal when his contract would begin. They had all signed up for different dates.

"Eighth of June."

"Mine's not till the 9th. Maybe you should go with Virg, too. His car is faster, and I'm in no hurry."

"Sure, okay by me," said Cal, working on a drumstick.

"Virg, how many do you want to take?"

"Oh, I think four at most in the Tudor, Mace."

"Cleve, you and Polly want to travel together, right? Then you'd better come with me: five would be an overload for Virg." The others looked at him, catching the drift.

"I'll be damned," laughed Marsh. "How about me? Did I figure in your calculations?"

"You'd better go with Virg, Marsh. I'm picking up a rider in Asheville tonight. That way there'll be four in each car." He couldn't quite suppress a satisfied smile.

Cleve cleared his throat. "That'll be fine, Mason." Then there was silence.

"Anyway," Mason added after a few seconds, "as far as lodging is concerned, Polly can be...suitably accommodated at the Dixon estate in western Tennessee - I mean, my grandparents will put her up. I'm planning to stop there tomorrow night." He gestured to the west.

"Oh?" and "Aha!" said Virg and Peter simultaneously, exchanging a look. Mason seemed startled.

"And where do they live, Mason?" asked Cal with a grin.

"In Obion."

"A fine town, I'm sure," giggled Marsh. Just like Mason, he thought, to overreach himself.

"Well, um, it's a pretty small house, actually, and I don't know...they're getting on..." He trailed off lamely and issued no invitation, but saw how it would be. Damn his blabbermouth: this need not have happened!

After dinner, Cal shifted his baggage from the station wagon to the coupe, Cleve and Polly put their things in Mason's car, and the three of them prepared to depart. "Thanks, Mrs. Vine, and goodbye, everyone," said Mason.

"Don't say goodbye, say *au revoir*," crowed Marsh as they rolled away, and the others laughed.

It was almost a hundred miles to Asheville, but they were off at the best moment of a southern summer. The warm twilight was rich with the fragrance of freshly-mown, sprinkler-moistened grass and - for those in the car - of the gardenia in Polly's hair. On her right, Cleve, tall and slender, surveyed the billboards and pastures and ruddy farmland rolling past, wondering, perhaps, if his high grades in pre-med chemistry courses could lift him above all this. With his horn-rimmed glasses down on his nose he looked severe and watchful - a scholarly Argus, thought Mason. Another South Carolina science whiz! He inhaled of the gardenia and grinned over at the averted head; Polly, catching his look, smiled enigmatically. Was that a slight press of thigh? Probably just his imagination - or *his* pressure - but they were getting on well, mostly talking about school. Might she come to Debrew? Well, she would like to, but her parents were talking about the state system for her: having two children in an expensive private university at once would strain their finances. Cleve stayed out of the discussion. In the dashboard the wonderful new speaker was vibrating to the passionate thumps of Li'l Richard down in Atlanta.

5

Out on the Interstate they could see in the last light stormclouds piled on the Smokies, and rain began to fall at dark. Engine laboring, gears grinding, the car climbed the long curving grades. Mason had had his used car only a few months; this was, would be, its biggest test yet. The right headlight turned out to have no low beam, and the windshield leaked a bit on the driver's side. This was not as much fun as sniffing a gardenia! Concentrate, he told himself. By the time they located Chris's address on a hilltop outside Asheville it was past 10 and they were all road-weary. Mason parked under a dripping oak next to the two-story frame house and switched off with a groan. Polly cooed sympathetically; Cleve snorted, waking bewildered. Then the kitchen door opened: Chris and his father, Reverend Jordan, stood silhouetted in a warm yellow rectangle.

The men carried suitcases in through the downpour while Mrs. Jordan fussed over Polly and patted her dry in front of an electric fire, a scene that warmed Mason's imagination. Once she was installed in the guest room, he and Cleve were shown to a loft with two cots and not much else, except a copy of *The Upper Room* on the bedside table. Chris, a shy freshman with bad acne, shifted his feet and gaze constantly, to all appearances the outsider here. He had asked the Debrew Placement Center to find him a ride, and this was the result. It had seemed a good idea to Mason at the time to have a paying passenger; only now did he feel its awkwardness. But a free night was not to be scorned! The Reverend, who looked as forlorn and unprepossessing as his son, was apologizing for the room's bareness and Mason was half-heartedly denying it when Cleve slumped onto the bed with a sigh. Their relieved hosts excused themselves promptly and in five minutes both travelers were asleep in their underwear. Mason's last thought was of the Bedouin, who were said to make the first stage of any trip a half-day, and that this had been a *long* half-day.

The storm passed during the night. In the hot fresh early-morning sunlight, Mason was trying to patch the leak around the windshield with friction tape when Polly joined him, sandy hair brushing his shoulder, looking up trustfully when he glanced down. Her square, healthy face looked even better outdoors than in, he thought. A few freckles, but good lines: the girl next door, with sex appeal. Doris Day! "The marrying kind." But I ain't the guy next door.... Inarticulate through his reverie, Mason became aware that she was speaking to him, saying polite things about his clumsy patch. Ah, the southern belle and her winning small talk: admired and envied for the hundredth time. Noting where the tape crimped making a corner, forming a perfect little rain catchment, he could not bring himself to agree, or disagree, but heard himself saying, "Today's my birthday."

"Oh?!" Polly leaned forward, seemingly about to bestow a birthday kiss, then drew back and looked down. The moment had passed. Later that day, in a small-town diner across the mountains, she produced a roll of film for his Brownie Hawkeye, tied round with a red ribbon. For an instant Mason thought that *he* might contrive an impulsive thank-you kiss, but that occasion passed too, and he wondered why. They had read *Paradise Lost* that year, and he remembered Adam telling the angel how abashed he felt in Eve's presence. He had known at once what Milton had gone through! But here it seemed a question of context, of atmosphere: a parson's neglected premises in one case, a dark-paneled drugstore café in the other; backcountry Presbyterians staring at a northern license plate; impoverished mining towns strewn among the verdant Smokies like fragments of eggshell. At that time, in that place, you didn't kiss a girl you met only yesterday. And if either kiss had transpired, who can say how their futures might have been different? Our destinies are finely balanced.

During the afternoon, as they swooped down through the red-clay foothills of east Tennessee, thundershowers bowled in from the west, leaving big pools of muddy water in the road's low spots. The Interstates had not yet reached this far. Once a trailer-truck just ahead threw a thin sheet of mud across the windshield and the speeding world disappeared for an instant. Mason stomped his left foot on the push-pedal window-cleaner, which sprayed enough water for the wipers to wash an opening, and visibility returned just in time: an oncoming car shot by on a narrow bridge. Mason and Cleve exchanged raised-eyebrow, eye-rolling glances. West of Knoxville the country leveled out and the clouds fell behind. Then on a flat stretch the left rear tire blew out with a mighty bang at 70 mph. Polly squealed and clutched Chris, who froze. There was a soft, slow weaving of the back end, like a hurt snake, but no skid, and they stopped safely. "Is someone trying to tell us something?" asked Cleve. Yet after changing the shredded tire they went on through the halcyon evening at a good clip, the car running quietly and well, with bluegrass coming in loud and clear from Nashville on the best of all possible radios.

They entered Obion, after one more deluge, at twilight, and in a few more minutes pulled up before the brick bungalow with a white porch on Church Street. Mason's grandparents, looking a bit frail, older than he remembered and very glad to see him, came out to the curb. "Did you get my letter, folks?"

"Yehs, grahnson. We were 'bout to staht worryin'." Mason blinked: it had been awhile since his last contact with that gentle drawl, that slightly old-world formality, and he wondered, as he hugged Gran and shook Grampa's hand, how the quite different worlds of Obion and Debrew would get along.

"Sorry, we had a flat tire. These are my friends. Polly... and Cleve, her brother, from Columbia, South Carolina."

"Ah," said Gran warmly, always quick to detect an acceptable relationship or approved family structure.

"And Chris Jordan, from Asheville."

"How do you do, son?" They all went inside, talking of the car and the trip, to the chintzy furniture and colonial Victorian bric-a-brac, familiar to Mason from childhood summers. He was starting to tell them about the other car when the phone rang. Grandad Dixon answered, but then offered the receiver to Mason. "For me? Hello?"

"Hi, Mace!"

"Oh hi, Virg! Uh, where are you?"

"Well, you know, we find ourselves on the outskirts of the great metropolis of Obion, and with dark coming on we thought we'd call our ol' buddy Mace." Guffaws and giggles were audible in the background. Then, reproachfully: "But Mace forgot to tell us his granddad's first name! Do you know how many Dixons there are in the Obion phone book?"

Mason flushed and stammered. "Gee, Virg, it's kind of a small house, one bathroom, or you know..." But his grandmother was at his shoulder, saying, "Awways room fo' yo' friens, grahnson," and the little voice in his ear was insisting that they could sleep on the floor, and a night's lodging wasn't peanuts. In the end, fairly trapped, he issued a lame invitation, and directions.

Virg's car drew up outside in a few minutes. The Dixons welcomed this second wave with undiminished hospitality, inviting everyone inside "if yawl ken *fiyut*." Mason's fears of a culture clash underestimated the well-oiled machine of southern manners; despite the numbers and various disparities the household bustled along smoothly, the Dixons treating the collegians like overgrown grandchildren and the students accepting the role. Mason was amazed at how polite and well-behaved his friends could be. Gran joked with Polly as they cooked ("You'll cernt'ly have a tahm rahdin' cross the country with awl these baweez"), while Granddad and Chris had a long talk about the future of the church - that is, of its Methodist and Presbyterian sects. At 10 PM Gran allocated sleeping places to the boys in a rattling fashion ("and one unduh the dahnin' table") while they laughingly complied; Polly, of course, had the guest room. Soon the darkened front rooms were a mass of huddled sleeping bags. When the others were settled Mason lay down on the front porch swing where he had rocked as a child and slowly relaxed into the lulling warmth. They had crossed their eastern mountains and were ready for the Big Muddy. Not a bad birthday. He drifted off to the slow blink of lightning bugs and the steady sawing of crickets.

*

Beatty and Henderson, who had met on the train, had an evening in St. Louis before their bus left and were looking for a bar or a brothel, whichever came first. Bastille had met a friendly divorcee as the Canadian Pacific train wound through the Rockies, and was considering her suggestion to break his journey in Calgary. A cool daddy in Daytona Beach had a final date with the Orange Bowl Queen and flaked out on a transcontinental Greyhound. A taciturn Wisconsinite named Hayward was already pumping gas at West Thumb, the only worker to appear so far. Pris, stretching her trim legs in Jackson Hole, had a line on a ride to the park. Out in Palo Alto, Will Harkness was memorizing his valedictory as the class walked through a boring rehearsal for graduation: the last event before he headed for Yellowstone.

3 Breaking Free

The morning was clear, then hot, then humid, as the sun drew moisture from the swamps and tall grasses of the low-lying countryside. Shortly after first light, Mason was awakened by a vision: Polly in a white summer blouse and khaki skirt, bringing him coffee. She even sat beside him on the swing and made conversation as he sipped. That was nice. Then he remembered the shredded tire: he would have to go and find a replacement first thing. Damn! Excusing himself with genuine regret, Mason went inside and through the waking crowd to find his grandfather. Together they drove the Ford down to Dixon Motors, the family's car and tractor dealership. Mason was amazed to find Uncle Wilbert - generally considered quite a dim bulb - apparently running the place. But he was as welcoming as always, and a new Goodrich tire was made available for only $20 - a suspiciously good price that he did not question. A mechanic mounted and installed it for him, disposed of the ruined tire, and restored the spare to its place, all free of charge. Family counted down here.

By the time they returned from town, Polly was helping to serve breakfast, her scoop-necked blouse falling slightly open as she bent over each diner, seemingly unconscious of the power of her curves. How to reconcile that constant sensual force with the demands and constraints of society - *that* was the trick! Her talk and laughter were mostly with Peter. Mason consoled himself by reflecting that such views would be *his* from here on, and by pushing for an early departure. Soon after breakfast they all went out to the concrete sidewalk, already heating up for the day; a few elderly neighbors looked on from shaded porches. The Dixons received a spontaneous round of applause at parting, whereupon Gran shed a few tears and told Mason he had "nass southun friends." She and Granddad stood on the curb as if on a pier, looking frailer and older than just the day before, as the cars pulled away with throaty roars.

"Real fahn folks, Mason," said Cleve, still waving out the window. "No wonder you're such a *decent* Yankee. Why did your branch of the family move north, anyhoo?"

"Not my family, just my father. Went to Harvard law school, did well, got a good job in Boston. Married the boss's daughter: patrician family." He paused to consider. "So if you're looking for motive, I'd say economic opportunity." This was received in silence. He glanced across and Cleve nodded, pursing his lips.

And then they were really away, driving northeast through the lush Mississippi bottomlands. Not far outside Obion the green Tudor passed the station wagon with much honking and waving. "That's the last we'll see of them until Wyoming," Mason predicted. It sounded more triumphant than he had intended, and the others looked surprised. The morning was exceptionally fine, they were cooled by the wind of their passage, and he felt more exultant than even a free hand with Polly could explain. Well, his last family tie had been cut! He had never been this much on his own before, had never set out anywhere without some watchful authority or educational goal waiting for him at the far end. This time, by God, there was nothing to limit or define him: only what he might make of the time and place. *This* was his birthday! He burst into song - "Let us take - the - road!" - startling his friends again. "The highway hath its own poetry," he explained. Cleve raised his eyebrows. He sometimes wondered if Mason, a Psych major, was entirely stable.

They angled through corners of Kentucky and Illinois, crossed the Ohio River and then, at Cape Girardeau, the Mississippi. "Muhsouruh," announced Cleve. "I pronounce this trip officially open."

"Oh, it *is* a mal wahd!" squealed Polly. "It *mus'* be!"

"In the west and on our own!" crowed Mason. "Who could ask for anything more?" Even Chris looked happy and hummed what might be a hymn. The day and the world seemed made for them, though after the dew burned off the cornfields the sun felt hot. They weren't all 21, but they *were* free and white and (marginally) solvent, and had a car and couldn't lose. When low on fuel they chanced on a gas war outside Jackson and filled up on regular at 19 cents a gallon. Later, in the Ozark hills west of Flat River, the radio picked up the "die-rect, awn-the-spot" broadcast of some burg's centennial jamboree, complete with cornball emcee, hillbilly guitar and fiddle, and contests for hog-calling and husband-summoning: "Heeey-YUH, Hiiirum! Yew come awn in heah out uv the south fohty rat naow ifn yuh wawnt yuh vittles!" It was the perfect accompaniment to their euphoria, the engine was humming like a Rolls Royce, and the car's lightness as it crested the hills made Mason giddy.

*

At this hour on the 5th of June, Ray's battered Dodge pickup - its temperature gauge poised between yellow and orange - was roaring across the Great Plains a few hundred miles west. Watching the gentle swell and fall of the prairie, Ray thought how closely it resembled the breathing of a great animal, and wished that Hole, stretched out on the front seat, wouldn't snore so much. Well, he needed the sleep, but someone had to be strong. Out in Palo Alto, Will was rising to deliver his valedictory address. Up in Calgary with his new friend, Bastille was going nowhere fast; maybe his editor would like a piece on divorced women in Alberta. Pris was checking in at the Ham's store in West Thumb, and across the road the service station, staffed by the manager, assistant manager, and Hayward, was serving a few early-season customers.

*

Meantime the station wagon was progressing slowly through a region of queer little hills - so abrupt that Mason would lean forward and peer over the hood before starting down - from whose tops they could see dark mounds heaped among the trees like volcano cones. Then came a black

11

metal frame over the road, proclaiming POTOSI – CAPITAL OF THE LEAD BELT. They idled slowly down Main St. - i.e. the highway, the only pavement in town - looking for a diner, conscious of stares. Dirt alleys opened off Main St. at irregular intervals; in the middle of each was a white post with some stenciling. The first read: NO MOTOR VEHICLES Town Ord. 137; the second, NO MOTOR VEHICLES Town Ord. 138, and so on. "I *have* to see more of this burg," declared Cleve. "There's food across the street." The locals lucky enough to be on hand watched the parking and locking of the car with the kind of silent attention usually given in westerns to the arrival of a noted lawman or desperado. Hands hung loosely by their thumbs from coverall tops; children peeked from behind mothers' skirts; even the chawing stopped.

The strangers crossed the street and entered a pink clapboard café whose signboard advertised a lunch counter. Its windows and shadowy interior were adorned with tobacco and cattlefeed ads, painted in garish colors on metal plaques; flies droned heavily while antique fans wheezed at dead slow. There wasn't room at the counter so they sat at a table. The waitress took their orders with a straight face, pretending not to know they were celebrities. When she withdrew, the heavy silence of the place began to infect them with giggles and they had to avoid meeting each other's eyes. Somehow laughter seemed sinful, heretical. A heavy-set fellow in the corner with a deputy sheriff's star on his shirt pocket kept looking them over. Best be careful. Foreigners in town. You never know. When the cokes and sandwiches finally came, they ate quickly, paid in small bills and left. Again heads turned slowly, like sunflowers on their stalks. The visitors did not resume normal breathing until they had pulled away from the curb and picked up speed. *"Lord,"* exclaimed Cleve when a wake of concrete was again flowing out behind them, "I bet they could float a new municipal bond issue now!" They all laughed, relieved to be out.

"I've read about limited gene pools," Mason reflected, "but this is the first time I've seen one."

As they neared the Missouri River there was more radio entertainment: a revival, quavering with evangelical fervor. *"Yes* Lord!" from the preacher, "Amen brother hallelujah Jesus *save* my soul" and so on from the congregation. Mason shook his head. "Pretty limited stock of ideas, I'd say."

"Oh come on," rejoined Cleve, who was driving. "Enter into the spirit of the Bible Belt. When in Rome, and all that." He began to pound time on the steering wheel and proselytize the passing countryside: "Yes, Lord, make it pay! Jesus saves, so will I! All-mighty dollar!" Ignoring Chris's forced smile, Mason reached back for his guitar and picked up the beat. Polly dug into her art supplies and lettered a big sign on a sheet from her drawing tablet:

SAVE-A-SOUL
MOBILE UNIT

Cleve pulled off on the shoulder so Mason could tape the sign to the right side of the car. Stepping outside, he was staggered by the fecund, sunflooded landscape - heatwaves boiling off the pavement, cicadas shrilling in the cornfields, birdsong from the beech woods farther back - but the sensation was brief: in a moment he was back in the car and they were rolling through central Missouri in their steel cocoon. While Chris squirmed, the others sang and shouted - until a State Police cruiser hove into view astern. Cleve slowed a bit and Mason hauled in the sign. They sat ramrod-straight and unsmiling as the car pulled alongside and hovered there. Faces and necks red, mouths thin-lipped, the officers checked them out from behind sunglasses. Had they tailed the Massachusetts car from Potosi, or was that paranoia? Was it only this morning that they had felt so free? After a few seconds the cruiser shot ahead. "Talk about seeing through glass darkly," muttered Cleve. Chris laughed - perhaps thinking that this was just retribution for sinners - but the mood in the wagon had sobered considerably.

They entered Kansas City at nightfall. It took an hour to find a reasonably-priced motel that Cleve considered "clean enough for Polly." Mason and Chris decided to sleep in the car when they heard the price, but first availed themselves of shower privileges. While Chris was scrubbing, Mason called home collect to check in, not knowing what the phone situation might be in Yellowstone, but soon wished he hadn't. His grades had arrived and they were not great. It was awkward, with Cleve and Polly in the room, to respond as his parents read out his grades (with commentary), asked about his social life and reminded him to write. "Yeah, okay. Me too. Sure will. You too. Byebye." He put down the phone with a 'whoof,' glad to break the connection, and grinned foolishly. "Think there's a steak house around here?"

"Let's see, will there be a steak house in Kansas City?" mused Cleve. "Tell you what: if we can't find one we ought to be locked up as mental defectives." They did indeed find a place within walking distance that supplied succulent juicy steaks at bargain prices, but what struck them most was that the room was organized around a great, gleaming stainless steel vat that dispensed glasses of the best cold milk any of them had ever had. Steak and milk! Truly, Kansas City *was* up to date, and easterners could learn from it.

After they returned to the motel and split up for the night, Chris and Mason talked for awhile before drifting off to sleep in the car: the most conversation they had ever had. Mason decided that there was more to Chris than he had realized, and hoped that Chris understood he was not the enemy of *all* religion. But when he mentioned that he was going to take a course in Non-Christian Religions, the younger man asked, seemingly without irony, "And what would they be?" Still, it's hard to spend a night in the back of a car with someone and not get to know them better.

*

Behind them, in a suburb of St. Louis, the "Best-Liked Boy" in his high-school class hugged his mother and sister and found a seat on the daycoach bound for "Independence and West." An engineering student from Ohio was tuning his pride and joy for the western expedition, and down in West Virginia a pre-med hopeful sank what he could afford in a used Chevy coupe. A young woman in Tucson caught the bus for Denver and points north. Girls from swish colleges in Columbia and Colorado Springs borrowed one of daddy's cars and set out for Wyoming in company with a plainer girlfriend. Bastille had left the affectionate divorcee (promising to stop on his way back) and was hitchhiking to Gardiner. Three Mormon girls from Logan assigned to missionary work in Yellowstone flew to Idaho Falls and caught a ride the rest of the way with a boy from a good LDS family there, but after they stayed two nights in Jackson one of the girls flew home and the other two weren't speaking. All across the continent they were cutting loose, breaking free, declaring independence. Fields of energy were starting to implode on the Park from every direction. What seemed to the Debruvians an exodus was really a gathering, a calling together of five thousand fledgling bodies and souls clamoring for food, though most of them knew no more of each other and the big picture than do electrons hurrying to their destinies.

*

14

West of Kansas City the roads ran north-south or east-west. Making good a northwest diagonal track meant going north then west, north then west, miles out of a direct route (Cleve informed them that having to go around two sides of a square instead of taking the diagonal added about one-third to the mileage, which didn't help morale at all). As the station wagon toiled through the corny state its occupants grew restive. The feeling of having a long way to go in a short time had come upon them - Cleve's contract would begin in two days - so they cursed the serrated route and fretted at the heat and the passing minutes. The sun was high over wheat and corn country, gently rolling endless miles of it, one prairie town and silo after another. Now and then they sang to keep up their spirits -

an' the wheat fields wavin', an' the dust clouds rollin' —

but they were tiring of the drive and each other. Even Polly and Mason, who had been flirting energetically for two days, became listless and sulky under the slow burn. The romance of the road had gone flat. At lunchtime, a little west of Lincoln, Nebraska, they ate quickly in a small diner and hurried back to get the ovenlike car rolling again. Two lanes of unevenly-patched concrete (*Ta-pocketa-pocketa-queep-pocketa-queep*) stretched to the ever-receding horizon.

After they crossed the Platte River and joined Route 30 at Grand Island, though, conditions began to improve. The road followed the river's gentle arc through verdant countryside - a great relief after the unvarying baked plains - and, better still, after a southwesterly dip it *curved* northwest toward Yellowstone. The car hummed along over smooth, recently-laid asphalt, and the heat began to abate. As the declining sun lengthened the shadows, the lines and colors of the landscape softened; long grasses waved by the roadside, and sycamores hung gracefully over the brown river's sluggish current.

"It's like a painting, or the Pastoral Symphony," enthused Mason. "In *Fantasia*, anyway."

Cleve frowned toward the radio, blaring #28 (#24 last week) on the country and western hit parade. "Yeah. But how can you think of Beethoven over that?" Mason nodded and switched it off.

Beyond North Platte the open rangeland to the north began to look the way "the West" *should* look, but the horizon remained as distant as ever and the miles of brute space went on and on, wearing them down. In a truck-stop café - a bright island surrounded by semi-trailers in the dusk

15

- they ate western omelets and discussed what to do next. For Cleve's sake, mainly, they needed to get farther that day, but suitable accommodation could be a problem. Cleve had picked up a list of Best Western motels in Kansas City, so he called ahead to the next one and made a reservation. It was in Torrington, Wyoming - still a couple of hours west.

They pushed on after dark with Chris at the wheel, Cleve riding shotgun. Near Scottsbluff they heard thunder rolling in the distance, and soon sheets of rain were splashing off the highway and driving at the windshield. Mason thought of taking over from the freshman, but it seemed too blatant a vote of non-confidence. The darkness was total except for their headlights - and the lightning. Every few seconds a vivid and prolonged flash would illumine miles of level plateau, a telephone pole and maybe a farmhouse, stark as a woodcut, all of which seemed to be annihilated by a tremendous thunderclap that followed immediately. Then they would again be alone with the torrents of rain in their moving circle of light. Polly and Mason were close together in the back seat, getting better acquainted. She confided in a whisper that she was terrified of lightning ("Don't tell Cleve how *silly* I am"), and cowered against him as a triple fork jerked down to the horizon. Mason found her fear and trust, her stroboscopic beauty, and the very *girlness* of her irresistible; he hugged her during the flashes and spoke soothingly between thunderclaps. This was just the kind of situation he had been hoping for. But the excitement carried him away. When a big bolt shredded the air and whumped the ground just ahead and right so that the car actually jumped, Polly screamed, and Mason tried to kiss her still-open mouth. "I didn't *mean* to bite you," she whispered later, giving him a peck on the cheek. The storm passed as they crossed the state line and entered Torrington, all too soon for Mason, but it was 10 PM before they found the motel. "Thank God," said Chris as he shut off the engine, and he meant it.

4 Immigration

Four hundred miles west, Yellowstone was beginning to quicken with its summer life. At the South entrance, Dan was relaxing on his bunk in the ranger cabin, reading a book by John Muir, having used his afternoon off to look for glacier lilies on Mt. Sheridan. Up at West Thumb, Hole was meeting his roommate, a bronzed, smiling native named L. B. Horn. "What's the L. B. stand for?" he asked.

"Little Big," replied Horn, flashing good teeth as he dropped his handgrip satchel onto the empty cot. Hole grinned appreciatively and Lou Fuller, the manager, slapped his thigh. "No shit? That's rich!"

Hayward came shambling in from the room next door and stuck out his hand to Horn. "Be good to have the help," he grunted. "Been workin' alone till Hole come."

Lou looked at his watch. "Wall, gotta go, jemman. Gotta late date."

Hole raised his eyebrows. "That Prissy chick?" Lou chortled. "Heavy. Hey but man, where ya gonna go? It's *cold* out there."

Lou grinned. "Jes' rat fer a *coolie*...yuh know, a quickie in the snow?" He snorted and went out, hurrying to make hay before his girlfriend arrived.

Across the Divide at Old Faithful, Ray was strolling through the geyser basin to get the effect by intermittent moonlight. Up in Gardiner, Morley Callahan, personnel manager for the Yellowstone Park Concession Corporation, having put in a good long day of checking supplies, contracts, uniforms, and station assignments, was sipping his usual at the Town Café, and bending the young waitress's ear about the declining morals and musical tastes of her generation. His topic tonight - the Peeve of the Eve, as the staff called it - was this new upstart Elvis. "Of all the," it began.

Meanwhile the implosion continued. Virg, Peter and Marsh were sitting at a big hardwood table at Curly's in downtown Casper, watching Cal make time with an older woman at the bar and looking forward to an easy day into Yellowstone. Marsh and Peter were debating the relative merits of drinking and abstention as they sipped beer and cider, respectively.

And in Rapid City, South Dakota, the Best-Liked Boy from Greenville, Missouri, was back at his hotel after seeing *Picnic* for the second time. While picking out the theme music on his accordion, he was also trying to fit his parents and his minister into the same universe as the scene where William Holden strips off his shirt above a reclining Kim Novak under a big shade tree in a meadow. Gair was sure that they would disapprove of it, but wondered if they would understand the strong, complicated emotions it aroused in him - stronger now, seeing it by himself, than when he watched it with his wide-eyed date back home. There came a rap on the wall and he closed the accordion. Just as well: the train for Gardiner would leave early.

*

Mason's carload awoke late, still groggy from having driven 700 miles the day before. They located a grill on the corner of First and Main, where none of them said much except "Scrambled eggs and coffee." That four characters up at the counter looked remarkably like cowboys, that the jukebox was crooning plaintive ballads of wrangler love, and that their eggs arrived with unordered hash browns, a sure sign of the true west, went undiscussed. When their plates were removed they still sat as if entranced. Then, "Well, I guess we'd better get started," said Mason, without enthusiasm.

"Oh man, I am sick of the car," moaned Cleve. "No offense intended, Mason."

Back on the road, though, they regained consciousness in a hurry. It was, after all, the Big Day at last, and no sentient being could miss the clues. Sagebrush! Arroyos! Range cattle! They seemed to have passed an undefined but crucial frontier in the storm and darkness; the Great Plains were just a formidable memory. Now the land was rising beneath them, opening to new possibilities, and exuding fragrant names like Fort Laramie and Powder River, more resonant and moving than born-and-bred easterners could express or admit. Each town-sign had an elevation more exalted than the last. And before the morning was half gone - about the time Horn was selling his first can of 10W-30 oil at West Thumb - Mason, scanning the horizon from the back seat, said, "Hey, those aren't clouds: they're *mountains!*"

"The Rockies!" exclaimed Cleve and Chris on cue.

"Snow," breathed Polly. And then, her voice breaking with excitement, "My first snow!"

Mason looked at her. "You've *never* seen it before?"

"Nevuh."

He shook his head and refolded the map. "Must be the Wind River Range."

They took a break - over Chris's mild objections - at Hell's Half Acre, a commercialized bit of badlands near the Powder River west of Casper, and walked stiffly to the edge of the cliff. There a sign painted on rough wood stated that the Indians had killed buffalo by driving them over the precipice onto the rocks below. They squinted down at gullies and mounds the color of bleached bones.

"Ugh, it's horrible," said Polly, wrinkling her nose and recoiling.

Chris seemed transfixed. "It *does* look like Hell," he said uneasily. "What's the use of land like that?"

"It was useful to the Indians," Mason pointed out.

"I mean, what's it good for *now*?"

No one answered. Too bad if they don't like it, Mason was thinking, because it sure is one kind of western scenery. We're not used to its sweep, or comfortable with its power: the car insulates you against the changes in topography. "They've crudded it up," he remarked, nodding toward the souvenir shop, café, gas pumps and coin binoculars.

"Looks like more than half an acre to me," said Cleve, surveying the topography with an empirical eye. "By gum, folks, the land surely is different here: *I've* never seen anything like it." He sniffed the breeze. "Air smells different, too…good. How high are we?"

"About 5000 feet," replied Mason.

"Ah've nevuh *bin* that hagh!" squealed Polly.

"Well, actually," laughed Mason, thinking of the Smokies, "we…" Then he caught a stern glance from Cleve and stopped. "We'll be going even higher!" he finished brightly, and they drifted back to the station wagon.

As the grades steepened and the air thinned, the country floated by more…gradually, which helped them savor the wealth of names: Shoshone, Lost Cabin, Crowheart, Badwater. At the ELEV. 6000 sign Cleve gave the dashboard an affectionate pat: "Hundred-thirty horses earnin' their keep today, Mason."

The registered owner was keeping a wary eye on the temperature gauge. "She's never had to work this hard before," he admitted. "I've got it on the floor." He switched off Overdrive so that 4th gear would not kick in at an inopportune moment. But the engine kept pulling, past the ELEV. 7000 sign, and lowland trees gradually yielded to evergreens so that the air became pine-scented. At eight thousand feet he turned on the heater for the first time. In the early afternoon they made Togwotee Pass, over 9600 feet high and still banked deep with plowed snow; rivulets of melt trickled across the steaming pavement.

"The Tetons!" Mason braked and pulled over. Everyone tumbled out, shivering in the breeze that came off the snow. Bred on smaller scales, accustomed to Appalachia's hills and dales, they stared across thirty miles of sun-washed alpine meadows to upthrust mountains, softened and bluish in the distance haze, and sparkling lakes that lay like precious rugs at their feet. Water was gurgling under the snow; the sun caressed them; a vegetable fragrance permeated the air. Silence prevailed for a few seconds, and Mason wondered if the others were also feeling - what? An obscure panic, a questioning of the whole enterprise, or of their fitness for it. Almost a fear. He suppressed a shudder. "It's not even summer here yet," he heard himself say.

Cleve had been molding a snowball, which he now lobbed. "There's some winter for you!" Mason dodged, muttered defiance and began making his own.

"Oh, it's so cold and funny!" cried Polly, touching a snowbank gingerly.

"Whoops!" Even Chris was larking about with unwonted gaiety, throwing aloft handfuls of powder.

"My hands are cold: let's go."

And so they went, down the Pacific side of the Continental Divide (which Cleve explained to Polly) to pastures dotted with wildflowers, past bogs and spruce forests toward the lakes. All were too excited to make intelligible noises, more deeply stirred than they could show or explain. The afternoon was wearing on, so despite the charms of Jackson Lake they turned north at once, through sleek-looking ranch country where every creek was lined with old cottonwoods. Soon the road began to climb through uncleared forest, deeply shadowed, where the noise of the laboring engine was sometimes echoed, sometimes deadened. At length a big sign - yellow letters painted on brown boards - slid into view:

YELLOWSTONE NATIONAL PARK

Trying to be cool, Mason pulled up to the rough-hewn tollbooth spanning the road and informed the tall ranger on duty that they, too, were working in the park.

He examined them for a moment before replying. "Pull off over there. I'll be with you in a minute." Mason opened his mouth, but changed his mind and did as he was told. When the ranger, a rugged, clean-cut, serious-looking fellow in a drab uniform and broad-brimmed hat, walked over, he asked to see their contracts, then started asking questions about each job, most of which they could not answer.

"I guess we really don't know much about what we're doing," Mason admitted. The ranger almost smiled, and told them to come into the office.

"Have we done anything wrong?" asked Polly in a small voice as they followed him toward a log cabin.

"No, it's just to fill out some forms," he answered without turning around. After they had done so, the ranger went over the park regulations with unflattering thoroughness. When he asked about firearms, Mason remembered that he had brought along his .22 for some reason. The ranger made him bring it in, and plugged the barrel. He used the word "savages" several times before they realized he was referring to *them* - not just to their party, but to all the young people with summer jobs in the park. Only when they had heard out the lecture and signed their ID cards did the ranger relax at all, though not to a fulsome degree. He simply held out a big hand, introduced himself as Dan; then nodded and said "I'll probably be seeing you" on his way out the door.

The four walked back to the car feeling somewhat chastened. It was, perhaps, not so much what had been said to them, as the loss of that heady sensation of breaking free - many miles east - that made the day seem less splendid than before. "Some welcome," grumbled Chris.

"Not what I'd call a smooth passage," Mason agreed. "*Savages*, indeed! Still: new name, new life."

"I'm guessing," said Cleve, "that savages are not considered an unmixed blessing."

"Good-*lookin'*," murmured Polly.

*

As the park received them, its gravity continued to pull others. In Deer Walk, West Virginia, Cyril added a quart of oil to his ill-starred Chevy coupe while a flat was being repaired and wondered if it would make Indianapolis, let alone Gardiner. Lois was guiding her convertible through western Missouri, a black beret perched aslant her auburn hair, and trying to ignore Fran, who was asleep with her mouth open. "The Mouth" was waving to assembled family as his Greyhound rolled out of West Unity, Ohio, alt. 789'. *Yellowstone or Bust* had busted in Barstow, where the Angelinos were debating whether to turn back, press on, or abandon the damn thing *and* their fantasies about wild orgies among bears and geysers. Beatty and Henderson were discovering that the fleshpots of Billings, Montana, had more to offer than they had managed to find in St. Louis or any other burg along their way.

Virg's sedan was parked in front of a motel in Gardiner. Bastille was sitting in the bar of the Old Faithful Lodge, trying to clear his head and write a backgrounder on the area. Jill had just reached West Thumb after a long ride from the Jackson Hole airport and was receiving a detailed account of her good buddy Pris's date with Lou the night before.

*

21

As the road from the South Entrance gained altitude, the savages had backward glimpses of thickly forested ridges flowing in dark-green waves down to the lake-plain of the Tetons - "Jackson's Hole" - before Lewis Canyon shut them in. A shaggy black bear with two cubs lumbered into the road and they stopped to gawk with other tourists - until they remembered who they were, and drove on. The car strained toward another divide, knocking softly. Eventually there was clear sky between the trees ahead; they achieved the pass and found themselves looking down on the broad expanse of Yellowstone Lake, rimmed by snowy peaks. Mason pulled over and stopped. They sat wordless at first, taking it all in, hearing the light wind soughing through the trees on the crest and the water simmering quietly in the radiator. In the distance, a few small clouds laid sliding patches of shadow like throw rugs on mountains, lake and forest.

Speech after long silence: "There is a certain sense of climax," said Mason, and trailed off.

Cleve nodded. "Umm. Suppose we had *flown* out here... think of all we would have missed! *This* would be different."

"Suppose we'd had to *walk* all this way, like the pioneers," said Chris. "They'd think *we've* had it easy."

Polly teared up and wept silently. She didn't know what had gotten into her.

Two: Mi tsi a-da-zi

"In the beginning," before the whites and the aboriginal tribes, the First Nations, was the land. The four eastern savages did not know that they were on the edge of the world's largest volcano crater, because geologists did not recognize it as such for another decade. What is now northwestern Wyoming was at an early period molded by enormous natural forces: what some call "the hand of God." Subterranean pressures formed a high plateau of rhyolite and basalt, and surrounded it with even higher mountains, the mightiest being the Absarokas to the east, a mile-high mass of volcanic breccia. Then, perhaps six hundred thousand years ago, a cataclysmic eruption blasted out the center of this plateau, leaving a caldera fifty miles across. Lava spread over several hundred square miles; ash fell on several of our modern states.

Thus Yellowstone was created as a mountain bowl that must be climbed into from any direction, while the forces that made it so have mellowed into tourist attractions. Today molten rock is still found at the relatively shallow depth of three miles, which explains why the park has three-fifths of the world's known geysers. The very fissures through which they play are left over from The Day of the Volcano. The *enfant terrible* lives to become the benign patriarch; the child is father to the man.

Later came glaciers, scooping, carving, depositing, and melting back, leaving Yellowstone Lake as a souvenir of the Ice Age. Where it lies, a glacial puddle in a volcanic cone, lava rests a thousand feet thick on the still older crust of earth. Its exit stream, draining northward, ran gently over the central plateau until it encountered thermally-weakened rock that it quickly eroded into a deep canyon. At the interface between harder and softer minerals, headwalls formed over which the Yellowstone River falls for hundreds of feet.

Time passed, water flowed, geysers played, flora grew, fauna roamed. More than ten thousand years ago, probably, people crossed the ice bridge from Siberia and worked their way south along the coast (by boat or on foot) or through low temperate valleys a little inland. In time some of these nomads began to make summer forays onto the plateau in pursuit of bison, mammoth, and other large game, but they did not settle: with an average elevation of over eight thousand feet and a harsh climate for nine months a year, the region was not and is not naturally hospitable to humans. On these trips they came across whole cliffs of obsidian, from which they could make good arrowheads, however, and this discovery made the plateau more attractive.

Both these hunters and their prey, however, disappear from the historical record about 5000 BC, a time of drought in the area. A few foragers may have kept the trails open, and when water was again abundant, animals and humans returned, at least in summer. Members of roaming tribes - including Bannock and Kiowa, Blackfeet, Crow and Dakota Sioux, Kalispell and Nez Percé - made transient visits as their people shifted territories. Only the Dukurika or Sheepeater Shoshones seem to have remained year-round in the vicinity of the present park, and they "left fewer enduring evidences of their occupancy than the beaver, badger and other animals on which they subsisted." Mindful of their oversight, the man who made that comment, Philetus W. Norris, second superintendent of Yellowstone National Park, sought to attach his own name to half the notable localities in his preserve, but it has stuck only to the geyser basin by the Gibbon River.

The first whites in the area were probably eighteenth-century French trappers. From the Minnetaree tribe downstream they learned to call the river *Pierre Jaune* or *Roche Jaune*, as they translated *Mi tsi a-da-zi*, but stayed only long enough to collect a load of pelts. "Yellow Stone" was first used by David Thompson, a British explorer, in 1798, and adopted by Lewis and Clark in their report to Pres. Jefferson (1806). None of them had been into what is now the park. Had these early "Long Knives" moved closer and made contact with a tribe who actually visited the plateau before adopting a name, we might call it "Elk River," the meaning of the Crow expression *As to pah oan zhah*.

Although the Louisiana Purchase (1803) technically opened the region to American exploration, it did not produce an immediate flood of explorers. The first European known to have seen Yellowstone was a French fur trader named Larocque (1805); John Colter, a veteran of the Lewis and Clark expedition who reached the lake from the south and followed the river as far as Tower Fall in 1807-08, was likely the first American. His descriptions of "infernal" landscapes (sulphur and brimstone) caused the place to be dubbed "Colter's Hell." They also began the tradition of tall tales that aroused both curiosity and scepticism until late in the century when the public was able to see for itself. For the moment - the War of 1812 was distracting the nation -

white visitors were few and mostly anonymous. One of them is known to posterity only because he set the dangerous precedent of carving his name on a tree. The inscription *J.O.R. Aug. 29, 1819* was found in the bark of a lodgepole pine a quarter of a mile from the Upper Falls of the Yellowstone by the Norris party in 1881. They verified the date by counting the annual growth rings of the tree, but never discovered who J.O.R. had been.

For the first two-thirds of the nineteenth century "white" knowledge of Yellowstone advanced slowly, more or less paralleling the nation's jerky movement toward the west. In 1825 moving to Missouri still qualified as "westward migration"; "the States" ended at Iowa until 1845. Yellowstone was in "unorganized territory," and its cartography was primitive and misleading. But in 1827 Philadelphians could read in their newspapers the first eyewitness description of it, written by Dan Potts, a fur trader, in 1822. Jedediah Smith and other trappers were operating on the plateau annually by then, despite many hazards. One party was scattered and two of its members killed by Blackfeet warriors near Mammoth in 1829: a harbinger of things to come. An illiterate trapper named Johnson Gardner followed a tributary of the Yellowstone into a valley he modestly called "Gardner's Hole" (1832). His name (with variant spellings) was eventually applied to both the river that flows past Mammoth through the "hole" and the town where it joins the Yellowstone.

The following year Manuel Alvarez led a party of trappers up the Firehole River to the Upper Geyser Basin and Old Faithful (all as yet unnamed). Their report had the significant effect of summoning the first tourist in 1834. Warren Ferris, a young clerk, was led there by two Pend'Oreille tribesmen, who reportedly warned him that evil spirits lived in the geysers. Historians disagree over whether this was an aboriginal belief or a notion picked up from Christian trappers. If the natives were superstitious about the geysers before contact, that evidently did not keep them from visiting the plateau to hunt, collect obsidian, and even - according to some - bathe in the warm springs.

The name most widely associated with Yellowstone during America's Great Leap Westward was that of Jim Bridger, trapper and tall-tale teller extraordinaire, who roamed the plateau sporadically for thirty years. It was Bridger, traveling with Kit Carson and others in 1849, who gave the name Fire Hole to the Old Faithful valley, Bridger who guided a topographical reconnaissance of the area in 1859-60, Bridger who passed through again as the Civil War drew to a close. His entertaining yarns stood up to sober scrutiny remarkably well, but he mixed fact with fiction and cockeyed explanations. Once he had told of "peetrified trees a-growing, with peetrified birds on 'em a-singing peetrified songs," or of a valley so big that if he shouted "Wake up, Jim!" as he went to bed, the echo would rouse him next morning, listeners could hardly be blamed for doubting the existence of a river running so fast that the stones of the streambed were heated by friction, or of a glass mountain, or of the hellacious region of smoke and brimstone. Yet the Firehole River, Obsidian Cliff and the Upper Geyser Basin are the recognizable kernels of truth inside Bridger's corny yarns, and more than one hungry expedition would later recall - with a shock of recognition - his story of country "so desolate that even the crows carry provisions when they fly over." Was Bridger a liar, a precursor of Mark Twain and Will Rogers, or a surrealist?

The discovery of gold along the tributaries of the Snake (1863) brought the first prospectors into Yellowstone. Little gold was found in the area, but the increased traffic (including the first known white woman, Jeannette Gemel, a trapper's daughter) produced more clashes with the natives. As usual the whites kept coming anyway, pushing onto the plateau with new vigor during Reconstruction, as men, energy, and technology that had been devoted to war were released for other purposes. The most important visit of the decade was that of Charley Cook and David Folsom (1869). Both had been miners, but curiosity about a fabled region appears to have been the main impetus for their trip. They published a detailed account of their month-long expedition, providing reliable information and a decent map, which interested future members of the Washburn party in the area. Aubrey Haines, the official park historian, calls this the beginning of "definitive exploration."

By 1870 there was enough public interest in Yellowstone to bring forth a real expedition, one whose findings could be trusted. The Washburn-Doane party was the largest and best-equipped white foray onto the plateau yet: nine reasonably sober citizens and four camp attendants under Gen. Washburn, with half a dozen of the Second Cavalry under Lt. Doane. This cross-section of frontier society spent about five weeks seeing most of the principal sights and lost one of its members. This turned out to be a fortunate mishap - he was found alive after 37 days - as it produced nationwide publicity and a ready audience for whatever expedition members said, wrote or drew after their return. They rose to the occasion with numerous articles, reports, lectures and illustrations. Never before had Americans heard so much they could believe about Yellowstone, and it began to look as if Colter and Bridger might not have been quite the consarned liars they had often been thought.

The most significant result of the expedition was to publicize the idea that Yellowstone was too extraordinary to be treated like just another piece of real estate. Nathaniel Langford, the party's principal chronicler, wrote an intriguing account of a campfire conversation at Madison Junction on September 19, 1870, as the men prepared to leave the plateau. It dramatizes some of the strong forces at work in American society at the time. Initially the talk was all of profit and utility, with several members suggesting that they all buy up quarter sections at Canyon and Old Faithful (which had just been named by Gen. Washburn), "develop" them and charge admission. The main issue was whether to proceed singly or collectively.

Mr. Hedges then said that he did not approve of any of these plans - that there ought to be no private ownership of any portion of that region, but that the whole of it ought to be set apart as a great National Park, and that each one of us ought to make an effort to have this accomplished. His suggestion met with an instantaneous and favorable response from all - except one - of the members of our party....

We do not know how trustworthy this report is - it could be apocryphal and is certainly not a verbatim transcript - but the idea attributed to Hedges was not unprecedented. The creation of Central Park in New York (1851) and the Yosemite Valley grant (1864) had already set aside land for public use; Acting Gov. Thomas Meagher of Montana had suggested (1865) that Yellowstone should be thus reserved, and David Folsom had said as much to some of Hedges' companions in 1869. Now, apparently, the idea's time had come. According to Langford, only one member of the party - which included mining and railroad interests - dissented. Several members worked for the proposal so hard and effectively after their return that in only two years Yellowstone National Park was a (legislative) reality.

There were, however, several problems: "the Indian question," for one. Both the Sioux and the Crows had been deemed "hostile" for several years, and in 1871 the Sheepeaters - Yellowstone's only resident tribe - were "removed" to a Shoshone reservation on the Wind River, though they had never been involved in an attack on whites. The year after the Battle of the Little Big Horn (1876) some of Chief Joseph's Nez Percés raided the park and killed two whites before their "uprising" was quashed. As a result the few remaining Sheepeaters were evacuated, though not far: Pres.

Arthur's guide through Yellowstone in 1883 was a Dukurika chief named Togwotee.

Another problem was white entrepreneurs. The fledgling park was immediately targeted by commercial free enterprise; its history has been a race between tourism and the nascent concept of a park. The trouble was that in 1870 few people had even a vague idea of what a "national park" might be, while many felt they knew exactly what should be *done* with or to Yellowstone. The Northern Pacific Railroad, which started building west from Lake Superior in 1870, was interested in the park as an enroute attraction for tourists, so it planned a branch line and various accommodations. In 1871, as the Hayden and Barlow parties conducted a survey of Yellowstone, enterprising spirits were already "improving" Mammoth Hot Springs with such features as McCartney's Hotel and McGuirk's Bathhouse, while Jack Baronett, the rescuer of Washburn's lost lamb in 1870, was bridging the Yellowstone. Developers did not cease when park status was granted, and they had the support of some reputable public figures. For the moment, the federal government had neither the will nor the knowledge to check individual or corporate initiative. It appointed Langford "Superintendent," but as it neither paid nor instructed him he could have little effect on events in his domain.

Philetus Norris (appointed 1877) was somewhat more fortunate, receiving sufficient funds for an administration building at Mammoth, so now the park at least had a resident ranger. Norris was energetic and dedicated, but corporate efforts to "develop" the park by laying track and putting elevators in the canyon, plus the depredations of hunters, fishers, campers and souvenir collectors, were too much for one man to control. The 1880s, when many public versus private issues were *sub judice*, proved critical in the struggle for Yellowstone, each side commanding some Congressional support and winning some skirmishes. The Northern Pacific dispatched F. Jay Haynes, the frontier photographer, to take pictures of the park; he returned repeatedly and became the park's first concessioner, founding Haynes, Inc. and publishing the Haynes Guides. By 1886 there were two hotels at Mammoth, steamer rides on Yellowstone Lake, and stagecoach tours of the park. The stage drivers called themselves "savages," and the tourists, "dudes." In the same period the conservationists managed to stop the Northern Pacific tracks at Gardiner, obtain a ban on hunting in the park, and secure the services of a detachment of Army cavalry in lieu of a superintendent.

These battles carried over into the 1890s, with the idea of governmental regulation gradually gaining ground. New concessioners were subject to stricter federal scrutiny, and older interests were brought into line with current policy. "Yellowstone Jack" Baronett was ruined by the confiscation of his toll bridge in 1894, Congress's $5000 compensation being less than his lawyers' fees. A US Commissioner (judge) appeared at Mammoth that year, wielding federal rather than state law because Yellowstone's parkhood preceded Wyoming's statehood (1890). By 1895 the park was able to organize a census, which counted over five thousand tourists. Serving them meant breaking new ground, and there was no shortage of developers, corporate and individual. The family interests that grew into the Yellowstone Park Company (YPC) can be traced back to 1891, while Ole Anderson built a café at Mammoth on his own in 1896. Haynes put up his first shop at Old Faithful the following year, when the census showed over 10,000 visitors to the park.

The new century began, significantly, with the laying out of the "Grand Loop" road system, whose first traffic consisted of horse-drawn wagons and coaches. In 1903 Teddy Roosevelt visited, the Weather Bureau established itself in Mammoth, and a young architect employed by the YPC began work on the Old Faithful Inn, which rose among the stunted trees of the basin like a lost Norwegian *stavekirke*. Though the dominance of the railroads was waning, the Union Pacific completed its spur to the park and created West Yellowstone as a terminus (1907). The park's popularity continued to grow: 26,000 tourists in 1905, 32,000 in 1909. One by one the individual concessioners sold out to larger operators or to conglomerates, who merged into larger groupings as the present commercial infrastructure of the park began to take shape.

If any period may be said to have begotten modern Yellowstone, it was the first half of World War I, which tore Europe apart while the US watched. Automobiles were first admitted to the park in 1915 over the protests of both conservationists and concessioners (who felt that their stagecoach trade would suffer). The number of tourists passed fifty thousand for the first time that summer, and Charles Hamilton, an enterprising young businessman who had started with the Yellowstone Park Association a decade earlier, opened the first Hamilton Store at Old Faithful. Stephen Mather, director of the newly-created National Park Service, assumed formal control of the park in 1916. He began releasing the cavalry who had been guarding the park since the 1880s for possible service in France, as

29

ripples from the Great War reached the Continental Divide. The soldiers were replaced by park rangers over the next few years.

Visits to Yellowstone fell off during the war, a boon for Mather, but burgeoned rapidly thereafter: 60,000 in 1919, 98,000 in 1922. Despite the fears of the concessioners, more savages were serving more dudes than ever before - just driving buses instead of stagecoaches and adjusting fan belts instead of saddle girths. The magnitude of the influx worried the Park Service, but Mather was creative: taking a lead from his European counterparts (with whom he had more contact after the war) he began opening museums and offering guided nature walks. In the early 1920s he had to fight off a rash of legislative proposals - spawned by the postwar surge of energy and prosperity - for dams, canals and reservoirs in the park. Mather was not a strict conservationist, however. Seeing the need to provide for the automobile tourist, he awarded a gasoline concession contract and opened a new south entrance to the park (1923), which immediately swelled his annual guest list to 138,000.

The private concessioners held the pace, with Hamilton opening seven stores at four areas (1916-17), and either building or taking over five more in 1930-31. The NPS encouraged chains, preferring a few large, presumably responsible concessions to the plethora of small operators who had provoked many complaints over the years, so the YPC was permitted to absorb a number of minor businesses, some of them dating from the 1890s. By the same token the NPS looked on corporate and governmental enterprise with favor. It turned over highway building and maintenance to the Bureau of Public Roads (1926) and had AT & T install telephones in 1927, the first year that 200,000 tourists entered the park. It was the era of Dempsey and Ruth, Red Grange and Knute Rockne, Bobby Jones and Bill Tilden: America had a passion for outdoor sports, and one of them was "roughing it."

The Great Depression, which cut the number of visitors (150,000 in 1932) and brought the Civilian Conservation Corps to the park, made concessioners pause to take stock. In 1935, however, the arrival of a record 317,000 tourists signaled the onset of Recovery, and play resumed. The return of prosperity, or at least solvency, was confirmed by the execution of a project to make the Cooke City-Mammoth highway a year-round operation (1938-39), extending the tourist season and giving Yellowstone a marginal winter income. The rise of Nazism and the Battles of France and Britain did not diminish the flow of visitors, who surpassed half a million in 1940 and set a new record in 1941; only Pearl Harbor, ending

American isolation from the conflict, did that. Somehow 64,000 tourists (the fewest since 1919) managed to reach the park in 1943, despite gasoline rationing, and there were already twenty thousand more the following year - the summer of D-Day.

It seemed that one of the things Americans wanted to do after the war was see Yellowstone: in 1946 over 800,000 visitors, half again as many as ever before, entered the park. The NPS and the concessioners responded by building more cabins, campgrounds, boardwalks and service stations, hiring more summer help, and regulating automobile traffic more strictly. Hamilton's and the YPC formed a special concession just to meet the needs of the automobile. Nothing they could do was too much: 1948, the year of the Berlin airlift, was Yellowstone's first million-visitor summer. Hamilton bought two more stores in 1952, but five years later the old concessioner died, ending not only a personal career that spanned two-thirds of the park's history, but an era of Yellowstone commerce.

In that tidewater summer of 1957, when over a million and a half tourists were expected to visit Mi tsi a-da-zi, our four travel-weary students came to the ridge above the lake and wondered at it all.

*

The sociology of Yellowstone Park begins with a distinction between three main groups: perennials or year-round employees, annuals or summer help, and tourists. Each sees and affects the park, and the other groups, in a different way. The few dozen rangers on "permanent" assignment may well be called The Few, in that they are asked to defend the realm against a massive invasion with absurdly inadequate numbers, though *they* must begin by allowing the invaders within the gates. The rangers are supported by many of the concessioners: business folk who take more than a business interest in Yellowstone. They are also, in a sense, perennials, albeit mostly absentee ones during the winter. So unequal do the odds become in summertime, however, that the residents must recruit temporary allies ("seasonals" or "savages"), fair-weather friends of dubious loyalty. The quiet dedication of the perennials is hardly audible during the summer; in the sound and fury of the tourist season, the rangers may seem background figures. Yet for the rest of the year, when deep snow blankets the park, discouraging automobiles and sending bison and elk in search of handouts, Yellowstone is mostly theirs. Annuals and tourists are transient phenomena of the brief mountain summer.

In 1957 this seasonal division was sharper than it is today. The advent of Snowcats and skidoo clubs, and the rise in popularity of snowshoeing and cross-country skiing, have given Yellowstone a modest winter tourist season. It mostly nibbles around the fringes, though, from Gardiner into Mammoth, and from West Yellowstone into Old Faithful. The great majority of the park remains silent, and human activity is as nothing compared to the summer.

The "dudes" are the automobile and bus tourists, mere passers-through: thousands a summer day, millions a season. The *Haynes Guide* tries to float the idea that the term *dude* "embodies respect and admiration," but it sinks. As in "dude ranch," it reeks of in-group condescension, even contempt. The muledrivers of the old Yellowstone Park Stage Company (an early Haynes enterprise) who coined the term were not long on respect and admiration for their paying customers or anyone else. "Dude" expresses perfectly the image that seasonals from the stagecoach driver to the gas-pump jockey have had of tourists: soft, wealthy, uninitiated, ignorant, lowland and (preferably) eastern.

Images are not realities, yet most tourists do remain insulated in cars and hotel rooms, seeing only the strip of the park visible from roads and windows. Their Yellowstone is apt to be high fuel prices, poor service by brash kids, Old Faithful a minute late, a hot walk to see the Falls, crowded everything, "something the children ought to see." (Two of their old standbys, "bear jams" and the anglers on Fishing Bridge, have now been banished by fun-hating rangers.) For the average dude - if such a construct may be admitted - the park is an unusual commodity, financed by his taxes, from which he is therefore entitled to extract as much use and pleasure as he can from the rangers and seasonals who stand in his way. A partial exception should be made for the camping crowd, some of whom bridge the gaps that usually separate dudes from the land.

The summer help hired by the NPS and the concessioners occupy an ambiguous middle ground. Neither fish nor fowl, they are viewed sceptically by both perennials and dudes. The seasonal rangers ("ninety-day wonders") whom the NPS takes on each year are a mixed lot: some are knowledgeable and efficient, some are not, and some become embittered by their duties. The "savages" proper - nominal descendants of Haynes's wranglers - are now (mainly) high school and college students employed by the concessions. Every summer thousands of them flock to the park - about 2000 at Old Faithful alone - to work at diverse jobs for marginal salaries. It is a chicken-and-egg question whether their nature or their name came first, but in some respects the label is appropriate. During their brief flowering the savages are the belongers, those in the know; they combine the terrible swift insolence and brittle sophistication of the parvenu with some of the rawness, if not the savvy, of their namesakes. Many savages view the park as a playground and dudes as second-rate Americana sent for their amusement or annoyance. They spend longer in Yellowstone than most dudes - three months versus three days, on average - so they often come to know it better, yet many head for the nearest bright lights at every opportunity. If they return in subsequent summers, however, savages may begin to move toward the values and attitudes of the perennials.

Neither dudes nor savages have much perspective: they tend to see the park and each other solely through their own prescription lenses, and the resulting images bring them into sporadic conflict. For dudes, most savages look like either the monopoly's hack, an example of cultural decay, or just a wiseacre kid. Savages in turn tend to see dudes as types: the purse-proud Texan in his Cadillac, the blustering vacationer from New York or Florida waving his gold-star credit card, the sweaty Utahite in his shoulder-strap undershirt. However few actually fit these stereotypes, the casual pigeonholing divides and dehumanizes. Their antagonism must have a place in any tale of modern Yellowstone, and sometimes feels like the great theme underlying and connecting the diverse events of an epic. This, however, is too simple and limited a view, for it neglects the land, which dwarfs all human actors (only about 3% of the park is "developed"), and the rangers, who constitute a third party. As they see it, there is often little to choose between seasonals and tourists; they have to police *all* the summerfolk, and the petty quarrels of malefactors are beside the point. While a sociologist may distinguish three groups, participants commonly have an "us-them" mindset. The rangers do perceive a triad, but the parkland itself is the third term, and their function is to mediate between Yellowstone and its visitors, giving protection, instruction, admonition or punishment as needed. They try to promote the view that the park is a community, a *polis,* an ecosystem to which all its human users belong and which is vulnerable to their abuse - a vision that does not come easily to dudes and savages.

33

Three: Rules of Thumb

Cleve looked at his watch. "I think we should get goin', Mason. We're not gonna make Gardiner today, and my contract starts tomorrow - which is Saturday, in case you've lost count - and who knows how things work around here? Maybe I should check in at this first place."

"Sure. I need gas anyway." Mason let out the clutch. The ornamental rocket on the hood - surely a bit of bravado on a Ford 'wagon - angled down at the corruscating lake, and the journey resumed. "This first place," aka West Thumb, presented itself as a gaggle of low wooden buildings by the shore. There was a general store, a ranger station, a campground, some log cabins and service buildings, but no hotel; lots of drifting steam from hot springs and mud pots, but no geyser, no colored terraces, no canyon, no falls.

"It's…undistinguished."

"I'm underwhelmed. What's the attraction? What do people do here?"

"Fish the lake?" Cleve scratched his head and examined the map. "Well, it's a highway junction: west to Faithful and north to everywhere else."

"Whagh do they cawl it Wes' Thu-umb?" asked Polly.

Cleve held up the map. "Look at the outline of the lake: sort of like a… maimed hand? We're here, on the swollen thumb. Gangrene, I'd say."

In the center of things, such as they were, the asphalt divided to flow around both sides of the service station: a pea-green shed of corrugated tin with a gravel front yard divided into lanes by three rows of pumps on concrete islands. Mason turned in and pulled up at the first pump, whistling at the price as an attendant clad in baggy green pinstripe overalls came sauntering over with a shy grin.

"Wow, 38 cents a gallon for regular! Is gas always this much around here?"

"Yeah man, the whole mountain area," said the youth, hands in pockets. "It's the transportation costs, I guess."

"And Comico? Comico gasoline?"

"That's what we sell. There's a lot of it around these parts. Ya want some?"

"Oh, yeah. Fill...no, wait." Mason did a quick calculation. "Three dollars of regular."

The passengers all got out to stretch. The attendant fumbled with the gas cap and untangled his leg from the pump hose.

"Been here long?" asked Mason politely when the gas was flowing.

"Na, coupla days." He looked up and chuckled. "Prob'ly shows." Then he noticed the decal on the rear window and did a double-take. "You from Debrew?"

"Yeah, three of us are."

"Me too. Thought ya looked familiar. Did you take Abnormal Psych last semester?"

"Yes! Funny we didn't meet." They laughed wrily: there had been about two hundred students in the medical building's foul-smelling lecture hall. "I'm Mason."

"I'm...well, people call me Hole." Mason introduced him to the others. Hole was blond and fair, a bit fleshy, and his blue eyes, which almost disappeared when he smiled or squinted, twinkled genially.

Polly, hugging her elbows as a breeze sprang up, asked how he had come to Yellowstone. Hole replied that he had driven out with a friend from Jacksonville. "Ray Jacobs, used to live in New York, goes to Debrew. Ya know him?"

Cleve and Chris shook their heads, but Mason said, "I saw him once in the bookstore, arguing with the manager." A remarkably intense young man with strong views and some general knowledge, eager to sound off. Deep-set hawk eyes that you didn't forget. "Is he here?"

"He's up at Faithful...with his truck, dammit." Hole grinned and shrugged.

"Listen," Cleve broke in, "we're gonna be gas jockeys too, and I need to report today. Is the manager around?"

"Yep." Hole nodded toward the shed. "The tall one - Lou." Suddenly he started, looked at the gas pump and released the trigger. "Oops! Uh, is three-fifty okay?"

Inside the shed Cleve and Mason found two utilitarian rooms with the usual paraphernalia of a rural gas station: fan belts on wall pegs, a tire-changing machine like a squat wrestler in one corner, tires and cases of oil stacked on the concrete floor in the semi-darkness of the back room. Up front, a long green wooden table holding a cash register and an adding machine, and a three-legged stool, stood in front of a large window overlooking the lanes. Two savages, dressed in the same green togs as Hole, were there: a short, heavy-set fellow with thick glasses laboring over the adding machine, and a lanky, well-built character who stopped coaching him and turned to them with a friendly, "Ken Ah hep yuh, sir?"

"Aha, a felluh westunuh!" exclaimed Cleve. "Atlanta?"

"Neah Macon, akshully."

Cleve performed the introductions and explained his situation. As soon as Lou heard that they were service-station savages his eyes began to appraise and his tone grew ingratiating. Turning to the other savage, he said, "This here's mah *assistant* manajuh, we callum Woo."

They shook hands with Thumb's #2, whose grip was considerably less crunching than Lou's. "Pleased ta meecha Cleve, Mason." His smile was warm but uncertain, almost deferential, and beads of sweat hung on his forehead. Mason guessed that he did not care for his nickname but was too amiable or self-effacing to say so.

Cleve returned to his priority. "Lou, what about our contracts? When and how do we report?"

Lou checked his big Mickey Mouse watch. "Wall, we jes have tahm tuh ring up the bawsman, ol' Morley in Gard'ner, 'fore he quitsun letum know yer here. Thetull take ker yer contrac, n yuh ken go up tomorra." He cranked vigorously at a black wall telephone such as you might have seen at a country cousin's place on a childhood visit, or in a museum of pioneer life. "Hey Lureen, this is Lou!" he yelled at the mouthpiece, jamming the cylindrical receiver against his ear. "Yeah, okay, how's it keepin? Good! Lissun Lureen, gimme Godnuh, willya? Gotta talk tuh...yeah, thanks. ...Hello, Godnuh? Gimme Morley... What? LAKE?! Dammit, Ah don't *want* Lake! Hey Lureen!" He cranked the handle again. "Thet wuz Lake! Gimme Godnuh!" He shook his head at the newcomers. "Hey Godnuh, I... FACEFULL?! Gawdammit, what's goin on *anyway*?" More cranking. "Lureen, gimme Godnuh rat now, er Ahm comin up thern clean house!"

The mysterious and playful Lureen finally connected Lou with the Corporation's head office in Gardiner, and thus with Morley. Both parties had to bellow so loud that there could be no secrets. Lou roared that he needed more men at Thumb and these two would do just fine; Morley squawked that he would see what he could do. Then Lou hung up emphatically and the phone jangled one belated protest. He wiped his brow and dusted his hands. "Wall, thet's thet: yer checked in awrat. Hill see ya tomorra mornin. Ah aist tuh have yuh rat heah."

"Yes, I heard," said Mason carefully. "I was sort of hoping for Faithful myself. I've heard that's where the action is, and most of the savages."

"Evrabody wants tuh go tuh Facefull, thet's a fac." Lou chuckled softly. "But there's lotsa action here too."

"Lou would know about that," interjected Woo.

The manager smiled benignly. "We're gonna have a real good station this yeah, probly win the sales race, n lak tuh have yabord. Yuh look lak nachurl salesmen." He sounded reasonable but determined.

"I guess Morley'll do what he wants with us anyway," said Cleve, staying above the argument.

"Thet's a fac," laughed Lou. "Say, ifn yuh wawntuh get anywhar close tuh Godnuh tuhnat, yuh mat wawnt tuh get stahted. Itsa lawng way up theah." He walked them out to their car, the only one in the lanes. Hole was talking to Polly. Chris had walked over to the nearest mud pot, a steaming pit behind a few fagged-looking spruces just beyond the gravel, and was watching bubbles surface through the grey muck with a syncopated 'thwup, thwup.' An elderly couple emerged from the store and walked slowly toward the cabins. "Not much going on now," Mason ventured.

"Naw, nothin but snow n rangers til the fuhst o' June. But come 'nother few days Ah'll need awl the hep Ah ken git. Wall, so lawng fer now, jemman." He offered them both his powerful hand for a final crunch.

A few hundred yards beyond Thumb the Old Faithful road began to climb toward the Continental Divide, and what with the grade and the bears it was a slow 17 miles. Any member of the *Ursidae* family who cared to shamble across the pavement could stop all the traffic in sight, which fortunately was not much. "Note," observed Cleve, waggling a pedantic finger, "the average tourist's assumption that if *he* stops to watch the bears, everyone else will want to. Thus there is no need to pull off on the shoulder: he can stay in his lane." Mason threaded through several of these "bear jams" and each time dudes turned to gape at them, astonished that anyone would pass up these wonderful bears.

Toward the end of the afternoon they reached the Upper Geyser Basin. After a quick impression of a broad valley with many smokes - Cleve irreverently compared it to Pittsburgh - they found themselves down among trees and dark cabins. At the great hulking lodge, Chris and Polly learned that they would both be working there, as a dishwasher and a waitress, respectively, and were assigned dormitory rooms. Cleve hovered about, trying to expedite, while Mason stood with his back to a big fire, gazing at the antlers and mighty log beams of the central hall. Impatient to push on, they lost no time in depositing their passengers at what looked like old wooden army barracks. Both of the drop-offs looked confused and out of place, especially Polly. Cleve hugged her and said that wherever he was stationed, he'd come see her whenever he could. Oh, and Virg would look in on her. Mason gave her a brotherly peck on the cheek and promised he would too. More than ever he hoped for Faithful. Then they departed, leaving her standing in the doorway like a stray waif, suitcase in one hand, hanky in the other.

Polly watched the blue car until it rounded a corner, then turned and walked down the dim corridor to her room, closing the door softly and setting her bag on the plank floor beside her paintbox. The room had the soft, acrid tang of a lumberyard - not unpleasant, but wistful - and the last rays of light from the window were melancholy. There came a knock on the door. She opened it immediately and saw two rather plain girls in gingham dresses. "Hello," said the one in front. "I'm Joanna and this is Patsy." Polly introduced herself. Joanna was holding a large leather-bound book which she now extended reverently with both hands, like an acolyte. "We don't know if you have read *The Book of Mormon*?" she said, "and we were wondering if we could say a few words to you about the Church of Jesus Christ of Latter-Day Saints?"

Polly burst into tears.

*

Driving north among geyser basins in the twilight, Cleve and Mason had only a dim sense of steaming pools, thick forests, and then meadows, with once some moose or elk feeding in the distance, the Firehole River cascading noisily nearby, a bear shuffling out of the headlight beams. At Madison Junction, Mason declared himself medically unfit to drive further, so Cleve took the wheel and tackled the last 35 miles in the darkness. They considered pulling over and sleeping beside the road, but - as law-abiding savages - hesitated to "camp" in an unauthorized spot. The road followed the Gibbon River to Norris, crossed a flat stretch, and descended through canyons to Mammoth. They could see little outside the headlight beams, but once Mason, waking from a fitful doze on the front seat, thought he looked up from the bottom of a deep narrow ravine and saw a cross gleaming in wan light far up on top of the cliff. Struggling for consciousness, he mumbled, "Whuzzat? Christians?"

"Or death," said Cleve. The next word intelligible to Mason was "Mammoth" as they pulled into a campground, and he remembered a sulfurous reek earlier.

"Dinner?" queried Cleve.

A food drive existed somewhere, but only on a secondary plane. It just seemed too much trouble. "Outa the question. Sleep." They laid the back seats flat, put their baggage in front, spread out the sleeping bags and dropped off at once.

Their first awareness of June the 8th was a spike of loud, angry voices nearby. The subject of the dispute was unclear, but not the emotions.

"Wull, I ain't goin again, that's all."

"Do like he says!"

"Fetch it yerself!" There was a smack and a howl.

Cleve propped himself up on his elbows with a groan. "Man," he exclaimed, "how can folks carry on that way in country like this?" Sunlight, bright but not hot, was streaming in the back window. They were on the western slope of a broad river valley fragrant with sage and pine; strong shadows cut across the greys and greens. Directly opposite, a chalk-colored ridge, gaunt and banded, rose almost clear of the last straggling evergreens. A magpie swooped across the view in a blur of black, white, and brilliant blue. The air was crisp and cool. The neighbors' argument reached a climax and trailed off, the males heading for the toilet block and the woman shouting after them.

"*Man!*" Cleve snorted. "Let's go look for breakfast. I could eat a bear."

"Uh-oh, now you've done it." Right on cue, a large black one ambled out from behind the next car, sniffed its exhaust pipe, pushed over a garbage can and nosed at its contents. The Angry Woman shrieked and ran into her trailer. The bear, obviously unimpressed with the quality of early-season refuse, cuffed the fallen can, scratched its right shoulder with its hind leg and sauntered away downhill. "You were saying?"

Cleve's eyes were wide. "Mama, I wanna go home to Carolina. Guess I'd better watch my mouth."

"Hard to do. By the way, where do we eat? We don't have a shred of food left."

"There's a big hotel back up the hill. Out of our league, but it's all I saw last night." He looked over at Mason. "How did you sleep? Heard you mumbling a couple of times."

"Sorry about that. Think I dreamed about that damned cross. But I slept okay, thanks."

39

"'That damned cross?' Hmm. You know, maybe you ought to take Remedial Theology next year."

Dressing in the uncurtained rear of the 'wagon meant awkward squirming in a sleeping bag, bridging to pull on pants, then sitting up too quickly and cracking the dome light with your forehead, but they were young and this was novel and it all seemed part of the adventure. Mason pushed open the tailgate and they crawled out, stiff and groggy, to stumble down to the basic facilities.

A commodious *toilette* was followed by a drive up to Mammoth Lodge. Morning was more advanced there; sunshine highlighted the steaming white mound of terraces and flooded over the pale-green grandeur of the hotel. They hesitated to sully such splendor in their wrinkled travel clothes, but the tourists were all casually dressed, so after a moment the gastric juices prevailed. They crossed the rustic, high-ceilinged lobby, ignoring the desk clerk, who seemed to be watching them. At the portals of the vast dining room, resplendent with crystal, silver, and white linen, Mason faltered. "God, Cleve, I don't know."

"Don't be overawed by conspicuous consumption," advised Cleve, leading the way to an inconspicuous corner table. He glanced over the menu. "Uh-oh, we *have* erred and strayed from our ways! But I guess there's no choice this morning. Think of it as dinner *and* breakfast."

"Agreed. Too late for escape now, anyway. Oh, but look here." A winsome young waitress in a crisp blue uniform was bearing down on them, order pad at the ready. Their eyes darted from straight, shoulder-length brown hair, curling up at the ends, to trim ankles, and returned more slowly.

"The makers of that uniform are much indebted to you, ma'am," said Cleve jovially. "Are you a savage?"

She thought it over for a moment, looking from one to the other with stunningly bright, and rather tough, brown eyes. "Yes," she said, and the curls swung.

"Well now, so are we! I'm Cleve, this is Mason, and we'd like the best *cheap* breakfast you have, Miss...?"

"Savage," she said, and turned on her heel. Later, after bringing them hot cereal and coffee, she identified herself as Sally. "And I have to be careful about customer contacts."

"Good policy!" exclaimed Cleve, bringing his palm down on the table emphatically. "You can't be too careful. Well, Sally Savage, have you any commands in Gardiner, whither we are proceeding, in Mr. Dixon's chariot, once this memorable repast is consumed?"

Dark eyes calculated briefly. "Actually, I wouldn't mind a lift into town, if you don't mind a short wait. I'll be off in half an hour."

As it happened, that fit their schedule well, half an hour being *exactly* the time they had planned to spend clambering around the limestone terraces near the lodge along with a few other tourists! One group from a chartered bus was being guided by a knowledgeable young woman with a geological-historical spiel of some interest. They hung around the fringes of the group until she gave them a hard look that sent them peeling off at the next boardwalk junction.

"What was all that stuff about calcium carbonate, Cleve? I couldn't follow."

"Oho, freshman chemistry, my boy! Most geysers are built from silica, but these are limestone, which is full of $CaCO_3$ - to wit, calcium carbonate. Underground gases, mainly carbon dioxide, heat whatever water they find down there, which reacts with the calcium carbonate to produce a carbonic acid solution. It stinks, and it dissolves limestone in a hurry. Are you following?"

"I didn't take freshman chemistry, but yes, I think so."

"Okay. Once this hot, carbonated, lime-rich water flows to the surface, it cools, loses some CO_2 and solidifies into these terraces. Then algae grow in the hot water, making the colors. You get different algae, hence different colors, in different-temperature pools. Presto! A color-coded hot spring."

"Cleve, that's a gas of a lecture. When's the quiz?"

Promptly at the end of half an hour they returned to the front entrance of the lodge to meet Sally, who appeared in white slacks and blouse, a vision of youth and health. "What are you staring at?" she asked, as if she really didn't know. "Have your plans changed, or do I still get a ride?"

Well, their plans had *not* changed. In high spirits with Sally gracing the middle of the front seat, they followed the bumpy tarmac along a hillside west of the river and down onto sagebrush plain, where a...something, an imposing but inexplicable construction, loomed up ahead. "What's that?" asked Mason. "A triumphal arch?"

"The north entrance to the park," said Sally primly.

"'Civilian Conservation Corps, 1933'," Cleve read off as they passed. "Man, times must have been *real* bad." A few low buildings occupied a slice of the plain at the foot of bare hills. "This must be the metropolis of Gardiner. Looks like a cow town, Sally."

"It isn't, though. Railroad terminus and some business, mostly tourist stuff."

""Does it swing?" asked Mason. "Bright lights? Where's the downtown?"

"You're looking at it. This street is all there is." Mason turned right and cruised slowly along Main, past cafés and motels and gas stations. "You can let me off right here."

Mason pulled over. "A bookshop! Is that where you're going?"

"Yes, I actually read," she replied tartly.

"That's *not* what I meant! It's the existence of a bookstore here that surprised me," he protested.

"Well, Sally, it's been a pleasure," said Cleve, bowing her out. "I hope to have the honor of paying my respects when I reach these parts again."

"That would be nice. Both of you gentlemen are welcome to call when you're in town. Oh, that's your building out there." She pointed a chord across the shallow arc of the road to a blocky warehouse where the town met the plain. "Thanks for the ride. Goodbye." She flashed the smile she had withheld until then and crossed to the bookstore.

"Cute girl!" exclaimed Cleve as he jumped back in.

"A real zinger," Mason agreed. "Though no cuter than your sister," he added, and was at once sorry. He had been looking for an opening to announce that he wanted to date Polly, but this had come out wrong. And was Polly really "cute," or just handsome and pleasingly constructed? He noticed that Cleve was looking at him in a sharp new way. "Hey look!" Mason blurted, grateful for a diversion. "The others are here!" Virg's car was indeed parked in front of the two-story edifice housing the Yellowstone Park Concession Corporation, and four familiar figures were lazing in the sunshine by the entrance.

"Ya made it!" called Virg as they drew up and got out.

"No sweat, Gen'l Vine, suh. Smooth as silk."

"P. Trueblood, as I live, and in a Stetson!" Cleve clapped him on the shoulder.

"When in Rome, yawl," grinned Peter, looking sturdy, upright, and comfortable in the role of cowboy.

Virg allowed about thirty or forty seconds for reunion banter. "Okay guys, let's go meet the boss." Very much the labor organizer, he led them into the office, a large, plain room with a view of the sagebrush flats; everything in it was wood except the file cabinets, typewriters, and a few desks. From behind one a balding, slightly plump man in his forties rose with a genial smile and an outstretched hand. Only his plaid shirt and string bowtie distinguished him from any other businessman in small-town America.

"Hello and welcome, Virg. Have a good year?"

"Not bad, thanks, Morley. You've lost some hair and gained some weight, I see."

"As have you!" laughed Morley. "Good to have you back. You want to introduce me to these gentlemen?" As each savage was presented, Morley confronted him directly for a few seconds, making small talk - he had clearly read their files - and listening to the replies. His manner was welcoming, his chatter pleasant, but the eyes behind rimless glasses were those of an estimator. He had them fill out forms and sign contracts, then conducted them to the cavernous supply shed and had them search for the least ill-fitting Green Hornets, two apiece. Derisive shouts greeted each savage as he paraded his choice of the green-pinstripe uniforms. Cleve pronounced them all "uniformly ridiculous."

"All right, gather round for a minute, will you?" called Morley, subduing the clamor with a beckoning arm. "Now, gentlemen, here are the ground rules." He didn't need to raise his voice in this warehouse-sized echo chamber. "You work at your assigned station eight hours a day, minus mealtimes, six days a week. Your schedules and days off will be arranged by your manager. You are responsible to him, as he is to me. Try to get along: if there's a problem, you'll probably be the one to go." He smiled benignly. "But it seldom comes to that. Now, on our side, I will see that you are paid!" A few quiet cheers. "You already know your princely salaries, but in addition you receive a bonus of 15% of the value of all sales other than gasoline." A few interested grunts and 'Hmms' were audible.

"Now don't worry about your inexperience: you'll be taught what you need to know, which isn't much...basic stuff, really, if you've been around cars at all. Any questions so far?" He paused and looked around. Some heads shook. "All right then, station assignments." Attentive shuffling.

"We don't like cliques, as Virg may have told you, so I've split you up and spread you around the park. You can meet on your days off or compare notes in September." Morley glanced at his clipboard. "You probably know that Virg will be back at Faithful, this time as assistant manager at #1." A scattering of applause. "Marsh, you're assigned to Mammoth, where I can keep an eye on you, and handy to the bright lights of Gardiner." He winked and everyone laughed - except Marsh, who smiled uncertainly.

43

"It's okay, Marsh: we can give you the name of a really keen girl there," said Cleve with an air of bestowing largesse; Mason nodded corroboration. Marsh looked suspicious and put-upon, but said nothing.

"Cleve, you'll work at Canyon, a beautiful spot and very busy: we're building a new station there." Cleve smiled and nodded. Having escaped West Thumb, he didn't mention that he had a sister at Old Faithful.

"Cal, you're going to be at Lake, a little quieter than Canyon, but also a lovely place and centrally located."

Cal grinned and gave the others a little 'Hey-I-can-handle-it' shrug. "Sounds good," he said.

Morley nodded. "Finally, Trueblood and Dixon are assigned to West Thumb." There were a couple of snickers; Mason snapped his fingers and Peter looked around blankly. Morley raised his hand. "Okay, it's not as big or famous as some other stations, but it's a lively spot near our busiest entrance. It has plenty of young people, without the nuisance of too many resident dudes - that's tourists." In-group laughter. "My most dynamic manager is down there because we expect Thumb will be humming this year. I think you two can help out and enjoy yourselves."

And that was that. Mason, his Faithful fantasies gone a-glimmering, saw that the matter was closed, and gave up any thought of arguing. "West Thumb it is," he said neutrally.

"Right." Morley smiled. "Now, are there any questions...no? Might as well go report, then. And I trust I'll be seeing you on social calls or routine business only." He escorted them out the front door, shook hands all around, waved as they drove off, and took a deep breath of the sage-scented air before going back into the office.

After self-consciously presenting their new employee cards to the ranger at the park entrance, they stopped at the Mammoth service station to deposit Marsh. He kept looking about in a puzzled fashion but managed a smile. "Well, men, have a great summer. Maybe see you now and then."

"Marsh, just ask for Sally at the dining room in the lodge," said Cleve grandly. "A *fahn* woman! Tell her Mason and I send our regards and hope she found what she wanted at the bookstore. You'll be glad you did."

"Sure, uh-huh." He sounded disconsolate, but roused himself a little. "There's a bookshop?"

"Sure, in Gardiner! Marsh, you're gonna have a *great* time!" enthused Virg, patting him on the shoulder.

"I'll be fine." Marsh picked up his duffel and went to find the manager.

For the first stage Cleve rode with Virg, and Peter and Cal with Mason, up into the mountains and across the plateau south of Kingman Pass. The weather was fine, and Mason was glad to see the country that he had missed last night, but found it less powerful by daylight than when he had half-dreamt it - as if a poem had been turned to prose. At Norris there was another parting of the ways: Cleve transferred back to the station wagon and Virg raised his hand in benediction. "Gentlemen, peace be with you. Good luck! I'll check on you when I can. And of course I'll look in on Polly, Cleve." Then he took the right fork to Faithful and the others turned east. As the intervening strip of sagebrush and grasses gradually widened they honked and waved until Virg's car disappeared behind lodgepole pines. Mason again had that exhilarating but slightly scary sense of cutting loose from support, from seniority, from the past.

"Well, there goes the vet'ran," remarked Peter, as if he were thinking along the same lines. "Guess we're on our own now. Say, has anyone seen a paper or heard the news?"

"Omigod no, what news? What's happened?" exclaimed Cleve, turning around to face him.

"Oh nothin', prob'ly, but how would we know? Bein' outa touch, I mean. I wouldn't know if enathin *had* happened, would you?"

"Jesus, boy, don't scare me like that," groaned Cleve. "I thought Suez or sumpun had blown up again an' I was about to read '*Greetings*'." Like most draft-age American males of the era, he followed closely any and all news that might call for an expansion of the army.

"Pete, didn't you guys listen to the radio?" asked Mason.

"Sure, but what do you get? Farm news, weather, what some state senator said, mebbe the stock market, but not much from Warshington, an' nothin' foreign."

"We can probably make it up," Cleve suggested. "Ike's just been golfin', but Tricky Dicky came back from Outer Slobovia with a trade treaty and a non-aggression pact. He promised them umpteen billion in foreign aid, and the papers say he's sounding presidential."

"Barf," said Mason. "Let's see...McCarthy died. I admit that's not exactly *new*..."

"About a month old," laughed Trueblood. "The last thing I heard was whatsisface on *Face the Nation* the night before we left...Kay of Bee and Kay?"

"Kruschev," said Cal.

"Right. He said our grandchildren would live under socialism."

Cleve chuckled. "Just let me beget the grandchildren! They can look after their own politics."

"You want to beget your *grand*children too?" exclaimed Mason. "Is that even legal?"

"If yawl will pipe down for a minute," said Cal, "I'll tell you what I read in the *Bozeman Gazette* this morning at the Town Café." The others turned to look at him. "Russia is sending submarines to Egypt..."

"That's just a rumor, isn't it?" asked Mason.

"...and Israel has accepted the Eisenhower Doctrine."

"Oh no," moaned Cleve. "Don't *do* that, guys. If anybody can get us into a war requiring warm bodies, it's Ike. Almost did it last year." They paused for reflection.

"They're having an election in Canada," said Mason.

"Do they *have* elections? I thought they had the Queen."

"Who cares, anyway?"

"I heard it on a Montana station, after the cattle prices."

Thus did they while away the twelve lodgepole miles to Canyon Village, a large, somewhat confusing area with a hotel, store, campground, cabins, lots of people bustling around, and an almost-completed new service station. Behind it was a pine grove, and behind that a clear space where the Grand Canyon of the Yellowstone fell open. They sensed the chasm's plunge, but not until later did it occur to them that they might at least have walked over for a look. Here Cleve and his single suitcase left the party.

"Envy, envy," chanted Peter. "Looks like great country, Cleve. We'll have to come back when we have tahm fer satseein'."

"Cleve, it's been real," said Mason, extending his hand. "Let's keep in touch. And don't forget about Polly."

Cleve laughed. "I think you men who are gonna be closer should look in on her - if you don't mind."

"No sweat, Brother Cleve." Cal nodded, grinning.

"Oh all right, Mason! I won't forget. Be seeing ya, guys. Keep outa trouble." He waved and turned away, evidently pleased with his prospects.

South of Canyon the loop road found the Yellowstone River moving placidly through broad, grassy meadows, and followed it up the Hayden Valley toward the lake. A few hip-booted fly fishermen stood immobile in the slow current, which gave no hint of the chaos a few miles downstream. Peter and Cal discussed when and how they might fish this stretch. After the transient stink of the Mud Volcano, the lake-vista suddenly burst upon them: an unforeseen expanse of scintillating blue, a flat plane that underlined the rearing curves of its mountainous rim. Then they were back among the trees. A road to the left gave a momentary glimpse of Fishing Bridge, half full of anglers and kibitzers, all quickly swallowed by the sliding screen of forest. A few minutes later they came back to the shore at Lake Station - "Another breathtaking panorama," said Mason, yawning - and began to hunt among dark old buildings for Cal's billet.

After inquiring at both the porticoed hotel and the humbler lodge, they were directed to a clutch of cabins set among pines behind the latter. The grove was humming with new arrivals; three laughing girls in jeans who were unpacking a car and chattering like birds at a feeding station waved amiably as they drew up. "Oh my," exclaimed Cal, "game on the wing! Looks like a busy summer." He heaved his duffel bag out of the rear with an exaggerated sigh. "A hunter's work is never done. Well, Mace, we've arrived at the same time. Guess I *could* have ridden with you after all." He grinned and put out his hand.

Mason took it, but was still trying to think of a smart comeback when Peter forestalled him. "Cal, let's keep in touch. It's only twenty miles."

"Sure enough - but *you've* got the car! So long, men: I'll be seeing you." He turned to the girls.

And then there were two, driving along the lake toward West Thumb. The road alternately traced the flat shoreline, revealing a range of snowy peaks to the east, then dodged inland through thick woods and over rock-spined promontories. A few miles before Thumb they came down to the shore to stay, passing among steam pools and fiumaroles whose noxious vapors occasionally drifted over the highway. Trueblood sniffed and snorted. "Pew, that's disgusting! Stinks like a fart."

Mason glanced over at him, startled: Peter, who had been silent since Lake, was usually polite and reserved in speech. Had Mason's abduction of Polly rankled him, too? Ah: but Virg's car had not passed by Thumb, so fiumaroles were a novelty for him. "Yes, it *does*, doesn't it," he said, like one who has been agreeably enlightened. Then Mason began telling him about people at Thumb, Hole and Woo and Lou, surprised at how proprietary and defensive he sounded.

A jumble of log cabins began to appear by the shore and among the trees. "West Thumb," Mason announced, adding - again to his amazement - "Home again."

Peter laughed. "There doesn't seem to be a lot here."

"Oh, it's all right, you'll see," Mason heard himself say. Where was this advocacy coming from? He parked in front of the dormitories, facing the high board fence, and switched off. Here, he thought, that long trip, all those weary, venturesome miles, finally ends. Whatever it might be, a new phase would begin now.

*

They walked across the road to the station, where an argument was in progress between Lou and a big fellow in a hunting shirt. Hole, gas nozzle in hand, was watching from the rear of the car, but not pumping. The driver had stepped out to confront Lou, who was saying, "Sir, the rule heah is thet yuh turn awf yuh motuh at the pump."

"It don't awways turn right back awn if I shet it down."

"Sir, ifn it don't staht will give yuh push, but it's a fiyuh hazud."

The driver's face reddened. "You kids like throwin' yer weight aroun... nobuddy ever tol' me I *had* to switch awf before!"

Lou glared back at him, arms akimbo, but spoke calmly. "Wall, yuh will heah, ifn yuh wawnt gice. Next station is 17 mahles awn at Faceful, sir. Mebbe theah moah cahless up theah."

The tourist held his stare for a moment, then swore, dove back into his car and slammed the door. The engine died. Lou nodded to Hole, who began to pump, and the manager strolled over to the newcomers. "Dumb dood," he muttered. "Utaw - wuncha know it?" He gave a warm, crooked smile.

"Stop motors in the lanes is rule #1, eh?" asked Mason.

"Wall, mebbe numbuh *two*. Numbuh one is, the *doods* is awways wrawng. No skin ofn ar back if he gices up somers else: we don make money awf gice anyhow. Sides, evrathin in the park is Comico, so we gotum wheah we wawntum. He needs us morn we need him: no cawl tuh letum get outa lahn."

Mason bit back a comment about monopolies and introduced Lou to Peter. They strained briefly at each others' right hands, triceps bulging, then relaxed into truce. "Pleased tuh meecha. Morley phoned yud be comin down," said Lou, his eyes twinkling. "Whyncha getuh room in the dorm over theah n staish yer stuff? Gray the house father'll fix yup, n after lunch Ah ken show yuh roun the station."

They carried their bags through a gate in the stockade, past a basketball backboard, across a paved courtyard flanked by two dormitories and the back of the Hamilton's store, and straight ahead into the dorm facing them.

48

Trueblood rubbed his fingers over the varnished knotty pine of the wall. "Building looks almost new."

"It is," said a voice from the landing. A balding, florid man was descending the stairs toward them. "They finished both dorms just last year so the wood's still light. 'Ja notice how much darker the old store is?" He stuck out his hand. "I'm Gray the so-called house father."

"How do you do? I'm Mason and this is Peter."

"Welcome. Welcome. You rooming together?" They looked at each other, caught unprepared, then nodded. "Follow me then: got a nice corner room at the far end. Let me help with those bags..."

Was he kidding? "No sir, that's all right, we can manage." Gray led the way upstairs and down a long hall - pointing out the bathroom in passing, and warning them about the slick toilet paper - to a pleasant sunny room with a southwest exposure whose window looked out on the station and a corner of the girls' dorm. "That's where you eat," he explained, "and do your washing - unless you can persuade a girl to do it for you. It's been known to happen! But all that stuff's on the first floor: the girls live upstairs and that's a no-no." He waggled a finger and chuckled. "Been no hanky-panky yet that I know of, but there's a laundry line between the dorms - runs from that hall window right outside your door - with a pulley at each end. I wouldn't advise trying to pull across, though: I used real lightweight line!" He shook with mirth. "Well, let me know if you need anything - 'cept heavy-duty cord! See you later, then. Oh, lunch in half an hour. If you can't wait there's a soda fountain in the store." He waved and left.

While unpacking they let the place soak in and exchanged first impressions, agreeing that Gray had pleasant, informal manners and a sense of humor. Down the hall someone arrived, someone left. A petite, pretty girl in a blue uniform switched across the courtyard in the sunshine; a basketball clanged on the hoop, and the girl dodged it with a little shriek. A motorist gunned out of the lanes and gravel clattered against the pumps - but these were brief interruptions of a greater stillness that came washing back each time. As they walked down the hall, notes from a guitar came eddying around them from the open door of number seven. Inside, on a bed, sat Hole, cradling a big guitar from which he coaxed, with great deliberation, intricate patterns of rhythm and sound. His fingers seemed to move independently of one another, falling like little hammers to strike the strings with marvelous precision. It seemed magical: hadn't he just been over at the station, pumping gas in his Green Hornets? The piece cadenced to a satisfying close. The newcomers applauded.

49

"My God, where did you learn to do that?" blurted Mason, beside himself with envy and admiration.

Hole looked up with a pleased grin. "Taught myself from a Segovia record. Played it till I memorized...well, something. S'posed to be a Bach gavotte."

"What do you mean, '*supposed* to be'? I *recognized* that!" Mason introduced Peter and then asked for an encore. Hole nodded, and they sat quietly on the other bed while he played it again. All animation in the room was suspended except for the hammer-fingers; time did not pass but stopped to listen, so that they did not lose a minute but gained one. "Terrific, Hole, what a gift! Play us another?"

"It's the only one I know," he confessed with a wry chuckle. "But I saw your guitar case, man. What have you got in there?"

"Oh, six steel strings. Not the top of Martin's line, but a good hard sound. Josh White's my hero. I've got Segovia records too, but I never thought of playing his pieces! What about yours? 'F. Ruiz'? Are those nylon strings?"

Hole nodded. "Classical. Mexican," he said proudly. "Got it down in Monterrey a year ago. Listen, I can prob'ly teach you that gavotte if you want."

"Oh, I don't know...I'm just a strummer and picker."

"No sweat. If *I* can learn it..." Hole left the obvious conclusion unstated. "Hey, chow time. You going over?"

"I guess *so!*" said Peter. "Seems like *days* since breakfast." As they walked over to the girls' dorm Mason idly hummed the gavotte: "dum-dum-dum daba daba dum ...".

Hole growled, "Hell, man, you've got it half memorized already."

Mason grinned but made himself stop as they went inside and entered the dining room: more knotty pine with a couple of long tables, a stainless-steel milk dispenser almost worthy of Kansas, and a pass-through opening from the gleaming kitchen. Among the diners Peter and Mason recognized only Lou and Gray, who rose and introduced them to his wife Kay ("She's an R.N.," he said proudly) and their tablemates: a quiet older couple and an attractive middle-aged woman from Florida. Lou said she was a widow or divorcee. Half a dozen girls in blue uniforms sat whispering and giggling at the far end of the other table, patently checking out the new arrivals, who emerged from the cafeteria line with heaping trays and joined Lou at the senior table, a little away from Gray's group.

After a few minutes of inarticulate munching and chomping, Lou observed, "Mountain air kinda gives yun *ap*petat, doan it?"

"Sure *does*," Peter agreed, between bites. Then his fork hand paused for a moment. "Say, that must be it. How hagh are we here?"

"Bout sebenty-eight hunnert. Caincha smell it? Gives yuh *awl* kinda appetats." He chuckled softly and asked, "Howja lack ar Ham's girls?"

Peter and Mason had been stealing glances toward the blue uniforms, but this seemed to stymy them. "They work over at the Hamilton general store," Hole explained. "There are other girls who work in the cabins - pillow punchers - but they don't live or eat here, so we don't see much of 'em."

"Oh," said Mason. "Well, I see one cute one."

"That's Prissy," chortled Lou.

"Do you know her?"

Hole laughed. "He knows her."

Gray and his party now rose, said polite goodbyes and left. "Nice legs on the Florida lady," remarked Mason judiciously.

"Wall, them's Floriddy legs," Lou explained. "It's all thet swimmin, wawduh skeen, aquaplaynin - thet's whagh we makum do it!" he chortled. "So, Pete, whacha thank of the gals?"

Trueblood, who had been silent but wide-eyed, cleared his throat. "Well, a little disappointing," he said. "Some not bad, but nothing spectacular. Of course they may be fine people," he added. They all looked at him, but his face was straight.

Lou leaned forward confidentially, pointing his knife at Peter. "Plain girls'll give yuh better lay, thet's a fac," he said softly. "As yuh know." Trueblood reddened, but Lou seemed not to notice. "Guess they're trine tuh proove sumpun." He shrugged and downed a bite of jello. "Course yuh doan *hev* tuh mess aroun with none uh these - they's un thousand moah up at Faceful."

Peter looked as if his milk might be sour. "Lou," cautioned Mason, "you're talking to the president of the Youth Fellowship of the First Methodist Church in Hillville, the pride of east Tennessee."

"Ain't sayin enathin evrybody doan awreddy know," chortled Lou.

"Lou, do you have a sister?" asked Trueblood carefully. "Or a girlfriend?"

"Yeah, sure Ah do!" he exclaimed impatiently. "She's a beaut n a lady n it's lack Ah said: yuh look but doan touch." Lou shook his head sadly, miles away for a moment. "Yull see, she's comin out heah from Floriddy later awn. But doan spread thet roun jes yet: Ah gotta few moah days." He laughed and finished his dessert.

The girls rose at that point and Lou hailed Pris to come over and meet the new guys. She turned out to be the pretty brunette they had seen crossing the courtyard, and to have mischievous eyes. Pris made her roommate Jill, a friendly, slightly chubby blonde, come over too. Mason and Peter stood for them, and both sides made polite noises of welcome and amity, but when they left Hole chuckled, "Tarts." Peter looked at him in surprise, opened his mouth, then closed it again without speaking.

"Wall, gents, lez get ovuh tuh the station n Ahl show yus aroun," said the manager. Crossing the courtyard he pointed to the basketball standard with its freshly netted hoop. "Fuss n bes thang Ah did heah wuz git thet up. Muh prahde n joy!" he chuckled. "Yawl play?"

Peter nodded uh-huh and Mason said, "Not much."

"Bettuh gitn practice," Lou advised. "It's the big nooz heah. Game goes awn the whole summuh."

"Who runs the station while you're away?" Mason asked.

"Woo'n whoevuh's awn. Hayward rat now, and the new guy, Hohn. Full-blood Injun from Oklyhomy, ain't thet a gas? He's larnin' the ropes. Quick, too." In the lanes and the shed Lou made short introductions; then said, "Cumawn, lesgo meet the pumps n stuff."

For an hour he demonstrated the high-speed gas pumps, showed them how to check and add oil to the engine, water to the battery and radiator, and how to run a chamois through the electric wringer without crushing their fingers. Next he taught them how to operate the grease rack and the tire-repair machine. Then, elementary salesmanship: push bug screens when the sun is shining and anti-freeze when it is not. Lou also explained the use of the cash register, the system of receipts and credit cards, and the schedule of shifts and days off. Each rookie was then issued a Red Flag oil dipstick wiper and appointed a hook on which to hang his uniforms. Tuhmorra they would work a reg'lar shift; rat now they mat wawnt tuh practice what they'd larned.

Insecure but eager, the fledgling gas jockeys donned their Green Hornets, brought Mason's wagon from across the street as their guinea pig, and spent the next hour probing its innards. They gassed it up, checked the oil and water, ran it up on the rack, greased the zerts and changed the oil. While it was up there (once Mason heard that he had a 15% employee discount on all purchases), they removed a tire, broke it down on the tire machine, threw away the patched tube and installed a new one. They were still apprehensive about serving real customers, but it had been a good afternoon for the car and for their morale.

Lou had been keeping an eye on them, and when the car came down he strolled over and asked how it was going. Mason said quite well, thanks, and Peter allowed as how he was at least feeling more confident than he had two hours ago. The manager seemed pleased by their enthusiasm, which they evidently overdid, because his next remark was, "Wall, tahm tuh hit the lanes, then!"

"What, you mean right now?" stammered Mason.

"Shur, rat naow, whagh not? Yuh gocher unyforms ahn."

"Well, I guess we were expecting a training period," said Trueblood. "You know, like an apprenticeship."

"Yuh just had it, Pete: craish course! Awl yuh need, n awl anyone gits. No tahm lack the present!" Lou was smiling, jollying them, but his voice had an edge, and they stopped unbuttoning their uniforms.

Woo and Horn had been observing all this, and now Horn stepped forward with a smile. "Pardon me, Lou, but if you like I could sort of advise on their first job or two."

"Good idee, Hohn, you do thet. Mason, Pete: you let Hohn heah take yuh through. Jes been wukkin a coupla days hisself, but he's uh faist lunnuh." Lou glanced out the front window. "Heah, take this Chevy cumin in naow. Hey Hay, take a break!"

As they hustled out to the lanes, nodding to Hayward, Horn spoke rapidly. "Pete, you pump. Get the driver's order. Filler pipe's behind the license plate. Mason, take the front. See if he wants the hood checked." Then he stepped back. The driver asked for $3 of regular and said the oil was all right, so Mason just dipped a chamois in the tub of soapy water, ran it through the wringer and cleaned the windshield. In no time at all the Chevrolet was back on the road and the cash was in the till.

"Well, *that* wasn't bad!" laughed Trueblood as he returned from the shed. "Heps when they have exact change. Say, thanks for the tip about the gas pipe, I might – uh oh, what's this?" A queer little bug of a foreign car was pulling in.

"Jesus, a Volkswagen," groaned Horn. "Okay, you pump, Mason, but listen..."

"Hey Hohn!" Lou was bellowing from the shed. "Come in heah uh minut!"

Horn closed his eyes. "I guess you're on your own," he said, and turned away.

The driver leaned out of the window, as if there were not room for his head in the car. "Fill it up regular," he said.

"Yessir, but could you pull forward a little?" asked Mason. "The hose won't reach the back from here."

"No, but it'll reach the front, which is where the gas cap is on these Folksvagens, you know." He pulled a release under the dashboard and the hood clinked a little open. Mason raised it, but all he could see was a pile of suitcases. Was this the trunk? He searched in desperate silence until the driver got out and pointed to the cap, hidden among the baggage. Mason unscrewed it with care, unhooked the hose nozzle from the pump, inserted it in the filler pipe and squeezed the trigger. Gas began to flow and he relaxed, sweating.

Trueblood had finished cleaning the windows, and as he passed Mason whispered, "The oil check must be in the *rear*." Peter grunted, went to the back and opened the engine compartment; Mason heard him talking to the driver. Then there was a sloshing sound and he looked down to see gasoline spilling out of the pipe and over bags and parcels. A sharp, sweet stench rose to his nostrils. He released the trigger, screwed the cap back on and got the hood down before the driver returned, smiling.

"Your friend suggested that I put in a can of anti-freeze," he said, "and I was explaining why that isn't necessary on this type of car."

"No sir, I see your point: the weather's warming up. But hot weather means bugs, and bugs mean a clogged radiator and a hot engine," replied Mason, amazed at how easy and natural it felt to swing into a sales pitch. He was oblivious to Peter's gestures, the driver's grimaces, and what he had seen under the hood - or whatever that was. "We have a nice little bug screen for 87 cents."

"Now wait a minute," said the dude, whose tolerant smile had faded. "Your buddy wants to sell me anti-freeze, and you want to sell me a bug screen - for an air-cooled, rear-mounted engine! What kind of place it this? Dammit, this car *has no radiator*! Here, just take your $2 for gas and I'll be off." He slapped the bills into Mason's palm, jumped back in the VW and peeled out, throwing up some gravel. Dazed, Mason carried the money in to Lou at the cash register.

"You didn't tell us about little foreign cars."

Lou's face was red and tears stood in his eyes. "He-he-he, larn bah doin!" he choked out, slapping his thigh as he rang up the sale. Obviously he had watched the whole scene from the window with great relish, as had the others; only Horn looked sympathetic. But in another moment Lou turned to the new team and with an air of solemn ritual held out his big hand. "Shake, Mason. Yer battle-tested! Done had yer bap-tism of far." His eyes twinkled shrewdly.

It *seemed* true. As if in a dream Mason heard the others murmur congratulations. Returning to the lanes he felt strange, different...a veteran, that was it: calm, confident, knowledgeable, tried and tested - a devoted servant of the American motorist. Well, of dudes, anyway. Peter was leaning against a pump and Mason joined him, popping his Red Flag oil rag and keeping an eye out for the next customer. Life as a gas jockey had fairly begun.

*

After another car or two Lou said they had done enough for the first day and cut them loose. They hung up their Green Hornets, took a closer look at the Mud Pot, then walked down to the shore to enjoy the vista, shooting a few baskets en route back to the dorm. Once showered and cleanly dressed, they went to check out the Hamilton General Store, Thumb's commercial hub. Entering from the courtyard via the back door and walking down a corridor past the wicket of the business office, you emerged into a large, high-ceilinged room with many gifts and souvenirs and some camping supplies for sale, a soda fountain, and a picture window looking out across the lake to the distant Absaroka Mountains. Gray happened to be in there, and he showed them where to pick up paychecks and buy stamps.

Then sprightly Pris, who was re-arranging displays, came over and invited them to stop by the soda fountain if they wanted to meet some more Ham's girls. Realizing that they *were* thirsty, they followed her to the counter, where she introduced Vicky, a lively, bubbling South Carolinian, and Barbara, aka Red, who came from Cheyenne. She was quieter, with a tough smile. Like Jill, both girls carried just enough baby fat to qualify as "pleasantly plump." The boys ordered a Coke and a milkshake, receiving "service with a smile," as the slogan went. Surveying the scene as they sipped, Peter laughed and remarked, "Yuh know, I think I can live here." It sounded like a declaration of acceptance. Mason was surprised at how relieved and grateful he felt.

As they walked along the dormitory hall to their room they heard music again: this time the drawn-out strains of *The St. Louis Blues* played on an accordion. The sounds were coming from the open door of #5, the room opposite theirs. Inside, sitting on his bed, was a genial-looking fellow who glanced up with a shy smile and ceased playing as they appeared. "Don't stop," said Mason.

"Oh. Not everybody likes it," laughed the player, who introduced himself as Gair from "near St. Louis." Mason asked if he could bring over his guitar and Gair brightened. They did *The St. Louis Blues* as a duet, then moved on to other standards: *Sunny Side of the Street, Blue Skies, St. James Infirmary*, and so on, discovering that they agreed on the chord progressions - a strong bond between musicians of any stripe. After a while Hole appeared, and it was his turn to marvel at people who could play by ear, adjusting, however crudely, to each other's keys and harmonic moves. They played until it was almost dinnertime. The visitors told Gair they'd stop by for him.

"We can introduce you to the girls," laughed Trueblood, and Mason thought, Yeah, I can live here.

Four: The Great Fast Flush War

In the middle of June, when most of the work crew had arrived, Lou held - or rather staged - a nocturnal "sales seminar" over in the tin icebox of the station house. Attendance was mandatory. After dinner they groped their ways across from the dormitories on a moonless Wyoming night - taking care to keep the plop/slurp of the invisible mudpot to their right - and found seats on cases of oil, fuel drums, stacked auto tires, or just the greasy floor. The shed had lights but no heat, and snow showers had been alternating with intermittent sleet for three days. While the white stuff was not sticking at Thumb as it did on the passes over to Faithful, nighttime temperatures still dipped into the 30s. Mason said it was no worse than mid-autumn in Boston, to which Trueblood retorted that the houses there were probably heated. "Just goes to show it's all relative, guys," chortled Hole, who had been acclimatizing for two weeks now. Hayward, inured to winters on a Wisconsin farm, and Horn, who had probably had it worse somewhere, kept their thoughts to themselves, as usual.

Additions to these "originals" or "core crew," as they liked to style themselves, had been straggling in almost daily. Gair, who was "honorary core," sat talking to a husky Canadian named Bastille, who had not been around much and was said to be a journalist; both of them were used to cold winters. The conditions were hardest on newly arrived southerners. "Jesus, it's cold," snarled Henderson, a North Carolinian who had been accepted at Debrew. He hugged his skinny body while his friend Beatty, a chubby Chattanoogan, moaned sympathetically. In one corner, Cyril and The Mouth sat silently on a stack of retreads. Cyril had nursed his Chevy across plains and up mountains for a week before abandoning it at a garage in eastern Wyoming and completing his journey to Thumb *by* thumb. His brush cut, as stiff and vertical as a field of corn, gave him an air of perpetual fright or alertness belied by his easy smile. The Mouth - aka Jake LaBouche - was a wide-lipped Ohioan who rarely opened them. Iowa had contributed Kramer, another very quiet individual, who was deemed strange and dubbed Creeper. Few real or full names could survive at Thumb; everyone needed a nickname, usually suggested by appearance, personality, homophony, or place of origin. Thus Mason was Boston, Bastille was Canuck, etc.

Lou and Woo came in a few minutes late with the newest arrival in tow, a tall, handsome character with a suntan and a shock of blond hair. "This heah's Will Hockness frum Califohny, gonna room with Gaih, play some baisketbawl, probly be the stah when *Ah* ain't playin, he he he!" Lou got out in one breath. There were murmurs of greeting. Will looked amused by it all as he shook hands with Gair and sat down by Mason with an urbane nod.

Meanwhile Lou was assuming his favorite perch: on the wooden table before the main window, beside the cash register, over which he draped an affectionate arm. "Now thet evrabody *knows* evrabody," he chuckled, then paused, his eyes bright, and asked more quietly, "Wudja lack tuh make some *muh*ney?" There were a few grunts from the keeners, which he took for Yes, and so launched into an explanation of the YPCC Sales Race. The corporation had assigned each of its seven stations a Quota: a cash value of products (other than gasoline) that it would try to attain or exceed. That quota was set at 10% above the previous summer's sales. The station that sold the highest percentage of or over its quota would receive a bonus on all salaries, plus a steak dinner in West Yellowstone, at summer's end. "Thet way a place lack Mammoth, thet wuz rock bottom lais cheer, got a chaince tuh beat Faceful, with awl its bizness," Lou explained.

"And that's how a monopoly fights lethargy," murmured Will, so softly that only Mason heard.

"N *we* gotta gud chaince too," the manager continued. "Caz we wuz purty far down the list lais cheer." Then he began to exhort his crew with gestures and inflections suggestive of revivalist preachers, stressing always the benefits to the converts. "So Ah figguh if yuh wuhk lack Yallerstone bee-vers," he concluded, "yuh could make n extry" - he looked up at the ceiling, then cocked an eye back down on them - "sixty dollahs!" Henderson whistled - it was about two weeks' salary - Mason laughed, Will sniffed. The others looked indifferent or mildly ironical.

When Lou began to offer advice on *how* to sell, though, interest picked up. "We bin piddlin so fah," he said. "Now we gonna get *serus*." His counsel brought to mind the door-to-door salesman (which Woo said he had been). Lou's analysis was colorful and shrewd, full of practical suggestions and warnings. You had to find a way to get friendly with the customer, slip the product smoothly into the conversation and make the sales pitch appealing. Reason was okay, but flattery and psychology were better. "Whate*v*ah yuh do," he warned, "don jes *say* the prass n leave it *hang*in theah. It's lack" - he heaved himself up into a commercial posture - "Yes

58

ma'am, with awl th'accesries weah awfrin it this month fer only nanta-nan nanta-fav BUT - Ah *cain't* promise duhlivry til nex *Toos*dee!" Lou smacked the cash register for emphasis, and it jangled a faint endorsement. "Yuh see?" he asked. Several savages nodded or grunted. "Will fine out bout thet." His narrowed eyes raked the assembly. "Beatty! Stan up n *sell* me sumpun."

There was an uneasy stir in the room, but Beatty rose at once, the movements of his rotund body surprisingly graceful, and began to speak in a fluid drawl: "Well sirrr, we have a deal with Farstone that lets us give yuh this tar fer twentuh-three nanta-fav AND theah's a two-yeah, fifteen-thousand mal guarantee." Where was this coming from?! Had he had the question in advance? Beatty spoke with unhesitating ease, his manner was charming, his delivery natural, and he sat down to applause.

"That's shonum, Chattanooga," said Lou, grinning. "Yull make it at Yew uv Tee all rat."

"Selling tires?" Mason's whisper was just audible.

"Awrat, Mason, yer tawkin anyhoo, let's hear *yew*." Flushing, Mason began to talk about bug screens in a tone of quiet persuasion, until Lou shook his head and snorted. "Nimmy, nimmy, nimmy," he mocked. "'Ts got no FAR! N *bug* screens!" He appealed to the others. "If we sold enathin *cheap*uh he'd be pushin *thet*!" The laughter was there but it was uncomfortable, and Lou visibly changed gears, his eyes twinkling. "Yew jes use some o thet Yankee wit, yull be awrat." Mason nodded slightly, still discomfited.

"Lessee...Hohn, show us how it's dood down on the...back whar yuh come frum." Horn stood up, looking strong and confident, and launched into a pitch for new tires, complete with technical commentary on tread wear.

"Pretty suave," whispered Peter. "Where'd he learn all that?"

Woo shook his head. "Business major, mebbe. Prob'ly be up in management next year." He spoke without enthusiasm, probably thinking of his own difficulties with accounts.

"Thet's good, Hohn, thet's the way. Jes not *too* smooth - thell thank yer trine tuh *sell*um sumpun!" He guffawed and slapped his thigh. Horn smiled, showing bright, even teeth, and sat down. "That's my roomie," Hole informed them.

"Okay Hole, yer ahn." And so all had their turns to stand up and sell something, while Lou coaxed, cajoled, jeered, grunted, criticized or comforted. It was an uneasy time - there seemed to be no escape - but it was also interesting, and quite a show. Behind the clown's mask Lou proved to be a close observer of styles: his observations were perceptive, prophetic, or both. Everyone except Beatty and Horn had room to improve. Henderson was kinda hangdawg, Peter a bit skwar. Hole and Gair could chahm the pints ofn yuh but mebbe too easy-goin. Only Will, as a new arrrival with no experience in the lanes, declined to participate, and after a tense moment Lou let him off.

Afterwards Will invited Mason and Peter across the hall to his and Gair's room. Closing the door behind them, he produced a bottle of Scotch from his still-packed luggage. Gair looked ill at ease, and Peter warned, "We can be thrown out of here for that, you know."

"Really!" murmured Will, raising his eyebrows as he poured a glassful. "Who's drinking?" Mason, used to a cocktail society, accepted and went for his glass; Gair said he'd try a bit. Peter refused politely. After two sips Gair opened his accordion and undertook a mournful blues. At the end Will nodded and said, "Nice progression. I liked that diminished chord in the last cadence."

Mason stated the obvious. "You must be a musician too."

"A little piano. How about you?"

"Singing, some folk guitar. Gave up piano long ago. They say there's a piano in the rec hall - we should find that."

Draining his glass, Will poured himself another short one. "Refill, anyone?" Mason and Gair, only half finished, shook their heads. Will began unpacking his suitcase, and a satchel of books.

Mason picked up some of the paperbacks and glanced through the titles. "Quite a reader, Will. Where are you going to school?"

"Off to Princeton in September."

"Baisketbawl scholarship?" drawled Peter.

Will gave him a sharp look and quickly saw that the question was not malicious. "Full academic."

Mason, rummaging through English, American, French and Russian novels, and some non-fiction, asked, "Majoring in English?"

"Maybe, or history. The humanities, anyway."

"Good luck." Peter rose. "'Night, men. You can bet the sales race starts tomorra for real."

He was right. In the morning Lou paired them up - often putting roommates together - and announced that the team logging the most dollars in bonus sales each day would earn an hour off. The selling soon became heavy; rare was the dude who escaped unsolicited. Mason and Peter took advantage of the unsettled weather (now sleet, now humid warmth) to sell several bug screens and some anti-freeze. Gair and Will made a rather languid pair, but did peddle a few cans of oil additive. Gair's Cheshire-cat grin as he returned to the lanes, gold can in hand, ought to have given the game away, but the dudes seemed not to notice. Horn was selling little for the moment but radiated self-assurance, like a good boxer just watching for a weakness. His partner was the unprepossessing Creeper. A pallid fellow of average height with a brush cut and a rural twang - seldom used - Creeper did not look or sound like a gifted salesman. It was quickly noted, however, that he drove a pretty blue Ford coupe only a year old, which seemed to constitute an eloquent plea against any hasty adverse judgment.

Lou prowled through the lanes and the shed restlessly, offering impromptu sermonettes full of mercantile philosophy and practical tips to any savage with an idle moment or just passing. Occasionally he moved in and sold something himself. "Rumembuh, Yallerstone is special," he told Peter as he rang up a sale. "Folks is awfun their home turf n awn ars, runnin skeered. Evrathins unfamiliar, ol buggy souns funny, they wanna know *whagh*. You givum some answers, yer gonna sellum sumpun."

By midday it was clear that Beatty and Henderson were the class of the field. While other teams experimented, they operated their system as if they had been rehearsing for years. Henderson the Respectful did all the pumping and sold 60-cent cans of gas additive with nearly every tank. (When Mason asked Lou if the stuff really improved mileage, the manager chuckled. If the dudes checked mileage, he said, they would think so, "caz they allus fergit tuh add in the volume uv the additive!") Beatty the Charming hovered around the hood, flourishing his Red Flag, poking into everything, selling anti-freeze, bug screens, oil, oil additives and spare oil. He could produce a shiny can from every pocket of his Green Hornets, as needed. The pair sent Lou into ecstasies of admiration. "Awmost thihty dollahs awreddy," he enthused as the first shift scoured hands for lunch. "That's *sell*un. Men, they's showin they backsads to yus!" They maintained their pace throughout the afternoon, easily winning the hour off with almost $50 of bonus sales. "They is the team tuh beat!" trumpeted Lou, dismissing them early while the others reflected on the personal qualities required for success at Thumb. And that, really, was the first day of the sales race.

Beatty's creativity was astonishing: the second day he discovered the Worn Fan Belt Replacement, and they won again with that. "This

61

could get *bor*in," sneered Henderson as they left early. Most fan belts cost around $3.50, well above the value of the "she-ut" they had been peddling yesterday. But Beatty realized at once that time spent *changing* a fan belt was dead, i.e. unremunerated, time - time lost from selling - so he moved into *spare* fan belts, "kanda lahk inshurrance." He would even mention that the customer could have the new belt installed at a rival YPCC station: let *them* lose valuable time. And the next day, when the rest were looking into fan belts, Beatty, never content to rest on yesterday's laurels, discovered Radiator Sludge and Fast Flush.

Fast Flush is a liquid chemical that is poured into the radiator, which it is said to clean as you drive. After a hundred miles you drain it, flush the system, refill with clean water or anti-freeze, and drive off with your cooling capacity rejuvenated. They all knew about the product from Lou or personal use (he had suggested with a straight face that they would make better salesmen if they tried their own merchandise), but they did not understand how to *sell* it until Beatty's inquiring spirit chanced upon Radiator Sludge. Scouting under the hood of an old Dodge he went to check the water, and stuck his finger down into the filler pipe because he could not see the level (a good way to get burned, but salesmen take risks). The finger came up with black goo adhering to it. For a moment Beatty stared at this revelation as a great idea was born; then sauntered around to the driver, held up the blackened finger and asked him if he knew what this stuff was.

"No, I sure don't," replied the dude.

"Kinda hoped you would, sirrr, seen as how it came out of *yore* radiator."

"Whaaat?!" The driver emerged at once, worried but sceptical, and hastened around to the hood. "My God, what *is* it? I've never had any… it's been runnin okay…long way from Topeka" and so on.

Beatty heard him out, then replied on cue at the first pause: "Well Sirrr, Ahve got a fahn product cawled Faist Flush fer only a dollahr'll surre hep a prollum lak this." Henderson reported that the man practically begged Beatty to dump the contents of the grey can into his radiator, and as he drove off, talking animatedly to his family, it was clear that he felt a disaster had been narrowly averted.

The Dynamite Duo, as Lou called them, could not help crowing about their discovery, so in the course of the afternoon the "sludge and flush" gambit spread to every team in the lanes. A Fast Flush brought in less than a fanbelt, but it sold easily, could be added in a minute, and would have to be drained and flushed by someone at another station. The fact that (as they soon learned) Radiator Sludge could be found in most cars if you knew where to look - and so could hardly indicate a pathological condition - did not detract from the appeal of purging it.

"But does it work?" Will asked the manager.

"Fars Ah know," said Lou, deadpan.

Let historians debate just how and when the Great Fast Flush War began; the savages were never sure. Its first skirmishes were mild and innocent, troubling no one's conscience in the prevailing ethical climate. It seemed reasonable to suggest to northbound dudes that the stuff be flushed at Mammoth, 91 miles away, though Lou had a phone call from their manager, who "sounded kinda noid," he chuckled, and Marsh, passing through on his day off, confirmed that Thumb's tactics were unpopular up there. Still, Mammoth began to return the fire, which appeared to sanction the arrangement by making it reciprocal. One morning Mason had to do a flush job from Mammoth, whereupon he and Beatty (Henderson being off) sold two girls from Texas a can of oil additive, five quarts of top-grade oil, a Fast Flush and a can of anti-rust to go into the clean radiator - all labor to be done at Mammoth. The selling was not difficult: worrying out loud about their car, the girls were grateful for suggestions. Price was no object. They drove away convinced that their red Pontiac convertible was running better. Beatty rang up the sales and told Lou that they had sent at least an hour's labor to Mammoth.

Thus far it appeared to be a fair contest between stations, with little collateral damage to the dudes caught in the middle. But several of the crew doubted the morality of opening a second front with Old Faithful #2: the Sarajevo of this war. One morning Beatty marched into the shed with a can of Fast Flush in hand and a mild-looking dude in tow. "Lou, this gemman wawnts tuh flush his radiator n he's headin out West Yellahstone," he announced. "Dja thank Faithful's too close fer a good flush?" He knew as well as Lou that Old Faithful - the only YPCC station the man would be passing - was only 17 miles away, and that 17 falls well short of 100, but both kept straight faces.

"Naw," said Lou after a moment, "ya got those two steep grades. Thet'd give it a gud cleanin. Old Faceful nummer tool be glad tuh do fer yuh, sir." He turned back to his accounts, and the die was cast. The manager at Faithful #2, a "damn Yankee," was of all YPCC's managers Lou's pet peeve. Mason - plugging a tubeless tire at the machine with the owner beside him, oblivious to the great moral struggle - stood open-mouthed. "Bedduh gedawn with thet tar," said Lou mildly. "N don swaller a flagh."

That afternoon an Idaho car pulled up beside the shed and the driver handed Mason a folded note addressed to Lou. "Frum the feller up at Faithful," he explained. "And yer supposed tuh drain this here flush outta my radiator." Mason delivered the note to Lou and set about flushing the Plymouth. A few minutes later Trueblood came around the corner of the shed looking both amused and alarmed. "I've never seen Lou so mad," he whispered. "Wait'll you see that note!" When Mason next went inside he found the piece of paper tacked to the wall above the cash register where its crude block lettering would be seen by every savage:

LOU:
    IF I GET ONE MORE OF THOSE FAST FLUSHES UP
HERE I'M COMING DOWN TO TAN YOUR REBEL HIDE.
MEANTIME HERE'S ONE UP YOURS.
    GUESS WHO

Lou had scrawled a postscript: "An hour off for every man who sends a Fast Flush to O.F. #2."

"Looks like the gauntlet is down," remarked Will, reading over his shoulder.

"Yes, but what do you think we should do?"

"I'm not having any part of it," said Hole, coming in from the lanes with a credit card.

Will nodded agreement. "A plague on both their houses."

"Sales race or not, it's an abuse."

But Beatty sent one before he went off duty, and Horn dispatched another at suppertime. An equal number came back during the evening. At closing time Lou had a shouted phone conversation with "that damn Yank" that could be heard clearly out in the lanes. "This is getting out of hand," said Gair gravely. The non-participants shook their heads and speculated on probable outcomes. Mason wondered aloud if the other manager would fight. He was certain that Lou would not back down.

"They won't let it come to that," Will scoffed. "A monopoly can't have its agents cutting each other up. The YPCC will intervene."

He was right. Early the next morning Lou had a phone call from Morley in Gardiner that could not have been more unlike the previous night's call. All an eavesdropper could tell was that Morley was doing the talking; Lou contributed only a few quiet replies, mostly "Yessir." When Mason next came in to the cash register Lou was staring vacantly over the lanes to the forested slope beyond. "No moah Faist Flushes tuh Faceful," he said mournfully.

Mason almost blurted "Why not?" but bit it back in time. He did briefly consider telling Lou that he had never sent any, and why. The manager probably knew that already, though, so Mason just said, "Righto," as neutrally as possible, and hastened back out to the lanes.

It was left to Will, the valedictorian, to pronounce the epitaph on this one: "It was a short war but a merry one."

Thus ended the hot and dirty phase of the trade wars. They could still harass their rivals with fan belts and oil changes, however, and send Fast Flushes to Mammoth. Since Lou believed that Mammoth, with its low quota, would provide their chief competition in the sales race, he was grateful for that dispensation, which led to a summerlong vendetta. He spent hours meditating on how to trip up "the Mammoths" as they tried to snatch the sales Grail from its rightful possessor. If he did not initiate or spread, he certainly welcomed the rumor that they were using hidden razors "up there" to slit fan belts as they checked under the hood. The mere possibility that it might be true fired his crew with moral indignation, and they pushed their products with the zeal of crusaders.

Most sales were easy: caught off guard by the hard sell, dudes often agreed to try a product without even asking the price. Lou told them to ask everyone, but never to persist beyond a "No." One afternoon Virg Vine stopped by and told Peter that Thumb's crew were regarded at Faithful as the fireballs of the Park, and Cal, who hitchhiked down on his day off, said there was nothing like it at Lake. "Good," growled Lou. Most of the crew reveled in their reputation, but a few, including Will and Mason, wondered what it would be like to work at a station where you just pumped gas and gave the dudes what they asked for. To them, the selling imperative was becoming burdensome.

The competitive adrenaline flowed faster as the Fourth of July weekend approached, which Lou had warned them from the beginning would be a madhouse. He treated it as the Big Game for which his team must be at their best. The scrimmages grew rougher: by late June the lanes were crowded for 8 hours a day, and all the savages had run-ins with hot, impatient dudes, but they had learned how to work and argue simultaneously.

On June 24th the crew finally reached full strength, the "parfic sixteen" for which Lou had been champing, and thus he was able to implement his high-summer schedule. Early shift began work at 6 AM, ate breakfast in two sittings around 7, lunch about noon, and came off duty at 3 PM. Second shift appeared at 1 and worked until closing time, 9 or 10 PM, with dinner at 6. The overlap between 1 and 3 provided extra hands to clean the station; the rest of the time there were just enough to keep all pumps going full blast as demand required. Two men were off each day, and with early shift before and late shift after their holiday it meant a break of almost 48 hours, ensuring that they would return to the lanes "lack taggers." Coach Fuller took considerable satisfaction in these logistical arrangements.

The late arrivals who brought him his full complement and made his system symmetrical were two Californians who materialized out of a late June snow shower. Actually there were four in the wheezing hot-rod and all wanted jobs, having spent their entire cash reserves on repairs to "this damn piece of junk." Lou culled the least scruffy two and sent the others on to Faithful. Then he called Morley, whom he had been begging for reinforcements, and told him he had found his own. They looked superficially alike - lean, tanned, healthy, with short blond hair - but "Schlitz" was quiet and pleasant, even when indulging in his favorite brew, while "Owl Brain" (the nicknames, again, were Henderson's) had lip and cheek enough for both. Tall, hard and brassy, he struck everyone as the quintessential Angelino, and no one expected him to last long on the job. Owl seemed not to care about that, or anything; he wasn't sure what he might do after high school. He hung out mostly with his roommate Hayward, who was said to be a dropout, a jailbird, and a veteran - at 18! "An *he's* doin' awright, ain't he?" demanded Owl. They made an odd couple, dubbed by Will "piano and forte." Schlitz was sent to room with Creeper.

The Fourth dawned clear and mild. Settled warm weather had replaced the wild early days when they sold bug screens at 10 and anti-freeze at 11; now they sweated in their coveralls and tried to dodge "dude-geysers": eruptions from boiling radiators when some idiot removed the cap. A blaring of horns over at the station jolted them awake, and Lou's dulcet tones floated down the hall. "Awrat, mens, les go serve thuh 'mercan public!"

"Christ, it's not even *six*!" yelled Owl.

"Git yer ice in geer!"

In a few minutes the first shift went stumbling across the road, watched with open hostility by four motorists standing beside their cars. "Fill er up high test," said a tall thin man in waders. "I been honkin' here 15 minutes."

"Is *that right?*" exclaimed Owl. "*Funny* we didn't hear you."

"The station opens at six, sir," said Horn with a winning smile.

"Fish don't have clocks," observed another dude.

A moment later they were pumping gas with one hand, buttoning up Green Hornets or rubbing eyes with the other. "This one don't start," said one driver apologetically as he paid Will.

"Oh Christ, men, here's a push job already!" Four of them gathered behind the old Studebaker and heaved, and ran, and finally sent it rolling and sputtering down the road toward the lake.

"Pushing cars at 7800 feet before breakfast!" gasped Mason. "I'd lose mine if I'd had any."

After the first wave of fishermen, business slacked off so they could eat in shifts as usual, beginning at 7, but when "second breakfast" returned at 8 an alarming number of cars sat backed up in the lanes and out into the street. Lou sent to the dormitory for reinforcements: as on a ship in peril, all able-bodied hands had to turn out. In a few minutes the ever-loyal Woo appeared, clumping along awkwardly because he had not even stopped to tie the laces of his clodhoppers. Some motorists - apparently assuming that he had overslept and was responsible for the long lines - honked and wagged fingers at him. Woo's first task was to explain to a fat man in a strap undershirt why he couldn't have a grease job right then. His reward was to have the car door slammed in his face. "Utah," sighed Woo as he went in the shed.

"Serves yuh rat fer spendin yer day awf at Thumb on the Fourth," chuckled Lou, which sounded ruthless. "But Ahl tragh tuh gecha some ovuhtahm, Woo. See whacha ken do with thet ol chamois-wranger, will yuh?"

"Ah Lou, is it broke again?"

"A dumb dood trad tuh wrang out his hand."

By 10 AM it was downright hot, and a solid mass of cars packed the gravel apron around the pump-islands. Then the only high-test pump in the outside lane broke, so Lou and Woo started trying to re-route "Ethyl" traffic to inner lanes, as well as cleaning windshields and soothing tempers. The lane changes increased the chaos, as dudes saw others apparently cutting in line and honked furiously. Meanwhile the savages were pumping gas as if their lives depended on it, and playing games they had devised as an antidote to the numbing routine. By now they had them down pat.

"Hey Pete, what time do you go on BEAR SHIFT?" Mason called over the luggage rack.

"Not workin' today. How 'bout you?"

"You're lucky, man. I'm on at 2. It'll be hot in that suit."

"Well, a job's a job. Gotta keep the tourists happy."

The children had been craning their necks from the rear window. Now one of them asked, "Hey mister, what's a bear shift, anyway?"

"Oh, that's when we put on bear suits and go along the road acting like bears: you know, sitting up on our hind legs, begging for food," said Mason. "Haven't you seen any bears yet?"

"Well, yeah, but we thought…" He whimpered and lay back in the seat, sulking.

"You ought to be ashamed of yourself," snapped the driver, putting *his* head out the window. "Don't forget our taxes pay for this park, including your wages!"

"Actually, it's your *gasoline* that does that, sir."

Woo passed by, smiling but concerned. "Mason, I don't know why you talk to people lak that."

"To keep our sanity," called Will from the next lane.

"An showum who's boss," muttered Lou, chamois in hand, from the other side.

At lunch the first shift looked burnt out; they ate silently or issued warnings to the late shift about what awaited them in the lanes. "It's incredible," said Trueblood, breaking bread. "Lou, how many gallons dyuh think we'll pump today?"

"Could pice six thousand, Pete."

"It would be okay if they'd just keep their tempers," Will reflected. "You'd think we were at war."

"We can handle 'em," snarled Owl Brain. "Bread!"

The "overlap hours," 1 to 3, provided some temporary relief. Business slacked off a bit; the balky pump and wringer were patched up; Bud, Comico's dyspeptic Canadian driver, arrived in the gas tanker to replenish their supply; and the shed was cleaned. There was even a little time to stand around and shoot the bull. But no sooner had the first shift stumbled away than a wave of cars rolled in and the war resumed. Owl Brain volunteered to help for an extra hour or two; he was in his element and even more outrageous than usual, stalking around to a woman driver with a black gob of radiator sludge displayed obscenely on his middle finger. "Did you know you had this crud in your radiator, *madam?*" he leered.

"Never mind that," she shot back, flushing. "Just give me directions to Old Faithful."

"Very well, *madam*, I'll tell you where to go." Owl straightened up, looked around, scratched his scalp, and bent down to the window again. "You go right up there" - pointing with that blackened finger - "and turn left. That's right: left. No, that's *not* right: I've left something out. That left is right after you've left a right *on* your right. Here, let me write it." He fumbled at his coveralls. "No, I've left my pen... The truth is, madam, you can't *get* there from here!" Owl just stood there and said all that to her face. No one else on the crew would have talked to a dude like that, or could have gone through such a routine without breaking up.

"Idiot!" she snapped, and went tearing off, flinging up gravel, which bounced off Owl. He stood unflinching and laughed until she turned left at the clearly-marked junction 50 yards west of the station and disappeared behind the trees.

Eventually there was such a backlog of cars waiting for gas that Lou told the crew to forget about selling and just pump. "Ah *don't* buh*lieve* mah *eahs*," said Beatty.

"Ain't no difference tuh me," snarled Henderson, slamming the nozzle back on the pump. "'S'day like all days." Not until suppertime did the lines shorten at all, giving some respite. The crew ate their roast beef in dogged silence, and served the last cars of the evening like automatons. Just before closing time an elderly man strolled over from the cabins, carrying a glass bottle and asking for white gas. Lou told him that, sorry, but it was illegal to put "gice in glice." The dude frowned, then looked around and demanded to know why they weren't flying a flag on the Fourth. Several of the savages hooted, and the man stalked away muttering unintelligibly.

At 10 PM Lou "stuck the tanks" with a calibrated pole to see how much gas they had sold, while the crew leaned against the still-warm pumps in the greenish-glowing twilight. "Seventy-six hunnert gallons, mens, a noo recud," he announced.

"F***g spirit uh seventy-six," crowed Owl Brain, who had stayed for the whole day, unable to resist such ample opportunities (and easy targets) for insult. "Woodena missed the goddam Fourth for the *world*!"

Five: Heart of the Summer

Selling fan belts was not where the savages lived, of course; they had more heart than that. Interwoven with work shifts, and more memorable than Fast Flushes, were social hours and love lives. The knowing reader will understand that these have been going on all this while, even as goods were being exchanged for money.

At the big hotel centers - Faithful, Canyon, Mammoth - social mechanisms were well established, and savages had access to a large dude population as well as to each other. If anything the boys *preferred* dude-dating: tourists being transients, inconvenient entanglements soon dissolved of their own accord. Working from the same data, "savage" girls shied away from tall, handsome but peripatetic strangers in favor of their own, more stable kind. Either way there was lots to do - sleeping-bag parties, hot-potting, savage shows, dances, excursions - and this was what most of them had come for. It was rather like attending a very educational summer school at a liberal college.

Organized socials were easy to come by at Old Faithful, where veterans such as Virg Vine abounded; it was they who brought people together and tried to pass on the traditions of savage social life. Virg's *forte* was hot-potting. He knew several spots along the Firehole River where boiling streams from the Midway Geyser Basin flowed in, creating a narrow habitable zone - a kind of dynamic sauna in which hot and cold were simultaneous instead of consecutive, spatial rather than temporal. It was tricky to reach the right spot and stay there, but, if you could manage, exciting to tread the flowing water and feel the cold slide along your back while the warmth fondled your front. The conditions were powerful teachers: two feet back you would freeze and shoot downstream, two feet forward you would boil, and the currents were constantly shifting. Not surprisingly, the rangers frowned on hot-potting as inherently unsafe (making it more attractive to some), so it had to be done at night, when it was trickier and more dangerous.

Early in the summer Virg led several parties to his favorite hot pot, where they peeled to swim suits, picked their way down slippery ledges and committed their shivering bodies to the dark waters. Quite hardy himself, he was always first in and last out, a patient coaxer of the timid, a kindly

P.E. instructor, admirably in his element while the diversion lasted. Most participants found that the best part was the afterglow, and the sharing of bodily warmth under a blanket in someone's cabin or car. Couples insisted that this was the best defense against hypothermia.

Because hot-potting was coeducational, nocturnal, and sensual, rumors of immorality began to circulate, and the rangers' frown turned to formal disapproval. They had better ways to proceed than a series of confrontations with individuals or parties, however; these savages had employers. One morning Virg had a call from Gardiner. "Immoral?!" he exclaimed into the station's phone. "Morley, what do you mean? What do you think we *do?*"

"I don't know, Virg, and I don't want to. But I hear what people are saying."

"Morley, boys and girls *will* get together, one way or another. But hot-potting's not immoral, it's fun!"

"The rangers say it's dangerous."

"Well…have you tried it yourself?"

"Mr. Vine, I didn't call to ask, but to tell you something."

"What's that?"

"We've decided that it's bad for the Corporation."

"Oh." And that was that: further discussion became pointless once Morley played his trump card. "It's really too bad," Virg told Cleve, for whom this all seemed very distant. "Hot-potting has been a Yellowstone tradition for a long time. Is 1957 so fastidious or squeamish that it can't maintain a colorful old custom?" But hot-potting parties were over - for that summer, at least.

Sleeping-bag parties, on the other hand, which anyone would tell you were more immoral (and less healthy), could be made legal: organizers booked a site such as Goose Lake near Faithful with the rangers in advance, invited friends and arranged rides. You brought a sleeping bag, something to drink, a date (if you were lucky), and/or a willingness to make music and keep the fire going. After that it ran itself - unless the invitations had been unwise or the crashers were rowdy. People talked or sang and roasted marshmallows for awhile; then the couples huddled down in their bags, which bulged ambiguously while the singles drank and poked the fire. Sometimes the rangers came around to check for drinking and sex, their truck headlights irrupting suddenly and rudely into the savages' evergreen Eden.

Of all their pastimes, "Savage Shows," another Yellowstone tradition, in which talented (or uninhibited) seasonals performed variety acts for mixed audiences of savages and dudes, were the least obnoxious to park officials. Both rangers and concessioners heartily endorsed them as "family entertainment." Even Thumb had some of these events in the communal recreation cabin, but at Mammoth, Canyon, and Faithful, Savage Shows were big productions. Polly got into the act - and gained a bit of notoriety - by slinking into the spotlight one Friday night in a black sheath and rendering "I'm Just a Girl Who Can't Say No" with confidence and panache. In the audience were three wide-eyed Thumbies: Mason, Peter, and Gair, who was instantly smitten (Mason wondered if she had been carrying that dress in her innocent-looking luggage on the cross-country trip). Most of the areas also had what passed for a dance band. The instrumentation was sometimes a bit odd, but the savages could keep a beat and rough out a recognizable tune - and dancers aren't particular.

Hot-potting, sleeping-bag parties, and savage shows had the merits of being cheap and local, but came well short of qualifying as *bright lights*. The closest spot for a "city date" with night clubs, dancing, and movies, or for bars and brothels, was West Yellowstone. It was especially popular with male savages not interested in taking "nice girls" to socials arranged by Virg and approved by Morley. Owl and Hayward went there as often as they could, occasionally followed by Schlitz, Henderson, or Beatty. Hole's friend Ray Jacobs from Faithful was a regular. Most of the Debrew contingent made occasional visits to "West," usually with a date. Marsh had the bad luck to be roughed up by a ranch hand on his first visit and never returned. West could be a tough town, particularly on weekend nights, when savages moved gingerly among hard-eyed cowboys eyeing their dates in The Lariat, Doc's, or the Frontier Bar, tried to look competent to hold on to their women, and hoped their bluffs would not be called. They had understood that their nickname was a joke, but in West they were reminded that *they* were dudes, and last year's movie over at the Bijou began to sound more interesting.

West was both a watering hole and a litmus test that distinguished the various strata of savage society. The main gulf was between daters and cruisers: the "respectables" who brought along young ladies and the "anti-socials" who were comfortable around drunks and whores. Also, there were those who would fight - a regular part of male bonding at Doc's - and those who would prefer not to. One Saturday night several of the Thumbies watched in amazement as Hayward refused to back down from a quarrel started by a pickled cowboy and got into a fistfight. Well, a fight, anyway. The Marquis of Queensbury didn't have a bar tab at Doc's; knees, bottles and chairs were as common as hooks and jabs. In any case Hayward emerged the victor, or at least the upright and less ghastly-looking survivor. "Don't f**k with a farmboy!" he crowed as Owl escorted him back to the bar. From that time Hayward was given a wider berth on "the strip" and at West Thumb.

*

Romance blossomed late at Thumb. Its savages, unless they had access to wheels, would have to choose amongst each other, and for most that meant a period of sniffing before the pairing-up began. Both the variety of regional sub-cultures, each with its own mores, and the many novel distractions combined to delay this. At first they learned their jobs and hiked the nearby trails in unisex pairs. Those lucky enough to own or borrow a car could check out the fabled attractions of Faithful and other areas, especially on their days off, when they "went dude" and tried to cover the Park. There was a lot to do besides court.

Dirty laundry proved to be the great socializer, as Gray had predicted. The laundry room was in the girls' dorm, and few of them seemed able to resist the spectacle of a male struggling to learn the regime of the washtub. As a result of the boys' well-known concern with clean socks and underwear, several more or less durable connections were formed. It was by the twin tubs that Woo encountered a tall, plain girl from North Dakota named Ellen, as sober and myopic as he; they soon became inseparable. It was over the sloping washboard that LaBouche first obtained the favor of conversation with Jane: a very silly female in the general opinion, but a veritable enchantress to The Mouth - proving again that there is someone for everybody. Pris and Jill, the Arizona cuties, revealed a domestic turn that soon gained them a wide following, as dazzled by dexterity with a steam iron as by twinkling smiles, nubile bodies or vivacious conversation. It was Jill's destiny, however, to spend the summer making unrequited mooneyes at Hole, who seemed oblivious to her charms - except on washday.

Lou's fling with Pris ended just before the arrival of his girlfriend from Florida. The gossips were divided: some said he had known all along and basely dallied with Pris, others that he had been caught by surprise and done what he had to. At any rate their parting was acrimonious. Pris retaliated by flaunting other boyfriends and encouraging a general female coolness to Lou. When Shelley arrived she tried to freeze her out too, and

73

did make her first days awkward, but Shelley was so genuinely sweet that no artificial chill could endure. Though she offended by having the face of Aphrodite, the figure of Demeter and the heart of Lou, she was also, as he had said, a lady: her manners were impeccable, she was charming, and scandal was powerless before her. Even Hole, who had high standards and a satirical style, pronounced her "a fahn woman," and Will said she had raised his opinion of Florida. Shelley also washed and ironed, so Lou did not suffer the retribution of the laundry room.

Mason, caught in a similar situation, did not get off so lightly. At the first opportunity he drove up to Faithful to see Polly. After the dining room closed they strolled among the buildings and geysers in the lingering summer twilight, conversing. As they talked of home and homesickness she began to cry. Mason took her hand, spoke comforting words, put his arm around her. Then they sat in the car for awhile. Warmth and affection came easily, and might have graduated to Eros, but he could not tell if that was what she wanted, and felt he might be taking advantage of her, so held back. All in all it seemed a promising start, though, and he had also begun to play the field at West Thumb when Virg Vine bustled into his room one morning in mid-June. Mason was lying on his bed, reading *Crime and Punishment.*

"Just on my way down to Jackson for station supplies, Mace, but I had to stop and deliver the great news: I got Liz a job in the Ham's store at Faithful! I kept working and it finally paid off! She'll be here Saturday morning!"

There was a pause. When they had first arrived, Virg had offered to ask "the Ham's lady" at Faithful - apparently a great buddy of his - to consider Liz for any cancellations, and Mason had casually assented, thinking that nothing would come of it. But he had been wrong: a cancellation had occurred, an offer had been wired, and an acceptance had been phoned. "Oh. That's great, Virg."

"Yep. Comin' into Gardiner by train. Too bad she won't be at Thumb, but..." Virg's cherub face still beamed, but his enlarged eyes now looked doubtful behind thick glasses. "Hope I did the right thing, Mace."

"Oh sure, Virg. Thanks a lot." Virg, like most men, had eyes for Liz, though he doubtless thought he was doing Mason a favor. "I - I was just thinking I won't be able to meet her. I'm on duty that morning."

"Oh, no problem! Morley or I will meet her, if that's all.... Listen, I've got to run. Be seeing you!" He was already hustling to the door.

"So long, Virg. Um, thanks again." After he disappeared Mason lay as if stunned, pondering a new course through rocky terrain. Virg didn't know that he and Liz had been on the verge of breaking up at the end of the school year. How could he? Mason hadn't told him. He should have nixed the idea of putting her on the cancellation list. But what was Liz thinking, to accept? That *he* had had a change of heart and was behind the offer, of course! Mason remained on the bed, staring out the window, the disregarded book on his lap, until Trueblood came in, chafing his hands.

"Hey, roomie." He flopped on his bed. "Boy, that's a cold rain! How 'bout a hot chocolate in the store? Gosh, Mason, what ails you?"

Mason stirred. "Liz is coming out. Virg got her a job."

"Hey, sounds great! Well, what's the problem?"

"Oh, it's okay, I guess: just not what I was expecting."

"Uh oh, now I remember." Peter sat up. "Yawl were gonna spend the summer apart, werncha?"

"Yeah, that was the idea - mine, anyway. We'd see how it went, then in September either split or commit. I was leaning to split. Liz was never very enthusiastic about it...maybe it *is* crazy."

Peter nodded. "Trial separation, huh?" He whistled softly. "I guess Virg put his foot in it this time."

Mason roused himself, shook his head. "No, it's not his fault. I knew what he was doing; I should have stopped him. Anyway, it's too late to do anything about it now."

Peter lay back down, chuckling. "Pris is gonna be disappointed again!"

Mason managed a feeble grin. "That lies not on my conscience. Anyway I was thinking more of Polly. Guess that goes by the boards now. I bequeath her to you."

Peter could not resist. "Tsk, tsk, and after all that work, too, Mason."

"You're right: I deserve this, in a way. Mentally I've been juggling Polly, Pris, Cheyenne Red, and Sally Savage up in Mammoth. Who did I think I was, a free agent?"

"That's bull, roomie, you *are* a free agent! Will you say anything to Virg?"

"What's the use? It would just be adding ingratitude to short-sightedness. You know, I think he likes having her around to look at."

Peter laughed. "Can't blame him for that."

*

They drove to Old Faithful together on Saturday afternoon. Peter went to look for Polly while Mason settled down on a sofa in the main lobby of the lodge to wait for Liz and Virg, trying to remember why they had chosen such a public place for the meeting. He forgot all that momentarily when she appeared, a petite, curvaceous brunette, and walked smiling into his arms, but their embrace had a required quality, and there was Virg, beaming as he held her suitcases, and a lobby full of dudes noticing. In her rumpled travel clothes, her eyes tired and uncertain, Liz looked less stunning than usual, and she said little. Watching them, Virg thought: 'My God, he doesn't want her here.' But all he said was, "It's started snowing," which sounded inane.

This re-introduction of the outside world came as a relief to Mason, however. "Let's get you settled, and then maybe go for a drive around the area?" Liz nodded wearily. Virg discreetly excused himself at the dormitory, brushing off their thanks. They walked through falling snow to the car. The tour was not a great success. Mason drove an unpaved track to one of the less-frequented geyser basins and parked there. Tired from two days on the train and hurt that Mason had not met her, Liz sat beside him with her legs pulled up, fingering a lock of hair and watching the hoary bears in silence. The passion of their reunion had been unconvincing, and the constraint was becoming awkward. Did he want her there or didn't he? Mason, torn between lust, regrets, and annoyance with Virg, wasn't sure himself. After a few perfunctory kisses he suggested that they go to the Ham's Store, where there were tables, snacks, and a jukebox. Liz nodded and reached for her cosmetic set.

In the store - where Liz would be working - they carried soup and coffee from the counter to a table. She asked for music, so Mason scanned the riches of the big Wurlitzer. There were Presley and Jerry Lee Lewis and other rockers, Boone and Eddie Fisher and other balladeers, but they weren't right. Then he saw a new one by the Coasters that Polly liked, "Searchin'," and dropped in his nickel. It had a classic beat, and some of the lyrics appealed to him.

> *I been searchin' (bum-dumpa-dum-dum)*
> *I gone searchin' (bum-dumpa-dum-dum)*
> *Searchin' ev-ry whi-i-ich a-way (yay-yay)*
> *But like a North West Mountie (bum)*
> *You know I'll bring her in some day!*
> *Gonna find her...*

At the table Liz was tapping her feet, but when he asked if she wanted to dance she shook her head. "Dix-on," she drawled, "can't you see Ahm beat? Let's cawl it a day. Take me home and tuck me in." She managed a smile.

"I'd like to, but they'll stop me at the common room." He left her there, promising to come back when he could, and returned to the lodge through stands of snowy evergreens - more like New Hampshire in December than anywhere he knew in June - to await his rider. Trueblood returned an hour later, looking a bit dazed, but exuding concern about Mason's afternoon.

"Howdjawl make out?" He laughed. "So to speak."

"Oh, it was okay. A little awkward, but I survived. What about you? Has something happened? How's Polly?"

"I didn't see her - but it's a lawng story. I better tell you on the way home. Hey, how 'bout this weather! Looks lak a Christmas card." As they drove away he began to narrate his adventure, a recital that lasted all the way to Thumb, even driving slowly in a couple of inches of snow. He had gone to Polly's dorm, but she was off somewhere with friends, according to her roommate, a tall, graceful girl with auburn hair. "So I got up my nerve an said, 'Then maybe *you'd* like to go for a wawk in the snow?"

"Hey, that *was* bold! You're getting to be a smoothie."

To his surprise she accepted. Her name was Lois and she was from Missouri, she said, though Peter was sure he had never encountered anything so exotic and sophisticated from that state before. "Muhsuruh!" he exclaimed. "That's hard to buhlieve. You don't sound lak it."

Her laughter was silvery. "One of the first tasks of a good women's college is to remove unwanted regional accents." She seemed to glide over the uneven white ground. Before the walk ended Peter was smitten. He asked her out for the following Saturday night and was again surprised when she agreed. As they putt-putted down the last slope to Thumb he said dreamily, "She reminds me of a willow tree."

"God, roomie, you have a bad case!"

"She also has a car."

"Aha! You *haven't* gone soft in the head, then."

"A white Thunderbird convertible."

"Jesus, you've struck it rich, Peter!"

*

When Mason met Lois he was impressed; with her beret, casual elegance and cultured speech, she was attractive in an almost Continental way.

Working from the same data, Hole declared her a "pseudo," but he was already notorious for his scathing opinions of Yellowstone girls. Priscilla and Jill were "Prissy and Flossy, the Tucson tarts," and Liz he considered "dotty." He had no criticisms, however, of Julia, a pony-tailed working girl from Idaho Falls whom he met on a blind date at Faithful: one of his attempts to escape Jill. "Man," he told his friends, "when you know what that chick knows, you don't *need* college." Hole wisely didn't say what this knowledge was, but tried to spend every spare hour in her company. He confided to Mason that he had never before dated such a wonderful conversationalist, but when Mason repeated that to Liz, she laughed.

"Oh, Mason! Have you ever talked to her?"

"Only a little. Struck me as rather quiet, but..."

"Don't you see? She's a good *listener*! Her talent is knowing when to keep quiet. Men! *They* talk and talk and think *she's* doing it all."

"Liz, you sound bitter."

"Well, I have to laugh at the way some people deceive themselves."

Be that as it may, Hole's devotion was both immediate and lasting; he had found his summer's romance. But there remained "the Polly problem," now that Mason and Peter had been rendered ineligible. Cleve, said to be much taken with a waitress at Canyon, was not getting over to Faithful. Peter and Mason decided that Gair was such a fine fellow that they would introduce him to Polly. It took, and in a couple of weeks they were dating regularly. People were pairing off; couples were forming.

During late June and July, when Mason's was the only car regularly on the Thumb-Faithful run, he and Hole and Trueblood spent many of their spare hours together. They frequently double- and triple-dated in the wagon, returning to Thumb as very late merged into very early, trying to pick up KSL Salt Lake City - 400 miles away - on the radio. One Tuesday Mason spent his day off with Liz and the others hitchhiked over after work. They agreed to meet outside Julia's cabin at 2 AM, but for one reason or another they were all late; it was nearly 3 when they began the long slow climb to Craig Pass. "I'm so beat," laughed Mason. "At least I can sleep till noon."

"Can you drive okay?" asked Peter. "Not that I'm any better."

"Yeah, I'll just roll down the window and leave the radio on." Cool, balsam-scented air flowed in as they plowed steadily up the grade behind the probing headlight beams, too tired to talk but feeling mellow. For miles there was only static on the radio, but atop the first divide KSL

78

suddenly came in loud and clear: mighty chords of piano and orchestra crashed down from the ether.

"Cool," chortled Hole. "What is that, anyway?"

"Beethoven. The Emperor Concerto, friends." Mason turned it up and they just listened - to one of the peaks of European classical art, miraculously delivered to the crest of the New World in the last watch of the night - on the descent from Craig Pass. Crossing the flats they could see false dawn in the northeast and groaned, as usual. The road tilted up again toward the second divide and there was movement ahead. Mason slowed, stopped, and turned down the radio. The biggest moose they had ever seen stalked ponderously across the pavement, looking at them up the shaft of the headlights. He turned them off, and the engine. As their eyes adjusted to the sudden darkness his antlers were silhouetted against the lightening sky, then slid left and merged into the forest. For a while the moose could be heard moving through the undergrowth before it was just birds twittering in the hush. "Well, that was a gift."

Mason started the car and gradually reintroduced the radio as they rose to the last divide. On top, for a moment, there was the spread of Yellowstone Lake, a pale still mirror in which the entire Absaroka Range, flushing rose and pink along the eastern horizon, was perfectly reflected. "Ah," they all said. The car seemed to float on the music and the dawn.

"You know, we owe this to the bitch - to the girls," said Hole. "What else would have us up and out at this hour?"

Mason thought, he's right. And will life ever get better than this? "Earth has not anything to show more fair," he quoted aloud. But doubt flickered through his mind: would the hushed, exalted minutes they had just lived through have been possible with girlfriends? Would they have been silent enough, open enough to the world, for the thing to have happened, or would they have been too wrapped up in themselves and each other, in trivia and plotting? More important, would it become possible, sometime, to have this closeness with a woman?

They putted and popped - Lou called it "backing off" - down the last grades in weary silence, at one with the Beethoven and each other. The concerto, the camaraderie, the dawn, the moose and the lake seemed woven into a grand design wherein each element was simultaneously theme and accompaniment. The last chords sounded as they coasted to a stop in front of the dormitories; then Mason turned off the radio and the mudpot farted a welcome.

*

Lou gave Mason and himself the same day off, suggesting that they and their girls could make up a foursome for drives around the park (one look at Shelley was enough to persuade Mason). For the first of these, Lou chose a small lake or large pond with "good fishing" down toward the South Entrance. They parked at the trailhead and loitered an easy mile or two through ragged stands of lodgepole pine to the swampy shoreline of Burnt Lake. The fishing turned out to be poor and the mosquitoes annoying, but they picnicked in the midday sun and strolled in the fragrant woods for a bit of romancing far from the smell of gasoline.

Walking out, they agreed it had been a pleasant getaway, and Shelley was enthusing about the pine-scented air when Lou said, "Uh-oh." An unsmiling park ranger was standing by the Ford.

"Whose car is this?" A thin voice from a thin body.

"Mine, sir." Mason recognized him as 'the other ranger' at the South Entrance. "Is something wrong?"

"Have you all been fishing at Burnt Lake?" Cold eyes behind rimless glasses.

"Thet's rat. Got lahcenses, too."

"Are you aware that trout season opens July the first?"

Lou reddened. "No suh. Guess weah few days shawt o thet, ahn't we?"

"Follow me in your car to West Thumb Ranger Station." He turned and walked to his pale green wagon.

"Thumb Station," sighed Lou. "Thet means Stony Simmons. Sorry, folks."

Stonewall Simmons, legendary for toughness with savages, lived with an unenvied junior ranger in a log cabin within sight of the pea-green shed, which suddenly looked like paradise lost. Heavy-set and scowling, he stood by the arresting officer behind his desk as they shuffled in, whereupon the thin ranger intoned formally, "I charge you with violating Section 4C of the Game Regulations of Yellowstone National Park."

"Uh look, Ranger" - Lou peered at his badge - "Curtis, we jes..."

"Shut up, Fuller!" snapped Simmons. "You'll get your chance. Tell on, Curt."

Ranger Curtis told his story while the savages shuffled their feet. When he finished, Simmons glared at Lou. "Okay, Fuller, what's your side?"

"Wall, ignorance, Mistuh Simmons. Ah shuda knowed the trout season but Ah didn't, thet's awl." Lou grinned and shrugged, which was a mistake.

"That's not good enough, Fuller," blazed Simmons. "You've been here before and you're *supposed* to know!"

"That's a hard look, mistuh." Lou glared back.

"Sir, Mr. Simmons," said Mason in his most conciliatory tones. "It's not as if we tried to get away with anything. We came down the trail and walked right up to Ranger Curtis, poles in hand. It was an honest mistake."

"It was a stupid mistake!" Simmons shot back.

"Yer wastin yer tahm, Mace. Look, Ah was th'onleh one what caught enathin."

"There were four poles and four licenses," said Curtis.

"You were all fishing? You don't deny that?" They nodded and then shook their heads. "The rest is just talk. Ten AM Wednesday at Mammoth courthouse. Now get out, and don't let me see you in here again."

"Stony Simmons," sneered Lou as Mason and Shelley pulled him out the door.

The next day they picked up Liz at Faithful and drove the 50 winding miles to Mammoth, mostly in glum silence. The weather was fine, but the holiday - all had had to rearrange their work schedules - and the landscapes gave them no pleasure. Geysers might play and rivers run to the sea, but they were criminals, miscreants, malefactors. In Mammoth they drove past the terraces - useless to them - and located the courthouse, a suitably stony little building. A green Ranger wagon was parked out front. Curtis rose as they entered the vestibule, said 'Hello' and sat down when the girls did. An awkward 10 minutes followed as the judge did something else; there was not much to say or do or look at. The room had two framed pictures of minimal interest, a copy of *Field and Stream* on a corner table, and no windows. Then Mason discovered books on a small shelf behind him: history, literature, philosophy! He had just pulled a volume of Hemingway when a young clerk opened an inner door and said gravely, "Judge Evans will see you now."

They entered not a courtroom but a plain office with a window, flag, desk and some straight chairs. The judge stood in his black robe as they came in and motioned them to sit. He looked like all their grandfathers, a kindly old man, firm yet mild, and sad to see them there. Mason thought, a patriarchal lawgiver, strength edging toward frailty. As ye are, so was I; as I am, so shall ye be. "Ranger?" said Evans.

Curtis narrated the Burnt Lake caper in almost the same words he had used at Thumb, as if he had it by rote now. Then Evans turned to the savages. "Well?" Each of the boys spoke briefly, resting their case on ignorance (Lou) and "moral innocence" (Mason); the girls remained silent. When he had heard them out impassively the judge looked at each in turn, removed his spectacles to rub his eyes, and cogitated for a few moments more.

"I'm sorry to see you here on this charge," he said at last, replacing the glasses. "I expect you are decent people who have not been in court before, and I trust won't be again. But ignorance of the law, you must know, is not an excuse, especially" - turning to Lou - "where we expected knowledge. If we bought that one, we would have lost the park long ago. Few of the misdemeanors that land people in this court arise from malice; most are trivial acts of thoughtlessness like yours. Unfortunately the sum total of such acts can damage our environment almost as badly as malice itself. Do you have any idea what early fishing can do to the trout population of a small lake?"

They shook their heads. "Thought not. I'm a fisherman, so I do." He smiled, and they smiled back. "As for you, young man" - turning to Mason - "you'll find that 'moral innocence' is not valid currency here or anywhere else, and if you try to pass it, you're counterfeiting." He shook his head. "To you it's just a phrase: better stop and think what it means. Boils down to ignorance again, and good intentions - remember what the road to hell is paved with! - or at least absence of malice, *plus* a dangerous abstract belief in your essential goodness. Your being good won't help the trout in Burnt Lake if you take them early! I don't know if any of us is 'morally innocent', but I know that behaving as if that were enough can get you into trouble. Are you a college man?"

Mason started. "Yes sir." He was shocked by how seriously the judge was taking this. The bored, pro forma sentencing he had expected would have been a relief.

"Thought so. Have you read Aristotle?"

"Well, he was assigned in one course, but..." Mason reddened. "No sir. Not yet." He wished a pit would open.

"Read the *Nicomachean Ethics* sometime, Book One. He says that in the Olympic games it is not the fastest man in Greece who wins the garland, but the one who shows up on the right day and wins the race.

That's because *performance*, not potential or ability, is what counts! He also says that human good is *an activity of the soul in accordance with virtue.* You see? Not virtue, but right action based on virtue. Now you won't tell me this is too serious for a fishing offense, because you're smart enough to see that I'm talking about the principle involved in your 'defense' - which worries me more than your offense. Anyway, if a man can't indulge his convictions and pontificate a bit at my age, when can he?"

He smiled at them again, and they smiled back. "All right. If you've nothing further to say? - the court levies a fine of $5 apiece, payable to the clerk, and releases you." Judge Evans tapped his gavel lightly on its base, stood and turned to gaze out the window at the bare ridge across the valley as if he would much rather be up there. Mason recognized it as the one he and Cleve had seen from the campground on that pristine first morning, long ago in the days of his innocence. He wished he were up there too, perhaps walking and talking with the judge.

The four of them tiptoed out of the office and - chivalry being still the rule - each of the boys gave the clerk $10. Ranger Curtis, hat in hand, waited for them by the cars. "No hard feelings, I hope. Line of duty." He extended his hand.

"Not at all," said Mason, taking it. "You've been very decent. Sorry to put you to all this trouble."

"You" - Curtis hesitated - "You might have gotten off with a warning."

"Wall, Ahl be daimed! Awrat!" Lou offered his hand.

"You've responded well, considering. Goodbye for now." He went to his car and rolled away.

Driving home the savages were again quiet. They reached Old Faithful just as the great geyser went up, and stopped to watch like any other tourists, as savages will. "My day to feel small!" blurted Mason when it ended.

Liz sat beside him, musing dreamily and toying with a jet-black curl. "The judge was *such* a *lovely* man," she murmured.

"But hard on Mason," said Shelley sympathetically. Mason glanced back at her, appreciating the support. Sweet *and* good-looking! It would be nice to be consoled by Shelley. How did Lou rate? Then he felt guilty.

"Actually I thought he was mostly right," Mason heard himself saying. "He taught like a good professor." They dropped Liz at the Ham's Store; then all three sat up front for the drive back to Thumb. Gradually the weight began to lift a little. As the station came into view Mason snorted, "At least we got off work, Lou!"

"Yep. Mornin, anyways. Yuh ken jus take second shift tuhday, Mace."

This *contretemps*, not to say *disaster*, in sortie #1 did not deter them from trying again. The next week they assembled at Faithful for an outing to the Grand Canyon of the Yellowstone. While the girls, harassed by Lou, shopped for picnic supplies in the Ham's Store, Mason headed for the jukebox and donated another coin to the Coasters:

> *Gonna find her (bum-dumpa-dum-dum)*
> *Gonna find her (bum-dumpa-dum-dum)*
> *If I have to swim a river, you know I will,*
> *An' if I have to climb a mountain, you know I will,*
> *An' if she's a-hidin' up on Blueberry Hill,*
> *How'm I gonna fin' her chil'?*
> *You know-wo-wo I will!*
> *'Cause I been searchin'...*

They drove up to Norris and over to Canyon, parked at Lookout Point and found a flat-topped promontory with a clear view of the Lower Falls that made a great picnic site. The day was so fine and their perch so spectacular that Lou kept looking for the catch. "Yuh spose this is *lee*-gal? Rangers ain't got a *rool* gainst it?" Mason took his Brownie Hawkeye to the very edge of the promontory and tried to line up a snapshot with the roll of color film Polly had given him while Lou urged him to back up farther and the girls set out a cold lunch. Before heading on to Thumb they stopped at Canyon Station and found Cleve on duty, looking tanned and happy. When Mason asked if the reports that he was having a high old time were true, he practically went orbital.

"Omigod yes! Terrific girls, wild times over in West, great country in every direction," he effervesced. "Best summer I ever had!"

"Been over to see Polly?"

"No, not yet. Been too busy. You know how 'tis."

"She seems a little homesick," said Liz softly.

"Big gal o' seventeen, she can take care of herself," laughed Cleve. "I hear *she's* havin' a hagh ol' time! Virg and Cal look in on her for me." Liz gave a little grunt and turned away, but Cleve, giving them a hurried account of his quest for a used car at a reasonable price, didn't notice. Then it was, "Well, back to the pumps. So long, guys. Good to see you again, Lou. Keep in touch, Mason."

"Nass feller," said Lou as they drove off. "Wish Ahda gotum." Shelley was sure that he really did care about his sister, and Mason, thinking how much he missed Cleve's liveliness and wit, agreed with her. Liz stared out the side window and was pointedly silent.

*

By early July there was more to do around Thumb. Its Friday night Savage Shows in the recreation cabin had begun to draw savages and young dudes from Lake and Faithful, attracted mainly by the resident "combo": Beatty on trumpet, Will on piano, and Gair on accordion, backed by guitars. Hole would sometimes sit in, though he didn't play "by ear." One "George of the cabins" was more useful, and Mason would come over after late shift. They were not talent shows - the ethic was collective - but occasionally there was a solo: Will playing Chopin or Joplin, Lou doing his Stan Freberg routine, George or Mason performing a folk song, singly or together. Once Hole was persuaded to try his Bach gavotte; nervous, he butchered it badly and received a standing ovation. The most unexpected star turn was by "Wanda of the cabins," a well-constructed Tennessee girl who put herself on everybody's map with a sultry rendition of "Stormy Weather," backed by the boys. Dudes were also welcome to perform, which several uninhibited souls did, and their participation enhanced the cooperative atmosphere. The spectators listened, danced, or sang, but always tried to pick up each other: the main reason for attending.

Afterwards some of the performers and audience members might walk down to the beach, build a big fire - igniting it with a quart of Comico regular - break out the beer and sleeping bags, and sing (a guitar generally came along) or make out until dawn. No one in Yellowstone seemed to care what time it was that year. Savages would come off work at 10 PM and party the rest of the night, even if they had to work again at 6 AM. They were young, and "We can sleep this afternoon" was their mantra.

On July 1st it was warm enough to have the season's first square dance in the courtyard before the dormitories. After work the boys scrubbed off their grease more thoroughly than usual and the girls donned calico while the musicians tuned up outside. Two rangers appeared to lead the local talent: a caller-fiddler known as Slim - the key man - and big Dan from the South Entrance, a banjoist. "Pillow punchers" from the cabins drifted in by twos and threes to join the pump jockeys and shake makers. The music began about 10:30, and it was soon clear that square dancing was a living folk art for some, but not for others. Slim was a real pro, Dan had obviously worked with him a lot, and George of the cabins, who came from small-town Nebraska, knew all the songs on the guitar. Because the music was simple Mason could usually follow, but Hole soon became discouraged and quit to join the dancers, where he was equally lost but had Julia to help him. Savages from the mountain west and plains states took the lead, teaching others the intricate patterns, but some of the dudes who were attracted by the noise and lights could hold their own. While bears roamed and mud pots slurped outside the stockade, the bright squares formed and dissolved at the urging of the music. The dancers' favorite, "Oh the sun shines down on pretty Redwing," was repeated twice, while in the cold sky a billion stars and one comet overhung the spot of light in the dark forest and were reflected in the lake's great mirror.

Liz came down for the dance and spent the night in Shelley's room; Lou had recommended an early start on their outing to Beartooth Pass. After breakfast Mason went over to gas up the car, and as he stood talking to Liz and several Thumbies Owl approached and handed him a folded note. Innocently Mason opened it, read, grimaced and guffawed. The conspirators roared - but when Liz grabbed the note they froze. She read it to herself - "Smile if you got much last night" - and turned slowly to Mason. "What are *you* smiling about?" she purred, then dropped the note and switched away. There were some snickers.

"Unspeakable bitch!" snapped Will, as Mason followed her silently.

The expedition moved off anyway. They skirted the lake and followed the river to Canyon, then continued north over Dunraven Pass into unfamiliar country. Mt. Washburn - said to be a great place to find antlers - loomed up ahead and right, over ten thousand feet. At Tower Junction Mason turned east across the river into rolling rangeland where scattered herds of buffalo (not yet being called bison) grazed and the air was fragrant with sage. There were few tourists around; the northeast entrance was nearly deserted. Lou, always happy to get away from rangers for awhile, sighed theatrically as they cleared the tollbooth.

The Absarokas grew more imposing, and beyond Cooke City the road wound higher in them. Making Colter Pass, they dove to cross Clark's Fork of the Yellowstone, then began to climb steeply again. It was a long haul to the top - the 'wagon was no ball of fire at these altitudes - so they broke for lunch at a log cabin café in the forest: a deserted place that seemed whole states removed from the madness of West Thumb. Afterwards Mason coaxed the car up more grades to Beartooth Pass, almost eleven thousand feet, where they all got out to stretch and gape at the vista.

"The top of the world!" exclaimed Liz.

"It's just lovely," Shelley agreed, snuggling against Lou in the cool wind.

"The best panorama since Togwotee Pass," pronounced Mason, ever the comparatist.

"*Better*un Toggity Pice, Mace. Yuh ken see thole dam Absorkies!"

"What are those place names, Lou?"

"Ts how folks roun heah sayum, Mace. You jes been *read*inum."

After a round of mixed-doubles snowballing in which they all got wet and chilled, Mason drove on down more switchbacks into Red Lodge, Montana. A block off the main drag Lou showed them The Old Bunkhouse, a log cabin done up as a night club, where they could eat, drink and dance. Shelley, who turned out to be a terrific dancer, showed Lou the "dirty bop" while Mason gawked. "This will be banned in Boston," he predicted. Liz let her annoyance show: he should not be admiring *Shelley's* hips.

By the time they started the climb back to Beartooth Pass night had fallen. Lou and Shelley necked quietly in back, while Liz tried to keep Mason awake. He required a coffee break at the cabin by the lake, so it was midnight when they reached the park and about 1 AM when the headlights revealed something large in the road ahead. Mason hit the brakes, bringing them all bolt upright and wide awake.

The biggest bull buffalo any of them had ever seen stood athwart the road, staring at them from one tiny eye almost lost in the curling fleece of his massive head. At the shoulder he was as high as the car. His tail switched once, twice. Dust swirled in the headlight beams. They were whispering about the likelihood of his charging when the buffalo turned tail - which seemed to halve his size - and resumed sauntering down the middle of the road. Mason inched up on his right flank. At a range of 10 yards, the buffalo stopped and turned again, growing huge, watching them. They could see fleas jump on his hindquarters. Mason switched off the lights. After a few seconds he could make out a sagebrush plain in the pale light of a quarter moon. The road crossed it on a raised bed, making a detour impossible. Directly ahead, the motionless black hulk looked larger than before. Mason turned the lights back on.

The bull started to walk again and the car crept up on his left. When they were 5 yards back he stopped, half-turned, and took one ponderous step back toward the car. Shelley gasped; Mason shifted into reverse, hoping it wouldn't come to that. For a few seconds they were motionless - the buffalo, the car, the headlight beams linking them - there on the most desolate stretch of road in the park. Then Liz reached over and pressed the center of the steering wheel. The horn blasted; the beast snorted and lumbered down the embankment; the car shot ahead. Mason pressed Liz's hand and said, "Thanks." Why hadn't he thought to do that? Well, because a part of him had been reveling in the close contact. He knew that the scene would stay with him, and suddenly missed the buffalo, back there in the moonlit sagebrush.

Dropping Lou and Shelley at Thumb, they began the long climb to the Divide between 2 and 3. "A great day but a long one," said Mason wearily.

"Yes. But I think we should take one with just ourselves."

"Oh." A pause. "Don't you like them?"

She laughed shortly. "Shelley's sweet. Lou's a goof. Anyway, we've seen them enough for awhile, you know?" Her hand rested lightly on his thigh.

Mason's heart sank. He had been enjoying the foursome, which helped divert Liz from grinding away at their problems. "Lou gave us the same day off so we could do this, you know. I quite liked our quartet."

"Yes, I noticed," she said icily, and pulled her hand away.

Ah: he had to pay for the dirty-bop episode. Or she didn't want to be diverted from working on their relationship. Or both. "Well, okay, if that's how you feel," he said. "I'll try to let Lou down easy." They crossed the passes in silence. Eventually the steamy plumes of Old Faithful drifted up toward them; silvery geysers played to an empty house.

"Full many a flower is born to blush unseen," she recited, "And waste its sweetness on the desert air."

Only it's *not* wasted, thought Mason. He pulled up behind her darkened dormitory but left the motor running. Liz reminded him of the Goose Lake party Thursday night, 10:30 at the store, don't forget to bring Gair for Polly; then kissed him briefly and got out.

Mason turned the car around and started up the homestretch, yelling to keep awake. Again it was false dawn on the divides, but this time there was no moose, and he never even thought to switch on the radio. How the devil would he break it to Lou?

*

Liz had a penchant for organizing large parties and loved to be called 'the hostess with the mostes'. She knew that the key to success was the guest list, and never made the same mistake twice: Owl was not asked a second time. Her ideal was a sweet, temperate guy such as Virg or Gair. The sleeping-bag party at Goose Lake was hailed as her best effort yet: all the "good people" were there but none of the misfits, the blind dates worked out and the rangers stayed away. Not even the leeches discovered on beer cans cooling in the lake could spoil it. The firelight revealed a circle of spruce boughs hanging gracefully from the blackness around a small clearing, evidently an ancient campsite. They sang old favorites and Kingston Trio hits to accordion and guitar accompaniment until it grew too cold for the instrumentalists' fingers. The only drunks were happy and fairly quiet. About 1 AM some of the guests departed, leaving the hard core to snuggle down in their bags for - whatever. To know what went on was difficult: it might have been almost everything or almost nothing. An observer would see only shapeless bundles flexing now and then, and hear only an occasional sigh or grunt. Some slept; some whispered; some listened to the loons or the whispers.

By 3 AM the clearing was quiet, the sleeping bags were motionless, and the fire had burned down to embers. A zipper was drawn its length, a bag opened, and Virg's round face peered out. Nothing stirred in the cold hour before dawn. Clad only in boxer shorts, T-shirt and white socks, he stood up and tiptoed toward the fire. Then another white face emerged from its cocoon: Polly's. "Virg!" she cried.

"Omigosh!" He stood rooted, hands crossed over his groin, as other faces appeared. "I'm not a virgin anymore!"

A peal of muffled laughter from Liz. "Don't you *love* him?"

*

Liz's desire to have Mason to herself on Tuesdays produced some serious consequences that she had not foreseen. On July 9th she hitched a ride to Thumb and found Mason waiting by the mudpot. They kissed. "How did Lou take it?" She pressed against him.

"Oh, pretty well. Just shrugged and nodded and said okay. He's a savvy guy after all." In fact it had been more difficult than that and Mason looked unhappy, but Liz just nodded. She had brought picnic makings from Faithful ("much more efficient than consulting with a committee!") and had their day all planned. They drove down to Jenny Lake and walked along the shore. Rugged mountains rose thousands of feet from the dancing glitter of the lake to summits of snow. The scenery was magnificent, the day perfect, and there was time for nuzzling in the woods beside the lake. But they were rather mechanical, and another couple chanced along at an inopportune moment. Mason sat up, and Liz stared at the Tetons with cold, dry eyes.

At noon they drove south to a ranch she had heard about and rented a couple of mild-looking horses for the afternoon. Following a path through forests of spruce and fir they rose onto the lower flanks of the Grand Teton; sloping meadows led up toward granite ramparts and veiling waterfalls too diaphanous to reach the ground. When the trail became steep they tied the horses to a tree as securely as possible and spread their picnic on the grass in the sun. A stream burbled past and a seasoned chipmunk accepted bits of bread. Again it was all quite wonderful, but they mostly gazed at the scenery in silence. Eventually Liz asked him what was wrong - the question Mason had been asking himself - and pressed for an answer. All he would say was that he didn't like to have his days off so thoroughly managed for him. It was only a small piece of the truth, he knew: the whole social-organizer side of her put him off, and he resented *having* to be with her, "going steady."

"*Some*body has to plan!" she hissed, exasperated. "All right, *you* choose for next week."

There was the rub, he realized: the assumption that they would still, again, be a couple next week. "I don't have any specific ideas..."

"Meaning you don't want to go anywhere with me?"

There was an opening, if he would but take it! Was he ready to break up? Pause. "How about Virginia City?"

So the next week they made the long, beautiful drive out the west gate and up the Madison River valley to Ennis, Montana, then west across rolling hills and down into Virginia City, which offered plenty of diversions. They explored the weather-beaten buildings, false facades and wooden sidewalks of the town, rode an elevator down into a silver mine, drove up sloping fields to read the grave markers on Boot Hill, drank beer in the old brewery and watched the melodrama put on by college students. "We *should* be having a ball," said Liz grimly. Mason did not reply; the shadow of silence often fell between them. During the interminable ride back to Faithful Liz laughed mirthlessly as it finally hit her: "Maybe we *needed* Shelley and Lou as a distraction from ourselves. We don't have much to say to each other any more, do we?"

"So it seems," he replied. She had brought it on herself, but it sounded so cold that he added, "Maybe it's a stage we're passing through."

"And what's on the other side, Dixon?"

"I don't know, Liz." We're *that* close to breaking up, he thought, but neither of us wants to say it first. Am I going to let her ruin my whole summer?

When Mason reached Thumb after midnight, full of dark thoughts, he discovered the other unintended effect of Liz's desire for privacy. In the courtyard he saw far too many lights for that hour and heard too much noise; steady screaming emanated from the girls' dorm. On the second floor of his own he found complete bedlam. Will Harkness was brandishing a bottle at the door of Lou's room, and judging by the uproar everyone else was inside. With unusual bonhomie Will threw a long arm around Mason's shoulders and hauled him into the press. A lot of people were drinking beer. "What the hell...?"

"Lou and Shelley got engaged!" yelled half a dozen voices. For a moment Mason was too shocked to react. People dated, broke up or got pinned, but *engagement*? That was definite and lasting, like *marriage*. Then he caught sight of Lou's beaming mug - streaked with lipstick and beer foam - in the center of it all and hurled himself forward.

"You old...son of a bear!" His hand was crushed. Then Beatty blew a blast on his trumpet and chaos broke out again. Henderson and Creeper and The Mouth were yelling aimlessly. Schlitz was pouring beer on people's heads as if West Thumb had won the world series, and Trueblood kept patting Lou on the shoulder. Suddenly Gair was heard to ask if they should be thinking of an engagement present for Shelley.

That seemed to stymie them for a few seconds. Then Bastille, the roving journalist who happened to be paying Thumb one of his periodic visits, remarked, "In Canada, an item of the gentleman's underwear would be considered appropriate." At once, half a dozen savages set upon Lou and bore him down. Fortunately he decided to cooperate, and soon Owl emerged from the scrum brandishing Lou's jockey shorts, raced down the hall holding his nose, threw open the window and pinned the underpants to the clothesline. "Prissy and Jill," he howled. "Come and getum while they're warm!" He rattled the line around the pulleys, sending the gift across to the girls' room, where heads quickly appeared. After a minute of fuss and confusion on the far side the pulleys squeaked again, and a pair of black silk panties crossed the gap.

Owl ran back to Lou's room and waved the panties at the door. Whistles and cheers. Several savages demanded that he put them on and began a ragged rhythmic clapping. Struggling into the lacy drawers, Lou performed a grotesque, suggestive dance to loud applause and cries of "Speech, speech!" The manager clambered onto a table and signaled for quiet. As they hushed each other, Gray appeared at the door to beseech them: "Boys! Boys! How about keeping it -" Then he caught sight of Lou. "Oh, Jesus." He leaned weakly against the door frame.

"Gray! Gray! Bes goddam house fathuh in thole..." He trailed off, as if merely contemplating the ineffable boundaries of Gray's supremacy had rendered him speechless. "Come awn in, man, it's mah en*gage*ment potty!" His hands resting on two nearby heads to steady himself, his nascent beer belly straining at the panties, Lou began to address the savages. "Mens! Ah jes wanna thank eachun ever oneuhyuh. Ah guess yer bout the bes dam crew any manajuh evuh had!" He brushed at his eyes. "Nuff o *thet*! Oh, we hev ar lil troubles aw rat, wi the dumb dudes n awl, but Ah guess they're okay, n..." For a moment he looked lost. " - n so are we, n thet's a fac!" Wild cheering. "Oh hail," said Lou, "Ah feel sick!" He was rushed to the bathroom and the party, deprived of its star, began to wind down.

The savages drifted off to bed. Mason walked back to his room deep in reflection. This was what came of leaving couples to themselves, then: they found out that they belonged together, or that they did not. Had Liz fully understood that? Did she really just want a clear yes or no from him? It bore thinking on.

He dropped into bed looking forward to sleeping late, but was jarred awake only a few hours later - which seemed but a few minutes - by the first shift's alarms going off and a new clamor in the hall. Lou was up - if he had ever been down - banging on doors and crooning, "Aw rat, mens! Tahm tuh hit the lanes! Les go see what the Mercan public wawnts tuhday an give it some *service*!" When he pushed their door open Lou was still wearing only Shelley's panties. Or maybe he only dreamed that part, Mason thought when he next woke up several hours later. A lot of the summer was like that.

Interlude

Peter Trueblood has come up to Old Faithful in Mason's car early on a Saturday morning to have a haircut - once or twice a summer a man may need that - and a few words with Miss Lois. Business before pleasure: and he needs to be back at Thumb in time to eat before work. Virg has warned him that Jimmy the barber will talk his head off about the old days, so he is forearmed and wary. Jimmy is a kindly-looking man in his sixties, probably, trim and white-haired, with a glint of amiable mischief in his eyes. Peter introduces himself and says that Virg sent him.

"Mornin', son." Jimmy whips the sheet around with a flourish. "Yes, Virg is a good boy. How do you like it? Short?" He switches on the clippers. "So you're a savage! Work around here? West Thumb?! Why, that was hardly big enough to rate a good-size gas pump a few years back. Now they got cabins an a store an evrythin…"

"Except a barber."

"But then evrythin's changed. You young fellers come an go so fast I never get to know yuh. Virg now, he comes back, an I remember him. But most o yuh…" Jimmy shakes his head and turns off the clippers. "Short all round and on top? Righto." He flashes the scissors and appears to think the job through. "I been watchin boys come an go here since, well, not long after the war, twenty-six, it musta been. Tell yuh, savages back then…they earned the name! Older boys then, yuh know, an tougher, no offense."

"None taken."

"Used tuh come back an back till they knew the place most as good as the rangers. Mighty tough on 'em sometimes, too. You boys are better behaved now - don't cut up so much - butcha don't have so much fun neither." He pauses in his snipping and chuckles. "Savage Day, now - used tuh have that."

Peter can recognize a cue. "Savage Day?"

"Tip fard a little, son. There. Yep, one day when they kinda let the savages take overn run the park. Oh gee" - he steps back and shakes with mirth - "what they wouldn't do! Cuttin up an scarin the dudes, actin like bears…"

"Like bears?" Peter twists around. "So they really did that in the old days? We still pretend we do it, an tell the dudes."

93

"Here, settle back a little, son. Yep, used tuh have a contest fer Miss Old Faithful, too. That was okay, the dudes liked that! But then they'd go roun tellin em they could collect peetrified lava out on geyser hill."

"Petrified lava here! Is that for real?"

"Nope, nothin but marmot turds, er marten, yuh know. An they'd tellum about the Montanny turd bird, an stuff like that. Here, hold still, son. Yep, finally went too far, though: so many complaints from dudes the rangers went an stopped it all. I dunno, though: lotta fun, too." He finishes cutting, whips the sheet off and gives it a shake. "Trim the sides? Righto." The depiliated sheet settles back on Trueblood's shoulders and Jimmy lathers up his sideburns, chuckling. "Yep, bes thing they ever did was run the geyser, though."

"Which geyser?"

"*Thee* geyser, son: Old Face-full."

"Hey, does Lou Fuller come to you?"

"Fuller, I know that name. Anyway I wuz sayin - ja hear bout this? No? Well, they got hold uh this big ol stagecoach wheel from somers in Montanny - brought it down in a truck an fixed it up on an axle they stuck down in a crack in the rock near Face-full. Get the picture? Put up a big sign:

OLD FACE-FULL VALVE. DANGER. KEEP AWAY.

Used tuh make like they wuz controllin the geyser with that wheel - drove the dudes an rangers crazy!" He cackles.

"Ow!"

"Sorry, son, just a little styptic pencil here, an trim behind the ears."

"How did they work it? I mean, how did they know when to turn the valve? I mean the wheel."

"Oh son, you've seen Face-full, how yuh allus get some little squirts first, up and down, an noise, then the big blow? Well, they'd have two savages turnin this wheel, an one up near the geyser, talkin em on, an they'd folla whatever he'd say, yuh know. 'Up a little, hold it'" - Jimmy stepped out in front of Trueblood to pantomime the action - "'Okay, a little more, back down, good' - just watchin the geyser an listnin, yuh know - 'stan by now - ready, folks? - LET ER GO!' An up she'd go, right on cue like they *made* it happen!" He snaps the sheet smartly off Trueblood. "There you are, son. One dollar."

Peter surveys his cropped head in the mirror, nods, smiles and pays the barber. "Who thought all that up?"

"Well, that was George Gosser, an Billy Hardin frum up Livinston way, an mebbe couple others."

"Did they get in trouble?"

"George now, he got off, but the rangers caught a couple others an thrown em out."

"Thanks, Jimmy."

"Good mornin, son."

*

It is late enough Saturday night to be Sunday. Will's day off began quite a few hours ago when he hitchhiked to Faithful with a friendly couple from Chicago. He has been socializing in the bar of the lodge since about 8 PM, but is now wandering around the area by himself, a bit unsteady on his feet. It's not that he wouldn't have liked a date - he isn't averse to girls - but all the fine ones are either taken (Shelley, Julia) or not to be found when he is available (Wanda of the cabins, the *chanteuse* at savage shows). Polly is nice, too, but she has paired off with his roommate. And so on and so forth, to the last syllable of recorded time. But no matter! Before the bar closed at midnight he met several congenial people, mostly dudes, and though he can't remember any names now they were far out, some of them, and he feels warm all through. Humanity is good, life is basically good. That includes life in the park.

Off to his left, a dozen or so cars are parked at discreet intervals along a railing with a good view of the geyser. All is dark and silent there. Will knows about this scene, though the fates have not yet given him a place in it. Coming closer, one sees silhouettes of closely-twinned heads in some cars. The ranger patrols do not mind those - they will even overlook some rocking and creaking - but the ones *without* silhouettes will draw their attention, and silhouetted *feet* upset them most of all. No rangers being in sight this evening, however, several of the passengers are apparently checking the floorboards or the seat springs, or watching the submarine races. Will notices a station wagon among them. That *could* be Mason's car...a possible ride back to Thumb... no telling who's using it tonight, of course.

Suddenly there is a roar like an approaching express train and he looks around wildly. Out on the bare rock a silver tower leaps up into the cold moonlight and stays there, pulsating against the stars. "My god!" shouts Will, stumbling and catching his balance. "Son of a bitch!" He hops precariously over a low split-rail fence and runs across a boardwalk onto smooth granite swells in the direction of Old Faithful, still thudding skyward. "You...*power*! You... ejaculation!" He feels a subterranean pounding and waves his fist excitedly, still staggering forward. "You big Yellowstone orgasm!" A shower of boiling water falls nearby and a few drops strike him; as he dodges left his foot catches in a fissure and he sprawls heavily on the rock. Will looks up at the fountain's final, subsiding surges. "*Élan vital*." He likes that. "You are the *élan vital* of nature." The spurts and noises gradually die away, leaving him alone and desolate on the unresponsive granite, sobering quickly. Rubbing his knee, he moans quietly to himself, "*Post coitum, triste*."

*

Chris Jordan of Asheville, the minister's son, is returning from Sunday morning service at the chapel along one of the boardwalks of the Upper Geyser Basin, humming the last hymn, "Faith of Our Fathers," as he thinks about the sermon: "Are We Here for a Purpose?" He wonders; he does wonder. Beneath the boardwalk's slats, warm rivulets trickle toward the river between banks of bright orange algae. He is bound for his single room in a dormitory behind the lodge and a period of solitary meditation, but as the boardwalk reaches its nearest approach to Old Faithful the geyser begins to spurt and rumble. Chris stops to watch, as people do, no matter how long they have been around. With a sound like a roll of timpani a great fleecy column heaves into the blue sky and flutters there, supported by the masses of hot water still surging from below.

"My God, my God," breathes Chris. He looks around, but no one is near. And if there were? He draws himself up. "For Thine is the power and the glory," he says as the eruption continues. "All Thy works are manifest in the earth to proclaim their great Original. Open Thou our lips, and our mouths shall pour forth Thy praise."

The power ebbs, the glory fades, the spout falls. Water runs steaming along channels and into fissures. He can smell the heated earth and stone. "Forever, Lord. Amen." Chris resumes his progress toward the dormitory, feeling that a pertinent comment has been made on his question. It is no accident that he passed by *at this time*. Light has been given. Let him who has eyes, see.

Six: What the Mountain Said

Teewinot (Shoshone for 'Pinnacles'): a 12,317' peak in the Teton Range standing almost directly in front of the Grand Teton. It rises 5600' from Lupine Meadows, from which it can normally be climbed in 6½-8 hours…. From the swamp, ascend the wooded triangular slope, then angle right up snowfields toward the peak…. Avoid the center of the snowfields where rockfall is common…. Many of the climbing accidents in the Park have occurred on this route's snowfields. No one without ice axe experience should attempt this climb.

- from *A Climber's Guide to the Tetons*

"Whar the hell's Hole, anyways?" Lou was in a foul temper. Less than a week earlier he had caught Hayward - the first of the crew to arrive - taking money from the till, and had fired him on the spot, spoiling the "perfect sixteen" rotation and darkening the mood at Thumb. Now another veteran - the second arrival - was delinquent. What the hell was going on? "Guy ken go enywharn do enathin on's day awf so longs he's back nex day fer late shift, yawl know thet!" Several of his men were standing in the lanes during the double-shift period. Yes, they knew that.

"Lou, yer preachin' tuh the kwar!" laughed Beatty.

"He was heading for the Tetons with his friend from Faithful," Mason remembered.

"Yeah, that's rat," said Woo. "He an that Ray guy from Debrew he drove out with. Yuh spose they had trouble?"

Mason shrugged. "All I know is they left Friday night. They were gonna climb yesterday and be back this morning." He paused, recollecting. "Hole sounded scared."

Lou had quieted down and become thoughtful. "Wall, we'll jes check thet out," he muttered, turning away. In the shed he yanked the receiver off the wall. They could hear him yell, "Lureen, gimme Tee-ton ranger station, willya?"

"Aw shit, he's just fartin' aroun with his girl someplace," Owl scoffed.

"I don't know, he *said* he was goin clahmin," said Trueblood. "Did you ever talk to that Ray? Stares right through ya. Hole says he's brilliant, but he looks crazy to me." Peter shook his head. "I wouldn't clahm with him."

"He's supposed to be the top-ranked pre-med at Debrew," Mason reported. "Lou, what's the word?"

The manager came slowly from the hut, his jaw working. "Ain't nobody down theah but some gal, caws awl the rangers been out since dawn, lookin fer two clahmers. Dunno who they ah - mus not uh registuhed. Aist me if Ah had a man missin. An Ah do." He chewed his lower lip. "Doan lack it, mens."

"Je-sus." Henderson exhaled the two syllables slowly.

Lou suddenly pulled himself up. "Hey, Henduhson, Beatty, get movin, got a customuh waitin! Rest uh yawl get the station cleaned up." He turned and began to walk toward the ranger cabin, shrugging and nodding as if in conversation. Most of the savages watched him go.

"Nevuh *have* unduhstood why people go clamin mountains anyway!" exclaimed Woo.

"I do," said Trueblood. "But the Smokies were hagh enough for me. I'd rather just *look* at the Tetons."

"What the hell do you suppose could have happened?" Mason stared beyond the cabins and the lake to the austere Absaroka peaks on the horizon, as if seeing them for the first time; then turned toward the shed to fetch a broom.

*

By noon Saturday Hole was ready to quit. They had been climbing steadily for nearly five hours, and he was dead tired in lung and leg. Also a little sick just now: maybe the altitude, he thought. The first two hours, on trails across meadows and up through forests of tall conifers, had been enjoyable, reminiscent of weekends in the Smokies. But what followed, the tortuous clambering up steep boulder-strewn gullies and over loose scree, had quickly become nightmarish. No trail, no scenery, every foot-placement a problem. And this last hour on the snowfield - which looked easy and innocent from below - had just about finished him: the unremitting glare, the slippery footing that forced him to crawl at times, and Ray always fifty feet ahead, climbing as if possessed. Hole stopped, panting.

"Ray!" The figure above halted and half turned, a frown just visible between goatee and deep-set eyes. "How high you figger we are?"

Ray glanced down to the rocks and trees and plains. "Maybe ten thousand, maybe eleven."

"How high do we have to go?" Hole could see granite battlements rising tier on tier above the snow.

"You know that, Hole," he said sharply. "Twelve-three."

Yes, he knew how high the mountain was. What he wanted to know was how high Ray would make him go. "It's noon. Let's eat lunch."

Ray stared at him. "Lunch on top, Hole. That's the plan."

"The plan," Hole repeated dully.

"But I dunno...I thought we'd be higher by now." For the first time Ray sounded uncertain. "Tell you what. We'll eat half our lunch up there, top of this snowfield, before we tackle the rock."

"Lead on, Jacobs!" Hole felt exhilarated. The journey was finite; it had stages. Maybe he could make it after all - or talk some sense into Ray. Ten minutes later he scrambled onto a flattish boulder near the top of the snowfield and flopped down beside Ray, his chest heaving. "I didn't know I was so out of shape," he gasped.

Ray was unpacking lunch from a worn knapsack. "In general we don't train our bodies carefully enough," he said calmly. "We take better care of our machines."

"Right now I could use an oil change," laughed Hole, popping his mouth full of snow.

"I wouldn't do that: it saps your energy." Sharp again.

"Why would it?" Hole demanded, rebellious. "Who says?"

"It's a matter of caloric economy. Snow chills your insides, so the body turns up the heat, trying to warm you. Net loss of BTUs. Here, have a sandwich."

"Yes, Dr. Jacobs." They began to chew in silence. Hole drank in the variegated colors and forms of the landscape spread beneath them. A small bird twittered across the snow. Now that they had stopped, he was able to enjoy the beauty they had won, which gave him the nerve to speak his mind. "Ray, why don't we call it a day? I mean, head back down. We've had a good climb; let's just enjoy it from here. It's already past noon, you know."

Ray had tensed for a second but did not even turn his head, just kept gazing out over the dappled ranchland with hawk eyes. "You know the trouble with you, Hole?" He gargled water and spat. "You listen to your body. Listen to your mind, your heart! You're forgetting the plan."

"Damn the *plan*! We made it before we *knew* anything," exclaimed Hole, his latent anger welling up. "Now that we're up here, we know more."

"What do we *know*?" Ray almost sneered.

"The reality, man! We know it's higher than we thought, and tougher than we are."

"Speak for yourself." Ray turned full upon him. "I didn't come this far to quit. Go down if you want. I'm going up."

Hole looked away and sighed. He should have known that Ray would not bend, and there was no resisting his will when he chose to exert it. Hole didn't want to climb, but he didn't want to abandon Ray and descend alone, either. "Well, how do you think we'd go up from here?" he asked lamely.

Noting the change in mood, Ray twisted around and pointed to a cleft in the rock wall behind them. "First part's tough: we bridge up that chimney, then go along that ledge. Around the corner it's more chimneys and clefts right to the top. Should be there in an hour or two." He chewed an orange slice.

But Hole was still staring at the first chimney. "Up *that*? Jesus, Ray." He surveyed the whole height of the dark barrier. It rose for hundreds of feet in irregular streaked cliffs crossed by snowy ledges, and he could not see the top. "Do you think we shoulda registered with the rangers?"

"Then we would have had to do their damned climbing school, and that would have meant half the summer. Anyway, I told that guy at the lodge where we were going."

"I wish we had ice axes, then," said Hole doggedly.

"Right, *and* crampons, and how about some oxygen?!" Ray's scorn flashed like sudden lightning. "Christ, Hole, we've been through all that! You can bury climbing under the damn gear until the whole point disappears! Don't forget what it's all about: men against mountains." He glared at Hole with what Julia called his madman's eyes. "We can't stay here all day…it won't get any easier." He pushed the knapsack to Hole. "You better carry this. I'll lead." His wiry frame was already moving up toward the cliff.

"Aye aye, sir," said Hole, only half ironically. They ascended the chimney by pressing their backs against one side, their boots against the other: "pressure-walking," Ray called it. Hard work, for which Hole had to put the surprisingly heavy knapsack on his chest. And now that the east face was in shadow the cold of the rock penetrated his jacket where it pressed on the cliff. After ten long minutes, Ray helped him haul out on the ledge. Hole stayed on his knees for a moment, panting, shivering, and trying to clear his head as he surveyed the twenty-foot drop to the steeply-inclined snowfield. "We have to go back down that, Ray?"

"Unless we find another way down, yes."

"That snow could be ice by then."

"Then we'll skate down!" Hole recognized that fierce gaiety and felt a pang of fear and admiration. Ray was testing handholds along the cliff face. "Follow me," he said.

"I have all summer." Hole lurched upright. The ledge was narrower than he had realized when seeing it from below. He moved forward in a half crouch, putting his hands and feet where Ray put his. Around the first corner it narrowed even more, and they turned to face the mountain. Hole put the knapsack on his back again. "Can we make this all right, Ray?"

"Yeah, it's the only way for awhile. I told you, this is the tough part." He began to edge along the granite wall sideways, both hands on the cliff, testing the lip with his feet. Hole glanced down and quickly back up. Immediately below, the snowfield angled sharply toward distant rocks. The drop was thirty feet now. He concentrated on Ray, who was trying to maneuver around a large boulder that jutted most of the way across what there was of the ledge.

"C'mon, Hole, don't stop!" His eyes blazed. "Ledge ends just up there" - he jerked his head onwards - "and there's another cleft." Ray settled both hands firmly on the two horns of the rock, shifted his weight to his right foot and swung the left around to join it. "C'mon!"

*

As soon as the old phone in the ranger cabin began to jangle, a big hand reached out from under the blanket and clamped onto it. "South Gate ranger station."

"Hello, Dan? Steve at Jenny Lake. Did I wake you?"

"Just drifting off."

"Glad you sacked early. We could use some help down here at dawn tomorrow."

"Is that right? What's the problem?"

"Had a call from Al at the lodge. Says a couple of fellas went off this morning to climb Teewinot and haven't come back."

"Maybe they didn't go."

"He watched them start, Dan."

"Oh, okay. What else do we have?"

"Fellow he talked to was vague and real casual. Told Al that *we* knew all about it, of course - was just telling him as an extra precaution. College guy, probably from Yellowstone, sounded inexperienced to Al. No names. Boots and jackets, a small knapsack, no other equipment in sight. They must be freezing their tails."

"If they're up there. Probably just didn't report back, like those last guys."

"I hope you're right. Anyway, with your search and rescue experience, old man…"

"Sure, I'll trade duties with Curt and be down first thing. Any guesses on a route?"

"Al says they were just going straight up from the meadows to the snowfields and try to climb the cliffs."

"Rotten rock - and no hardware!"

"If they even got that high."

"Right, See you about six, then?"

"No later. Thanks, Dan."

"'Night, Steve." He hung up, turned on the bedside light, and rang the tollbooth to give Curt the bad news. Then he padded over to his desk, pulled one topo map from a pile in the bottom drawer and scuttled back to the warmth of his bed. Dan unrolled the Teewinot-Grand Teton quadrangle in the lamplight and began to study the delicate calligraphy of its contours.

*

It was clear to Hole that they were coming down now, but the rest was hazy. Altitude, Ray said. Up top he had described how lower pressure and less oxygen affect the body, which would diminish as they came down… that is, the *effects* would! Funny he hadn't mentioned those earlier. Hole had been surprised to find himself at the top - at least he didn't remember seeing any more of Teewinot to climb. But he had been astonished when Ray pulled a *movie camera* out of the knapsack and filmed the panorama! Unreal, man! What an amazing fellow! And then produced a *rope* for the descent! The ends were still tied around their waists, Hole noticed. Still, he would be glad when they got down from these clefts that required bridging, and rock ledges that you inched along sideways, onto some surface where they could walk *naturally*. By then he might feel better.

They were making progress, though: the highest snowfield was not far below now. In fact, this ledge looked a lot like the one they did right after first lunch. Same big slab that narrowed it. "Hey Ray, is this the same ledge that...?"

"Shhh!" Frowning with concentration, Ray gave him one fierce glance. "Not now. Gimme some slack."

Crouching cautiously, Hole moved forward a few feet. Well, it looked like the same one...especially the yellowish boulder, ochre maybe, that Ray was trying to work around. With both hands on two of its prongs, he reached his left leg around it, settled his weight on that side, and swung the right leg around to join it.

As the slab pulled away from the cliff and carried Ray off the ledge, the world as Hole had known it ended. His senses seceded from the government of his mind. Time slowed, judgment went catatonic, perception intensified. Ray and his boulder, locked in a silent embrace, swung, slowly and majestically, through a spiral arc centered on his pivoting feet. Hole saw - too clearly to forget, ever - the flared nostrils and wide-open mouth, the acne and reddish facial hair, the blue of Jenny Lake momentarily encircling the head. He reached out toward the arc, a gesture that destroyed his equilibrium, already disturbed by the sudden unexpected movement and his awareness of other rocks pulling loose and falling with clacks and soft susurrations. Hole felt himself slipping as Ray lost contact with his rock; then the rope yanked him and a sickening somersault made his vision spin. From somewhere came a wild yell of terror or exultation.

His mind revived: land on your feet! By wrenching his legs around he did so, more or less, but his knees were driven into his belly and he grunted with pain - a deep '*Hough*' like a bear's. As he fell sideways onto the ice and hard snow his left leg twisted and a deeper stab made him cry out. His cheek struck once before he could ball up, and then he simply endured the pounding, like a fighter on the defensive against a much stronger opponent, while he rolled and bounced forever down into the lap of Wyoming, waiting for the big bruiser to punch himself out.

Hole became conscious of a great peace. He had stopped rolling, had been hunched up here for some time, had *survived*. He took a deep breath, and gasped. *Pain*. In his lung? He felt. In his rib. Broken rib? Hurt, then, but alive. Particles of ice inches from his open eye. Focus. Color, form - marvelous. A million billion, a mountainfull, like these but different. Sentience. Apprehension. Look around. Dark cliffs far above. Icy slope. Lying nearer bottom. Going down now, dammit, not up. No more climbing! Fell, hurt - but *alive*! Ray? Where? Ah...a little downslope, over, 50 yards maybe. Was the rope that long? He looked down at his waist. No rope. Ah...no good at knots. Ray was stretched out motionless. Below him, rocks, large and small, at the end of tracks in the snow. Rockfall. Long way to bottom of snow, but less steep here. Go see how Ray is. Get up? Ooh, no, uh-uh. Side and leg no good. On all fours, then? Not so bad. Possible.

He began crawling toward Ray, his eyes trained, his mind sifting evidence. Motion? Yes: a twitch. Good. More? No. Blood all over his back. Bad. And head. Worse. Pulsing out? No, flowing. Ugh. Back and head injuries, worse than mine. Blood in the snow, uphill and down. Big rock, smaller rocks down there, same track as Ray. How badly injured? He reached Ray and made himself enlarge the tear in the back of his wool shirt. Nice red plaid. Ugh. Big wound, blood oozing slowly. Neck too, deep. Can't move him. Then what? Ray would know. Pre-med. Always has an answer.

"Ray, I need a pre-med!" The sound of his own voice: loud, startling, thin. "Ray!" No response. Ice crystals tinkled downhill. Yes...down. He twisted to look back up. Sun sinking toward peak, shadow stretching this way. Cold soon, then dark. Better go down, get help. Can't spend night up here. Ray too weak to move or talk. Unconscious. "Going for help, Ray. Hang on, man."

He started to crawl down the slope, but stopped fifty feet away as a thought formed. I'm in shock. Injury, trauma, shock. Not thinking clearly. About what? Ray. He isn't just unconscious. Well, then...dead? Maybe Ray's dead. Double-check: you're in shock. Hole made a painful U-turn and hauled back up to Ray. Not moving, flow of blood almost stopped. "Ray, it's Hole." He made himself thrust a hand under the left side of Ray's shirt, waited. Nothing. A flutter? No. He took Ray's wrist. No pulse. Breath? No, not his face ...yes. He slipped his hand under Ray's nose, could feel no breath, and slowly pulled the face around toward him. The lips pallid, the eyes open, staring madly into the snow. Hole jerked back with a cry. "Ray, if you hear me, it's Hole. Going for help. Be back."

He began to crawl, squirm, roll downhill. Once he had circled around the fallen rocks, the panic eased and he tried to think. Going too slow. Must get way down before night: could freeze. May be far gone already. Freaking out, man. Can't be seeing a boat down on Jackson Lake! Try to stand up, walk. Aah! Oops! Useless. Ankle sprained or broken. As he sat, he slid a few inches. He pushed and slid a foot. Hmm. Pushing harder and pulling with his good foot, he slid almost a yard. Far out! It'll work if the crust is hard enough. And if my ass holds out. "Ass-walking," he heard himself say, and giggled. He pushed again and slid another yard.

Hole and the shadow reached the bottom of the snowfield at the same time, and he decided to stop for the night. It would be dangerous to try to come down scree and boulders in the uncertain light remaining. Maybe he was low enough to survive a night out, though the wind was colder now that the sun had set, and flying ice particles stung his neck. Anyway, wasn't snow a good insulator? Or did it steal calories? Shit, man, just admit you're too tired to go on. Probably blood all over my ass. Stayed off the front, though, saved the family jewels. If ever…Julia.

A large rock protruded through the last patch of snow above the first of the hated gullies. Hole crawled into a curving snow-pocket just below the rock and found that he was also in its lee. Shelter from the wind, by God! Propping his back against the granite he rediscovered the knapsack. Forgot about that. Remains of lunch: mine and…. Eat the half PBJ now for bulk, orange for fluids, chase it with some snow, no offence, Ray. None taken. His denim jacket: good. No matches, in fact nothing else. God, were we smart!

He pulled on the jacket, squirmed into a half-reclining position, wrapped the empty knapsack around his feet and jammed his hands into his armpits. Not bad. Everything being used. Gloves would be nice, but… not bad. And how's that for timing? A full moon rising over Togwotee Pass. Watching it slide up, he tried to conceive of the earth rotating, his horizon dipping. It made him dizzy. Saturday night, he thought. Julia? Maybe out on a date with somebody else. Thumb? Lou sticking the tanks before closing. Horn on his day off, probably camping miles from the road, downwind of some buffalo. Will in a bar, boozing, holding forth. Ray's body stiffening on the snowfield. Hole shivered, and his rear began to ache. Soon he would have to change positions, move, flail to keep warm. He closed his eyes and began to hum a tune that came into his head: dum-dum-dum daba daba dum…the Bach gavotte, man! The moon poured its cold light over the Tetons.

*

Dan swung the chestnut's head back toward the mountain for the dozenth time and tried to be patient. It was a stable horse and wanted to go home. Sensibly. Climbing the forest trail had gone smoothly, but once the horse realized where Dan wanted to go - it had been on other searches - the balking had begun. Steve had ridden somewhat ahead on his own well-disciplined mare. There was no trail through the stony rubble below the gullies, it was getting hot, and they were all sick of the jumbled moraine. This was as high up as the horses could find any footing; the rangers were hoping for a sign, a clue - something that would give them a reason to dismount and start up a particular gully. Hell, thought Dan, they're not up there anyway: they're in some dormitory at Faithful or Canyon, sleeping late, waking up sore. This would not be his first wild savage chase.

The chestnut pricked his ears. "Yes? What is it?" Snuffle and stamp, but not the pull toward home. Dan laid the reins gently on the damp brown neck and the ears pricked again. "Okay, amigo, it's all yours." After a moment the horse began to walk forward, sometimes bobbing its head, holding their previous course for 50 yards, then veering inslope for another hundred. It halted at the foot of a gully where a rivulet of snow melt plashed among the rocks, lowered its head and began to drink. "Why, you deceiving scapegrace," laughed Dan, tightening the reins. Then he heard it: a faint high-pitched wail, then silence, and then another wail. Despite himself, he shuddered. It seemed to come from such an immense distance, and in such stony reverberations - as if it were emanating from within the mountain itself.

"Steve!" Two hundred yards ahead the horse and rider stopped, turned. "Did-you-hear-that?" Steve cupped hand to ear, waited, then turned thumbs down. "I'm-going-up-here!" Steve waved and dismounted. Dan swung down, unstrapped the blanket and first-aid kit, then dug in his pocket for the sugar lumps. "Here, these are for you, with my apologies." The horse lipped them impassively. "Well, that isn't the Old Man of the Mountain, you know." Again the wail echoed down the gully: "hey!" or "help!" or just a bellow. The chestnut pricked his ears, wide-eyed. Dan double-looped the reins around a boulder and started climbing.

*

Hole squinted at the rising sun, which had roused him from his best doze of the night. A dozen times, whenever he got too cold, he had pushed and hauled himself upright against the rock to flap his arms and kick; later he just crawled in a circle and howled. Finally he became too tired and weak and numb to care: if his body wanted to freeze, let it freeze and be damned. But now by the first light he soberly examined his hands for signs of frostbite, wishing that he knew what to look for. White? Grey? Ray, of course, would know, would have known, having memorized a passage in a medical dictionary. Those French guys in *Annapurna* probably said what color frostbite was, and they should know. His own hands were mottled purple, blue, grey and white. "Well, they are or they aren't," he croaked, flexing his fingers and whooping with the pain. He warmed them inside his shirt for a few minutes, then ate the chocolate bar, trussed the knapsack around his seat like a pair of diapers and pushed off down the hill.

But on rock the going was tougher, much more fatiguing than the snowfield; his stiff limbs constantly had to reach, brace, support. Yesterday's exertion was today's soreness. His injured leg ached dully and the good one began to complain. Soon he was shaking, partly from exertion, partly from the discovery that he was leaving spots of blood wherever he sat or slid. His jeans were torn up the back; the knapsack was frayed almost through. After half an hour he threw up the chocolate. Hanging onto a rock, panting and dry-heaving, he heard himself moan, "I can't take much more of this," and wondered if that was true. Some part of him thought that he *could* keep doing this, all day and tomorrow too, if necessary. After that, the thought continued, the machine might run out of fuel. "What I meant was that I don't *want* to take much more of this." Ah, laughed the thought, that's different. "Oh Jesus, here we go." He swallowed a handful of snow, noticing that there was less of it around now. This time he didn't bother to apologize to Ray. "Get moving."

Some time later he deepened a cut on his right buttock and bellowed at the top of his voice. The sound went echoing down the gully for several long seconds: AGH-Agh-agh…. "Freaky, man." He did it again, and heard the noise bouncing off rocks far below. It gave a kind of relief, and a feeling of extension, almost of power. How far down? Maybe…. He decided to scream every time he rested, just in case. During his next rest he could see trees at the bottom of the gully, distant but clear, and he thought, I'm getting somewhere. If we fell at ten-five or eleven, would I be down to nine? Weren't the meadows at seven? How long to lose two thousand feet, going like this? He remembered The Plan. "A party in good condition gains a thousand feet an hour. Leaving the meadows at seven, we should make Teewinot at noon, lunchtime." But are we in good condition, Hole had asked. Ray had just turned away. "We certainly aren't in great shape now, are we?" he giggled. And suppose he was wrong about the altitude where they fell? Maybe it was eleven-five. "Then I might still be at ten."

Suddenly tired and dizzy and sick of it all, he lay across a sunny rock and howled intermittently. Didn't anyone else ever climb by this route? Maybe they would on a nice sunny day. They *should*, dammit!

107

Both legs throbbed and he sat up, fighting back nausea. He drew in his breath for one last yell before starting and a movement caught his eye. Down in the gully something…a man?…was moving, climbing toward him…a man, in a ranger hat. "Yaaagh!" He heard his yell trail off into inarticulate blubbering. The man looked up, shaded his eyes, waved, and yelled something. Below him, another man, also climbing. The nearer man climbed steadily until he was a few yards away, then stopped to remove his hat and wipe his brow.

"Hello there," he said calmly, as if he were not the broadest-shouldered hero and finest human being the world has ever known. "Could you use some assistance?"

"You - you're the f-freakin' b-banjo player!" sobbed Hole.

*

No one had much to say on the way down to Jackson. They didn't know what they would find. The rangers had told Lou that Ray had died and Hole was injured, but not how badly. Julia sat in front between Mason and Peter, her ponytail swaying slightly as they made the curves. Lou and Will were in back; the manager had juggled shifts so that the four men could go. (Jill wanted to come too, but wasn't quite brave enough to ask once she heard that Julia was going.) South of Yellowstone the road followed the Lewis River down toward the Jackson Hole ranch country, bent around a hill, and finally revealed the long file of Tetons brooding over their lakes. A sound just audible - not quite a gasp - passed through the car, a sound of shocked recognition such as you might make on seeing an old acquaintance for the first time after learning a sinister fact about him. The afternoon was placid, but dark clouds lay massed on the peaks, and the slow turning of the panorama as the car descended the curves onto the plain felt like the unfolding of some great tragic drama. Twilight of the Gods, thought Will. Mason repressed a shudder. *I came and gamboled on your flanks like a lamb dancing before the wolf. Now it's different: I know you.* Bullshit, he thought, but shuddered again.

At dusk they reached Jackson and followed signs to the new hospital, a handsome two-story affair. Climbing stairs to the orthopedic ward they were hushed and restrained; only the sight of Hole in a corner bed, his encased leg elevated, released them. Savages and words rushed at him as he awkwardly levered up on one elbow, his face creasing in a pained grin. Julia carefully hugged him and kissed his less-damaged cheek. Then she tried to step aside, but Hole kept her hand as the boys came forward, muttering anything. He grasped each hand feebly, nodding but not speaking. After they propped him up and found chairs, silence fell. Julia stood holding his hand, facing the others.

"Looks like an FDR press conference," said Will. The others laughed inordinately.

"Well, men," croaked Hole, wiping his eyes, "Guess you could say I really screwed up this time."

"You had us all worried," Mason told him. "Horn and everybody wanted to come."

"Yeah, but Ah said somebuddy hadda run the station, so th'others just say hello."

"Bastille was here this mornin," said Hole. "I think."

"Wall, Ahm glad *some*buddy's seen the durn Canuck!"

"Hole, what's the damage?" asked Peter. "You hurt bad?"

"Actually they haven' tol me much, an I forget what they say." He tried to laugh and grimaced. "I'm so woozy on this morphine… Think I've got a broken rib, an prolly somethin broken down there" - he wriggled his toes - "from the fall, an cuts from slidin down…"

Where did you fall? Where did you slide? they asked. What happened up there? Hole stared at them, tears welling up. Of course they didn't know. His friends were ignorant of what was now almost the whole of his consciousness. With Ray gone, *no* one else could ever know what he knew. Another price to pay. If you'd rather not talk about it, they said kindly. "No, I should. Gotta try." He squirmed into a more comfortable position, took a firm grip on Julia and a deep breath, and told his story, from Thumb to the rescue. Some parts were more coherent than others, and his voice gave out at the point where Dan found him. It was a long narration, and when it ended he slumped, visibly fatigued.

Trueblood cleared his throat. "Hole, I'm sorry, we're sorry as heck about Ray." Murmurs of assent. "I know he was a good friend of yours."

"He led me out here from Florida and up that mountain," Hole said huskily.

"He almost killed you." It was Julia. They all looked at her.

"I chose to go. Ray had a lot to offer. He was a brilliant guy."

"And he was mad," she said firmly.

Hole glanced up and squeezed her hand. "Guess he cared more 'bout adventures, an doin things the right way, than about livin." Julia turned half aside to look out at the silhouetted Tetons. "Anyway, he paid for it."

Much of the light had faded. They sat quietly in the darkening ward until a ranger appeared at the door, hat in hand. "Dan! It's my rescuer! Come in, man." They all rose.

Nodding to the others, Dan crossed to the bed and took the outstretched hand. "How are you feeling, Hole? What do they say about your leg?"

"Uh, sprain or fracture. Or maybe sprain *and* fracture? Sorry, this morphine…"

Dan smiled. "It's okay, I'll ask the doctors. Hmm, you won't lose much skin off your face or hands, I think. Now your backside's another matter."

"Dan, these are my Yellowstone friends. Julia…"

"Thank you, Dan. Just thank you." She shook his hand and met his eye.

"Line o' duty, ma'am, as they say." The others introduced themselves. "Ah, Fuller and Dixon: the fishermen." They stared at him. "You know I share the South Entrance cabin with Ranger Curtis."

Mason laughed uneasily. "We paid our debt to society."

"Of course. Just a mnemonic. I think I remember your arrival. You had a rifle?"

"Yes…and the square dance. The second guitar?"

"Right. Shall we sit down? I can't stay long: Hole looks tired, and I have to get back to Yellowstone." When everyone was settled he turned to the patient. "Hole, what do you think now about what you and Ray did on Saturday?"

Hole squirmed and grimaced. "Pretty stupid, I guess."

Dan nodded. "Uh-huh, and illegal, by the way. No climbing school, lied to a clerk at the lodge about that, failure to register. If you'd both come back alive you could have been charged with breaking National Park regulations."

"Mistuh," blurted Lou, his face reddening to a degree not seen since Stony Simmons called it forth, "thoser hahd words to a sick man."

Dan glanced at him. "Yes, sick - but recovering, out of danger, *not dead*. Hole knows that he's lucky to be able to hear my "hard" little speech. Do you all realize how seldom we get 24 hours of clear weather up there? Not to mention a freak echo." He gazed steadily but not unkindly at Hole, who looked unhappy.

"But do you have to lecture him in front of his friends?" asked Julia plaintively.

"Yes, actually I do, because the lecture is for them, too." He looked around the circle. "How many of you knew where Hole was going and why? Mason? Peter? Julia? Did anyone say a cautionary word to him?"

"Of course!" exclaimed Julia.

"Good! Good for you. What about you, Lou?"

The manager blushed. "Ah doan tell mah men whar they ken go an what they ken do when they're awf," he growled.

"No, but a veteran can always give a word of friendly warning. Might have been all he needed. And a manager *can* veto a dangerous plan, or report it."

Hole stirred uneasily. "Dan, please lay off Lou. It was my mistake. I don't remember tellin him where I was headin."

"That's right," said Mason. "When Hole didn't show for work on Sunday, Lou had to ask us where he was. *I* told him that he was heading down here."

"All right: I'm sorry, Lou. But *you* knew then, Mason. Did you try to warn him?"

It was Mason's turn to look discomfited. "Well, no, because I didn't know enough. I'm not a mountaineer, and I don't know the Tetons. He just said "climbing." Even if he had said Teewinot it wouldn't have meant anything to me."

Dan nodded. "Okay. All I'm saying is, everybody has to take these mountains seriously. We can't treat them like a playground for our amusement. They can kill."

A middle-aged woman with steel-grey hair, wearing a white uniform, bustled through the doorway and took in the situation at a glance, as nurses will. "Visiting hours are over for this patient," she announced firmly. "He's tired, *as you can see*. Thank you for coming." She began to plump his pillows and prepare an injection.

Now it was Dan who looked uncomfortable. "Yes, sure, sorry," he mumbled, heading for the door.

"She means it. You better go before she pulls down my pansh - pants." Hole grinned painfully. "Thanks for comin. Hey, can't you wait till my friends leave?" He waved them out the door, uttering brief farewells.

In the hall, Dan spotted a doctor and peeled off for a consultation. The savages hesitated on the stairs. "I guess we should wait for him?" ventured Mason.

"Aw, like hail we should…"

"He's only doing his job," said Julia. "And he may have saved Holey's life." Lou harumphed significantly, but they waited, and in a minute the ranger joined them.

"Walking into town? I can show you a good café on my way to the ranger office." They followed him outside and along the sidewalk from lightpool to lightpool under the dense foliage of shade trees toward the glow of First Avenue. Peter asked what he had learned from the doctor. "Well, he has a bad ankle sprain and a fracture of the lower tibia, so he'll be on crutches for a good while. Then there's the broken rib, facial cuts, shock, exposure, some frostbite, and multiple lacerations of the backside. He lost some blood, and still has lots of pain. Quite a banging-up, but probably nothing serious in the long run. Fortunately he's young and healthy! But even so, if he hadn't managed to descend a couple of thousand feet from where they fell, it might have been a lot worse by the time we found him. Overall, I'd say he was lucky."

They emerged from the side street into the garish lights of First, thronged with cars and tourists. "Life goes on, you see. Well, there's your place yonder, the Saddle Grill. I have to get over to our local headquarters and requisition some transport north. Early duty tomorrow."

A slight pause, then Mason spoke hesitantly. "Look, we'll be heading north after dinner and I have an extra seat. You could just, uh, eat with us and then ride along." He looked around for support.

"Sure," said Will. "Some of my best friends are rangers."

Dan smiled. "Fine with me, if that's *generally* agreeable. But I understand that nobody likes being lectured to. For that matter, I don't much like dishing out the lectures."

Lou cleared his throat. "Hail, come awn along, Dan."

"All right, thanks. We may be in time for the Frontier Days skit." The Saddle Grill was crowded with men in Hawaiian shirts, women who didn't belong in the pedal pushers they were wearing, and roving bands of children; the only customer who looked as if he might be a local was a drunk on a barstool. But it was the place to be, the prices were right, and the food was good enough. At Dan's urging, they took a table by the front window.

As they were working through hamburger steaks, hash browns and cole slaw, Peter glanced outside and exclaimed, "Hey!" A *Wells Fargo & Co.* stagecoach was drawing up to the curb. In the strange light compounded of the streetlight and the greenish glow still emanating from the northwest sky, the coach looked unearthly, a mirage, a time machine; yet they could see gobs of grease and cotter pins at the hubs, and gilt paint flaking off the ampersand. The driver hung up the reins, jumped down and held up his hands to receive the strongbox from the guard. Suddenly two men stood up on the roof of the building across the street and began firing six-guns at the stagecoach. The savages stopped chewing in mid-mouthful. The driver struck an agonized attitude and fell, but the guard and one passenger returned fire. One bandit was hit and crumpled on the roof, whereupon the other jumped nimbly onto a low shed, thence to the ground, and fled, firing back. The guard and passenger loaded the groaning driver into the coach and drove off at a terrific clip, firing into the air just to be on the safe side. Most of the passersby had stopped, and some applauded.

"Tourist entertainment," explained Dan. "So they'll know we still value our tradition of lawless violence."

"Notice that in this version the attempted robbery fails, though," Will observed.

"Crahm don't pay, Will," said Lou. "It's a fam'ly show."

Driving north they were silent until the moon shone through a few attendant clouds onto the Tetons, now almost abreast of them. "Beautiful," murmured Julia; then, after a pause, "But killers, too." She turned slightly toward Dan, sitting beside her up front. "How do *you* feel about them? Especially after what just happened."

"Ambiguous, as you said. Nobody loves the mountains more than I do, but you take the good and the bad together, as with anything you love."

"I like that."

"How long have you been a climber?" asked Will.

"Oh, half my life. I've climbed every summer and most winters since I was fourteen or so. Mostly in the Rockies." He chuckled. "Can't seem to shake the habit."

"I don't understand mountaineering," Mason admitted. "It's not a compulsion I've ever felt. Seems to me a form of egoism, imposing your will on nature."

"Ah, the psych major," laughed Peter.

But Mason persisted. "What's the appeal for you, Dan?"

"Oh, it's hard to say: you either feel the pull or you don't. For me it's adventure, physical challenge, beauty…exercise…initiative. And a little spirit-stretching, I guess."

"That's how Ray used to talk," said Julia quietly.

"Then I'd say he was on the right track, but his ambition outran his knowledge. We see a lot like that: eager, stubborn, self-centered. I'll bet *he* had an ego."

"That was Ray."

As the car labored up the grades to Yellowstone, the Tetons disappeared and the scent of resin grew stronger. Eventually dim lights showed ahead. Mason pulled over by the ranger cabin and Dan paused with his hand on the door. "Thanks for the ride, Mason. Glad to have met you all. I'm sure Hole will be okay. A fine fellow, too."

Trueblood spoke from the back. "Bye, Dan. Can't thank you enough. Words don't do it."

"That's for sure." Dan opened the door. "Listen, I don't really have to say goodbye. I'm being transferred to Thumb on the first. Ranger Simmons is moving to Gardiner."

"Hot dawg!" Lou came to life. "Stony Simmons gettin the boot!" He thrust his right arm into the front seat. "Dan, yuh ken count awn the red cahpet the day yuh arrahve at Thumb."

Dan twisted to accept the handshake. "Lou, your support will be a red-carpet welcome in itself." Small bones could be heard crunching and Julia laughed. Dan eased his torso outside and closed the door. "See you all in a few days, then. Goodnight." He took the three wooden steps in one long stride and waved before he disappeared into the cabin.

They were halfway to Thumb when Julia pointed up through the windshield and said, "There it is. The comet." They had been seeing it from Thumb, but this was "out in the country," away from the "brat lats," as Beatty said, so Mason stopped and everyone climbed out to look. On either side, black evergreens rose halfway to the zenith and converged up and down the road, leaving a rhombus of starlit sky, a lighter dark, overhead. In the middle foreground of their starscape hung the bright visitor, like a tiny diamond fan.

"What's it called?" asked a voice in the obscurity.

"Something 1957 something."

"Who cares about the name?"

"The papers say it was last visible 5000 years ago," Mason reported, "and won't come back for another 5000, if at all. It goes millions of miles outside the solar system, maybe to other galaxies. And it's going 25 miles a second."

Lou whistled. "Now thet's hawlin tail!"

"Let no men say / 'These are their reasons; they are natural'," Will advised. "For I believe they are portentous things / Unto the climate that they point upon."

Silence fell. The comet streamed its brilliance coldly in the far-off sky. A breeze carried the fragrance of pines across the road, and a loon laughed somewhere. Julia shivered. "Could we go now? I'm cold." Mason felt an urge to put his arm around her, but didn't dare.

*

The next morning Mason drove to Old Faithful to spend the day with Liz. He knew it was a mistake: the accident made everything else seem trivial. But, he told himself, she was expecting him, and it was easier to go than to call it off. Besides, Julia, who had spent the night in Shelley's room, needed a ride back to Faithful. So he gave her a lift, and found her all that Hole had said; though they spoke little, there was no awkwardness and Mason felt very close to her. Liz was partly right: Julia was a good listener. But she said enough, at the right times, to let you know she was there, and it was always on key and worth hearing. He was amazed at how sorry he felt to leave her at the lodge, and that regret darkened his mood further.

For much of the day he and Liz wandered among the geysers, sometimes holding hands and talking but making little contact. Somehow everything was poisoned. She wanted to hear about the accident and he complied, but with obvious reluctance. She thought they should "do something" as a distraction, but neither of them could think of what. Yet she could not let him go, and he could not quite bring himself to leave. Mason said that he was preoccupied with the fall, that it had drained him; Liz responded that couples *should* be brought together by crises. Mason snapped that he was tired of hearing about what couples *should* do; the accident and Ray's death made all that stuff seem superficial. Liz screamed in rage and frustration. Around in circles they went, making no progress.

At midnight they were parked at the end of a dirt lane in a remote pine grove where the rangers seldom came, a favorite spot for savage couples that they had used in better times. This was not one of them. Liz stared out the window, wiping her eyes; Mason slumped behind the wheel, wondering what had become of the girl who helped him with Renaissance poetry and could recommend interesting books on Africa. "Liz, we've been flogging ourselves for hours," he groaned finally. "Let's quit for the night."

She suddenly turned on him. "Is it just for tonight you want to quit? The whole day's been a nightmare."

"Yes. I've been very bad. My mind's not on us."

"People who don't turn to each other when things go wrong aren't in love."

"You're probably right."

"They don't belong together."

"No, I suppose not."

"Damn it, is that all you can say, Dixon? Did you mean quit for tonight or quit for good?" Mason tried to remember which he had meant, but as he paused to consider, Liz pounced: "*Do you think we should break up?*"

He took a deep breath. "Probably, yes."

"Probably yes," she mocked, sobbing. "*Of course yes!*" she shrieked. "It's written all over your face. Has been the whole summer." Liz sat up and wiped her eyes. "It's not your mind that isn't on it. Your heart's not in it. Take me home."

Outside her dormitory Liz leaned over and kissed his cheek before getting out. "Goodbye, Dixon," she said tonelessly. "Isn't it nice that we have half the summer left?" Then she walked away into the darkness - not to the building, but toward the trees.

Watching her curves recede, Mason felt a pang of regret and called her name. She kept walking. He lay on the seat, motionless and silent, for several minutes, but she did not reappear, so he sat up and started the engine. Driving slowly away, he could feel only relief. It had been done. Said and done. Up on Craig Pass a line from an old sonnet came to mind: "Since there's no help, come let us kiss and part." But how did it go on? Did it offer any useful advice? Did it end happily? He wondered what would constitute a "happy ending," the right ending, for him and for Liz.

After parking in front of the stockade, Mason stood in the cold and watched the comet twinkle in the void for several minutes. He tried to imagine the sizes and distances and speeds out there, but failed, of course, and had to come back down to earth, which is what he wanted to avoid. In the morning he should tell Peter and perhaps some others, who would be sympathetic, and he would have to respond.

Mason woke late from a dream, after a night of disturbing dreams, and lay looking out at the tops of the conifers. For a moment, to his confused perception, their tips looked like roots. Yes, he felt, the trees *ought* to grow upside-down today: a topsy-turvy, Alice-in-Wonderland world. He got dressed, made the bed, wrote a letter to Liz, tore it up, lay down again. Hell, they'd only been together for nine months!

116

Surely they'd go on to live long, full lives with other people and barely remember this episode? But right now it was hard, dammit. And the trees still looked odd, their edges harder or softer than usual: he couldn't tell which.

After a while Trueblood came in, chuckling at someone's joke in the hall. "Hey roomie, we missed you at breakfast. How 'bout some lunch? Gosh, Mason, what's the matter?"

"Do I look *that* bad? Okay: Liz and I broke up last night."

Peter froze. "Oh, no! That's a shame, Mace. I never thought...I mean, I knew...well, why?"

Mason shrugged. "You know, it's hard to say. We had something once...last winter I was thinking we'd probably get married someday. But it's been love-hate this summer." His voice trembled. "I'm all shook up, as the man says."

"Man, that's rough." Trueblood came forward and patted his shoulder: the strongest expression of sympathetic solidarity permitted them in 1957. Mason nodded dumbly, overcome. After a moment Peter said, "Maybe Will was right about the comet."

Mason looked blank. "About the comet...what?"

"You know, about it being a bad omen. He meant for mountaineers, I think, but maybe it's for lovers, too."

"In that case the rest of you better watch out. For Liz and me, I think this was in the stars from the day she arrived."

There was a knock at the door. Peter stepped back as Will came in. "Hey, gents, how about...God, men, what *is* it?"

Mason was unresponsive so Peter spoke up. "Mason and Liz broke up last night. He's feelin kinda rocky."

"Ah. That's tough, Mace." Will paused for a moment. "Although as you know I think you're better off without her. God, won't it be nice when the puppy-love agonies of our teen years are over?!"

"Hate to tell you, but I'm 20. They go on."

"Oh." Will shrugged. "So, who's up for some basketball after lunch?"

"Yeah, but lunch first," said Peter. "You coming, Mason? Pris'll want to know that you're available."

Mason managed a thin smile and stood up. "No appetite, but..." He grimaced and followed them out. It appeared, as Dan had said, that life would go on.

Seven: And the Rains Came

"Over here, Will! Hey, interference, Lou! Ugh!" Trueblood took the pass, drove around the corner and made his lay-up. "Awrat!" Sweating profusely, he paused to catch his breath and let his heart slow down, but Lou had already taken the ball out and was charging the backboard again. "Get him! Pick him up!" Lou sent Gair sprawling, double-dribbled, missed a jump shot, but elbowed Will for inside position and tapped in his own rebound. "Hey!" Peter tried to protest but was laughing and panting too much.

For a week after the accident, basketball was Thumb's one acceptable diversion. Romance curdled, dude-baiting seemed in poor taste, music was out of the question. It was as if they had been hit in the solar plexus during a good laugh. What had seemed a mostly light-hearted summer was something else now; a shadow had fallen. Hole was lying in Jackson hospital. A few made the somber trek to attend the memorial service for Ray Jacobs at Faithful ("for Hole's sake") and returned looking gloomier than ever. The best outlet - for the boys - was basketball, as therapy and recreation.

Ever since the advent of hot weather a running pick-up game had flowed from day to day, involving almost everyone at some time and stopping only for darkness. "Individuals come and go, but The Game is eternal," Will announced. The sounds of basketball - pat-thud, pat-thud, squeak, smack, whang! Grunt, swish, yell - bored into every consciousness, like an insidiously catchy theme on a soundtrack. They had already worn out one basketball, and Lou was talking about putting up "lats fer nex season." But "after Teewinot" (as the accident was now called) they played with heightened ferocity from mid-morning until dusk while a few off-duty girls watched, silent and intense.

Lou fired the ball back into Trueblood's midriff. "Come awn, Pete: cain't quit whilst yer ahead!" He ruled the court as firmly as he did the station: his ability made him a dominant player, while his authority and availability often made him a "choosing captain." The other would usually be Trueblood - a good player but too incorrigibly clean to be effective against Lou - or Will, who had made All-State his senior year. Younger and fitter than Lou, Will was an inch taller and a better shot, but Lou's elbows, tripping, and loud yells at crucial moments could frequently offset these advantages. "Hey, whereya goan, Mace?"

Mason was limping off the half-court toward the dormitory. "To rest this ankle and read a book, Lou. Henderson can take my place."

"Hokay, Mace. Gotta getcha some decent sneaks. Jesus, Ah need some hat awn mah sahde!"

"Let's even up the teams," Will suggested. "You take Owl and Henderson can play with us."

"Ahl take Pete."

Will laughed. "Lou, you know that's absurd! You'd do *anything* to win, wouldn't you? Game like this, what difference does it make?"

"Any man what won't get down in the dirt tuh win doan duh*serve* victrih." Lou chuckled. "Tell yuh, in the counteh champeenships, rat afore the fust tipawf, Ah laid mah foot uvuh t'utha centuh's, reel cazhullack. Huh! Shoulda seed him: yelled, jumped back lack Ahda *goosed* him an staimped on *mah* foot. Ol ref blows his whistle: 'Technical foul: one shot.' Ahm the bes foul shot in the counteh! One tuh nothin, an they's still wundrin wh'hoppen. Nevuh did recovuh."

Will smiled indulgently. "But are you *proud* of that? Anybody can go around fouling people. That's no test of abilities."

"Huhbilities! If yer Superman thet's hokay, but us mortals gotta cut some cohnuhs!"

"I'm afraid you'd foul out a lot on the Coast, Lou."

"Mebbe. But chewd take yer lumps in Geawja."

"I might at that. If you're rested enough, let's play. You can take Owl."

"Huh, *Ahm* ready if *yew* are!" And they returned to battle as opposing centers, a study in contrasting styles, pretty evenly matched after all. Usually the winner would be the one who procured the services of Trueblood or of Bastille, when he was around, although with personnel shifting so often, the very concept of a "winning team" was porous. Owl was also valued, as a fouler and an intimidator, like an "enforcer" in hockey. Beyond them the material fell off sharply, which did not keep Lou from dreaming that he would someday challenge and crush the Mammoths, the Lakers, the canyon Fallguys or the Geyser Hotshots, should any of those areas have the temerity to form a team. Mason had suggested that their squad be named the All-Thumbs, but he was a sarco and a lousy shot. Jesus, with Will and Peter and Bastille, and mebbe Owl or Horn, he could...

"Hey, he's heah, yawl!" Lou held the ball and the game screeched to a halt. Beatty's moonface was peering at them from the gate in the palisade. "Come awn!"

"Who's here, man? Hole?"

"Yeah, Hole's back, come awn!" They followed him across the road in time to see Hole struggling out of a car and onto his crutches, looking clumsy and somewhat wasted, but smiling. A middle-aged woman in professional clothes emerged from the driver's side.

"This is my mom, guys," he said, with an introductory wave. "She's come to collect me."

"Welcome to Yellowstone, ma'am," said Gair politely.

"It's all a bit confusing," she replied vaguely, shading her eyes and looking around at the mountains and mud pots.

"Culture shock," chortled Hole. "Doesn't look much like Florida, does it, mom?"

"God, the blind leading the halt," murmured Will.

"Hole, you took…quite a beating." Gair winced sympathetically.

By then the word had spread, and savages came streaming from the dormitories and the store, leaving dudes to look after themselves. But those who had not been down to Jackson hospital stopped short and fell silent when they drew near enough to see what one brush with a big mountain had done to the plump, healthy young man who had left them a week earlier still carrying his baby fat. Conversation was difficult, since it had to skirt so much. Many a girl kept one hand over her mouth. Would he never go?

"Well, we'd better be on our way," he said at last, and savages crowded around to say goodbye.

Mason put out his hand. "I'll miss that big guitar, Hole."

"See you back in the hallowed halls," promised Trueblood - and was startled by the thought of that distant re-entry.

"You'll leave a big hole," Will assured him. Snickers and groans. Lou could only grip Hole's hand and gulp.

"I put your guitar and the bags with your clothes in the car," said Horn quietly.

"Say, roomie, thanks, I'll…oh, screw the goodbyes!" he laughed, squinting more inscrutably than ever.

Suddenly Jill darted forward and gave him a peck on the cheek. "Bye, Holey." She had never given up hope, and now she cried into her apron, comforted by Pris and observed closely by Hole's mother.

Nonplussed by this mark of affection from a Tucson tart, Hole stammered toward a comeback. "Oh, hey, Flossie, listen, I…I'll go back up there and break the *other* leg!" He waved a one-crutch salute as he bent to get in. In a few moments the car rolled off toward Old Faithful and Julia, with Hole waving until they disappeared around the turn.

"Those whom the gods love get it in the ass," declared Will.

"Oh will you *stop that!*" Jill shrieked through her tears and ran toward the dormitory. The other girls gave Will dirty looks and followed her.

"Shee-ut," said Beatty. "Just shee-ut."

Relief from the blues was at hand, however, and also relief from the "manpar crahsis" created by the loss of Hayward and Hole. Lou twice called Gardiner to plead for reinforcements; Morley said he would enlist veterans, including Virg Vine, to broadcast on the old-boy network. Just hours after Hole's departure Lou had a call to say that help had been procured. At dinner he announced that yet another Debruvian was coming.

Mason and Peter looked up in surprise. "Who's that?"

"Friend uh yers, Ah guess," said Lou, slurping his chicken soup. "Fella frum Atlanta, name uh Clay."

"Red Clay!" exclaimed Trueblood. "No kidding?"

"He's a good singer, and a bit of a ladies' man," Mason informed the company. "When's he coming, Lou?"

"S'drivin out with a buddy. Be heah ez quick ez they ken."

"Then it won't be long," chorussed Mason and Peter.

On Friday morning, the 26th of July, a white station wagon with New York plates pulled up to the pumps. On its rear window was a decal: *Universitas Debruviensis - Sic Friat Crustulum.* Inside were a pale, dark-haired fellow and a pretty blonde. "Debrew is always welcome," said Mason. "What'll it be?" At the sound of his voice the girl leaned forward to look at him and he recognized her. "Hello, Jacky. Haven't seen you since that madrigal group last year."

"Mason! What are you doing here?"

It seemed obvious. "Summer job *alfresco.* And you?"

"Just married." She blushed becomingly. "This is Bill."

"Hi, congratulations. What'll it be?"

"Hello, thanks. Just a dollar of regular." Tense forehead.

"That won't get you far out here."

"I know," said Bill anxiously, "but we're down to ten dollars. You don't know of any temporary work around here, do you?"

"Wait: did Morley send you?"

"Who's Morley?"

Mason straightened up and laughed. "Hey, Lou!" he called. "Another Debrew man looking for work." Lou came striding from the shed with a wide grin.

"Gawd," said Beatty. "Theah evrawheah!"

In the space of an hour Bill was hired for the station and Jacky for the store. Gray allotted them the large "couple's room" over the grocery ("Just waiting for you to show up," he said). Hayward's Green Hornets were about the right size for Bill, who found himself a lane apprentice that afternoon. With everyone trying to help him at once he tended to become confused, and Lou pronounced him "a worriuh," but he was a warm body, he'd do. Jacky was an instant hit: in her blue Ham's uniform, with rosy cheeks and a seraphic smile, she looked like a Dresden doll, and her sweetness was as unfailing as Shelley's. She had even brought along her own man, so the girls liked her, too. At dinner the first night she tried to thank the whole company for this shower of good fortune. "And that lovely room!" she gushed. "How can we ever repay you?"

"Ho ho, ha ha! Easy," replied the savages, rolling their eyes. "You can throw parties!" Bill and Jacky looked startled, but the idea had already been widely discussed since their arrival. One of Thumb's most lamented weaknesses was its shortage of good places where the sexes could gather to socialize at night, and the suitability of the couple's room for this purpose had escaped no one. The welcome for Bill and Jacky was both sincere and self-interested. Nobody asked for a party that first night, but no one turned down an invitation after that. There was only another month.

During double shift on the afternoon of Sunday the 28th a white Ford coupe raced onto the apron, heeled steeply and skidded to a stop by the grease rack, flinging pebbles against the tin shed. As Lou came boiling out, both doors swung open; from the passenger side staggered a pudgy, carrot-topped youth who fell theatrically into Trueblood's arms. "Two days and two nights from Atlanta!" he gasped.

Peter turned to Lou, who was glaring on, arms akimbo. "Lou, this is Clay," he announced, as if that explained everything. "And who is your friend, Clay?"

"Oh yeah, sorry." Clay straightened up and brushed himself off. "This is Tech," adding, "that's where he goes."

A tall, heavy-set hulker, Tech smiled amiably and offered a big paw around. "Glad tuh meechah. Pleased tuh be heah."

Lou stepped forward, shook their hands and took control. "Ahm Lou the manajuh," he said. "Clay, putcher thangs in the dorm an ruhpoat back heah. Ahl show yuh the ropes this aftuhnoon. Tech, they wawnt you up at Facefull numbuh one rat away."

A quick study, Clay read his distaste and became at once the responsible employee. "Shurr, Lou, Al just stow muh stuff an be rat back," he said, in what seemed to Mason a deeper drawl than usual. Lou nodded and strode off to yell at a dude who was trying to pump his own gas in a blocked-off lane. Clay pulled his Air Force-blue Valpak out of the trunk. "See yuh, Tech. Keep in touch."

"Tech, try to get Satuddys off," said Peter. "That'll be Clay's day. Maybe we can work something."

Tech beamed. "Swell idea. See yuh, men." And he peeled away, again scratching gravel.

In the course of showing Clay the ropes that afternoon Lou lost his angry edge: after all, the manpar crahsis was over. That evening he stuck his head in the doorway of #4, where Clay was visiting with his buddies and new friends, to ask, "Gettin settled in awrat, Clay?"

"Shurr thang, Lou, thank yuh kindly." The manager waved and withdrew.

"You and Lou on good terms now?" asked Trueblood.

"Oh yeah, reglur peachtree buddies!" chuckled Clay. "But he gave me a goin-ovuh this aftuhnoon…!" His rising inflection invited them to imagine - or remember - the thoroughness of that drill. Then he went back to regaling his listeners with tales of the westward dash. Once he heard that his friends needed help, speed was the watchword. He convinced Tech to come, and Tech had a fast car. Once, said Clay, they covered 200 miles in 2 hours and 20 minutes - not on Interstates, mind you, but on two-lane roads with towns and stoplights. Sleep was limited to cat-naps for the off-duty driver; meals were snacks at gas stops. Stopping to change drivers would have wasted time, so the new driver slid along the top and back of the seat into position, then dropped down as the retiring driver slid right. To lose more than 5 mph in the process was a disgrace. Small towns with 25 mph speed limits were their bane. They would creep through, then floor it when they spotted the "Resume Speed" sign ahead - hoping that it wouldn't say "School Zone." Somehow they were never stopped by the police for anything. Clay's audience was enthralled: he managed to make this material seem both entertaining and epic.

"Hey, when do I meet my roommate?" asked Clay.

"Oh, he's over in West, be back late." Peter laughed. "He lacks the ..."

"He likes the movies," Mason interjected. "Probably went to see *The Bad Seed*, or that Italian film."

"What?" blurted Peter. "Owl?"

Clay looked doubtfully from one to the other. "What sort of gah is he?"

"The shy, quiet type," replied Mason. "You'll have to draw him out. Owl Brain is his nickname: a brain, but owlish, reclusive."

Peter nodded. "Yeah, you should make quat a pair."

Clay relaxed on a bed, arms behind his head. "You got a nass-lookin bunch uh girls here," he observed.

"We do?" exclaimed the others.

"Shurr, from what I saw at dinner, they'll do - just fer now, yuh know." He grinned. "So what duh yuh have in the way of pahties roun heah? Social laf?"

"Good question," said Mason. "It *has* been limited, but I think it's about to improve."

Bill and Jacky began by inviting the other Debruvians and an equal number of girls to come by after work the next evening. Clay and Pris hit it off at once, Peter was very gallant with the grieving Jill, and Mason joked around with Vicky, who was even jollier than he had realized. What a relief to flirt a bit without tripping over tangled *issues*! Maybe there *could* be life after Liz. The three-room apartment, redolent of pine and recent varnish, struck them as posh, opulent, luxurious. Beer, wine and song flowed freely. Fresh-faced Jacky turned out to know a remarkable number of dirty songs, which she sang in her clear soprano and accompanied prettily on the guitar. Her *succès d'estime* was a ballad about Aunt Rosie, whose errant career began when, as a choirgirl, she and the bishop were discovered in the loft investigating a mysterious organ. The catchy chorus ran:

> *We never mention Aunt Rosie:*
> *Her picture is turned to the wall.*
> *Though she lives on the French Riviera,*
> *Mother says she is lost to us all!*

Woo and Ellen, who had turned up late, giggled with embarrassment.

The party went on until 2 AM, by which time there was strong sentiment among those present for more and larger parties, so the following night the doors were pretty well thrown open. Gair came and played his accordion, Beatty brought "Stormy-Weather" Wanda of the Cabins, Owl got drunk and maudlin, then sick; Lou and Shelley made a rare public appearance. An obscure couple necked in a corner so devotedly that it was hard to see who...could that be Jane and The Mouth? In truth the cloud of Hole's accident seemed to have passed over, along with the manpar crahsis, and West Thumb, basking in the warmth of its new arrivals, thirsting for the upper room, opened itself to a revival of romance...or at least of sexual sociability.

One morning Mason woke with a vague recollection of having been disturbed by Clay during the night and asked for his car keys. When he found that they were indeed missing he padded down the hall to #6 and returned the favor. "Oh yeah," mumbled Clay sleepily. "On the table there. Didn't think ya even woke up."

"I just remember saying, 'They're in my pants'. How 'bout some gas money?"

Clay laughed. "Actually, you know, I never even turned on the motor. Just used the back."

"Ah." Mason searched for signs of a joke. "Prissy?"

"Wouldn't say yes, couldn't say no. God, she's hot!"

"Oh, shit, man!" Owl, half-awake, pounded his pillow hysterically.

Coming off work that afternoon Mason walked by his car and noticed a small black object on the blue carpeting in back, still made up into a bed. Not knowing what it was, he opened the tailgate and picked up...the heel of a woman's shoe. Directly above it was a small tear in the ceiling fabric. He stuck the evidence in his pocket and headed for the store. Trueblood was sitting at the counter with a soda; Mason took the next stool and laid the heel on the countertop.

"Hey Mason, hot in the lanes today. What's that?"

"Oh, just a little present for Pris. Speaking of hot."

"She's around - just served me."

"Fortunate fellow! Ah..."

As if on cue Priscilla issued from the kitchen and stood before him, cute and defiant, awaiting his order. Her manner toward him had had an edge ever since Liz's arrival, but especially since their break-up. Now, as she stared at the object lying on the counter between them, her cheeks were coloring. "Yes?" she said faintly.

"Oh, I was just wondering if this could be yours," said Mason politely. "It didn't fit either of your sisters, so…"

"Where did you find this?"

"In the back of my car." Priscilla snatched the heel from the counter and marched away without a word, short hair swinging as she flounced into the kitchen. Mason watched the rhythms and shapes in the blue uniform until she disappeared through the swinging doors. After a moment squeals were heard.

"God, what was that all about?" Trueblood asked.

Mason, busy inside, did not answer. *That bitch,* he caught himself thinking, *I'd like to have a go at her sometime!* His reaction surprised him: where had it come from? Was he jealous of Clay? What was he repressing? Okay, Mr. Psych Major, but still…. One evening he had brought his guitar down to the courtyard and sat playing. After a while Pris came out and joined him. She didn't interfere, just smiled and sat quietly, listening, yet when he finished that song he made some silly excuse and walked away without looking back. *Why?* For the dubious pleasure of cutting her? Because he was ill at ease? It had been rude and stupid: why come out there, if not for company? Now he saw that he had been attracted to her, like other guys, but was ashamed of it, and shame had caused him to treat her crudely. He owed her an apology for that, and now he had added another insult. But Trueblood was asking him something.

"Oh, Mason…Mason? Hello? Can I borrow your car tonight? If I put some gas in it? Big date…"

"Shoot, you too? Well, okay, here." He handed over the keys. "How's it going with you and Lois, anyway? We haven't been anywhere together since Goose Lake."

"Good. Maybe too good." He laughed, blushed, shrugged.

"Great…but watch yourself. Plenty of high-level competition for a classy girl like that."

"Don't I know it!" Peter rose. "Gotta check for mail."

Mason got up too. "Guess I'll go buy an Old Faithful paperweight or a little birch bark canoe: not gonna get any service here." He went off to look for Jacky; the store was more interesting these days. But where had she been when he needed her? Two years ahead of him, that's where. A pretty blonde who sang and played the guitar! Maybe he'd seen her before

Bill! Well, he had had his opportunity in that singing group, and as usual had let it pass.

While The Parties lasted they were a hothouse for couples, speeding their growth and their decay. Within ten days of meeting, both Pris and Clay were looking around. She made eyes in several directions, including Mason's, while Clay took up with Barbara, a well-padded redhead who resembled him so closely that people had matched them up from the first. They called each other "Red." She looked like a formidable vamp, which was enough to scare off most. That she always behaved as a perfect lady around Thumb only aroused anxieties that when she did cut loose she would be more than they could handle. After all, a woman from Cheyenne had to be wild, didn't she? It took self-confidence like Clay's to take her on. He reported that their fears and his hopes were well-founded, yet in a week or so he was on the loose again. Clay hinted that she was boring, but Cal, who saw them in West, told Peter that Barbara drank like a fish and Clay was tired of buying her liquor. Either way, he was finished at Thumb; a deep-freeze there obliged him to seek his fortunes at Faithful. He began to date Lois's friend Fran: "a sport" and "a good-time girl" in his lexicon. The gossips predicted that he - and Peter and Gair - would come to grief dating at Faithful. What else could they expect after spurning the local girls? Why, just look at Mason!

Clay occupied one end of the spectrum of in/fidelity, at whose opposite end were the "old marrieds." Lou and Shelley, Woo and Ellen, Trueblood and Lois, Gair and Polly, The Mouth and Jane turned up together if they turned up at all. The consensus at Thumb was that Lou and Peter were reaching too high, would fall and be hurt, a prospect that cost the consensus no sleep. And then there was Bastille, considered a unique case. He was dating a cute *chicana* from Faithful named Paquita - but since he was a rover and a Canadian, ordinary standards of morality did not apply.

Two other couples crystallized during Bill and Jacky's parties. Beatty's social stock rose whenever he showed up with Wanda, generally agreed to be a knockout and a good singer. (Jealousy explained his success in terms of their being fellow Tennesseans; Will joked, "They can understand each other.") Beatty's muted trumpet played sexy arabesques around her vocals, but apparently they were "just good friends," and she was a pillow puncher down in the cabins, so a more exemplary match was that of Creeper and Gail, neither of whom had had a date until they found each other. The girls had dismissed Creeper as hopeless, while the boys thought Gail the plainest and dippiest of the Ham's girls. No matter: the couple clearly felt that they had come home. Oblivious to everyone else, they doted on each other. Gail no longer felt homely - if she had - and Creeper had something to look at in his Ford other than the manifold pressure gauge. Both glowed with inner light. Amazingly, others then began to see them as they saw each other. The boys wondered how they had missed her winsome smile; the girls noticed his "bedroom eyes". More "lak a dyin cayf in a hailstorm," chortled Lou.

But The Parties that nurtured these couples did not please everyone: they grew controversial as they became larger, louder and later. The last of them - two dozen people, two cases of beer, two guitars and singing until past 2 AM - disturbed an older couple who worked and slept in the store. They complained to Jack the store manager, who called in Lou and Gray. Lou took Bill aside at lunch the next day and informed him that The Parties were over. Always eager to please (and perhaps short of sleep), he agreed, but other savages were outraged. Stop The Parties? Well then, stop the gas! There were rumbles of rebellion, of a work slowdown. Who did they think they were, anyway? Service was unusually sloppy that afternoon: hamburgers burned and gasoline sloshed out as savages seethed and jawed.

This storm, like most at Thumb, blew over quickly: in a night or two the party culture was thriving again where it had begun. The savages recalled that they *had* managed to amuse themselves before Bill and Jacky arrived, and found that the lakeshore was still within walking distance. For the first few minutes there would be starlit vistas of water and mountains; then someone would toss a lighted match onto a gasoline-soaked bonfire, producing a garish tableau of couples in warm dumpy clothes leaning on one another or opening beer cans or guitar cases and shielding their eyes against the sudden glare, like people caught by the flashbulb in an old snapshot. Once the fire settled down it was best to get into a sleeping bag or cuddle with someone to combat the chill that made guitar-playing a contact sport; Mason and George of the cabins strummed and picked until the flesh of their brittle fingers looked flayed. The beach was colder and less convenient than Bill and Jackie's, but it was also dark, and distant from authorities and light sleepers. The lake served as a refrigerator for beer, pop, and the occasional unlucky victim of a group toss-in.

So the beach party was once again a flourishing institution, and never handier than the evening three young Alabama beauties pulled in for gas after dinner and asked if "yawl know wheah we could fahn tuh sleep tonat?" The pause that followed was a measure of the crew's growing maturity; at one time the question would have drawn an unprintable reply. True, Owl was off duty.

Reeling a bit from the perfume, Woo shook his head. "Believe our cabins are full up tonight, ma'am. There's the campground."

The girls hesitated. "We do have sleepin bags," the driver admitted. "But it's so *cold* heah, an theah's *beahs*."

"If you're going to have to camp, why not just come to our beach party?" suggested Mason. "We build a big fire to keep warm, and bears never come around."

"Ooh, yawl *tawk* so funny!" giggled the girl in the middle, crinkling her nose at Mason, who gaped as the savages roared. Still the girls seemed uncertain.

"We could bring lots of extra blankets," offered Cyril.

"You could go over to the soda fountain in the store until closing time, then come to the beach with some of the girls," said Gair, and they were won over.

"Aw ra-at," trilled the driver. "Weeyul see yawl down theah, then."

And they did show up, very much under the protection of the Ham's girls, who were anxious lest they form entangling alliances that might prolong their stay. After some jockeying for position, Clay managed to cut the driver out of the herd and monopolize her, but the other two remained aloof among the sistren. Still, they looked gorgeous by firelight. Song and liquor were abundant that night, and after the flames and noise had died down there were still two hours for the girls to sleep on the beach, encircled by the "bear guard," before the sun rose over the Absarokas. Clay's date wanted to stay over, of course, but she was outvoted. "They really should've had a lube job," he mourned as they drove off. "I woulda greased all their zerts for free."

As the trauma of Hole's accident faded, salesmanship revived. Dudes might again be imposed on, for the sales race still had to be won. Horn had overtaken Beatty as the individual leader by virtue of his prowess at spotting worn tires and persuading car owners to replace them; his concerned frown and judicious headshake as he approached the driver with news of balding tread and bad roads ahead were the envy of the crew. "I'll see about it when I get home" was the usual defence, but Horn would already have noted the license plate and seemed to carry a Triple-A research bureau in his head. "Well, but Arizona is a long way off, sir, and highway 89 is in bad shape this summer, with all the construction," he would say. "If you go back through California, it's 66, or 60-70, or 80, isn't it? All pretty far south, and you know what heat does to rubber. One thing if it's just yourself, sir, but with your family along..."

As Horn emerged from the shed one afternoon carrying the third tire he had sold that day, he was met by Will. "Your official portrait should be painted just like that, Horn: a helpful, even benevolent smile on your face, a spare tire on your arm but not on your waist, a *Comico* man." Horn smiled and nodded without breaking stride. He could afford to take any ribbing in good-natured silence: tires were by far the most expensive items they carried. If he sold even one a day he could usually win the hour off. Most of his buyers looked happy and satisfied with their purchase, almost relieved - as if he had tapped into a secret anxiety they had been nursing. The word around the station was that he could return next year as an assistant manager if he wished.

Beatty had never quite graduated from fan belts, but in that field he was still peerless, and merciless. Even Lou winced the day the Chattanooga kid sold *two* spare fan belts to four elderly ladies in a brand-new Plymouth, and did not mark it up entirely to his credit. He considered Beatty ambitious, and certainly a good salesman, but a bit of a sharper, perhaps not quite "leaduhship muhtirul." And behind him and Horn, he felt, the drive, the "sales aptitood," fell off sharply. True, Will had qualities that could make him a good assistant or manager, were it not for his mild disdain of the business, which was also Mason's problem.

Lou spent hours perched on the stool by the cash register watching them all: analyzing performance, assessing potential. Gair and Cyril and The Mouth were good as crew, but too nice or simple or passive to rise to command. Trueblood? Mebbe.... Owl, of course, was unthinkable - though not as bad as at first - and Henderson a born loser. Unfortunately Clay was too busy having fun to take the job seriously or think higher. He had an abundance of easy charm and nearly everyone liked him, yet he made few sales, and those mainly when dudes asked *him* for goods they saw other savages pushing - they thought they were being left out of something. His great contribution was to keep people laughing, as when he rounded up the crew to see four nuns from Ontario in a snappy new red and white Oldsmobile Holiday whose rear window bore a decal with the legend "Supercharged by McCullough."

Lou considered them all: Creeper, a competent mechanic (his skills wasted here) but a deadbeat; Schlitz, an amiable goof-off; and Bill, who was just dropping in for a few weeks on his way to law school and higher things. Bastille didn't count: not a regular employee, not getting much work experience, not even an American. Nope, aside from Woo - who was not exactly burning up the place - there was really just Horn, Pete, and maybe Beatty. Too bad he had to leave early: Lou would have liked more time to observe him.

Beatty's contract ended the 11th of August so that he could reach Tennessee in time for his Army Reserve training. No one at Thumb liked the idea. What, lose their star trumpeter? Surely the summer was longer than that! Were their own returns to duty just around the corner, then? Savages shook their heads and felt uneasy, but there it was: nothing to do but throw a big farewell party. Bill and Jacky were given special dispensation to host it. Wanda and George of the cabins attended, as well as most of the Ham's girls and gas jockeys. They stood around drinking something and talking seriously like adults at a cocktail party. Beatty seemed pleased by the turnout, though morose over his departure. "Nipped in the bud uv a promisin sales career," he lamented. "But Ah gotta have that scholuhship."

"Gotta do yer dooty fer yer country, too." Owl waggled a patriotic finger - the index, surprisingly. "Might hafta teach them Mau Maus a lesson!"

"Mau Maus!" exclaimed Mason, startled. "Hey, that's a British problem, not ours."

"We almost got into Suez nonetheless," Will pointed out.

"There's no tellin what that new Secretary of Defence will do," added Peter. "The soap man. Though I spose he won't be worse than Engine Charlie."

"There's one difference," said Will. "With Wilson, we had to keep the world safe for General Motors. With McElroy, we have to protect the detergent market."

"Whoa men, jes whoa theah." Beatty held up a pacifying hand. "Yawl talk lak Ah was goan awn active dooty, fuh Chrassake. Ahm jes goan awn summuh muhnoovuhs."

"Yuh hope," said Henderson darkly. As he saw it, his bonus money and hours off were departing.

"Wall, Ahm jes sorreh tuh lose yuh, Beatty. Shur could use yer hep winnin the sales race."

"How're we doin, Lou?" asked Cyril earnestly.

"Fust in June, fust in Joo-lie, total sales, butcha know thet doan cut it. It's thet low Mammoth quota Ahm skeered uv."

Beatty sighed. "Shurr hate tuh leave with that still hangin. Jes thank uv awl those fain belts won't get sold! Sorry Lou, sorry guys." He moved away to find Wanda in the crush; early the next morning he was gone.

On the 13th of August the summer weather broke. Clouds suddenly materialized over the Continental Divide to the south and west, accumulating into thunderheads with surprising swiftness. Old hands - Lou, Woo, Gray - sniffed the air warily. Within a half-hour rain began to pelt down, quickly turning the lanes into a slough. As the storm roared and the crew moved in and out of the shed Lou kept up a running commentary from his perch by the front window: "Wall, there goes the dry weathuh an the bee-ball, gents. Will, get cherself a slickuh frum outa the back. Not mucha summuh left when it stahts in lack this. Shur makes it fun wukkin the lanes, doan it, Pete? Mason, theah's sou'westuhs in back. Yuh ken spec lease one uh these a day frum heah awn. One thang: business'll fawl awf now. Rain an doods doan mix. Hey, yuh shur look cute in yaller, Hohn! Tell yuh what, mens: bedduh get out an see whacher gonna see purty soon. Tamsuh gettin shawt."

It fell out much as he said. Thunderstorms hit almost every afternoon from then on, and the supply of dudes declined steadily. For the first time since late June raindrops found paths down savage necks to their backs, hose nozzles were frigid, and anti-freeze could be sold. But it also became possible to break the lock-step schedule of high summer and arrange a different day off to go somewhere with a friend. Owl and Will surprised everyone by organizing an overnight backpack together. "He's been a pariah long enough," Will told Mason. "Can't you see he's trying to change? He *likes* us - and we won't give him the time of day."

"Well, good luck," said Mason doubtfully. Dan - by then living at Thumb's ranger station - briefed them on the abundance of game in the Shoshone Geyser Basin and helped them gather equipment. Mason, who gave them a lift to the trailhead, came back shaking his head and saying that he still didn't understand their group dynamics.

Cursing the clumsy packs, the adventurers trudged in for several miles through coniferous forest to the meadows near Shoshone Lake, making camp just short of the swamp. "At least it was fuckin downhill *pardon* my French," said Owl, dropping his pack. "But we'll hafta climb out."

"The weather's holding," observed Will, determined to stay positive. Evening and night remained clear. They saw a bear, an elk, several deer and beaver, and some small animals they could not identify. "We'll have to ask Dan," was their chorus. Later, sleeping out, they had unmitigated stars.

"This is cool," Owl admitted.

"Like something out of Hemingway," said Will. He lay awake in his bag for hours, watching, thinking and feeling, far too excited to sleep.

At dawn they were watching a bull moose drink from the lake when it caught their scent, wheeled and charged. They managed to scramble into a nearby tree, whence they watched the moose trample their sleeping bags and rifle their packs of everything edible. Then he seemed to catch another scent and trotted away, so they were able to come down, but had to set off without breaking their fast. Water and a few shriveled berries were the whole menu until they reached the highway, where a passing dude gave them some crackers and a ride to Thumb. The lunch table looked like a cornucopia, and came equipped with an attentive audience. "Never saw sumpun so big move so bitchin *fast*," chortled Owl. "That sucker really lightened our loads. Made good time climbin out, though!"

"Dan *told* us we'd see game," Will reminded him. "Too bad about his rucksack." They both looked a bit stunned. The episode got everyone's attention, reminding them that the off-road world was not entirely benign.

One Friday afternoon Mason, Peter and Clay drove to Old Faithful to rendezvous with Tech for their excursion to Virginia City, whose praises Mason had been singing for a month. Virg and Tech had found them bunks; Mason and Trueblood had worked on their usual days off to make it possible. Since breaking up with Liz, Mason's days off had been largely wasted. One had been completely utilitarian: down to Jackson to have some work done on the car. Another had been rather pointlessly spent in West Yellowstone - though he had managed to see Julia at Old Faithful on that one. Come on, Mace, that *was* the point! The days-off question was just part of a larger issue: what to do with himself socially in the post-Liz era. He couldn't see himself going with anyone at Thumb. Sally Savage was too far away, Polly too heavily involved with Gair. His thoughts kept turning to Julia: he wished she were closer to him, farther from Liz, and not still known as "Hole's girl." But Virginia City would be lively, and he hoped it might take him out of himself.

Peter and Clay borrowed the car and went off to watch the submarine races at the Lone Star geyser with Lois and Fran. Mason would have liked to call on Julia, but he felt constrained about that with Hole's friends around, so he caught up on gossip in Virg's comfortable room, i.e Virg told him what was going on in the park. Cal was playing the field and having a ball. No one had seen Marsh recently, but he was said to have a girlfriend at Mammoth. Cleve was head over heels in love with a Canyon girl and had bought an old car in Bozeman. He had come over to see Polly once or twice. Mason interjected that she was going with one of Thumb's finest, but of course Virg already knew that, and just nodded. "Oh, I guess you heard that that fellow you brought out didn't make it."

"What? Didn't make it?!" Mason's heart skipped a beat: Ray Jacobs hadn't made it. "You mean Chris? No, what happened?"

"Chris, that's it. Well, he broke his contract, left on a bus a couple of weeks ago. Seems he was never happy here - homesick, I guess. Thought westerners were aloof, and didn't like the immorality, I heard. Very religious, apparently."

"Yes, he was - is - quite religious, a minister's son. I hadn't heard. That's too bad." Suddenly Mason felt...what *was* the word? Callow, probably. He had a sense of vast gaps - between then and now, Chris and himself - that he might have tried to bridge. Maybe he would drop in on Chris back at Debrew? But no...he would never go, and why add hypocrisy to neglect? "Do you see much of Liz?"

"A fair amount, Mace. She dates, but she doesn't look happy. I've heard she's planning to leave early."

Mason looked a bit unhappy himself. "Yes, well...." There was much he could say on that subject - about how ill-starred her coming to Yellowstone had been, about how Virg should take her out himself since he liked her so much - things of that sort. It might become a really interesting conversation, but it was a painful subject about which he was harboring a surplus of resentment, so he veered off sharply. "Aren't those new glasses, Virg?"

"Oh, those." He removed them, laughing self-consciously, and wiped them on his shirt. "Yes, and they cost me a trip down to Jackson. Did you hear how I broke the old ones? No? Ah, Mason." He shook his head and settled the glasses back on his nose. "Well, you know how when you sell a bug screen, you clean the radiator grille first?"

"Yes, you whisk it off."

"Right - but for rich-looking customers who might tip we clean it with a compressed-air hose behind the station house. Well, about a week ago in comes this snappy new Lincoln, New York plates, well-dressed woman driver, no one else. And I sold her a bug screen. Then she asked if we had a rest room - or so they tell me, and I guess they're right. But I thought she asked for a *whisk broom*. So I said, 'Just drive around back and we'll *blow* it out.' Well, she jumped out of that car and slapped me *so* hard it knocked my glasses off! Sure, you can laugh - they all did - but that's when they got broken. She drove over them on the way out."

"Virg, that's a wonderful story," gasped Mason, trying to compose his features.

"So they tell me," said Virg stoically. "I guess it has a moral…against greed?"

"Or against deafness," whispered Mason.

On Saturday the weather was perfect, and by 9 AM the Virginia City Expedition was underway in Tech's white Ford coupe. They sang and chatted, certain of a prodigiously good time. Driving through West Yellowstone without stopping, they took Route 287 up through the Madison River valley. Once free of the park's 45 mph speed limit, the car leapt across the sagebrush miles. Spirits soared as they passed between beautiful parklike hills covered with wild grasses and isolated stands of piñon and ponderosa pine and red cedar. "What gorgeous grassy hills!" enthused Mason. "They look like breasts."

"Grassy breasts!" shrieked Tech, pounding the steering wheel. Trueblood guffawed.

"Do you think Mason misses a steady girl?" asked Clay.

Coming into Ennis, where the road to Virginia City branched off, Peter saw a sign for the Lewis and Clark caverns, 35 miles ahead. Since Mason said that the old brewery in "VC" - their first target - did not open until 1, they decided to go spelunking. Tech stumbled around the caves like a circus clown and was suitably terrified when the others doused both flashlights. "Hey, men, it's dark! Hey, that's enough! Not funny. Ouch!" He tripped over a stalagmite, breaking it off. Savages to the core now, they smuggled it out as a trophy; then raced south at 80 mph to make the opening of the brewery.

The range of steep hills between Ennis and Virginia City slowed them down, however, and it was 1:15 before they walked through the sagging double doorway into a large room lit only by what sunlight came through a few small dusty windows to fall on the old planking. The rich odor of beer-soaked wooden casks permeated the air.

"Beer! Beer!" croaked Tech. The good-looking young woman behind the bar smiled tolerantly and began filling steins from a dark keg.

"I guess we just missed your opening," remarked Peter.

She looked at him for a moment, obviously puzzled. "We've been open since 11, you know."

They all turned on Mason, who slumped in a chair. "I knew it had ones in it," he said lamely.

"A serious offence: misremembering vital information," said Clay. "Calls for a stiff penalty, eh men?"

"Coulda been drinkin insteada kickin rocks in that cave!" wailed Tech.

Clay pointed sternly at the criminal. "Your sentence is two hours of guitar playing or until your fingers bleed, whichever comes last, and a number of chuggalugs to be determined. It's all right for us to play and sing here, isn't it, Miss... I'm sorry, I didn't catch your name." He grinned at the barmaid.

She produced another tolerant smile. "That's because I didn't throw it, Red, as you know. Anyway, it's Ann. Yes, you can sing at any of these tables, except when other customers want to listen to the nickleodeon. Then you can go down those stairs to the big tables in the back room."

"Well thanks, Miss Ann," said Clay easily. "Mm, that's good cold beer. Here's to you."

"What's all that stuff?" Tech was pointing and peering into the dusky gloom down the stairs.

"That's the machinery of the original brewery. This is quite an old place, actually."

"Yes," said Mason, pulling himself together. "The oldest brewery in the state, right?"

"They *think* we were the first," she stipulated. "You were in here earlier this summer, weren't you? With a girl?"

"Yes, but I'm surprised you remember me."

"I remember your accent," she laughed, and the others joined in. "Bahston, isn't it?"

"*My* accent!" Mason gaped. There it was again: *his* accent!

"Gosh, I like all this wood," said Peter, feeling his way down into the semi-darkness of the sunken room, where the aroma of hops and beer-cured wood was stronger and the old brewing vats sat ready for inspection.

Mason was sent for the guitar and another round was ordered. They drank, sang or played the nickleodeon, and flirted with Ann until Mason said that it was time for the matinee over at the thee-ay-ter in the hotel. Doubts were loudly expressed about the reliability of his memory on such a point.

"He's right this time," came Ann's clear voice. "Every afternoon at 4, all summer."

"Beer, beer!" bawled Tech, banging his mug on the table.

"Uh oh. Not now, Tech. We're going to the *play* now. See you later, Annie," said Clay jauntily. "Thanks for the beer."

"We close at six, fellas."

"Oh." Mason went over to her. "Then we'll miss you, I guess. Say... are you busy tonight? After you close?"

"Sorry, I'm married." She looked down demurely, then up, and smiled. "But thanks anyway."

"Oh, well." He shrugged. "I'm sorry too. G'bye, Mrs. Annie."

"Watch the step, fellas! So long."

They stumbled out into the parking lot, laughing, sun-dazzled, a bit unsteady, and decided not to drive to the show. It was only a short ramble over to Main Street and down to the hotel. They negotiated the route with noisy panache, arguing over whether buildings had been restored or antiqued, attracting some attention. Tech kept moaning for beer, and Mason kept telling him that he could drink during the performance, "cause the stage is *in the goddamned bar*, Tech!" As soon as they flopped down at a table in that establishment, done up in garish gay-nineties gilt and plush, and ordered three more beers and a cider, Tech was happy.

"Now let's have this play," said Clay, surveying the scene with an air of proprietary or even imperial complacency.

"Don't expect too much," warned Mason, suddenly concerned that he had gone overboard in building it up. "It's melodrama, and pretty hammy."

He needn't have worried: the actors, drama students from the state university, knew their stuff. The villain twirled his mustache and elicited a chorus of boos, the heroine was irresistibly helpless, the hero showed surprising backbone at the crisis, the theme - innocent good vs. jaded evil - was of general interest, and the action was suitably accompanied on a honky-tonk piano by a dapper fellow with a red garter around the bicep of his striped silk shirt, and a pungent cigar that he alternately puffed and waved like a baton.

When it ended Mason took a chance and led the party over to the piano. "Hello, Berny, another great show! I'm Mason, remember? About a month ago. This is Peter…and Clay…and that's Tech over at…on the table."

Berny said he remembered. As they talked, a delectable redhead, recognizable as the heroine of the play, came toward them. "Fellas," said Berny, "I'd like you to meet Madelaine." They slipped their arms around each other with easy familiarity.

"Wow," said Clay. "I mean, pleased to meet you." They introduced themselves, drinking her in shamelessly.

"Hewwo, boys." She spoke, as she sang, with a slight lisp, the effect, perhaps, of a pouting underlip. "Enjoy the show?"

They nodded dumbly. Mason half-remembered some lines from an old ballad about a bride at her wedding.

> *Her lips were red, and one was thin,*
> *Compared to that was next her chin;*
> *(Some bee had stung it newly.)*

"Listen, fellas, we need to get some rest before the second show," said the fortunate Berny. "But if you're staying, maybe you'd like to come to the party afterwards. There'll probably be singing, and the bar's open till midnight."

The savages quickly decided that none of their Yellowstone engagements was so pressing as to prevent their accepting the kind invitation of, etc. They passed the interval over at Gert's Bar & Grill, where hot beef sandwiches helped soak up the afternoon's beer. The conversation centered on Madelaine's charms, which seemed to have deepened Clay's drawl. Men had *daed* for less, he assured them, and "She's got the cutest ice Ah've evuh seen!"

"Hagh praise from Clay," chortled Tech, startling them. "That's after seeing her once in a full skirt."

"You know what anthropologists say?" Mason inquired. "That we *think* we like tits and ass, but what we really like are the small waists that show them off, and indicate that a woman is healthy and fit to bear children."

"That's what an-thro-PO-lo-gists say," crooned Tech.

Mason smiled and sipped his beer. He was thinking about Ann the bartender: her casual warmth, her friendliness. "What about Ann at the brewery?" he asked them.

"Maybe a little on the tough side?" ventured Peter.

"Hey, she's a bartender! But a really nice, *slightly* older woman," Mason insisted. "Competent, solid, attractive."

"And married," Clay reminded him. "But if you really like her, why don't you go say hello?" He nodded toward the bar, and they all turned to follow his gaze. At the far end of the counter, her back to them, sat a woman who did indeed look like Ann, sitting between two empty stools. As they watched, a man from a nearby table came forward and hung over her; she yelled something at him, and he slunk back to the laughter of his companions.

Mason's eyes widened and he checked his watch: just an hour since the brewery had closed. Was that enough time for her to change clothes and get sloshed? "All right, I will." Not much choice, he thought, but from up close he still wasn't sure. Tendrils of brown hair clung to her damp neck and forehead; her head lolled a bit. Ann, or a parody of Ann? She was drinking a brown liquid - rye or bourbon or scotch - from a glass with ice cubes. He *had* to try. "Ann?"

She turned and focused her eyes on him. "Well, well, here's a nighsh-looking boy!" Some of the barflies guffawed.

Watch it, Mason told himself. It didn't look as tough as the crowd at Doc's down in West, but maybe not far from it, either. "Didn't you say you were married?" Whoa, where had *that* come from?! Was he applying to be her moral guardian or something?

"Married!" she said angrily. "What do *you* know about *married*?" More laughter rippled along the bar, and she took another belt of her drink.

Mason felt hot and flushed, and well out of his depth. "Listen," he said quietly, "do you need any help?"

"Help!" Her bloodshot eyes narrowed. "Get lost." She paused and added, more loudly, "Creep." The bar broke up.

"Hey, is this guy both'rin yuh?" someone called.

"Sorry, I thought you were someone else." Mason heard the stiffness in his voice and walked back to their table, conscious of stares, feeling ridiculous. Would he *ever* learn to handle a situation like this?

"Tough," said Clay, not quite acknowledging the bum steer, and Peter grunted sympathetically.

"It wasn't Ann," said Mason, trying to sound confident. "Let's get our check."

They sat through the melodrama again, leading the cheers and boos, then joined the cast and others around the piano for two more hours of boisterous song. Clay buzzed vainly around Madelaine, hissing like a foiled villain when she and Berny sang their polished love duets. The closing of the bar at 12 ended the party. The savages found themselves outside in the darkening, emptying street, saying goodbye to their musical buddies, and knowing that while the actors would still have each other, and other performances and audiences and parties, *they* had to go back to work and not return. It felt like being ejected from the garden. *And* it was 125 dark miles to Thumb. They gradually became subdued as they led the somnolent Tech over to the brewery and the car.

Clay, who had stayed reasonably sober, undertook to drive while Tech snoozed in the suicide seat. Mason and Peter sat quietly in back, dozing from time to time. The sky had clouded over, the night was tar-black, and there was little traffic to slow them down. They were barreling along near Hutchins Ranch at 80 mph when the headlights suddenly glared on a yellow road sign, dead ahead at no great distance. The odd thing was that it seemed to be in the middle of the road. It said SHARP CURVE, and the arrow underneath made a right angle to the left. Clay braked hard, but they were still doing about 60 as they entered the turn. In the back, Mason and Peter clung to each other like Hansel and Gretel. Clay swung the wheel hard left, locked his arms and floored the accelerator. "The sweat's on!" he called out. Tires screeched, the rear end broke free and the car slewed around, straightening out with a jerk on the new course, 90 degrees to port of the last one and perfectly aligned for the next stretch. They were even in the right lane.

Clay relaxed and grinned over his shoulder. "Close one," he admitted.

"Are you telling me we *made* that?!" asked Mason incredulously. He had never felt so close to becoming a statistic. Part of him was wondering if they *had* made it; maybe this was just a post-crash dream of life? Noticing that he was still clutching Trueblood, he let go. Tech stirred, grunted, and curled up again.

Rain began falling as they finally, wearily, entered the Upper Geyser Basin. Leaving Tech asleep in the car outside his dormitory at Faithful, they transferred to Mason's wagon for the final leg. Rain fell harder as they climbed, with a few flakes of wet snow around the passes. It would be a bitch of a day in the lanes, Mason thought, but they could sleep till noon. He took the slick curves of the descent with great caution, trying to regain his grip on reality, still unable to shake the idea that they had *not* made the turn. Maybe he was dying and his life was flashing before him. How could he be sure? Tunneling through this rain-streaked blackness was no help. He tried the radio: just static. Hmm, not good.

But finally he was parking in front of the dormitories, switching off. *Plop, ffttt.* The mudfart was reassuring - that wouldn't be in the afterlife, would it? "Hell of a trip, men!" enthused Clay. "That Madelaine...Jesus!"

Peter said something, but Mason was not there; he was winging back to Hutchins Ranch, where a yellow sign leaped at him out of the blackness. Was this the way it worked, then? He was about to wake up in heaven, or hell, or blood and pain and glass and steel. One of their favorite songs that summer was "Crash on the Highway." He had sung it at sleeping bag parties, at Bill and Jackie's, on the beach, even at savage shows, with a cheeky preface by a hillbilly preacher sanctimoniously warning sinful drivers.

> *I heard the crash on the highway,*
> *I knowed what it was from the start!*
> *I saw the wreck on the highway,*
> *The picture is stamped on my heart:*
>
> *There was whiskey and blood all together,*
> *Mixed with the glass where they lay!*
> *I heard the crash on the highway,*
> *But I didn't hear nobody pray!*
>
> *No, I didn't hear nobody pray, dear brother!*
> *I didn't heard nobody pray.*
> *I heard the groans of the dying -*
> *But I didn't hear nobody pray.*

Mason realized that the others were talking to him, and that he was just sitting and staring. "All out here?" Clay was asking. Silence. They were back at Thumb, but he couldn't speak yet. "The Turn?"

"The Turn," Mason croaked, and the spell was broken.

Peter opened his door and got a shower off the roof. "This dawgawn rain!" he grumbled.

Mason opened his door and let the stuff run down his upturned face, thinking he had never felt anything so good. Rain, just rain, clean and cold. Real rain. But he knew then, with the absolute certainty of a zealot, that for the rest of the summer - maybe for the rest of his life - he would wonder which was the dream.

Eight: Yellowstone Christmas

It was the best and giddiest of times, the saddest and soberest of times. The weather fell apart, dudes went crazy, and savages were easily moved to laughter or tears. Yellowstone was a zany place they must soon leave, a battle zone where they skirmished with *exotica americana*, and a power they would never forget - not one *or* the other, not sequentially, but all at once.

At the station, business was often conducted in freezing rain. The chamois wringer, the pneumatic grease gun, and one gas pump broke down, but Lou's repeated *fortissimo* calls to the Comico service unit produced no palpable results. One morning Mason blinked the water from his eyes as a plain brown sedan pulled up to his island and uttered his usual "High-test or regular?"

"*Comico* or regular," said the driver.

"Yeah. What? Which do you want?"

"You said 'High-test or regular.' It should be *Comico* or regular," he explained pedantically.

"I don't know about that." Will came around from the front, dipstick in hand. "All summer the great philosophical question has been 'High-test or regular?' Seemed to sum it all up, really. Somehow 'Comico or regular' doesn't do it. Your oil's fine, sir: a little dirty, but full up."

"Wait a minute, let's be open-minded," said Mason, with the air of a man committed to reason. "Doesn't it all depend on what you *mean* by 'Comico'? If we understand it as a symbol of excellence, an allegory of high-testedness, as it were... Is that how you intended it, sir?"

"Nonsense!" snapped Will, sounding like one who does not suffer fools gladly. "'Comico' evokes low-life farce. What kind of symbol...?"

The driver had been looking from one to the other with narrowing eyes and hardening jaw. Now he jabbed a finger out into the rain. "Never wise off to a customer!" he snapped. "That's the first rule of Comico policy. Who trained you guys, anyway?"

Will examined him with interest. "And might you be the legendary, frequently-needed and oft-called but seldom-seen Comico repairman?" he asked sweetly.

The driver sighed. "I am the Comico *service representative*," he specified in a tone of evaporating patience.

"Hey, Lou!" bawled Mason, "there's a Comico rep here, and *he* doesn't like *our* service!"

Lou erupted from the shed, brandishing a sheaf of requisitions on his clipboard and yelling, "Hold awntuh him!" In other lanes savages looked up from their work.

"Well, *well*," said Owl, with his diamond-cutting grin, "things must be *real* slow up at headquarters for you to look in on the likes of *us*."

"Okay, Owl." Lou's voice had a hard edge, as when you call off the dog so you can interrogate the intruder yourself. "Mistuh, Ah got broken pumps, broken lube, shawt supplaz uh awl an fahn belts, an Ah dunno what else..."

"Tires," said Horn succinctly. "We need tires."

"An tars," Lou agreed. "Howm Ah spoz tuh operate? An yew complain bout *ar* service? Huh, yer lucky we ken pump yer *gice!*"

The driver regarded them warily. "Never mind about the gas. Close the hood," he said, rolling up his window. The motor started and the car accelerated away. But the next day a repairman finally arrived, driving the supply truck. Lou was surly with him, and inclined to yell at his crew on the slightest provocation. Woo explained that he was unhappy with the latest park-wide sales figures.

Fortunately the sun was out and the mood relatively mellow the afternoon the Contentious Canadian appeared. He was, they learned, the Finance Minister of one of the prairie provinces, a tall, greying man with a quiet manner - until he heard that his Canadian dollar was worth only 90 cents US here. "Look here, son, that's plain robbery!" he exclaimed to Creeper. "I can't accept an exchange rate I *know* to be false. You're shortchanging me!"

"Sorry, sir, you'll need to talk to the manager," answered Creeper politely, signaling to the shed. The man climbed out of his car as Lou approached with his standard "Ken Ah hep yuh, sir?"

"I certainly hope so. It's about the exchange rate. Do you know that the Canadian dollar, which you're valuing at only 90 of your cents, is currently worth $1.04 US on the world's money markets?"

"Wall, no, fac is, Ah didn," replied Lou genially. "But it doan mattuh none. See, thet ten purr cent awf is standud YPCC polucy *through*awt the Pahk, all summuh, evruh yeah Ah been heah. Ifn yuh thank it's wrawng, bedduh go tuh headquawtuhs in Godnuh an tell Mistuh Galluhtun."

"All right, I may do that on my way home," answered the minister. "But *you* are implementing the policy. Does it seem fair to you to discount my currency 14 percent?"

To the savages' surprise Lou stayed calm. Business was light, the double shift was on, they didn't need the lane. Motioning for Creeper to block it off, Lou replied, "Ain't none uh *mah* bizness, sir."

"Ah, but I think it *is*, since you are in effect exchanging currencies," insisted the Canadian, who, seeing that he was granted a hearing, launched into a lecture on economics, focusing on exchange rates, and some international relations thrown in. Lou excused himself after a while, but various savages hung around to listen or argue or ask questions. Clay confessed to being an Economics major, and the minister, smiling, said, "Then you can understand that I would be taking a loss even by settling for par, and that would be unjust." Clay responded that the owners of the world's top currency had rights that trumped the vagaries of global currency exchanges. The debate had been simmering for half an hour when Lou returned to say that the lane and the attendants were needed now. The minister bade them a civil farewell and drove slowly away with his patient wife.

The punch line was delivered an hour later, after the first shift finished work, when Will came back from the store with a Bozeman *Gazette* and asked the gas jockeys what they thought the Canadian dollar was *really* worth. No one had any idea, unless it was 90 cents, as the YPCC said. Will grinned. "It floated to a dollar *five* yesterday!" Some shrugged and others said, "Hmm."

"Where's Canuck when we need him?" asked Mason. No one knew; the elusive one was often "somers else," as Lou said. Clearly Bastille did not punch a YPCC clock. But the episode seemed to underscore what Paul sometimes hinted: that they knew next to nothing about their northern neighbor, whose border was only one state away. Aside from Mason, who had made a couple of visits, none of them had ever "crossed over"; it was a cipher. For the southerners, Canada might as well have been Xanadu. One afternoon Henderson asked Cyril if he recognized the license plate of the car pulling into their lane. It read "Sask."

Cyril shook his head. "Why don't you ask the driver?"

So when the gas was flowing and Henderson had checked the oil, he strolled around to the open window and inquired sociably, "Wherebouts yawl frum?"

The driver turned to him and replied, "Saskatoon…Saskatchewan?"

Henderson looked blank. "Uh, thank you. 'Scuse me." He walked quickly to the back of the car.

"Well, where are they from?" asked Cyril.

"I dunno," said Henderson. "I don't think they speak English." His sheepish grin revealed a young man once more out of his depth. Since the break-up of his profitable mercantile partnership with Beatty he seemed resigned to his role as the station's fall guy. Clay's unkind catalog had stuck: no brains, no charm, no luck (to which Will added, "And guess who'll inherit the earth").

Yet Henderson kept plugging away with what little he had. Pretty girls who stopped just long enough to refuel had been a source of frustration all summer. The only recourse was to persuade them (or their parents) that they should not race past Thumb's many attractions. It was a challenge to male ingenuity that they all accepted a few times when moved by pulchritude - "even Henderson," as the saying went. One day he tried to convince a carload of Texans pulling a horse trailer to lay over for a night.

"Naw, gotta get awn up tuh Narse er someplace Ah ken run mah mar, son," said the Texan, removing a tan Stetson to scratch his sweating head. "Mah dotter's gotta rad er she pahnes."

Henderson, ogling the olive-skinned girl in tight riding pants who was pouting in the back seat, sighed, "Shur is beautiful, sir."

"Yay-uh," drawled the Texan, reaching into the trailer to pat the mare. "Fahnest lahns uh any filly in West Texas."

"Yessir! I'm shur she'd fand sumpun tuh do roun heah…"

"Naw, she's gotta *run* er she ain't happy, son."

"Well, if yuh need any help wither, sir…"

"Thanks enaway, son, but Ah gen'ally handler muhself. So lawng now."

"What was that all about?" asked Clay, taking an unusual interest in Henderson's affairs after obtaining a quick glimpse of the girl.

"I wanted tuh meet his dawter," moaned Henderson, "an he couldn't see paist the tail uv his hawrse." Will predicted that it would prove to be his best line of the summer.

The next morning Horn got a chance to demonstrate how such affairs should be managed. He happened to serve a carload of New Mexico Apaches, proud and handsome and rather fierce-looking people who spoke about "the Indian nations" and "ancestral lands." Picking up on Horn's physiognomy, they began to question him. He hit it off with them at once, and the Apaches actually did lay over for a day. The sixteen-year-old daughter, dressed in traditional Apache costume, was generally acknowledged to be a raving beauty, and Horn was for a short time the envy of the gas jockeys as he squired her around Thumb's scenic beauties, from the mud pot to the lakeshore. After they left he seemed more reserved and solitary than usual.

Later that day there was a commotion in the thermal area between the store and the lake: some kind of accident, they said. But none of the savages witnessed it, and at dinner they were still trying to piece together what had happened from third-hand accounts that sounded far-fetched. According to Vicky, who heard it from Dan, a dude was photographing his family when he fell backwards into a steam pot, immersing himself in scalding water. At first this was not believed - too much like the old gag about backing over a cliff, and Vicky could not entirely control her giggle and mobile face - but the rangers confirmed that the man had been fished out in sad shape and rushed to Gardiner hospital, where his condition was listed as "fair."

"Dumb dood," they said automatically, and filed it away in that overstuffed folder.

The next afternoon Trueblood and Lois were strolling along a back road near Old Faithful when they came upon some dudes feeding and photographing an old black bear. Suddenly one man walked up behind the bear with his young daughter, set her astride its back, and retreated to picture-taking distance. In the stunned pause that followed, the bear raised its head, sniffed, and looked back. Then Peter made a dash tangent to the bear's rump, hooking off the little girl as he went by. The bear resumed eating, the child ran crying to her parents, and the dudes fell to discussing Peter's action. Some praised his presence of mind; others blamed his interference. The man himself yelled that this idiot had spoiled his picture and scared his kid. Peter clenched his fists. "You're a darn fool!" he blazed. Lois pulled him away.

At lunchtime the following day Vicky came into the dining hall a few minutes late. "Did you hear about the dude who fell in the steam pot?" she asked the assembled diners. Again it sounded like a joke: had she said, "the one about..."? Pris giggled nervously.

"No, what happened?" asked Gair.

"He died," said Vicky.

In a moment the savages were convulsed with hysterical laughter. None could have said why. Maybe it was Vicky's moon face and too-straight delivery, or the run of crazy dudes they'd been having, or end-of-the-summer fatigue. But they laughed, laughed till they cried, despite disapproving looks from the senior table. When the first gale subsided, some *sotto voce* witticism set them off again. Vicky was offended; she thought they didn't believe her. "Well, Dan *said* that he died," she insisted. They tried to sober up, but for the rest of the meal there were sporadic outbursts of giggles and wiping of eyes. Everyone noticed that emotions were closer to the surface in those last weeks of the summer.

For some, August was the Month of Dan. The first pleasant and accessible ranger most Thumbies had met, he was soon established as the station's mentor - and most eligible bachelor. Several of the girls cast eyes in his direction, but though he was always civil to them, he was never more than that, and claimed to have no time for dating. The boys saw more of him: he would occasionally drop by the dormitory, and they would return those visits to hear more about his summers as a fire lookout in Montana, his test run and rejection of law school, and winters in Yellowstone. He soon came to seem larger than life, an almost legendary character, starring in his own myth.

If Dan had business elsewhere in the park and a spare seat or two in the pickup, he would usually take along whoever had the time and inclination to go. That was how several of them first managed to get off the road and learn more about what rangers did: checking on a seeding project, a wilderness campsite or a herd of bison; investigating a poaching incident; returning a troublesome bear to the deep forest. And with Dan there were always the flowers. He claimed to be scandalized that the savages knew so little about Yellowstone's flora. "What *have* you been doing?" he asked Will and Mason. On any outing he would point to his favorites: marsh marigolds near a pond, white columbines in the woods, bright stalks of Indian paintbrush in a meadow, a cluster of sky-blue alpine forget-me-nots on the shoulder of Mt. Washburn. For his sake a few of them tried to learn how to distinguish the different ferns and conifers, and how to tell an aspen from a birch.

He would lament that they and other summer visitors came too late for anemones, calypso orchids and glacier lilies, which bloomed through the last snows in May and were thus seen only by the year-rounders, never by seasonals and dudes. That often led into what Will called Dan's Discourse on Winter: a panygeric on the deep snowdrifts of February, the hand-feeding of elk and bison, half-tamed by their hunger, the camaraderie of the few wintering rangers, their propellor-driven sledges, geysers erupting white on white, the stark simplicity of it all. "*That's* a life for a man," he declared. "'No more frontiers,' indeed!"

"Is winter your favorite season, then?" asked Mason.

147

"Wouldn't say that. Don't like *one* season, but seasons - the full cycle. Autumn may seem sad, but there's a great peace after the crowds leave. Winter is survival, but it has many compensations and doesn't last forever. Spring is, well, joyful, the way it's balanced between death and life."

Will waggled his finger. "April is the cruelest month," he intoned magisterially.

"Only from a narrowly human point of view, and a very pessimistic one: that it raises false hopes. To a naturalist April is the culmination, the month worth waiting for. It proves that the sap still flows, that the annual cycle is still intact." Dan laughed. "Eliot is a lousy naturalist - and a rather dessicated poet, in my opinion. A dried voice."

Will nodded. "A hollow man."

Mason looked thoughtful. "Okay, what *don't* you like about the life of a ranger?"

"Oh, not all of the dudes are roses, you know, and we even have trouble with the odd savage!" Mason blushed. "It can be lonely, too. I mean women...domestic comforts. You don't see that many ranger wives or children, do you? Women who will settle down with a husband working in a place like this are *not* a dime a dozen."

Trueblood could not help smiling. "I think you have some possibilities around here, Dan, if you want 'em."

"Ah, that. And some nice girls among them. But you can bet not a one wants to *live* in the park. They see me in their home towns, giving up rangering for something respectable. Nope, better put down solitude on the negative side. If you want to start a family early, do something else."

Directly or indirectly, Dan figured in most of Thumb's August expeditions: the Great Antler Hunt, for example, likely to be the last big escapade of the summer. Virg Vine had gotten Peter interested in obtaining moose antlers as a souvenir of Yellowstone, and they manipulated days off so as to team up with Horn and Cal. Then Virg and Peter approached Dan for technical advice. "Do you prefer your antlers with or without the moose?" he asked.

They laughed and opted for the discarded type.

"Try the meadows on the south slope of Mt. Washburn - you know the area, Virg - around the nine-thousand foot level. They often drop 'em there. Don't know why: some moose reason, probably connected with mating displays."

He was right, as usual, but the antlers were not easy to find, and by the time the group broke off the hunt only three hours remained before the

Thumbies were due back at work. They raced down the meadows to Virg's car, carrying two pairs of antlers and a buffalo skull, and drove pell-mell to Canyon. While they refueled, Cleve phoned Lou to assure him that his crew members were on their way and would arrive by 1 PM.

"Ifn they know what's good fer their ices they shur will!" shouted Lou. Out in the lanes a few bets were offered and taken on whether the hunters would make it. At 12:25 Cal phoned from Lake to report that Virg had just dropped him off and was speeding toward Thumb. There was more wagering, now at two to one on Virg. At 12:53 the green and white Ford was seen rounding a headland across the bay, and five minutes later it drew up on the apron to a mixture of cheers and boos. Horn and Peter spilled out, brandishing their dirty antlers, caught a glimpse of Lou's face and dashed inside to don their Green Hornets.

Virg apologized to Lou for cutting it so close. "I was really pushing to get here on time."

"And you made it!" exclaimed Mason. "We win!"

Virg glanced at his watch. "Pretty darn close! I have 1:02."

"The station clock is slow - I don't gotta pay!" crowed Owl.

"Wait a minute," Clay objected. "We're *going* by the station clock." The argument dragged on through the afternoon like some lingering international dispute, and no money ever changed hands.

As for the antlers, they were cleaned up and exhibited to an admiring public in the dining hall that evening, and later in the ranger cabin. "Well, looks like you fellows are coming along as outdoorsmen," mused Dan, running his fingers over the pitted bone, his eyes closed, as if visualizing the former owner ranging over meadow and forest in sunshine or snow. "I think you're ready to meet the Old Timer. I'm going up to Mammoth Sunday: we could drop in on him then." He looked around. "Who's available?"

"Who's the Old Timer?" asked Mason.

"You know him," said Dan. "The judge in Mammoth."

"Oh, him. Right, we've met."

"Yes, Judge Evans. So, would you like to go - a purely social call this time?"

"I would, Dan, but I work Sunday."

"All right," said Dan easily. "Any takers? Will, you have Sundays off, don't you?"

Will nodded. "I'm free. But who *is* this guy?"

"You haven't heard of him? Man who wrote *Sketches of Old Yellowstone?*" Blank looks all around. "Ah, gentlemen. Well, it's a rare book now, but a minor classic, I'd say. And the author is a judge who lives in Gardiner."

"Sounds splendid!" exclaimed Will. "Count me in."

En route to Gardiner they made brief stops at Beryl Spring, one of Dan's favorites, and Mammoth, where he had business at the ranger station. Will strolled around the hot springs and then over to the busy service station, whose *porte cochère* and freshly-painted wood siding on a neat stone base possessed a good deal more panache than Thumb's tin shed. A savage whose sallow face looked vaguely familiar glanced at him a couple of times and then came over. "Hi, don't you work at West Thumb?" he asked.

"Right. I've seen you down there, I think."

"Yeah, visiting Trueblood and Dixon, frat brothers. Name's Marshall King."

"Ah, another Debruvian! Will Harkness." They shook hands. "You people seem pretty active. Selling a lot?"

"Yeah, maybe win the sales race, they say." Marsh shrugged. "What are you doing up here, just duding around?"

"A ranger from Thumb is taking me to meet somebody called the Old Timer."

"Ah, Judge Evans! I met him. He's all right." Will had a feeling that this might be high praise from Marsh.

Dan's truck appeared, pulled into a lane and stopped; Will hailed him and waved as he got out. The ranger spoke to the attending savage before joining them. "Wow, you risk YPCC service on a ranger truck?"

Dan shook his head. "Can you believe our maintenance shed is out of anti-freeze?"

"A commission sale!" crowed Marsh.

"Dan, this is Marshall King, a friend of Mason and Peter's at Debrew. Marsh, meet Dan MacLeod, Thumb's answer to James Arness."

"Hi. Say, didn't you give a slide lecture on flowers here a while back?"

"Why yes, were you there?" replied Dan, with a significant glance at Will.

"Sure, and you know, I found a flower you said I wouldn't: a calypso orchid."

"Really?! Where?"

"In the woods over near Tower Gate. Wouldn't keep, though."

"No, they won't," Dan agreed in a tone of condolence. "When was this?"

"Not long after you were here. About...early August?"

"Say, that's late for calypso! Thanks for telling me. You know, I've been trying to get these Thumbies interested in our flora, without much success, so far."

Marsh snickered. "Pretty unpromising material, all right."

"Oh, not so bad," said Dan, with a smile at Will. "Listen, you haven't by any chance in your rambles come across one of those..."

"Uh oh," groaned Will. "If you guys get started on flowers I'll never get to meet the Old Timer."

"He's not expecting us till after lunch," Dan protested. His tone suggested injury.

"Maybe I could join you when I get off at three?" asked Marsh. "And bring a girl? The Judge likes her. If you don't think that's too many."

"Not at all. When the Old Timer holds forth he likes an audience!"

The Old Timer found in the living room of his cabin up Clematis Gulch bore only a faint resemblance to Judge Evans in his courthouse chambers. He had exchanged judicial robes for a plaid shirt and jeans, and was stirring up a fire on his hearth, surrounded by books and chairs and memorabilia. On either side of a massive stone chimney, large windows looked out on the lower gulch, Mammoth Hot Springs and Gardiner Valley. "Chilly day, Dan," he said, rising slowly.

"It is, judge, touch of autumn. Feeling your joints?"

"A bit." Evans felt his joints. "Who's your friend?"

"Andy, this is Will Harkness, a mighty literate fellow for eighteen, and a musician too. Piano player."

"Always a pleasure to meet a civilized savage," said the judge as they shook hands. "Do you also read the book of nature?" He gestured to a chair.

Will pondered his answer as he sat down. "Can't say I knew it *existed* before this summer. Dan's been trying to teach me - teach us - something, but we're raw recruits."

Evans settled a benign look on the ranger. "Might make an old timer himself in another few decades - if we *have* that long! When are you going to finish law school, Dan?"

The ranger looked startled, and hesitated a moment before replying. "No plans to right now, Andy. Couldn't leave the woods that long."

"All the same, I'll be needing a replacement one of these years." He shrugged. "How are Fuller and Dixon? Notice my restraint in *not* asking after their gorgeous girlfriends."

"Oh, Lou's much the same: been very friendly since I moved to Thumb. Mason's coming along, I think."

"Kinda thought *he* might come along with you."

"I invited him, but he works Sunday."

"Oh well." There was a pause while Evans lit his pipe.

"Judge," began Will, "you said we might not *have* another few decades. Did you mean…do you really think…?"

"No, no." Evans waved him off, laughing. "The Old Timer's no prophet. It was a passing remark, a fashionable one: the bomb, you know. Never trust the fashionable!"

Will regrouped. "Could I pick your brains about books for a few minutes, then?"

The host settled more comfortably in his armchair. "Long as you keep to *American* literature. Don't know the others."

"Uh-huh," said Dan, putting his scepticism on record.

Will glanced from one to the other, puzzled. "Right, then, nothing east of Maine." He cogitated briefly. "Okay, what's your reaction to Hemingway's statement that all American literature comes from *Huck Finn*?"

"That's from *Green Hills of Africa* - well east of Maine!" declared Evans, chuckling. "And it was just a remark made during a campfire conversation."

"That's how the idea of Yellowstone National Park was first broached," Dan reminded him.

"Quite true, if that account is accurate." The judge puffed in silence for a few seconds. "All right, seriously, then…fact is, I don't buy his 'statement.' People who play that game - and it *is* a game - generally mean that's where my, or my friends', or my favorite kind of writing starts." He pointed his pipestem at Will. "Now we know what Ernest meant by that, and it may have seemed truer when he wrote it in the '30s than it does now. But if I wanted to play that game - and I don't - I could make a pretty fair case that it starts with Cooper, or Dreiser, or parts of Hemingway himself." He drew on the pipe and looked at Dan. "Or with somebody else, if I were in a different mood. Emerson."

"Wouldn't that be *theory* of American literature?" ventured Will.

The judge raised his eyebrows at Dan. "Very good," he muttered around the pipestem. "Quite right."

"Andy, what's your favorite Hemingway novel?" asked Dan.

"You know, I really don't care that much for his novels. Sometimes admire the style, but not his plots. Don't have much use for his expatriate stuff. Big stories, some of them, but European material, mostly, and Europeans do it better. *All Quiet on the Western Front*, *Paths of Glory*, *Homage to Catalonia* - those are the war books. Ernest's experience over there was too narrow, really. It's his short stories like "Two-Hearted River" and "Up in Michigan" that are important, and I told him so. They're authentic, and distinctive, and as American as *Huckleberry Finn*."

But Will had gone rigid. "You *know* Hemingway?"

"Well, he's practically a neighbor when he's over in Ketchum. We've fished together, and exchanged books." He stretched for a volume on the nearest shelf and handed Will a well-thumbed copy of *The First Fifty-One Stories*. "Here, look at the inscription."

Will opened the book and read out what was scrawled on the flyleaf: "For Andy Evans, with the affection & respect of a fellow western writer, EH."

"See what I mean?" asked the judge. "Fellow *western* writer. To me, *that's* the important Hemingway: not all the European and African and Cuban stuff, good as it is."

"How did you inscribe your book to him, Andy?" prompted Dan.

"To the better craftsman." Judge Evans smiled.

Will brightened. "I get it!" he cried. "Eliot to Pound in *The Wasteland*! Only it's in Italian, isn't it?"

"Good again," chortled the judge. "Now, enough of picking my brain: let's talk about you. Have you actually *read* Emerson, or just read *about* him?"

Will's reply launched them on a winding stream of talk until Marsh arrived, along with a slender, pretty girl, half an hour later. The Old Timer received them warmly, as friends. "Marshall, come in. Sally, Sally my dear, welcome!"

Sally gave Evans a kiss on the forehead, then went straight to his desk and seized a rumpled newspaper. "Judge, you're subscribing to the *TLS*?" she cried.

The judge's eyes followed her and he nodded approval, but his voice was stern. "Sally! Meet Dan MacLeod and Will Harkness." She put down the paper at once and there were handshakes and polite greetings. Evans removed his pipe. "Now that true civility has arrived," he told the men, "we may consider what is going on in the literary world."

Will cleared his throat. "Steinbeck has a new book out."

"*Pippin IV*," said Sally quickly.

"Is that the one about apple-pickers in Washington?"

"Judge! What do you think of it?"

Evans smiled at her. "He's coasting."

"That's what Bart says. He runs the Gardiner bookstore," she explained to Will. "He's lent me his copy of the new Lawrence Durrell: *Bitter Lemons*. God, he can write."

"Haven't seen that." The judge relit his pipe. "Baruch's autobiography is out, volume one. There's a long review of it in there." He nodded toward the *TLS*. "You can have that if you'll pass the Durrell on to me next."

"Thought you stuck to *American* literature," queried Will.

"That's a good one!" Marsh giggled. "He's got half of Aristotle memorized."

Evans smiled but shook his head; then said to Will, "I just meant I wouldn't play oracle on European literature."

The conversation flowed on around books and authors, with occasional shoals of politics and park gossip, until Dan said he had to leave. Will decided that he would like to stay longer even if it meant hitching back to Thumb, whereupon the judge invited him to spend the night in his spare room. That being settled, Dan departed. The remaining four enjoyed a noisy dinner at the Old Town Café in Gardiner, after which Will stayed up late talking to the judge. He fell asleep wondering if Princeton could possibly be this good.

On Monday Will reached Thumb in time for lunch and spent the overlap shift enthusing to any savages who would listen about the Old Timer. "Best day off I've had," he declared, showing his autographed copy of *Sketches of Old Yellowstone*. "Oh, and I met a friend of yours," he told the Debruvians. "Marshall King."

"Oh, Marsh," said Clay.

"Yep. Nice guy. Pretty sharp."

"Marsh?" Trueblood sounded surprised.

"He was with a really attractive girl too, and a smart one. Best thing I've seen all summer. I really envied him."

"*Marsh*?!" It was Mason's turn.

"She said she met you way back in early June. Asked if you remembered Sally Savage."

"Oh. Jesus, yes." Mason looked puzzled and thoughtful.

"You should really try to get up there yourself. Judge Evans remembers you and says the welcome mat's out. An interesting man."

"I'll see if I can fit it in," said Mason, heading off to serve a customer.

"People get jealous bout their days awf towards th'end," remarked Woo. "Let's clean the grease rack, men."

Actually Mason had already made plans to spend his next day off with Julia, but was reluctant to say so. His crewmates were still very protective of her and would not, he thought, look kindly on individual initiatives. Under the banner of "Look After Hole's Girl," they made sure that she had invitations and rides to Thumb for any social function, and sometimes she accepted, with an air of gravely pleased surprise. She had attended a beach party and a savage show, and had somehow smitten most of the station's males, to the annoyance of its females. Pris (like Liz) pointed out that Julia spoke very little - but she always watched and listened to the speaker, which Pris (and Liz) did not. Will had a theory, of course: "It's her little smile and sympathetic expression that draw people out. You know she's paying attention." Several savages spent the evening telling Julia about themselves and then praised her conversational powers. At the beach party Mason talked to her until the sky paled and thought her amazing, mystical, profound, though he could not recall anything specific she had said.

Perhaps the greatest tribute came from Owl. "That's one chick I wouldn't even try to make," he assured Dan, to whom Julia always paid her respects when visiting Thumb. Dan nodded but did not reply; he had his own views on Julia. The station's usual adjective for her was "easy-going," but once when Mason used that phrase Dan asked, "Don't you think there's a certain tension underneath?" No one else had observed that, and he would not elaborate, but seemed to enjoy her visits. For everyone she was set apart: there were Yellowstone girls and there was Julia.

Driving to Old Faithful, Mason had time to think about Julia's boyfriends and his place among them. She and Will sometimes read poetry together, Dan had at least noticed her, and he even wondered if civilizing Owl to some extent could have left her unaffected. Plus she must have beaux at Faithful. Of course they were *all* snaking on Hole. But really, what chance did a battered boy in Florida have with an Idaho girl? Very little: no more than a shy Massachusetts boy, about to head back east. "So, being one face in her crowd is no longer good enough, eh?" he muttered.

Was it time to speak to her about his feelings, then? Or would that be an awful mistake that would damage their friendship? So which was better: too hot or too cool? He was sure to blow it somehow, his social skills being what they were. The whole summer had been disastrous: breaking up with Liz, missing out on Polly and Sally Savage, angering Pris. Why couldn't he just fall for a nice, healthy, affectionate girl at Thumb? Tune in tomorrow for another episode of *All My Savages*.

Julia had to work that afternoon, so there was no opportunity to go anywhere. Instead, Mason chose a trail that led away from roads and cabins and dudes, past an obscure geyser to a hilltop with a view of the basin. Along the way they tried to identify flowers and trees, gossiped a bit, discussed what made some people better than others, wondered how the summer would look in retrospect, and so on. Dissatisfied, wanting more, Mason kept probing her feelings for Hole and Will and whoever she was seeing at Faithful until Julia grew visibly uneasy. At last she shook her head. "Why are you so full of personal questions today, Mason? It's not like you."

His first impulse was to hide behind lightness. "Sorry, must be the end of summer. Christmas is comin' kind of thing?"

"Maybe." She stooped to examine a flower. Her tone said, Maybe not.

Mason took a deep breath. This was it, then. There is a fortune in the affairs of men...no, a tide, which, taken at the full...damn. He hesitated, and heard the unasked question resonate down through the years. "Well then, how about *us*?" he croaked, his voice oddly thin.

"Us?" She looked up at him quizzically, her face as open and guileless as always.

"You and me. What are we?" His voice rang in his ears as from a distance, just audible over the pounding of his heart.

"Ah. Well, we're friends, of course...good friends." She turned back to the flower.

Well, there it was! Or was it? "And so we are!" he might say heartily. Or (gently), "*How* good, Julia?" But how much could he expect *her* to say, caught unawares like this? Perhaps he shouldn't be asking, but declaring? That is, it should be a declaration, not a question. Were there no manuals on how to do this, no models but soap operas? And all the time he knew he was saying nothing.

She glanced at him briefly, then at the flower. "What are these tall ones with the six yellow petals?"

"Oh, those." He flung himself on his knees beside her with relief. "I haven't the slightest idea."

She laughed and tapped his hand. "You're funny," she said, looking him full in the face, again warm and open; then rose and resumed the walk. Choking on a mouthful of possible responses, Mason followed dumbly. At the top they were again constrained, exchanging moody glances but little else. On the way back down Mason wondered, not *whether* he had missed his way, but *how*. Had he gone too far or not far enough? As usual Julia was content with long silences, and this time Mason could not fill them. Had he ruined everything? Only, when they parted at her door, she said, "Very good friends." Now what was *that* supposed to mean?! He gaped after her, again speechless.

At loose ends now, and looking for some diversion, Mason walked over to the store: he should try to say a civil farewell to Liz. But she was working, and couldn't or wouldn't take a break to see him. Nor did he find Polly either in the dining room or in her dorm, so he walked over to service station #1 to find Virg. A savage there said, or rather giggled, that the assistant manager was "taking stock in the back room." Something was up.

Then Tech emerged from the station house and caught sight of Mason. "Watch this," he beamed, raising his arm to reveal a good-sized box wrench up his sleeve, and walked toward an old blue sedan with Minnesota plates.

"What is going on?" Mason asked the first savage.

"An old tradition, knibbling the escutcheon. Just watch."

After checking the oil and water Tech spoke with the driver, whose responses apparently satisfied him on some point, because when he came back around front to replace the dipstick and was screened from the driver by the lifted hood he gave them a big thumbs-up. Then he shook his sleeve and there was a great clanging in the engine. Everyone in the station turned around, and several savages came running over on cue.

"Whuzzat?!" The driver popped out, a balding middle-aged man of medium height.

Tech scratched his head. "Looks lak yuh dropped yer knibblin' pin, suh."

"Is thet bad?" An anxious voice: Walter Mitty on vacation. Tech had chosen well.

"Holds the 'schutcheon rod in place," explained another savage in sepulchral tones.

"Ah. Can yuh fix it?"

Shrugs, clucks, raised eyebrows. "We ken shore tragh," said Tech: John Wayne rallying the battered troops. "Gimme hand, fellers." Four of them pushed the sedan around to the side apron, hooked up a battery tester, flourished a timing device and began swarming over the engine while the driver looked on with a resigned air.

"I *told* 'em to check thet thing afore we came," he remarked angrily to Mason, who grunted sympathetically, trying to keep a straight face. After ten minutes the savages closed the hood and wiped their hands.

"Tragh it naow, suh," suggested Tech. To everyone's delight the engine started and idled as smoothly as before the knibbling pin and escutcheon rod parted company.

The driver jumped out again, beaming. "Thet's terrific!" Then his face fell. "How much do I owe yuh?" But the savages backed away, giving their palms-out, 'Satan-hence-avaunt' gesture.

"No chahge, suh," said Tech. "Glad tuh hep." He was palming the wrench. The driver shook his head, scarcely able to believe this magnanimity, thanked them again, and drove away carefully. Only then did Virg complete his inventory and reappear, just as Mason was thanking Tech and the others for the show.

"Show? What show?" asked Virg. The savages all shook their heads, mumbled unintelligibly and walked away.

"Oh, nothing much," said Mason. "A dude had trouble with his knibbling pin, but they fixed it."

"Ah, and saved the escutcheon rod, I trust." Virg grinned and lowered his voice. "You know, Mace, this stuff is harmless: what worries me is real incompetence. Last week a dude asked one of our younger guys for an oil change. The idiot drained the *transmission* oil and was trying to add engine oil through the dipstick hole."

"Virg, that's incredible! In June a rookie *might* do that, but in mid-August?"

"Indeed. I tell you, we'll be lucky to get out of that one without a lawsuit. The dude is *pissed*."

Mason stayed until 3 PM, when Virg's shift ended, and after he cleaned up they walked to the snack bar in the store for sodas and gossip. No sign of Liz there, so no goodbyes today: he would have to look her up at Debrew. Mason brought up Julia, but since to Virg she was still "Hole's girl" it was not a very satisfactory topic. They ran over the usual list of friends' names instead. Cal was still having a great time and staying free of entangling alliances; Marsh and Cleve both had steady girlfriends. "Oh, have you heard that Cleve has decided to leave early?"

Mason started. "I have not! Why would he do that? He seemed to be having such a good time."

"Yep, going in that old Ford coupe he calls the White Fright. Taking Polly with him, and maybe Liz, he says."

"But *why*, Virg?"

"Ah well, that's the question, 'cause it makes waves up in Gardiner... means bad recs and no re-hire, you know. Not that he cares, probably, but Morley doesn't like broken contracts." He removed his glasses to wipe them. "I'm not sure, Mace. Family problems, something that needs doing back home? Must be important to bolt like this! Maybe...I don't know." Virg looked uncertain and checked his watch. "Listen, I have to run along and do some errands. Hope you have a good Christmas. Looking forward to it?"

"Haven't given it much thought."

"Well, it's your first - we veterans get more excited. It's an old savage tradition, you know."

"Ah, like knibbling the escutcheon?"

"Well, yeah...but don't be such a Scrooge, Mason! There'll be presents and speeches and Christmas trees and all. Sometimes it even snows."

"Sounds good. Have a cool Yule, then. Good to see you, Virg." Left alone, Mason considered searching for Polly or Liz again, but felt inhibited and lethargic. Enough tension for one day! His whole plan had been stupid; he should have taken Dan's advice, gone to Gardiner and sat at Judge Evans's feet. *Maybe* looked up Sally Savage. He wandered into the general store and scanned the titles on the jukebox. Yep, still there: "*Searchin'*" by The Coasters. He dropped in his nickel and gift-shopped as it played.

> *Sherlock Holmes, Sam Spade got nuthin' chil' on me,*
> *Sgt. Friday, Charley Chan an' Boston Blackie,*
> *No matter where's she's hidin' she's gonna hear me a-comin'*
> *Gonna walk right down that street like...Bulldog Drummond!*
> *'Cause I bin searchin'...*

Mason found himself singing the introduction: "Gonna find her..." He had heard it with Polly, with Liz, with Julia, and by himself. If the summer needed a theme song, this would do as well as any - along with the Emperor Concerto, plucked from a clear dawn after it had soared over hundreds of empty miles of mountain and desert. *If* it needed one! He noticed that an approaching thunderstorm had brought on a premature dusk, and set off for Thumb as the first raindrops fell. At the pass it was snowing.

Saturday the 24th was Yellowstone "Christmas Eve." When the early shift straggled into the dining room around four that afternoon they found Clay and Dan trying to keep a young fir tree vertical against the increasing weight and imbalance of ornaments, and guard against the possibility of pushes or slips. The decoration was being done by several of the Ham's employees, directed after a fashion by Will as he worked through a glass of apple juice, probably: "Mason, lend a hand here! This tannenbaum must be ready by 10 PM. Whoa, steady there, Jill! Push comes to shove. Bare spot in the upper left center, ladies."

Florida Lady was there, her shapely calves on display as she stretched to hang an ornament on a high branch. For some reason, instead of simply enjoying the show, Mason took it from her and hung it up there himself, winning a smile and a chance to talk. He had heard that her name was Millicent or Henrietta, something awkward and unworthy: hence the generic title Florida Lady. She was as quiet a person as he; usually they just smiled and said hello as they passed in the courtyard or the store. Now he learned that she preferred her middle name, Elizabeth, and that her husband had been killed in the war. When he gallantly suggested that Florida men must be blind if she was still walking around on her own, she teared up and couldn't speak. After she left, Mason joined Jill and Barbara in hanging tinsel. "At last we've found something we can all do together!" he exclaimed. The girls laughed and rolled their eyes, and he saw that he had stepped in it again.

Though several of the girls found that they had to go soon after Dan left, by dinnertime the tree was splendid enough to produce admiration and further recruits. Bill, Jacky, Woo and Ellen helped from then on; Gray found a string of lights from Christmases past; even Jack the store manager - a distant, slightly ogrish figure - came by with a *crèche*. As well he might, said some cynics: all day and into the evening, savages paraded through the store, buying knick-knacks and having them gift-wrapped. In Yellowstone as elsewhere, Christmas was good business.

The festive fir was a blaze of incandescent lights and tinseled reflections by the time the late shift appeared, chafing their hands. They reported freezing rain: there was hope for a white Christmas. Rushing to the window, Pris and Jill claimed to see an occasional snowflake melting on the glass. Shrieks of excitement from Shelley and Jane. A hot rum punch, sanctioned by the management, was handed around; it delighted everyone, especially the newly-arrived work crew, chilled to the bone, but finished off Will Harkness. With his arm around Horn's shoulders he bid the company goodnight, explaining that he must work on his Christmas address, and retired looking unwell.

Then Clay, serving as unofficial Lord of the Feast, called for music. The traditional carols were duly sung, accompanied by guitar and accordion, after which Gray produced a big old tape recorder and called for quiet. There were murmurs of speculation as he started the machine, but a hush fell as a solo trumpet began to play *Adeste Fideles*: slowly, clearly, flawlessly, each note a thrilling drop of golden nectar. At the second line a few began to sing, and by "*venite adoremus*" everyone had joined in. In the silence after the final note and the slow dying-away of the trumpet, the voice of Beatty himself intoned, "Merruh Christmus, Wes Thumb, an to awl a good nat."

"He recorded it before he left," said Gray solemnly. "It's his gift to evrabody." Someone stifled a sob.

"I knew I heard that one day!" blurted Creeper. Everyone turned to look at him, and he blushed and fell silent again.

As a finale Lou gave a spirited reading of "The Gnat Before Christmas," undeterred by Mason's pretending not to understand certain key words. The party lost momentum when a few churchgoers left for the midnight service at Faithful, and broke up at 12 with calls of "Merry Christmas!" and a few under-the-mistletoe kisses. But some savages, too wound up to quit, started a snowball fight, using the wet, easily-packed stuff in the courtyard. At one point Mason chased Vicky out of the stockade and around the store into a dark corner where the fence made a right angle behind the dormitories. They were alone, panting, holding their snowballs, a few feet apart, when Mason felt a sudden impulse to drop his snowball and kiss her. For a few seconds he wondered if, after all, *she*, the lively South Carolinian with bodacious hips, was The One he'd been searchin' for. Then she took off in another direction with her trademark hysterical squeal. Mason stayed put, the snowball melting in his fist, again wondering what would have happened if he had made his move instead of just thinking about it.

By the time he reached the courtyard again the fun was over; people were heading off to bed. For some reason he entered the girls' dorm and went into the dining room. Why? Was he hungry? The food had been put away. To see the decorations again? With the lights off, the tree looked ghostly. To stand under the mistletoe? He heard a slight noise behind him and turned. It was Florida Lady, Elizabeth, coming toward him quietly with a strange smile. She did not stop until she could kiss him on the lips. "Merry Christmas," she whispered, and looked up, still smiling. He followed her glance. He *was* under the mistletoe. Then she took his hand and gently led him out the door, down the hall to her first-floor single; the girls lived upstairs. Elizabeth pushed the door open and led him into the dark room.

"Would you like me to turn on the light?" he asked.

"Just close the door."

It was the nicest Christmas present anyone could have given him.

Christmas itself might well have been an anti-climax, but in the rarefied atmosphere of novelty the spirit carried over. Will awoke looking terrible, but assured everyone that he had never felt better. Clay, who had made up with Barbara - they left the party together - told Horn that he had already enjoyed Christmas "to the hilt." Mason slept in. At lunch he was silent, staring at his plate and wondering if he had dreamt it all. The girls hugged one another. All day savages were wishing dudes Christmas cheer, which forced them to explain the custom, i.e. to fraternize a bit. Dan, an amused observer of this new fellowship in the lanes, told Lou that it reminded him of stories about British and German troops calling a truce and playing soccer between the front lines on the first Christmas of the Great War. Periodic snow showers throughout the day draped a thin white blanket over the scene by nightfall. Mudpots burbled weirdly through ragged white collars; the weighted evergreen forest looked like a *Weihnachtskart* from Bavaria. The savages hardly recognized their workaday world in such a disguise.

The party began with the serving of YPCC-blessed rum toddies at 10:30, and proceeded to presents and speeches. Most of the gifts were anonymous, with good reason. Clay received a packet of prophylactics from "Amanda," causing an uneasy stir among the older set. Who was Amanda, anyway? "The Boys" gave Shelley a pair of panties, while "The Girls" presented Lou with a large pair of jockey shorts. Pris was given a pair of heels (shrieks and blushes), Henderson a gift-wrapped yellow can of gas additive (snarls), Owl Brain a small wooden owl bearing the legend, "With All Thy Getting, Get Understanding," and so on. A large mystery package proved to be a box of Florida fruit from Hole to everyone. There was another momentary hush. Jill sniffled, and had to be comforted.

Then Lou cleared his throat. "Gray! Gotta formal ree-quest. Whagh doncha tell us sumpun huhbout Yallerstone Chrismus? With awl these young rookies, *some*buddy's gotta speak fer age an tradition."

Gray pretended surprise but rose readily, hitched up his baggy khakis and looked around at the roomful of attentive faces, savoring his not unforeseen moment in the limelight. "It's not just here, yuh know, but all over," he began, rather obscurely. "I mean, there's parties like this at ev'ry station in the park tonight - an it's been like that ever since I bin comin' here - turn o the century er so! Oh, just a chance to get sent-eye-mental at the end, I guess, and get presents, an give 'em - really *nail* somebuddy! - an snow fer the grits. No offence, Lou!" Gray paused for the laughter as if he had apprenticed in stand-up comedy. "So, we're kinda" - he paused and swallowed before his big flight - "*united* with all those good folks - I mean, at other stations *an* other years. Like the ghost of Christmas past, yuh know?" Mason and Will exchanged a raised-eyebrows glance: they had not expected this. And Gray knew when to quit. "So, well, Merry Christmas!" He waved and sat down to cheers.

Lou then prevailed upon Will Harkness to draw on his recent experience as a valedictorian and respond for youth. Will struggled to his feet with an assist from Horn, keeping one arm around him, partly for support. As soon as he began to speak it was clear that he had drunk deep of the punch, though whether he would have spoken better or worse had he been sober is difficult to say. "Now we've spent a lot of time working and playing with each other" - he paused for howls of laughter - "but do we really know one another? Take L. B. here, for instance." He hugged Horn. "A fine man and a good friend, but can I say what goes on inside his head? Do I understand what makes him tick? Do I really know him - I mean you?"

Horn flashed his dazzling smile. "No," he said, disengaging himself, and sat down. There were more howls.

Deprived of his support, Will staggered, and seemed momentarily confused by the noise, but recovered his balance and continued gamely. "What I mean is, there just hasn't been enough time. Look at all this!" His sweeping gesture took in the tree, his audience, the torn gift wrappings, windows wet with snowflakes. "All the trappings of a family Christmas, civilization in the wilderness, and in another week - a *week* - where will it all be?" People looked at each other, not sure of the right answer. Here?

There? Nowhere? Will himself seemed momentarily confused by his own leap.

Mason resisted the urge to raise his hand. "With the snows of yesteryear?" he asked.

"Exactly!" yelped Will, pointing at Mason as if he were an example to the class or had scored at charades. "All gone! Our part of it, anyway. In a week *we*'ll be gone, probably never meet again, and the wilderness will be left to itself." He paused to sip his punch, and the savages shifted restlessly.

"What the eff *are* you talkin' about?" asked Owl, but not unkindly, for him.

"Glad you asked," replied Will suavely, in control now. "What I'm trying to say is that time, no, *the sense of time*, has been the important hidden element in this summer for all of us - the kicker, if you like. At first we didn't think about it, but these last few weeks have been different, haven't they?" He let the question hang, and his audience was quiet. "We've had good times and bad, joy and sorrow, so much packed into - what? less than three months - and the specter of *the end* hanging over it all, like…a dark storm coming over the pass." He gestured to the window again, where sleet was clicking on the pane. Jill sobbed; tears were running down her chubby face. "Sad, yes, think about it, the evanescence! We always knew it couldn't last, didn't we? But the beauty, too…it's Keats's 'Ode on Melancholy' all over, isn't it? 'Joy's hand is ever at his lips, bidding adieu'."

"Oh God, here we go," groaned Henderson.

"Bear with me, Carolina," asked Will. "Keats says the best times pass quickest, and maybe they're the best times *because* they're so fleeting and we *know* they can't last. They're beautiful *because* their quick passage is inevabul - sorry, things were going so well! - in-ev-i-table, and then they're gone. One more quote, friends: 'Ay, in the very temple of delight, veiled melancholy has her sovereign shrine.' There it is: *Melancholy lives in the temple of Delight.* Do you see? What that means, what I'm saying, is that this summer is unique and unforgettable *because* our time here is so inexab - damn! - in-ex-or-ably short, and our partings are final."

Most of the savages were silent, but Pris and Jill were crying openly now, and Woo felt moved to intervene. "Nobody but a drunk would talk like that!" he called out, as if disapproving, but he sounded amused.

"That doesn't make what he's saying any less true," said Dan quietly.

"By God, you're *both* right!" cried Will, raising his glass.

"Merry Christmas, Will," said Gair.

"Merry Christmas, everyone." Will sat down a bit unsteadily, almost tipping over his chair, which served to break the spell by letting them laugh. As the crowd dispersed, Mason looked for Elizabeth, but didn't see her, and was too timid to knock on her door. The party was over...the parties were over. The gas jockeys had time for a few hours of sleep before their alarms woke them at 6 to go out and work in the slush. Of course it would probably melt by noon. *Où sont les neiges d'antan?* as Will would say.

Nine: Exit, Pursued by a Bear

Few times and places feel as melancholy as a summer resort at the end of summer. Yes, the days dwindle down to a precious few: they also shorten and cool, plant life fades, and winter can be sensed around the corner. The idea that the resort will live again next year is too abstract to comfort those who are scattering to the four winds, blown elsewhere by the demands of work or study, and who may not return when the days lengthen again. An unsettling period of entropy, of disintegration, and a strong sense of inhabiting a space whose spirit has migrated followed hard upon Yellowstone Christmas. The weather was full of freakish shifts, trade was dying back, savages were making travel plans, having final flings and parting from friends. Only the rangers looked happier in late August - Dan seemed to exult in the approach of autumn - whereas seasonals, seeing that they were doing things for the last time, tried to remember how they were done "on the outside." Could they adjust to life without mudpots?

The morning after the Christmas party Gair borrowed Mason's car to spend his last day off with Polly, and when he returned that evening he handed over three dollars for gas. Mason looked at the bills and back at Gair. "That's a lot for a trip to Faithful, amigo. Eight gallons for 34 miles? A buck will do."

Gair blushed. "Well, actually, um, we went to West, so it's about right."

Trueblood looked up from his paperback. "West? That's not your usual style, Gair. In the daytime, too." He grinned.

Gair reddened more deeply. "Oh, there's lots to do there in the daytime, actually. Well, gotta get some rest. Thanks again, Mason. 'Night, men." He waved and went out.

Mason and Peter looked at each other. "That was funny," whispered Trueblood. "I wonder if somethin's wrong."

When the door across the hall closed Mason answered. "Something's wrong for sure, but I have no idea what. Have you noticed how tense and drawn he looks these days? As I remember, in June he was a relaxed, easy-going guy."

Peter shook his head. "Hope my last day off goes betterun *that*."

"Mine too." Mason glanced at his watch. "Think I'll try to catch Dan as he comes off duty and find out where I'm going tomorrow."

But for once the ranger was not particularly helpful. "Well, if you're not going up to see Judge Evans" - he paused briefly, eyebrows raised - "I think you should probably go off somewhere by yourself, away from dudes and savages, and listen to the still, small voice." When Mason asked *where*, Dan insisted that it did not matter, as long as it was lonesome. "Know thyself, as Socrates said. And for you and me, at least, that's best done alone."

So when Mason started his car the next morning, he still did not know where he was going, and if Dan was right he should not even care. True, he *had* spent most of his time with other people; alone, he *might* begin to see what - if anything - it all meant. Yet one had to go in a particular direction, no? He could "give the car its head," Dan had joked, as riders sometimes did their horses. That was silly, of course, especially when one had to start in reverse. Give the car its tail? Yet he waited until there was no traffic, then backed up slowly, keeping his hands in his lap, and gradually the stern swung north, which left the hood ornament pointing south. All right! Mason shifted, eased the clutch out and followed his star. At first he took this as a turning away from Old Faithful and Liz, or an alignment problem; not until he left the park did he feel the pull of the Tetons.

Descending onto the lake plain, Mason passed the lodge, turned right on a dirt road, left the car by a gate at the trailhead, and began walking through a narrow belt of forest toward Jenny Lake. The day was fair and mild, a touch of Indian summer after the alternation of hot days with early snows; the fragility of the sunshine made the air more invigorating than ever. There were no fallen or turning leaves to confirm the seasonal change, so that nature seemed unaltered since his last visit. If he knew the flowers, of course - and for the *n*th time he regretted that ignorance. If he knew the flowers...if he were another person.

The trees thinned out and he emerged on the shore of the never-disappointing lake. Across the sundance of the waves, the mighty Tetons, outgrowing their trees, thrust up to daunting heights; fresh snow on their summits was etched against the sky's deep blue. *Dangerous* heights, where Hole and - well, they, the survivors, had all gained new respect for mountains. Mason found a pine-needle-carpeted hollow like the one he had shared with Liz and lay down, hands behind his head. If they hadn't been interrupted there... Yes? What? Would that have made things better, clearer, or just more complicated? The air felt pleasantly warm at this lower elevation. Time passed as he watched colors and shadows change up on the high cliffs, halfway to the zenith. At moments they became a screen on which his mind could project its own tableaux.

Liz...how futile that had all been. This is where I started to know that it was not just sick but dying, dead. Arranging deck chairs on the Titanic. She shouldn't have come...damn meddlesome Virg. But no, it was bound to happen, better to get it over with. Why did she have to ruin my summer, though? There could have been Polly, or Julia....
It was all focused here, really: that first view, with Polly, the day with Liz, the trip to see Hole with Julia when we met Dan. And ever since, dreams: huge granite ramparts, impending. The Tetons had been like giant magnets, attracting seriousness, repelling levity. Were they a test, a standard against which we were measured? Some mountaineer said that he climbed to see if he was worthy, that up there he gave back everything he had been given and then tried to survive. "My God!" I thought. But mountains were holy places in ancient times - I shall lift up mine eyes unto the hills, from whence cometh my help - and still were for some people. What about for me? Well, here I am, lifting up my eyes! And even churches make artificial mountains, which they call steeples.

Mason stared at the summits, trying to connect with them, to send or receive...what? A message? But they seemed terribly far and cold, part of a pure, inhuman realm, like mathematical laws or the vast empty spaces between stars where the gods sit aloof. That was some Greek philosopher's idea: Judge Evans would know which one. Maybe Dan, too. An icy glint, more silver than white, flashed from time to time, as if someone up there were signaling, but it was random, patternless. He was half blind from concentrating on the radiant whiteness. Blanched, *blanc*, blank. A cold no-color. And yet, *les grands tetons*: the big breasts. Someone - a Frenchman, of course! - had seen them as warm, life-sustaining, the Earth Mother. Could they be that, too? Had he been searchin' in the wrong places? He reached toward the peaks; his vision swam and the mountains seemed to stoop over him. Mason closed his eyes in terror, but the image of the stony bulk pressed on his body. For a moment he felt warm and fused. Coherent. Then he shuddered and opened his eyes: the mountains were again distant and he was cold. More time passed.

*What was that all about? How long have I been here? The sun and my
watch say mid-afternoon. I can't have been lying here for five hours! But I'm
hungry...you blinking idiot, get up and go home before you freeze or starve.
And stop talking to yourself!*

Back at the main road, however, he found himself turning right
- the alignment again? - and driving farther south, to the Chapel of
the Transfiguration. Liz had coaxed him there once and had knelt to
pray while he stood awkwardly at the back, unable to participate in her
devotion, but equally unable to gauge or articulate his own feelings. He
had not expected to return, but submitted to the impulse. It was, after all,
a uniquely spectacular place: behind the altar table with its simple wooden
cross, a picture window framed the classic view of the Tetons. That sight
again stopped him at the door, but this time his revulsion was instinctive
and immediate. The mountains seemed to hang on the far wall like a huge
postcard, cramped by those right angles, and the cross lay on them like a
grid. "Blasphemy," he muttered to the empty room. The chapel had turned
its back on Calvary, far to the east, and was trying to Christianize those
mountains to the west. "No," he said loudly. If we're going to worship
mountains, this isn't the way. He turned on his heel and reached Thumb
in time for dinner, which he wolfed down with a healthy appetite.

When Dan asked about his day off, Mason replied simply, "I took your
advice, and it was good."

"I'm glad. Where did you wind up going?"

"It doesn't matter, does it?"

"Touché."

Then Mason relented and said, "The Tetons."

Dan nodded. He seemed almost impressed.

The Farewell Season began in earnest the next day. In the morning
Trueblood went off in Mason's car for a last visit with Lois, who would be
leaving with Fran the following day. Tech arrived loudly at noon to pick
up Clay, their month being up. The Debruvians' goodbyes were low-key:
they would soon be meeting back at school, and there was talk of a reunion
with Tech at their football game in October. Only Gair seemed moved,
but everyone agreed that he had gotten emotional recently. Pris came over
to give Clay a parting peck, which was quite decent of her, considering,
and (he claimed) invited him to Tucson *sotto voce*. Barbara was nowhere
to be seen. Lou advised Tech to see about a new muffler purty soon,
and Tech, amiable as ever, agreed effusively. Then Clay slung his Valpak

into the trunk and they peeled out, scratching gravel, waving from both windows.

Lou, who had never seen reason to change his first opinion of Tech, shook his head and spat, dust to dust. "Ifn there wuz *law* in this countreh they'd nevuh make it," he muttered.

Trueblood returned from Old Faithful at an ominously early hour and came unstrung when Mason asked him how it had gone. "I awways *knew* it wouldn't outlast the summer an I *thought* I was reconciled to that" came pouring out. But when he had actually *seen* that it was only a summer fling for her.... His voice caught, and he could not continue.

Faced with so much emotion - and given an opportunity to repay the support he had received a month earlier - Mason found himself at a loss. Their culture provided no models for this scene: a guy didn't choke up over losing a girl, and if he did another guy didn't hug him. "But surely you can meet again if you want?" he ventured. "Go and see her?"

Fighting for control, Peter raised his head. "She said she'd *wrat* to me if Ad *wrat* to her," he said miserably.

"What did you say?"

"Ah said, awrat," choked Peter. "What else could Ah do?"

Mason reviewed various other consolations, but rejected them as unconvincing - and probably unconsoling. How to indicate sympathy, solidarity, the need to accept and resign oneself to reality, the metaphysical inscrutability of the universe? Finally he waved his hand. "What the hell, roomie, life goes on." It was good to know that his day of retreat and meditation had not been entirely unproductive of wisdom. But we live in the body, too, so for the moment he prescribed aspirin and sleep.

The next day he tried to distract him with work on the gift album for Lou. Several of the savages had been collecting snapshots (a tedious process, as film had to be mailed to and from Bozeman) and money to make a souvenir for the manager. The job of gluing in pictures and writing clever captions had fallen to Will and Mason, who now drew Peter into the task. He saw through their therapeutic motive, of course, but took it in good part. That and basketball in the morning, work in the afternoon, and a long bull session - elucidating the problems affecting gender relations in the mobile, evolving society of postwar America - that night, pulled him through the first, worst day, while the next provided diversions of its own. An early-morning snow encouraged anti-freeze sales and snowball fights; then the sun came out, the air turned muggy and every dude needed a bug screen. "This is a reel shit-kicker," Lou snorted. It was early June all over again.

But the mood was relaxed and the double shift was idling in warm sunshine when an apparition drew nigh from the east shortly after lunch. "God," blurted Peter, his woes momentarily forgotten, "look at Wanda!" The statuesque singer was dressed to kill in a well-tailored, form-fitting suit and heels. Tagging along, though looking quite colorless beside her, was George of the cabins, who explained that they had come to say goodbye before catching their ride to the Gardiner railroad station. A swarm of Green Hornets - who had seen nothing like this for many a day - encircled Wanda likes drones eager for flight, and wondered why they hadn't gotten over to the cabins more often.

"We'll be seeing you on the cover of a record album one of these days," said Will with rare gallantry.

"Mm, an Al be lookin' fo' you, playin duets with Erroll Gahnuh," she smiled. "Thanks fo' awl the musical suppoht, baweez." The instrumentalists beamed. Mason and George shook hands with the special caution of fellow guitarists, and gave their long-running joke one last airing.

"Take care now, Chet."

"See you round, Josh."

The couple then departed, under close scrutiny. "Mat as well go home now," said Peter contentedly, as if he had suddenly recalled, or accepted, that pretty girls really are a dime a dozen. "She's a gal from Tennuhsee-ee..."

"She's lawng an she's tawl," finished Mason, dodging a poke. "Okay, gents, when shall we give the album to Lou?"

"How about tomorrow, before anyone else leaves?" suggested Horn.

"Hope he can still enjoy it," said Gair. "He looks kinda low these days."

Horn and Schlitz thought that Lou was worried about the outcome of the sales race, while Gair and Creeper leaned to the view that he was having Shelley problems, but The Mouth said they were all imagining things. "Just because a guy doesn't *say* much doesn't mean there's something *wrong* with him," he announced tartly.

On the last day of August, thunderheads came sailing over Craig Pass every hour or two with loads of sleet or snow; after a while they just left their rainslickers on. In mid-morning Lou had a phone call from Morley that left him glum and distant, but the savages decided to go ahead with the presentation anyway. During the two o'clock lull the whole crew gathered at the middle pump island; then Will escorted Lou out from the shed and Woo produced the album from its waterproof bag. Purchased at Thumb's own gift shop, it had black pages and covers of varnished pine with "Souvenir of Yellowstone" burnt into the wood. Woo proferred it to the manager with a crooked smile. "Uh, Lou, it's just a token of, well, a souvenir of the summer. It's frum the whole crew, to show ar 'priciation." He stopped and looked around. "Will an these guys made it."

Lou stared at the gift and flipped through some pages. "Gosh, yawl been tuh lot uh trouble." He glanced up, nodding approval.

"The hwat ink *was* a pain in the butt," Trueblood chuckled, "but it's a worthy cause."

"Lou, it's been a pleasure working for you," said Will.

"We coulda done lots wuss," Henderson conceded.

Gair cleared his throat. "We think you're an excellent manager."

"Lou, it's been real," said Cyril, and there were murmurs of assent.

"Goddam, men!" Lou stopped looking at pictures, coughed, straightened up and met their eyes. "Don't know how tuh thank yuh. Said afore you wuz the best crew a manajuh could wawnt, an Ah still thank so. 'Ts jes a damn shame we couldna won the sales race." Mutters of consternation or disbelief, looks of dismay. "Yep: Morley cawled this mornin. We sol' the mos' by a mahle, but Mammoth won it awn puhcentage. *They* gets the steak dinnuh an the bonus."

A moment of quiet ensued as the savages tried to read each others' expressions. A month or six weeks earlier this outcome would have seemed unbearable, but now.... An invisible shrug made the rounds. "What the hell," said Owl, and spat. "They won on a fuckin' technicality, just caz they was so shitty last year!"

"Thet's rat," chortled Lou. "Jez wait'll next yeah!"

"Anyway the spruces are still in place," said Will. They looked at him blankly. "Winning isn't everything! We had a lot of fun. Let's see the album."

Most of them had not seen it yet. The circle closed around Lou for the last time. There were pictures of Gair hamming it up as he pretended to catch his fingers in the chamois wringer; Clay sloshing gasoline out of the horizontal filler pipe behind the rear licence plate of a '56 Chevy; Beatty brandishing a fan belt and Horn accepting a wad of money; Hole and Hayward standing forlornly in an early June snowstorm, sans customers; Cyril and Peter under the hoist, laughing and pointing to the bottom of a dude's car; and The Mouth looking suave as he talked to a dudette in the lanes. There was Will rebounding with Lou's elbow in his ribs, Owl and Schlitz toasting the camera in a West Yellowstone bar. Bill with his eyes closed sitting on the bed next to Jacky, who was playing the guitar and singing during one of The Parties. Mason and Woo clowning with Pris and Jill by the mudpot. Bastille talking to Bud, who was almost smiling. Lou at the Christmas party with one arm around Shelley and the other around - could that be Ranger Curtis? Now freezing drops from the next shower began to hit the yellow sou'westers, and a car honked in the outside lane. Closing the book, Lou slipped it back into the cover with a sigh. "Well, back tuh work, gemman. An thanks fer evrathin." He walked slowly back to the shed, occasionally shaking his head.

The slight increase in tourist traffic over the Labor Day weekend was barely noticed in the bustle of impending departures. Ten of the gas jockeys were scheduled to leave within four days; by the end of the week, Lou, Owl and Woo would be running the station. Most of the Ham's girls and pillow punchers were due to depart that weekend. The Park was shedding them like dead leaves.

At midday on the first of September a white '39 Ford coupe pulled up to the pumps and Cleve emerged, grinning broadly, his arms outspread. Crammed in with him and the luggage were Polly and - to Mason's discomfiture - Liz. All three stood talking in the lanes while the White Fright was refueled and checked over. Cleve was optimistic about reaching the Carolinas; he had had the "Bozeman Beauty" out for several spins and she had performed flawlessly. No, he didn't think he would need a spare fan belt or a new tire - the last twitch of Thumb's dying sales drive. The old incentive had just drained away.

"How's Mary?" asked Peter. "We keep hearin' about this Mary."

"Ah, and well you might!" beamed Cleve. "A prassless girl, gentlemen, prassless." He gestured expansively. "But I can't take her home, you see - not yet, anyway! We'll keep in touch, though, you can bet on that."

Polly and Gair stood some way off, holding hands, saying little, obviously fighting for control. In another lane, Mason and Liz enacted their own *agon*. Twisting a jet-black curl around her forefinger and sometimes saying "Uh-huh" or laughing demurely at nothing, Liz marveled that he could be so gauche and tongue-tied; Mason felt her resentment like a cold blast from a freezer and wondered what she expected of him now. All he could say was that he would call her back at Debrew and they would talk - about what, he didn't know. It was an awkward interval.

173

At last Cleve held up his arms - the "Eisenhower wave" - and summoned his passengers aboard. "Men, we'll see you back at the hallowed halls. Mason, Cal will be calling you about a ride east."

"He already has, Cleve. We're all set."

"Great, don't spare the horses! We need him in Charleston for a big weddin' the night of the 6th. I'm the best man! Pete, wish us luck. Gair, nice knowin' you. Lou, a real pleasure. 'Board!"

Polly kissed Gair on the cheek and jumped into the car with a wave to Mason. He and Liz said a brief, tense farewell. Both girls were weeping as the White Fright pulled out and honked away toward the south entrance.

"Awrat, les get back tuh work," said Lou heavily. "Mason, clean up the grease rack. Henduhson, sweep the shed. Gair...take five. Come back when yuh feel bedduh."

But Gair did not get better, at least not before he left. All efforts either to comfort him or to get him to open up failed; he remained bleary-eyed and uncommunicative the next day - his last. Creeper kindly offered to drive him to Gardiner for his train, as he and Gail had the day off. Gair went around shaking hands solemnly with every boy and girl, man and woman he had met at Thumb, saying, "Goodbye. Nice to have known you," with a sad smile.

"I'll miss you and your accordion," Mason told him. "Of course I'll miss a lot of what's leaving every day now."

"Yes," replied Gair. He waved languidly from the passenger side as Creeper turned his car northward.

"Takin' it purty hard," observed Woo. "Must be in love." Other savages nodded. There was consensus on that.

The departures had begun to thin out the mealtime crowds in the cafeteria: an attrition too visible to ignore. At lunch and dinner there was an air of almost wartime sombreness about the empty seats and missing faces, one of which was Florida Lady's. Mason found an opportunity to ask Gray discreetly where she was.

"Oh, she left yesterday," said the house father. "Didn't she...ah." His face registered a recollection. "Actually, she asked me to tell you goodbye, which was nice: she didn't ask me to say goodbye to anyone else!"

"Maybe she said goodbye to the others herself."

"Mebbe. Anyway, she thought of you before she left."

"That's good. Where does she live, Gray?"

"Oh, around Orlando, I think. Or mebbe Jacksonville? I just see her up here." He peered at Mason more closely. "Why, ya wanna send her a Christmas card?"

"Yes, she should definitely be on my Christmas list."

"The Ham's people must have her address. Don't know if they'd give it out, though."

Will Harkness had changed his plans: instead of returning to California for a few days before flying off to college, he decided to accept Mason's offer of a lift straight to Princeton. It made sense, he wrote his parents: it would be cheap and direct, with good company. They could just ship his trunk to Princeton: it was nearly packed. His parents disagreed, occasioning a rare and (by Harkness standards) rather stormy phone call, but Will stood his ground, and in the end his elders gave way. "The financial argument got to my dad," Will told Mason, "and that was that."

On the eve of their departure, Mason and Will walked over to the ranger cabin to take leave of Dan. "Running off, are you?" he chuckled.

"You don't seem particularly upset by our departure," laughed Will.

"That's because I think you've seen the light! I don't worry about someone once they've got natural religion."

"Thanks to you," said Mason.

Dan smiled but shook his head. "Will here is completely hooked: a convert. And maybe you…I'm not sure."

Will looked delighted. "So you think I'll be back?"

Dan shrugged. "I didn't say *that*. Don't know where you'll go or what you'll do. But that's between you and yourself: you're hooked anyway."

The next morning Mason was packing when Henderson came by, incongruously resplendent in his travel outfit: blue-jean suit and regimental-stripe tie. There wasn't much to say, but they agreed to look for one another at Debrew and walked outside together. Henderson was hitching a ride to Gardiner aboard the gasoline tanker, a violation of Comico policy and thus an irresistible temptation to Bud, the surly Canuck driver, who could never pass up a chance to "f**k the company." He was waiting with one foot on the running board, chewing tobacco, his sour face topped by the blue wool cap he had worn all summer. "Lesgo," he said.

"Guess I'll say goodbye, Bud. I'm leaving today too." Mason extended his hand.

Bud touched it briefly. "Gonna try an make it in that Dee-troit bathtub?" He nodded toward the blue wagon and spat brown juice in the mud.

"Sure, why not?" Mason flared. "It got me out here."

"Luck," said Bud, without specifying any particular kind. He swung aboard and slammed the door. "Lesgo, grit."

"Au 'voir, Bud!" called Bastille from the next lane, and the driver raised a clenched-fist salute out the window. Henderson rasped his last farewells to the crew and hauled himself up into the cab, settling the duffel bag on his narrow lap. The truck went growling away toward the pass.

Then Creeper pulled his immaculate Ford into the lanes to fill up for the trip east. Savages who had not exchanged ten sentences with him the whole summer came forward to wish him well, but they could not get his attention. Gail was with him; they hugged and kissed while the gas flowed and assorted Green Hornets said goodbye at the windows. At last Gail jumped out and ran back to her dormitory, weeping uncontrollably. Creeper paid up, said "So long, fellows," and drove slowly away to the north, watching the manifold pressure gauge.

"How little we know of our fellow men, some of them," remarked Will. "But I suppose you would know him better," he said deferentially to Schlitz, "being his roommate."

"Not really."

A few minutes later, an old convertible with California plates drove in, top down to receive the benison of a sunny hour. In the passenger seat sat a languid blonde; the driver was an olive-skinned girl with dark hair and bright brown eyes. The contrast with her white blouse was stunning. "Hey, *chico*," she called in a low, rather sultry voice.

"*Hola*, Paquita," said Trueblood, clearly pleased with the greeting. "Hey Paul, your girl's here."

"*His girl*, I like that!" she laughed. "Is he *my boy*?"

"I could go for that." Bastille surveyed the car's contents, shaking his head as if to clear it from a blow. "You look great, *chica*. Sure wish I were coming along."

"Why not?" She cocked her head up at him. "You can write stories in L.A. What's stopping you?"

Bastille froze. After a long moment he said, "Nothing." Then, "Packy," and leaning down he kissed her. She kissed him back. Some whistles and hoots from the less mature members of the crew. Bastille straightened up and turned to the manager. "Lou, I'd like to...end my duties now."

"Shur, Pawl, take awf. Don't eggzakly depend on yuh anyhoo," he chuckled.

"I'll just pack. Won't take five minutes." The savages cheered as Bastille peeled off his overalls, handed them to Peter and sprinted for the stockade. Paquita pulled the car off to the side, where she was surrounded by well-wishers. Within fifteen minutes Bastille returned, slung his duffel bag in the trunk and climbed into the back seat with a sheepish grin. "This is not my usual style," he announced.

"You won't be sorry," Peter predicted.

"Go get it, Canuck!" called Owl as they rolled away, waving.

"There goes probably the most interesting savage I *didn't* get to know this summer," Will remarked.

"How couldja?" asked Lou. "He waren't in, mostly."

At lunch there were more leave-takings. "Oh, what a sad day," sighed Shelley, looking more beautiful than ever in her grief. "Everyone's going away. Goodbye, Will, and good luck. Goodbye, L.B., I know you'll do well. Goodbye, Mason, and thanks for all the rides and songs." A hug from Shelley, he reflected, was the best thing that had happened to him since, well, Christmas. Jill gave each of the boys a peck on the cheek, but Pris, aloof at the last, shook hands rather formally. Mason could not blame her: his offences had been many and grave. After all the boys who had fluttered around at one time or another, she seemed to be on her own now.

Gray walked back into the dorm with Mason and helped by carrying a light bag out to the car. "Tell me," he said jovially, "is it true that you've slept with every girl at West Thumb this summer?"

Mason smiled, considered the question carefully, did some mental arithmetic and ticked off a few fingers before replying as cautiously as a trial witness, "No, not every one."

Gray nodded sympathetically. "Some of 'em belong to other guys, eh?"

"Exactly. That's what held me back." Jacky crossed the courtyard on a diagonal course and Mason waved. "See you at Debrew this fall?"

She smiled and nodded. "Bill's in law school, you know. Maybe you can come over for dinner! See you there."

"Great, it's been great." Jacky disappeared into the back of the store. "As we were saying..."

Half an hour after the early shift returned from lunch Lou dismissed Horn and Will, chortling at the speed with which they stripped off their Green Hornets for the last time. In another half-hour the three departees were ready to leave and walked over to the station to say their goodbyes. Horn, his duffel bag on his shoulder, still moved springily. "Well, gentlemen," he said, flashing his splendid teeth and gripping their hands strongly, "if you're ever down on the reservation …". In five minutes he had thumbed a ride south and was gone. Woo became sentimental and morose; he *hoped* to be back at Debrew in the fall, but there was that failure in biochem, and it could go either way. You just never knew.

"So long, Mace…stay cool, man," said Owl, affably enough. "Hey, what's the matter?"

Mason had winced at how tightly the skin was drawn over Owl's face and head. It looked like a skull. "You've lost weight, man."

"Mebbe so. The broads take it outa ya," he grinned. Then he turned to Will, and Mason to Lou. With solemn faces they pumped each others' hands.

"Well, Lou, looks like the end of the line."

"Shore is, Mace. You guys tuhday, Cyrl tuhmorra, an Mouth, then Pete an Bill."

"Thanks for everything, man. It's been real."

"A shitkicker," Lou agreed, grinning broadly. "Come awn back next yeah, will have a bawl."

"Mebbe…*maybe* I will," laughed Mason. "Lou, I'm sorry about that days-off thing," he added lamely.

Lou shrugged. "Wall, we know whar *thet* came frum!"

As Mason turned away to shake the few remaining hands, a pang sliced through his innards. Friends were melting away like snow showers when the sun came out. Abruptly he headed for the car. He was going to be lonely! Already he missed Cleve and Polly, who had made the drive out interesting, and felt nostalgia for the pastoral idyll of early June, when the summer lay all before them. Idiot, to be the plaything of these moods! When Will climbed into the car, a wave of gratitude to him washed over Mason.

The last goodbye had been said. They drove slowly past the shed, where Owl covered his ears and the others waved, then headed north along the lake. Mason sighed. "Finally made our getaway."

"Maybe," said Will. "I keep thinking about what Dan said…hooked even if we don't come back? We'll see if we get away." Then he was silent, watching the Absarokas.

Driving on, Mason was again ambushed by an empty feeling. The familiar scene was as beautiful as ever, but he was leaving and did not know when he would return. That was the problem, the darkness, and there was no escaping it. He tried telling Will a bit about the other riders. "Um," said Will. Maybe he had his own darkness just now.

When they pulled up to the cabin-dormitory at Lake Station, Cal and a tall, slender fellow whom he introduced as Perry were already outside with their bags. Mason shook hands with Perry and introduced Will. "Full circle, Cal."

"Just about." He looked rather glum. Several pretty girls were loitering about, apparently to say goodbye, and sunshine was slanting through the pines with a mellow brilliance, as on the day they left Debrew. It seemed a shame to have to leave and return to duty. For a moment they stood rooted.

Then Mason bestirred himself. "I hear that wedding in Charleston will be a blast, Cal. Cleve says I'm to get you to the church on time."

Cal brightened. "Yeah, that's right! Three days, though. Can we make it?"

"Maybe - if we hop to it and the travel gods are with us." They put the back of the car down flat, piled their mostly-soft luggage along both sides, and laid an air mattress and sleeping bag down the middle so one person could sleep or at least rest. Will crawled in there, the others sat up front, and off they went. Mason negotiated the gauntlet of well-wishing savages out to the shore road, skirted the north end of the lake and crossed the Yellowstone River at Fishing Bridge. A few fisherfolk were dangling their lines in the slow-moving waters or loitering along the roadway itself.

"Dumb dudes," they chorussed automatically.

"We can only talk like that for another half hour," Will pointed out from his bunk.

At least this stretch will be new, thought Mason. The road ran east, then south along the shoreline for a few miles before turning east into the Absarokas. Soon Yellowstone Lake disappeared behind the mountains: another friend gone. After some slow climbing they crossed Sylvan Pass, casting a long shadow ahead, and dropped steeply to the East Entrance. At the tollbooth all four turned in their employee cards to an unfamiliar ranger, who waved them through impassively, and Mason gunned the car downhill alongside a tumbling creek, beyond the lip of the mountain bowl.

"No more ranger rules," said Perry cheerfully. "Hey, look at that!" Not far ahead, a car had stopped in the right-hand lane so its occupants could feed two black bear cubs. "God, they're cute!"

179

"Shades of Yellowstone," said Mason. Dudes who didn't even pull off on the shoulder to play with the bears were one of the rangers' pet peeves - and his. But maybe the bears had been out in the road? One cub, his front paws on a window sill, was eating a sandwich from someone's hand. The other was sitting up like a baby on the side of the road, tearing at a package of crackers, but dropped it and came ambling over hopefully as the second car stopped.

"Mason? What are you doing?" asked Will plaintively.

"Our lane's blocked and there's oncoming traffic," replied the driver, which was true - but then events began to shape themselves. Perry rolled down his window and the cub stood up to sniff his fingers.

"Well, this is appropriate," sighed Will. "*We* are dudes now."

"No dudes and savages out here," Perry retorted. "We're not employees any more. We're outa the park, and the rangers aren't the law."

"Hey, Mason," exclaimed Cal, grinning. "This cub's as tame as a puppy. Do you suppose...?"

"Uh, Liz tried that once and it didn't work so well," said Mason, remembering the only time he had ever yelled at her. "Isn't your buffalo skull enough of a souvenir?"

"C'mon, if he doesn't like it we'll let him out. Open your door, Will. We don't have room up here."

"This is crazy," said Will, but to Mason's astonishment he complied. The cub put his front paws on the door sill, sniffed at a duffel bag and began to lick Will's fingers. "God, it *is* cute," he said. "I wonder..."

Mason finally woke up. "This is *crazy!*" he snapped. "We're going ..."

"ON YOUR LEFT!" yelled Cal. Mason whipped around and found himself looking into the eyes of a large black bear two feet away, behind the window. Her breath was steaming the glass, her lolling pink tongue dripped saliva, and she was trying to work her left front paw in through the no-draft vent. Mason hit the accelerator and pulled the wheel to the left. They shot forward around the other car, the paw slipped from the window, there was a scrambling sound from the back, and Will's door slammed shut.

Cal turned around to peer in back. "Did we get the cub?"

"No, thank God." Will sat up, facing backwards. "I just hope he's okay. Yes, there he goes, into the long grass. But Christ, look at mama bear!" The mother was coming after them at a shambling gallop and had not yet fallen far behind. "Men, that was a pretty dumb play," said Will emphatically. "We were suckered but good, and it serves us right. I'm just glad Dan's not here."

"Who's Dan?" asked Perry and Cal.

"A ranger. God, we must be *nuts!*"

No one answered. When Mason glanced in the rear-view mirror before the first curve hid her from view, the mother bear had slowed to an amble. She would not go far from the cubs. Imagining Dan shaking his head, poised between laughter and tears, Mason felt sick to his stomach. *Where there are cubs there is a mother!* Why hadn't he or any of them thought of that? And even if she hadn't been there, why mess with the cubs? Had they learned *anything* that summer? Were they really, or again, just dudes after all? He pounded the steering wheel and dared not speak.

They all observed several minutes of silence.

Ten: Home from the Hill

As they descended the eastern slopes of the Absarokas, the high peaks behind them blocked the setting sun and night fell swiftly: it was dark before they reached Cody. Midway along the Las Vegas-style strip, garish with neon cowboys and stallions that galloped jerkily, they ate cheap hamburgers, then refueled (drawing on "the gas kitty": $5 each, renewable) and changed places. Already Yellowstone Park seemed very distant, an unlikely vision. Cal drove on through Greybull and over the Bighorns to Sheridan - a rugged 135 miles, with a high pass - while Mason rested in back. At first the air felt strangely thick and close, almost balmy, although Cody sat at about five thousand feet. He tossed and dozed fitfully, dreaming a weird melange of Julia and Dan and Hole's fall, Liz crying in the Tetons, the taut drum of Owl's head. Somewhere in the mountains he awoke on a sharp curve and looked around feverishly. Before him glowed a horned skull, its jaw thrust forward in a hideous grimace, its gaze blank and pitiless. He stifled a cry as he recognized Cal's buffalo head, ashen in the moonlight and rocking slightly with the car's motion. He covered it with a sweater, then sat up and watched the twisting descent into Sheridan.

It was midnight and most gas stations had closed, but they found an all-night Comico where they filled up (feeling unexpectedly clan-loyal) and drank vending machine coffee while they looked at the map. Over half of Wyoming and most of the big mountains lay behind them; ahead, the empty plains rolled eastward at about four thousand feet. The hundred-odd miles to Gillette were a good stretch for Will, a fast, casual driver who cruised at 75 mph along a nearly deserted road through open rangeland. Occasionally a jackrabbit would start from the side of the highway, which was smeared with blood and fur; Will hit one rather than swerve or slow down. On a long straightaway they saw headlights in the distance and clocked eight miles before a pickup materialized and shot by in a flash of light.

"If we assume equal speeds, he was 16 miles away when we first saw him, and our closing speed was 150 miles an hour," announced the Physics major from the back.

"You know, that always bothered me in physics courses," Mason reflected. "The neat assumptions that enable you to solve what are really quite complex problems."

"Those are introductory courses," Cal retorted.

Fortunately the overloaded Ford loped along like a wolfhound with a scent through the smallest hours.

Then the lights began, starting as a greenish glow in the northeastern sky, mistakable for a reflection of their illuminated panel instruments. Not until the flickering began did they realize that it was the *aurora borealis*. A scintillating curtain of green and gold soon spread along the entire northern horizon. They woke Cal, who agreed that the spectacle was worth watching, and explained it in terms of solar storms and electromagnetic activity.

"Yeah, but give him the Shakespearean quotation, Will," said Mason. "The one you used coming back from Jackson."

The driver thought a moment. "Ah, you mean 'Let no men say / "These are their reasons; they are natural", / For I believe they are portentous things / Unto the climate that they point upon.' However, I'm bound to point out that that is specifically about comets, not about northern lights."

Miles slid by as they tried to name the colors, or silently drank in the shifting display. Will dimmed the panel lights, and when the sky was brightest would slow a bit and switch off the headlights for a few seconds; then the car seemed to float through blackness before a cosmic tapestry in a simulacrum of space flight. Mason shivered, thinking how lucky they were. The romance of the road! He had forgotten how it felt to be on a trip, *going* somewhere. Great things could happen. Except for the scent of sage this was more like being an aeronaut of some kind, one of St. Exupéry's aviators, than an earthbound traveler.

By degrees the vision faded and the terrestrial world resumed. Their odyssey depended on gasoline, so when they saw a 24-hour truck stop between Gillette and Moorcroft Will turned in to refuel, and they went into the café. At first the neon glare and truckers' stares made them self-conscious, but once the coffee arrived they forgot that they were tired and out of place, and began to laugh and gabble, high on the drive and the hour and the caffeine and the northern lights. Will took a nip from his pocket flask. Perry watched impassively and Cal raised an eyebrow.

"I'm next," said Perry.

"Sure!" Will proffered the flask.

"I meant driving."

So Perry drove the last of Wyoming and through a corner of the Black Hills, obscure silhouettes against a lightening sky, in the pre-dawn hours. When Mason took over to begin the second cycle the road was rising and falling with the long swells of the Dakota wheat plains - the last time they would feel the Rockies - and he was squinting into a clear sunrise.

"Gonna be bitchin' hot," Cal predicted.

"And the car stinks of gas," Will complained. "Let's jettison that spare can."

"I'll pour it in at the next stop," said Mason drearily. Having mistaken the smell for engine exhaust, he had been expecting to die of asphyxiation, which would at least put an end to this infernal trip. "Half in love with easeful death": was that Keats? His mouth seemed to be growing some exotic culture, the valves were pinging nastily - fit retribution for his demented attempt to adjust them without a gauge at Thumb - and all the exhilaration of the night had dissipated. This was *Men without Women*, as Hemingway called a group of his stories, and made the drive out with Cleve and Polly seem a highly civilized affair

They ate breakfast listlessly in some greasy spoon - no one even knew where - and pushed on east, eyes screwed achingly against the sun. Miles of two-lane, patched-up concrete pavement shimmering with heat bumped along undertread, driving turns came to seem too long and were shortened to an hour, while time in back was already too brief. Somehow they crossed Nebraska and entered Iowa, paying them no mind, pressing hard. The radio was stupid and boring; Cal and Perry were silent and boring; and, Mason felt, it was stupid to be traveling like this, boring through the country as if through a tunnel.

But Will was neither stupid nor boring nor silent. He had been tippling from his flask (his resignation from the driving pool had been accepted without regret), and although he could be articulate anytime, liquor did seem to rev him up. He grew loquacious about life, art, nature, their summer in Yellowstone, and tried to get the others to discuss those topics, or even the passing countryside, which was growing flatter and tamer, with farms and fences. "This is insane!" he exclaimed from the back. "We're privileged people, the cream of the richest middle class in the world, this trip should be a wondrous thing, and all we do is drive ourselves into the ground! We're moles, not humans!"

Cal and Perry sat silent but looked annoyed; Mason felt both sympathetic to Will and embarrassed by him. Finally, in an effort to turn the monologue into at least a dialogue, he said, "You know, I do have trouble taking this kind of countryside on its own terms. I keep comparing it to the park, to the standards of *western* landscape." Cal and Perry looked at him, then away. "I mean, as if we were still there," he added lamely, and lapsed.

Will cleared his throat. "Well, Yellowstone is a state of mind. You take it with you, like a touchstone. Other landscapes with less power, less - I don't know, grandeur? - won't satisfy you once you've known it." Cal and Perry turned to look at him, and Will craned around to see their expressions. "You know what I mean?" They looked at each other, shook their heads, and turned back to the road, chuckling. Evidently they did *not* know, were either baffled, or writing it off as drunken gabble, or both.

A bit annoyed himself now, and challenged, Will began to cross-examine them. Had they enjoyed Yellowstone? Sure, it had been a great summer. What about Lake Station? A nice place. The people? Some neat girls and crazy characters. The mountains? Fine. But that seemed to be it, despite the Mt. Washburn expedition that had produced Cal's buffalo skull. The Yellowstone that Dan and the Old Timer felt and taught, with its mystique of "the west," had not been imprinted on them. Was it Dan who made the difference? Or Hole and a death on Teewinot? Anyway, Mason thought, Will did achieve a result, revealing something about where they all stood. But he was glad when Will desisted with a puzzled "Hmm." In the long silence that followed, he tried the radio again. They needed *something*.

Towards evening on the 4th of September, twenty-seven hours after leaving Lake, Perry drove them with his usual excruciating, not-a-mile-over-the-limit caution into his home town of Davenport, Iowa, which had been twinkling at them through the prairie twilight for half an hour. He apologized for not being able to offer them a home-cooked meal, but things weren't so good at home, so they had a steak dinner at his favorite restaurant while the Ford enjoyed a professional lube and oil change at a nearby Sunoco station. Mason called attention to the special quality of the light, the way street lamps and commercial signs glowed warmly in the soft dusk, while high above, the sky was not yet dark. "Probably it's the last sunlight passing through all that agricultural dust," said Cal. The mood was mellow: they seemed to have come a great way and spent a long time together; surely the differences between them were unimportant in the continental perspective they were acquiring.

Afterwards they dropped Perry at his mom's bungalow, and for the first time everyone could sit up front. Will proclaimed Perry "a good man" who might have had only "a small role in the great drama of the summer" but had played it well, which was received in silence. The car rattled across the Mississippi River bridge into Rock Island, Illinois. "Well, that's it: we're in the east now." Will sighed. "Looks dull. Aren't you guys tired?"

They agreed that they were, too tired to drive, and started searching for a place to bed down as soon as Route 6 hit open country. There were no campgrounds, but after miles of low-speed hunting, Mason pulled off and down onto a dirt turnout beside a dike or levee, and cut the engine. Crickets chirped loudly in the sudden stillness; dark masses of foliage overhung and encircled the car. It was a good place: they were in luck. Cal and Will crawled in the back, now more spacious, while Mason fell insensate across the front seat.

*

Tap. Tap tap. Mason opened his eyes to grey light. Will was waggling his fingers at the driver's window; in the back Cal stirred and moaned. A muggy, overcast morn, heavy with green fecundity. He sat up and rolled the glass down.

"Good morning. Don't you think we should be getting underway?" Will was freshly attired and had washed his face somewhere. His manner was almost brisk.

Anger welled up in Mason: to be *tidy* at this of all times! It must be early, not much past dawn. "Aren't you hung over?" he snarled as viciously as he could manage.

"Not at all," replied Will suavely. "That's all past. I'm ready to help with the driving now."

"He must think we'll be in Princeton today," groaned Cal.

"Then he's dreaming. But Jesus, if you think you can drive, be my guest." Giving him the keys, Mason got in the back with Cal and fell asleep again as soon as the car established a regular ta-pocketa-pocketa rhythm on the segmented concrete.

Tap…tap TAP tap. Mason struggled up from the fibrous embrace of his dreams and the sleeping bag, shielding his eyes against bright sunlight. The others were smirking at him through the tailgate window. He grabbed his Brownie Hawkeye and snapped them - the only known photograph of their mad cross-country dash - then pressed the hatch release with his toe so that the tailgate swung up in their faces. They jumped back. "Where are we?" he croaked.

"Gas station, Route 6, central Illinois," replied Cal crisply.

"The place names don't help much," said Will, surveying the cornfields. "All of this country seems to be the same. East Cob, West Cob. Amid the Illini corn." He smiled, obviously pleased with himself.

Mason propped himself on his elbows. "The breadbasket of America. I'm hungry."

"There should be food down there." Cal nodded east, toward where a water tank and a grain silo rose above shade trees a mile or so ahead. "In Seneca."

"Now, *there* is a place name that can tell us something!" Will observed.

A few minutes later they were ordering big breakfasts in The Transcontinental Diner while a technicolor Wurlitzer beside the counter played "Heartbreak Hotel." Mason, scanning the listings on the selector in their booth, discovered that country and western had not yet reached corn country. Cal bought a Chicago *Tribune* from the rack by the door and announced that it was September 5th.

"The fifth." Will considered. "Cyril and Mouth will be on the road by now. Gair should be home...Creeper too, I'd guess, even at 50."

"Peter and Virg and Marsh'll be leaving soon," Mason added. "And Cleve should get home today, if the White Fright held out."

"Uh oh." Cal was frowning at his paper. "There's trouble in Little Rock."

"I thought there would be, after Strom Thurmond shot his filibustering mouth off," said Mason carelessly, forgetting that the senator's home state was Cal's as well. The representative of South Carolina informed the gentleman from Massachusetts that the origin of the trouble was Congress abrogating states' rights. The two then had a short, unpleasant argument about segregation that surprised both because it was without precedent between them. Of course it *would* happen "out here," thought Mason: at Debrew it wouldn't even have come up.

"Well, well, I see we have division on this point," observed the representative of California. "But what, pray tell, is the issue, if it can be stated?"

The gentleman from South Carolina informed him that some Negro students in Little Rock wanted to attend Central High School, that Gov. Faubus and many white Arkansans were opposed to that, but that Pres. Eisenhower said they must be allowed to attend and was prepared to call out federal troops - an account to which the representative of Massachusetts stipulated, effectively ending the argument.

The diversionary tactic of the gentleman from California was ably seconded by the arrival of their breakfasts, a welcome development. The food looked and smelled good, but Mason and Will exchanged a look and shook their heads when they saw the plates. After the waitress left, Mason said, "No hash browns."

"What the hell!" laughed Cal, digging into his omlet. "Can't you guys leave the west behind?"

"Now *that*," replied Will, pointing his fork at Cal, "is a good question. Glad you asked."

"Course you *are* a westerner of sorts," Cal conceded, obviously trying to head off a lecture. "But Mason here...he's just an easterner like me."

Will and Mason both hesitated for a moment, considering whether to enter these lists, but decided to eat instead. To win an argument and then find that your eggs are cold is a hollow victory. So they tackled their hot food, chewing also on the news in the sports pages that somebody named Ibbotson had run a mile in 3:57, a new record, and on the need to replenish the gas kitty before the next fill-up.

All day they plowed east along 6 and 30, through the small towns and sometimes (unwillingly) the larger ones of the cornbelt and the industrial Midwest. Lunch was eaten at an A & W outside Ft. Wayne, dinner at a Toddle House close enough to Akron for the fumes of a tire factory to be mingled with the aroma of their minute steaks. The romance had gone out of their journey, lamented Will. No shit, said the others. In the heat of the afternoon they passed the time by arguing. Will tried to convince Mason that poetry was superior to prose, and Cal that the arts were a higher form of knowledge than the sciences. The topic of segregation came up again once, but was quickly dropped by all participants as the hot potato it was.

Instead they scanned maps and debated a question closer to home: where Cal should break off for South Carolina. Pittsburgh would be closest to Charleston, but they were not sanguine about the rail connections between them. New York would have better connections, but was farther northeast than Cal needed to go. On the whole, Philadelphia looked like his best option. After dinner they tackled the Pennsylvania Turnpike, glad to have three drivers, and drove more than half of it that night. Somewhere in the Alleghenies they pulled off at a roadside rest and made up the car for three to sleep. "*Now* we should be oblivious; *now* it's a nightmare," grumbled Will as he tried to get comfortable.

At first light on the 6th they were up and off again, barreling east at over a mile a minute, feeling the pull of the Great Eastern Megalopolis. They stared straight ahead or read the map, sat silent or communicated tersely about where to turn. As the traffic increased and progress slowed, their pulse rates increased. "What a way to live!" exclaimed Will. They managed to inquire their way to the main railway terminal, though, and it was still early when Mason stopped in one of the unloading areas. The sun glowed through a shroud of haze or fog or mist.

"It looks like Dickens's London," said Will suspiciously. "Is this smog?"

"It smells bad enough," said Mason evasively. "Well, Cal, do you have everything?"

"Think so: two arms' worth, anyhow."

"Do you think you'll make the wedding?"

Cal shrugged. "Maybe not - but I'll make the parties! Anyway, we gave it our best shot. Thanks for the ride. See you in a week or so." They shook hands briefly, and then he turned to Will. "Good meeting you, Will. You certainly made the drive more interesting! Good luck at Princeton."

"Thanks, Cal, I enjoyed talking to you. And I hope you find a train going your way soon."

"Better go see, I guess. So long, men." He swung the duffel bag onto his left shoulder, tucked the buffalo skull under his right arm like a football, and joined the crowd heading into the station. When he was 50 yards away and on the steps, Mason called out, "That was a helluva good shot, Cal!" It turned some heads, and Cal waved the skull on high without looking back.

Will navigated, or at least held the map and talked, as Mason picked his way through traffic to the nearest bridge over the Delaware, trundled across into New Jersey and started following signs to the Turnpike. "Should be about an hour from here," he estimated. "I don't know what happens after we turn off to Princeton, though. That looks like a fair stretch on secondary roads."

"Hmm, yeah, we'll see," mused Will, with the air of a man whose mind is elsewhere. "That was interesting - with Cal, I mean. Especially when you argued about segregation. I've met people like you before, but not like him. I guess he's considered pretty bright in his field?"

"Oh, absolutely. First-rate in math and physics, they say, and I believe it. Headed for graduate work."

"Okay, a promising scientist, but maybe a bit narrow? His social views seem very much of his time and place."

"Yes, you might say that," replied Mason drily. "It surprised me, frankly. States' rights!"

"You've never talked to him about this before?"

"No, this is not a topic that you discuss at Debrew."

"How could it *not* be, in times like these?! Jackie Robinson, Rosa Parks, civil rights marches..."

"Hard to say, Will. Debrew is a southern school, after all, a segregationist consensus is assumed, and it's just too divisive." Mason maneuvered into the right-hand lane for their turnoff. "There are private bull sessions in dormitory rooms, of course. With good friends."

"What do the Negro students say, though? How do *they* handle that silence?"

Mason glanced over at him to make sure he was serious. "There are no colored students at Debrew, Will."

The Californian turned to look at him, eyebrows raised, wondering if *he* was serious. "I did not know that," he said finally. "It never even occurred to me."

"I've heard that our Divinity School is considering whether to integrate," said Mason, thinking how pathetic that sounded. Then they were quiet for some time.

Curving onto the turnpike, they boomed along northeast for half an hour, took the Princeton turnoff and motored northwest more sedately for thirty minutes more, delighting to pass through Grovers Mills, where the Martians land in American versions of *The War of the Worlds*. Will advanced the hypothesis that the Martians were trying to get into Princeton, but were unfamiliar with our admission procedures. It was the middle of a hot, humid morning when the first university towers rose above the shade trees. "The Debrew of the north, in all its ivied glory," crooned Mason. "Where to now?"

"Nassau Hall, of course. But don't ask me where that is."

They parked where the town abutted on the campus; then, glad to walk, followed signs for information, room assignments, and post-office boxes. Mason enjoyed playing the role of Will's elder brother, who'd done this sort of thing before. Reparking as close to Will's dormitory as possible, they carried his few belongings upstairs. The single window of his somber garret really did look out through ivy to the campus and, farther off, a slice of the town.

"My compliments on your prospect and plantation," said Mason. "Fine old trees. Elms, I believe."

190

"Yes, thank you," replied Will graciously. "But really, you know, my reeve sees to all…" He broke off abruptly and looked around. "God, it's oppressive!"

"The room? The atmosphere?"

"The air, the climate, the antiquity. I feel weighed down… as if I were carrying a backpack."

Mason examined the dark old wood of the wainscot. "I suppose this room *could* get you down in winter."

"It'll be livelier when everybody arrives, I guess."

Mason tried to rouse himself, them, the mood. "Hey, let's drive to the railroad station. Your trunk may be here by now." It crossed his mind that he might be hanging on to the last vestige of West Thumb.

Will shook his head, laughing. "No, you've done enough! Go home!" They walked out to the car together. "All right," he said, "this is it. Time to cut loose, go our separate ways."

"Agreed. And after all, what's to be said now?"

"Right: the summer was what it was. And we shared it."

"You made it more interesting. And your valediction will remain a part of it - in my memory, at least."

"Oh, God. You may remember more of it than I do."

"Let's keep in touch. Who knows?"

"I'll drink to that." Will grinned and put out his hand.

And then there was one. Before leaving Princeton, Mason filled up, using the last two dollars in the kitty plus two of his own. Hoping that he hadn't drawn New Jersey's answer to Owl Brain, he asked the attendant for the fastest, easiest way to the George Washington Bridge. Should he go back to the Turnpike on 571, as he had come in?

"Na, I wooden, 's outta ya way," said the skinny youth. "I'd take One Nath till it hits Gaden State: slowah, but ya get moa sehvices. Coahse ya can't get roun the city," he warned. "Ya got Nurk." His twang was as colorful as any heard at West Thumb, but more familiar - though with his dark Mediterranean complexion, he might have some exotic roots himself.

Mason traced the route on his map and nodded: this would be more direct, though there was indeed no way to bypass Newark. "Thanks, man."

He paid up, backtracked a couple of miles and joined the traffic on #1, most of it streaming northeast into the thickly-huddled, overlapping cities. This was the historic Boston Post Road, but neither history nor the plenitude of services could disguise or redeem what it had become. This had never been his favorite part of America, and, fresh from the mountain west, braving the megalopolis for the first time in six months, he was hit by a wave of revulsion against the honking masses of cars and trucks surging from green to red, the hurrying crowds, the smells and aerial pollution, the crush of tall buildings on the eastern skyline exuding their powerful sense of concentrated capital. And he was trapped in it all, deprived of choices, forced to endure. Mason felt like an alien, a stranger in a familiar land.

Bone-tired and hungry, he still had a strong aversion to stopping here: he must purge this urban excess somehow. The Garden State Parkway allowed him to make better progress, but he still had to negotiate Newark's sprawl and get over to the Hudson. Only time and perseverance would do. Finding decent stuff on the radio - news, music, a baseball game - helped: something New York did well. He left the Garden State, following signs to the George Washington Bridge, and eventually its towers appeared ahead. Paying the toll, he crossed the Hudson into New York and embarked on its 1930s network of parkways, laughing to find himself bouncing over the bumpiest pavement of the trip on the Cross Bronx Expressway.

Knowing there would be no diners on such a road, he cut over to the Post Road again, found the Palermo Delicatessen in a dingy immigrant section of the upper Bronx and purchased a big *prosciutto* sandwich and a beer. That took care of his hunger, but left him feeling more displaced than ever as he reached the Hutchinson River Parkway and exchanged the urban area for its bedrooms. So there he was, cruising up a verdant boulevard through some of the richest counties in America - heading home to one of them, in fact - greedily munching his Sicilian sandwich, with all this western supercargo bouncing around inside him and no place to store it. Gradually Mason realized that he must be in a kind of shock. "Compound cultural fracture," he pronounced with his mouth full of ham.

The commuting suburbs fell behind and the highway flowed prettily enough over low wooded hills. Milford, Wallingford, Hartford. Yes, it was clear what had happened here: early settlers had founded villages at the fords of streams and rivers, naming them as in England; later some of the villages became mill towns. Historical Geography 101. Now and then he would top a rise and glimpse a million deciduous trees and a steeple, then drop down among them again, feeling slightly smothered, as Will had at Princeton. The humid air, palpable and oppressive, made him conscious of breathing. Claustrophobia must begin like this! He had never liked humidity, but this was worse than before. It was the fault of the west, of course, whose pure, arid medium had spoiled his lungs for Atlantic seaboard air.

But was it only the air? Certainly he was missing the rarefied, translucent mountain atmosphere, but also something else more subtle... perhaps the sense of separation in landscape, of here- and thereness, to which he had unconsciously become accustomed. He wanted *breathing space* with equal stress on both words; wanted to breathe space, to see that places were discrete, not all connected and continuous. New England: maybe that was his trouble. These treed and gentle hills, rolling to a near horizon, gave his untutored eye no clues to their real age, but they were old in terms of human habitation, and the weight of history pressed on them. The place names clung to anything-but-merry old England: New York, New Jersey, Maryland, Virginia, Carolina, Georgia - those awful Georges! Certain doors were closed, certain possibilities excluded, by all that had gone before. In the west the European veneer was thin, the earth bare, and he had a sense that great things could happen. Yet terrible things had happened there too - upheavals, genocide - so was his reaction logical or paradoxical? He could not make it out, lacked the tools. But Europe did not have a counterpart of the West: he was sure of that. Maybe this was what Will meant when he spoke about Judge Evans and Hemingway and "real American writers" gravitating west.

What his father might say of this reverie suddenly popped into his head: "Too introspective by far, Mason." He laughed, but it sounded forced. All summer, out there, he had not thought of how his father would react to anything he said or did or imagined. But with Boston just over the horizon, of course.... "You really don't want to go home, do you?" he asked the unshaven face in the rear-view mirror.

The stimulus of finding his way through unfamiliar territory had passed, and fatigue was setting in more strongly. A few thoughts glowed through his mental haze. One: shower, shave and sleep. Two: get somebody to adjust those pinging valves (the mechanic would shake his head: "Jeez, whoever set these really screwed 'em down tight. It's a wonder you made it," while Mason stood by, the picture of wronged innocence, and raged, "I *told* him not to set 'em unless he knew what he was doing!"). Three: come up with some snappy answers to the inevitable questions: How was your summer? What's Yellowstone like? Whadja find to do out there? Maybe the Coasters could help him with that one: "I bin searchin' ev'ry whi-i-ich a-way, yay, yay."

Thus did he put in the requisite number of hours, detached from his surroundings and only half-believing in the reality of Sturbridge, Worcester and Wellesley Hills, until his parkway fed into the circumferential skirting Boston. "Newton Highlands" made him laugh again. All right, it was snobbish, but - highlands in Massachusetts? If the west was raw and untamed, then the east was well-cooked and thoroughly domesticated. Mason turned off into his suburb and followed familiar streets to the Dixon house. The neighborhood had the eerie emptiness of suburban bedrooms in the daytime: fathers were in the city until 6 o'clock or so, mothers were doing errands or socializing, and the kids - by the time their parents could afford to live here - were off working at summer jobs.

His home looked deserted but expectant, with organdy curtains stirring at open second-floor windows. Obviously security was not a problem here! Seen after a six-month absence and a wide displacement, the house struck him as quintessentially New England: white frame, two-story, gables. Hawthorne could have lived there. Mason parked in the *porte-cochère* and let himself in the front door, using the key under the doormat. Was there a thief in the world who didn't know that "the key is under the mat"? Wiping his shoes on it, he proceeded into the carpeted quiet of the entrance hall. "Anybody home?" he called - though the absence of cars told him that no one was. He carried his duffel bag and guitar upstairs over more carpet. His room was as neat as a museum exhibit. Well, a deserted house was useful, a relief, really. Depositing his baggage, he took his razor into the bathroom. Shower and shave!

When he emerged, his was still the only car in the driveway. He put on clean clothes from the dresser and closet, lay down on the bed and closed his eyes. Let fatigue be unconfined! So, what had the summer amounted to? He'd driven a long way, pumped a lot of gas, made a few friends, lost one girl and missed several others, developed some attitudes that might make life around Boston more difficult, and put off clerking at Copley, Dixon & Sons, Attorneys-at-Law, for at least a year. Had encountered other ways of life, and some splendid country...don't forget that. He could see it on the screen of his eyelids: he was trying to drive his car up an insanely steep mountainside where someone was climbing, someone was falling. Dan, seated on a motionless horse but always alongside, watched him silently. Horn was insisting that he would need new tires now for sure. Behind him there was laughing, or maybe crying, but he could not turn his head to see who it was. A bear - or someone in a bear suit - emerged from a cave and Mason had to back all the way down. Of course when he stopped and turned around there was no one in the rear. But whose deep voice was booming in the background, like a speaker behind the screen, "Go northwest, young man?" God's? Or was there something about Aristotle?

The noise of an engine and tires crunching over gravel awakened him. The sunlight had a flatter slant. He went to the window and faced a hazy prospect of white frame houses in an ocean of hardwood trees. His mother had pulled her car into the driveway and was getting out, still in her equestrienne costume; when she caught sight of him she waved. Mason waved back. In a minute he would have to face her and say something coherent about the summer, his job, Liz - trying to keep his words from destroying or distorting any more of the fragile, irreplaceable materials he was carrying than necessary. When his father came home the questions would be about his plans for the future, his courses, his next job. The brief interval was his. Mason went into the bathroom and splashed cold water on his face before going down to meet his mother.

*

Mason's arrival on a Friday afternoon gave him a respite from business, at least. He slept in on Saturday morning, and by the time he came downstairs both parents had gone out to recreational appointments. He spent the weekend catching up on sleep and friends, which gave him a chance to try out various answers to very nearly the questions he had anticipated. For the most part his friends' reactions to what they thought of as his western *shtik* were puzzled or dismissive, although a couple of them who had actually been out west nodded as if they understood. The only tense times were with his parents. His father clearly considered that he had wasted his summer and wanted to know when he was going to settle down and "apply himself" to serious work. What seemed to rankle him most was Mason's having declared a Psychology major. "*You* don't need *that*," he warned. His mother responded to the news of his break-up with Liz by reviewing triumphantly all her misgivings about "that girl." Both were unhappy with his spotty academic performance over the last year.

It was with some relief, then, that Mason drove off early Monday morning to the nearest Ford dealer to have his faithful station wagon serviced and its long-suffering valves adjusted. By the time he made his way home by bus and on foot the house was empty and the mail had come. There were two items for him: a postcard from South Carolina and a letter from Yellowstone. He took them upstairs and flopped on his bed to read. The postcard was from Cleve, announcing his safe arrival home and eulogizing the White Fright for burning only one quart of oil on the trip. Clay had just called; he and Tech had made it back to Atlanta all right, though a speeding ticket in Missouri had kept them from equaling their westbound time. Cleve was already missing his "Canyon sweetie," and Liz, in the writer's humble opinion, was still nuts about Mason. Christ! Not a word of Polly.

The letter was from Dan. Mason read it slowly, pausing frequently to reread or stare out the window.

Dear Mason,

This is a difficult letter to write, so I'll come straight to the point: Julia and I are engaged. I know that will come as a shock to you. My main concern is to assure you that it just happened, the day you left, in fact. No secrets were kept from you. We had no understanding before. I hope you will trust me on that. I was very surprised when it happened. I'm not sure if Julia was surprised. Quite a girl.

Then Julia told me that you once hinted at having feelings for her. She fears they may have been, may be, strong feelings, and blames herself for not clearing the air, but says she didn't see you again. I wish I had known about those feelings, though in retrospect they seem obvious enough. I suppose that I couldn't see around my own emotions to yours. Now I can only hope that I - we - have not hurt you. This should be a joyous occasion, and instead it is troubling my conscience.

We are in no hurry: the idea needs living with for awhile. Julia will be heading home tomorrow, and I'll be going over to meet her folks when I can get away. We're very happy, and hope you'll be able to join in that happiness. Julia is writing to Hole, and I should add a postscript to that, as she will to this. More trouble for the conscience!

Things are pretty quiet around here now. Your roommate left today, so at the station Lou and Woo just have Owl, I think. Most of the girls have left too, and tourists are becoming scarce. It is snowing, and of course it is beautiful. Why not work in Yellowstone again next summer? Think about it! Apart from other attractions, Julia and I would both love to see you.

Sincerely,
Dan

There was a postscript in another hand.

> *When I said "very good friends" I meant exactly that - no more, no less. I didn't know how else to put it (you caught me by surprise). Okay?*

> *Affectionately, Julia*

Well, well, well! The letter signaled the end of one line of inquiry, a closing of accounts. He could not say that he had lost a girl, since she had never been his to lose, but this definitely made him zero for whatever on the romantic scoreboard. Of course the letter must be answered in some fashion, and the postscript. He ought to write Hole, too: they could commiserate about being losers in the Julia sweepstakes. Neither letter would be easy, or light.

But Dan's letter could also be a beginning. "Why not work in Yellowstone again next summer?" He sounded serious. "Well, why not?" Mason asked the ceiling. What, as a pump jockey? He giggled. Perhaps as an assistant manager, then - if Lou had thought that highly of him - or perhaps in Morley's office? As a ranger, or a fire lookout?! He had some connections now, how good and how well-disposed he didn't know. Why not, indeed. His father would have a few choice words on *that*.

Mason rolled off the bed, went over to his desk and starting going through the drawers, looking for pen and paper: he had big letters to write. Or perhaps he should use his typewriter? No, that would send the wrong signals. Letters like these had better be handwritten.

Eleven: The Pool of Light

"I'll be in the study, dear. Call me for dinner?" Mason, already half inside the room, allowed himself to slump against the edge of the carved oaken door. Fatigue seemed to creep up from the green carpet and spread through his legs. The trim figure of his wife confronted him in the dark hall.

"All right, Mason. You look tired." Eve smiled with a sweet expression he had learned to distrust. "Did you work hard today? Or just the usual?" And what did *that* mean? As if he didn't know. He let a few moments pass.

"About as usual, I guess. It *seemed* hard."

"Anyway, *rest* hard," she said. "The variety will do you good."

"What does...?" But she had pivoted on one heel and was walking with rhythmic grace toward the kitchen. She walks well, he thought, watching her silhouette, momentarily clear against the bright rectangle of the open kitchen door. When it closed, he was left in blinding darkness.

"A lovely girl," he mused aloud, pulling the study door shut behind him. "Perhaps a bit sharp when she has a point to make. Resentments that never sleep...the Argus of Beacon Street." Though in her defence it had to be conceded that he wasn't exactly burning up the offices of Copley, Dixon, which was her point. Mason sighed as he turned on the green-shaded lamp on his big desk. He had been talking to himself as long as he could remember, and while he thought it harmless, his friends - well, Eve's friends - made fun of the habit, calling it a sign of ego-fixation, a symptom of a well-developed fantasy life, or some other such psycho-babble. "But then our friends are terribly clever where I'm concerned," he said. Which sounded bitter.

He set the leather briefcase he was carrying on the desk. A dull-gold *Copley, Dixon, Montagu* nameplate stood out nicely from its brown animal hide; it did not quite blaze, but silently screamed, CLASS! Sinking into the well-upholstered swivel chair behind the desk, he very briefly considered reading the Leggatt-Burns affadavits, but instead dropped the briefcase to the floor from about two feet up. The carpet gave back a loud thud, and the lampshade rattled noisily. From the kitchen came a gay "Tra la!" that sounded both reproachful and triumphant. "Go to hell," he muttered. It

198

was exasperating: he couldn't even let loose in his "private study" without being overheard!

Leaning on his desk, Mason stared a circle around the shadowy, knotty-pine room. The walls to his left and right were entirely covered with bookshelves seven rows high, and they were almost full. The facing wall contained the door, with an antique carriage light above it and an expensively-framed Winslow Homer reproduction on either side. In the corner to his left stood a stereo console: radio, phonograph and tape player. The dark-curtained bay window behind him looked out on Beacon Street and the Commons, only a few feet below. "A library and a sound studio," said Mason emphatically, "but primarily a haven." During their - well, Eve's - frequent cocktail and dinner parties, teas, open houses, and pretentious intellectual/cultural gatherings by any other name, this room always remained closed to what he called "the general public." This rankled not only Eve, who was proud of the *whole* house, but Mr. Robert E. Dixon, who, being one of Mason's bosses as well as his sire, felt entitled to sound off. "A man's home *is* his castle," he once said in his most resonant tones, "but drawbridges are out of style, sir." Who did he think he was, Dr. Johnson?

Their friends just laughed and needled him about what was in his study that they couldn't see. Discomfited, he would smile and say, "Oh, it's pretty esoteric." Once Jacques Beauxeaux told the others, "That means he washes his underwear in there": an old joke, Jacques having once defined esoteric nihilism as "washing your underwear without believing in the ultimate value of it." Jacques wasn't really French, though he wished he were. He was rather what preppies called a pseudo, a fake. Some people said he hailed from Quebec, which could be true, but Mason harbored a suspicion, or a hope, that he might prove to be from small-town America, and that one day an old friend of his from Dubuque or Decatur or Dekalb or Perth Amboy would see him on the streets of Boston and call out, "Well, as I live and breathe, if it isn't Jack Bozo." Oh, to be there that day!

A lot of our friends are like that, thought Mason. Pseudos. He felt vaguely restless, a feeling too apathetic to call for a drink or a sad piece of music. "Just a sit in my study." Leaning back in his chair, his fingers resting on the desk to steady himself, he twisted far enough to look out the foot-wide space between the maroon drapes. Beacon Street was still clogged with rush-hour traffic at a quarter to six.

"Another damn, dank, dark, damp day," he muttered slowly. Intrigued by the alliteration, he tried to continue. "Dualistic, dyhedral, dehydrated... Darwinistic...day! Oh hell," said Mason. Then, decisively, "It was that scene with father dear that did it." He stood up, leaning on the desk, fingers spread to steady himself. "Gentlemen of the jury," he began, addressing the bookshelves, "This is a clear case of justifiable - regrettable but justifiable - patricide. Robert Everhardt Dixon - had he lived - could have been charged with mental cruelty to the defendant, his son and junior associate. On the day of his death, the father stormed into the office of his son, *demanding* an explanation - no, an apology - for the latter's considered interpretation of a lawsuit. Picture, gentlemen, the difficulties inherent in a father-son *business* relationship, augmented by this sort of dictatorial and uncompromising attitude toward the younger man's work! And there is more, gentlemen..."

Much more, thought Mason, sitting down, leaning back in his chair, shutting his eyes and rather enjoying his improvisation. But I'd never kill him for it. I can't even really get mad. He's not malicious, just trying to make a good lawyer out of me. *In nomine patris, et filii*. Maybe I don't even *want* to be a good lawyer, in his sense. *Et legu sanctu*...I should never have worked for him...*Amen.*

These reflections were too depressing, and Mason opened his eyes to escape them. Humming, he opened the desk's bottom drawer and began turning over papers, shuffling aimlessly through drafts, folders, memos, newspaper clippings, pencils, tools of the trade. In a back corner he touched something thick and dusty, which he drew out. It was a small notebook bound in cheap brown leather. On its cover was a strip of peeling adhesive tape, on which *The Yellowstone Summer* was written in his neat youthful hand. "Ten years," he said softly. "Long..." He blew dust off the cover and watched the motes settle onto the green desk blotter. "Must be years since I even looked at this." Leaning forward to rest his arms on the desk, Mason carefully opened the cover. Alone in his pool of light in the dark room, he began to read.

June 7, midnight - Reached the park this PM, & I've been busy ever since. At midday we crossed Togwotee Pass, where snow-fed rivulets ran fast across the road in the sunshine. From there we caught our first glimpse of the Tetons, and stopped. Cramped inside & out from 4 days in the car, we piled out & gazed - a little panic-stricken - over 30 miles of sunny wildflower meadows to jewel lakes and snowy mountains. Bluish & stark, they thrust upward, past natural beauty, toward...? I thought, "I hope you're up to this." Meaning?! Are they symbols? Of what? Think Jung in New Mex.

Mason pushed back from the desk, laughing. "Oh God, Jacques, would you love to see that! What a hopeless romantic!" But his face darkened quickly. "Go to hell, Bozo," he snapped. Bending again over the notebook, he flipped several pages, skimming, and laughed once more before settling on folded arms again.

June 21 - Jim died yesterday in a mountain-climbing accident. He told me before he left that he was scared as hell & that Bill Mosher from Lake had talked him into it. Jim led me out here, & then left me to go die on a mountain. I love the park & the country, but I hate the mountains, & this is mountain country, so where to turn?

June 23 - We have just come back from Jim's funeral. Yesterday they got his body down off the mountain, & at sunset today he was buried. A ranger said he was found in a snowfield thousands of feet above the valley with a broken back and a large hole in his head. Mosher was also injured, but managed to climb down. Jim was my best friend; the mountains are beautiful, they are nature, but they killed Jim. There is much I don't understand. It is as if the trees were growing upside down.

Mason looked up slowly from the notebook, like a man waking from a bad dream, and shrugged his jacket off onto the chair back. He squinted through the semi-darkness of the room at the painting beside the door, where a powerfully-built black man in rags, lying on a drifting raft, rolled white eyeballs at a shark fin cutting the grey waves nearby. "A third world," said Mason.

July 7, 2 AM - Tonight we had a square dance in the courtyard under the sharp, cold stars. A comet trailed toward the horizon in the northern sky. While bears prowled at the edge of the forest & a geyser spat periodically, we danced to a score of folk-tunes. The band was guitars, a banjo, a fiddle & a caller. I had never square-danced before, & it was great! So communal - There was a really appealing girl there. Her name is Julia. She has a nice voice & a brown ponytail. I hope to see her some more, but she works over at Faithful.

201

Mason loosened his tie. He could hear Eve singing one of her favorite songs, "The Lady Is a Tramp," in the kitchen as she cooked. The hall clock struck the half-hour.

July 10, 3 AM - A new ranger has moved to our station: Dan, who found Jim on Teewinot. He is a great bear of a man, whose craggy eyebrows are as expressive as his eyes. Dan is 28, & put himself through college by spending 4 summers in a mountaintop fire lookout in Montana. He got a degree in history & did a year of law school, but came running when he was offered a ranger job; now he hasn't left this area, winter or summer, for 3 years. We talked tonight about the Park, & how I'm getting to love it despite Jim's death. He says that it's in his blood & it'll get in mine, too, especially if I see it in winter: snow halfway up the pines, geysers erupting through snow, white on white, traveling on big sleds with airplane motors on them, herds of bison & elk drinking from the springs in back of the Faithful lodge & being fed by hand, the mountains a wall of sheer white from base to peak & looking twice as high. Dan said that if I think the country makes me expand now, come in winter next year.

The telephone beside him rang with a jarring noise, breaking the spell; Dan and his ideas shot away into empty space. Mason blinked, gritted his teeth, and touched a button on the phone's base. The clatter stopped, and he did not pick up the receiver. It would be his father, of course, calling about a brief. Calling at the dinner hour, as usual, to keep him on his toes, "thinking business." Let Eve deal with him; she knew the drill. But his father could not be dismissed by a button…

…Robert Dixon clapped his son smartly on the shoulder and the younger man winced. "He's well-preserved," thought Mason as his father's remonstrance flowed over him. "Hard and handsome. Doubtless a demon on the squash court. Greying hair becomes him." Except for the hair, the two men, both wearing dark brown suits, appeared generally similar. Their solid-stock features were respectable, efficient, and dry, but the elder Dixon was slightly red in the face as he leaned over his son. Mason looked pale and almost phlegmatic by comparison as he sat still in his office chair, watching his father warily.

"…is simply not adequate," Mr. Dixon was saying. "Your commentary on this suit demonstrates little research into precedent, a tenuous grasp of the legal principles at issue here, and very little application of your fine mind. You cannot *coast* in this profession, Mason, and you're long overdue to realize it. There are other associates out there" - he gestured to the door and the rest of the plush office - "hungry to get hold of the Lyman brief and run with it!"

Mason coughed and tried to stay calm. "I'm not coasting, sir. That's my honest opinion of the case. Lyman strikes me as a crook. I've talked to Riley. Have you? He makes some strong arguments."

"Talked to Riley? George Lyman is our *client*, Mason! Are you putting your character judgments of them up against the body of the law? That's rather presumptuous, I'd say. A holdover from your days in psychology, perhaps? This is *not* an extraordinary case; the precedents are clear and ample." He hesitated microscopically. "I *know* that at your age it seems natural to revolt against historical precedents, to question and take flights of fancy, but..."

"Let's leave my tender age out of this." Mason was surprised to find himself on his feet, to feel his color rising, to hear the testiness in his voice. "No one here but you uses it against me. I just want to inject into this profession something fresh, some individual initiative, a touch of human feeling, a little imagination..."

His father straightened up, paler. "The twenties are also a time of life in which you could *imagine* yourself right out of an excellent position."

Mason couldn't resist. "I'm thirty, by the way."

Robert Dixon bit his lip, moved his mouth silently, then turned and left....

Fingering the journal, Mason smiled crookedly. "He wanted to make amends." Or perhaps *amends* was too strong. He would have been glad to find a compromise, though, to make it up. "He has more feeling for me than he would admit. But I pissed him off." I know how to do that, he thought; I'm pretty good at it. Actually I rather enjoy it.... His eyes came back to the tattered journal. "I wonder where Dan is. I hope he stayed in the park." Mason turned a few more fading pages and read where his glance fell.

July 20, 7 AM - Julia is amazing & mystical. Though she hasn't been to college & seems to care little for books, we have a chemical bond that's absolutely molecular. With little in common, we talk for hours about nothing & everything, and enjoy it immensely. She is the most instinctively - intuitively? - profound person I have ever known. This must be love! Last night we sat on the lakeshore & watched the northern lights play in fantastic white folds. We told each other all

*we could think of about ourselves until daylight. I held nothing back;
I feel clean. I want to marry her.*

Rubbing his neck, Mason grimaced. "A fine idea - for one night! I hope to God *she* stayed out there. She'd be no good here." He stopped rubbing his neck and frowned. Opening the journal further on, he bent over it again.

July 29 - As the summer wears on, I feel as if all that I value inside me - heart, soul, intelligence - is expanding, growing deeper & wider, up & out. I feel increasingly the gap between those who live in the park, & the hurried, angry, small people who pass through. I am trying to meet more of the rangers & year-round residents. In most of them, I find in some degree the sense of freedom, the love of nature, the magnitude & depth, that I find most fully in Dan.

Tight-lipped and white-faced, his body hunched defensively, Mason flipped pages until almost the end of the notebook, then paused over one of the last entries.

August 20 - Dan says that there's no one working in the park who doesn't want to be here, no one whose job was forced on him or who wants to leave & do something else. I asked about Bud! He laughed & said don't be fooled: sure, we have drifters, misfits & anti-socials, but none who would change his job here for anything else. He said that makes for sincere, worthwhile people, of a certain magnitude, & (in the main) honest. I was sceptical, but he insisted that those who don't like mountain country don't stay long. His theory is that unless your spirit can grow in proportion to the mountains, you aren't a big enough speck to constitute an existence, & you leave. (I remembered my reaction the 1st day we saw the Tetons: 'Am I up to this?') Later he talked about "the dark side": finding a wife. He believes that few women have "the spirit & the stuff" to settle down here, & warned me not to expect just any girl I fell for to be willing to try. Dan admitted that he hasn't found one yet, but says when he does "it'll be worth the wait."

Eve pushed open the big door and peered in at him. "I've called you twice for dinner, Mason. Do your ears quit at five, too?" Silence. "My

God," she blurted, "you look like you're on an island. Don't you want a light on?" Mason did not reply. "Dinner," she said flatly, and left, leaving the door open.

Again Mason's eyes fell on Winslow Homer's painting of the shipwrecked man adrift, hanging beside the door. "The sharks are circling," he intoned. Well, he *had* married the boss's daughter, hadn't he? *A* boss's daughter. Eve Montagu. Like Copley, Montagu was a name to conjure with in Massachusetts; it reeked of history. His father had done well to bring his family name into conjunction with those stars. But he himself had gone farther, had he not...sleeping with the enemy. "The dining room," said Mason, his eyes closed. "Forward, march."

In the dark-paneled, high-ceilinged dining room, his wife and son were already seated at the table. "Hi Pop," said Tommy. He was just learning to sit up at the table with the family and play the casual adult.

"Tommy," said Eve, "don't call your father 'Pop.'"

"Hi, Tom-Tom," replied Mason. He rumpled the boy's hair before dropping into the chair at the opposite end of the table from Eve.

"The chairs, Mason," said Eve quickly.

"Are chairs," he responded, and immediately wished he could recall the words. He felt absurdly surrounded. The room was dark, darker than his den, lit only by three tall white candles on the table. Eve's eyes were narrowed, her forehead creased.

"Would you say grace, please, Mason?" she asked in her flat Boston twang.

He muttered the petition, stumbling a bit over the words as they danced in the flames of a campfire on the shore of a mountain lake. He felt the cold, saw the aurora, heard a loon wail, watched firelight illumine a circle of faces as they sang. The singing grew louder, until he felt sure that his family could hear. He finished the blessing, but the music and the loon calls continued. Mason stared at his plate, slowly tracing with his fingernail the large blue *M* in its center and the elegant old pattern around its circumference. "The pull of the past," he said softly, as if continuing the grace.

"Did you want something, Mason?" Eve was watching him, holding a silver serving tray just above the tablecloth. Candlelight reflected by the tray flickered over her face, throwing fugitive patterns on her features.

"Nothing," he said aloud. "Just talking to myself, you know. *Ubi sunt?*" he asked Tommy, drawling and rolling his eyes so that the boy laughed.

Twelve: Epilogue

1 Re-entry Shock

At least the tollbooths at the South Entrance had not changed much, which came as a relief after the jarring catalogue of "progress" in Morley's letter. On the drive north from Jackson I had been bracing myself for the alterations, the *improvements* that would make me regret this venture into the past, but the neat wooden hokiness - had we known that word? - of the signs and booths and ranger cabin gave me a delicious tingle of familiarity. *Not* because that style has since been copied on rural diners and motel cabins, but something deeper and older. Every rough-hewn line was etched in my neurons; it was the pleasure of bringing together the image and its tracing. But look here: the young ranger collecting entrance fees wore sideburns and a mustache. No longer anything strange about that, of course, even in the civil service - except, for one returning after a long absence, against the backdrop of Yellowstone. There was no hair below male ears in '57, by God. "I guess things have changed a lot since I worked here."

The ranger glanced up from the cash register. "When was that, sir?" I told him and he laughed. "Well, you'll find, let's see, about half again as many people and cars. And you'll need this" - handing me a slick colored map - "to figure out the bypasses."

"*Bypasses?* In Yellowstone? Really?"

"Yep." He handed me my auto permit. "Look sharp, or you'll miss your exit off the Old Faithful Freeway."

"God!" I gasped - just the effect he wanted. "Well, Faithful was already a bit of a zoo in the 'fifties. I pumped gas at West Thumb."

"Ah, then you'll want to stop there and have a chat with the station manager. Have a good day." He chuckled and waved me on; traffic was beginning to pile up behind.

A little way past the entrance I pulled over to examine the map. The same tangy resinous scent still emanated from dense stands of conifers, a wall on each side, but otherwise it seemed a chapter of novelties. Entire new tourist areas at Grant Village and Tower Falls with service stations since my time. Automobile bypasses around Thumb, Faithful and Canyon. A network of signed hiking trails. Low-power AM transmitters broadcasting local information. Strict admonitions NOT to feed the bears. Yellowstone without "bear jams"? Maybe I *had* better ask the manager at Thumb for some orientation before pushing on to Gardiner.

As the Volvo flowed easily up the grades to the Divide, I remembered coaxing a long-departed station wagon up there, its valves clicking, having to drop a gear. The familiar postcard vista of Yellowstone Lake at the top actually surprised me a bit: I was rattled enough to feel grateful that it was still there. Then down past a series of signs for Grant Village to a glimpse of lakeshore and the turnoff to West Thumb, which I almost missed.

Away from the main road, however, Thumb had the same spooky familiarity as the South Gate, as if Time itself had taken the bypass. The homely straggle of old brown-stained buildings still overlooked the lake, and I parked near them, in the row of spaces where those blessed with wheels had done some of their courting. That custom might have survived! In the paved court before the dormitories stood a weather-beaten backboard, a netless hoop protruding from its face. Across the street "our" little mud pot, seemingly unaffected by the earthquakes that sometimes made the news, thwocked and slurped its unpredictable but catchy syncopation, like a drummer from another culture. And surely that was our old station house underneath a recent coat of peasoup paint! The lanes and pumps were laid out as before, although the two innermost lanes had been paved. With the cabins gone from the field beyond the station, however, Thumb looked more than ever like a backwater, or the hangdog employee whose raises never quite match the rate of inflation.

I walked over to the station, where an RV was being serviced by two savages. Their coveralls were different from ours: less memorable, I thought, less...*flaky*. Did we know that word back then? Inside, the ceiling of the main hut was almost entirely covered by bright, naïve, whimsical paintings, signed by whole crews of savages and dating back through several seasons. I tried to imagine Lou's reaction to that much freedom and self-expression in 1957. *Doin' their own thang, huh?* In the back room two savages were quietly inventorying stacks of tires and cases of oil. Both had long blond hair; one was a girl. Actually, I now realized, the new uniforms were not bad at all. She looked up and asked, in a forthright and slightly challenging way that reminded me of Lou, "Can I help you, sir?"

"Pretty quiet here for the 20th of August," I observed.

"Traffic just peaked," she said briskly. "Are you looking for someone?"

207

"I was hoping to have a few words with the manager."

She smiled slightly. "I am the manager."

"Aha." I leaned against the doorframe. That smartass ranger…. The other savage, a tall fellow with a shoulder-length pigtail, was watching me.

"Everything okay, sir?"

"Yeah. Yes. Just that things have changed so much. I used to work here myself."

"Oh, hey." He smiled and bobbed his head. "When was that?" A thought struck me and I asked him how old he was. He exchanged a brief glance with the girl before answering. "Nineteen."

"Whoa." I sat down on a handy bench, and when I looked up after a moment saw concern on their faces. "It was before you were born."

2 The Old Timer

Although I had mixed feelings about Ron and Sandy's suggestion (over coffee in the Ham's store) that I talk to a ranger at Faithful who was collecting stories about "early days" in the park, several developments conspired to put the idea in a different light by the time I got there. Mainly I was beginning to like the new Yellowstone. The kids at Thumb were easy and natural, and seemed more comfortable with the outdoors than we had been. There were knots of hikers conferring at the trailheads, nature talks on the radio, and *no* bear jams between Thumb and Faithful: the bears were back in the forest where they belonged. The bypass, it turned out, allowed through-traffic to skirt the hotels, so that the number of cars and tourists around the main geysers did not *seem* to have increased much, though I knew it had. The old buildings at Faithful immediately struck me as *campy:* another concept we had lacked. (I started a list of words that had been needed in 1957.) The network of concrete ramps and boardwalks encircling Old Faithful was rather hideous, but the new Visitors' Center won me over: the right building in the right place. I was standing at the information counter, skimming the Park Service newspaper, when a public notice caught my attention:

> *Visitors with anecdotes or facts about old times in Yellowstone are invited to contact Ranger Ted Simms, who is gathering materials for an historical volume about the Park.*

Then I glanced up at the clean-cut young man behind the counter; his nameplate said *Ted Simms*. This began to feel like destiny, which it is wise to accept as gracefully as possible. "How far back does 'historical' start?" I asked him. "Do the 'fifties qualify as 'old times'?"

Ted made a funny face, as if the idea - put that way - struck him as odd, too. "Well, yeah, could be, I guess." He didn't look a day over 30, and spoke with what sounded like a western twang. "What were you doing here?"

"Oh, pumping gas at Thumb and seeing the park. But the old timers I met sure had some stories you could use. People like Morley Gallatin at YPCC in Gardiner and Judge Evans up in Mammoth. Well, he died, but you know his book? Um, Bud the Comico driver, over in West? And there used to be a barber here named Jimmy who was a walking, talking archive. Don't know if he's still…"

Ted's interest appeared to grow as I spoke, and now he cut in. "Listen, maybe I should get some of this down, if you can spare a few minutes. Roger, can you take over here for a bit? I've got a contact. Would you come with me, sir?"

So I followed Ted to his office, noting the reappearance of the word "sir." And now I was a "contact"! People looked at me differently once I started talking about "my time in the park." For hours a pattern had been forming, and now it had developed to a point where I could recognize it. In a quiet way I had infiltrated the ranks of the old timers.

3 Interrogation

Ted seemed to know less about "old times" in the Park than I had expected, but perhaps he knew more than he let on. His style was laconic: mostly just nods and "Uh-huh" as I talked and he wrote. But the interview set me to examining my own motives. Driving up to Gardiner I thought so much about what had drawn me back that a couple of times I admonished myself to watch the scenery. Whenever I did, though, I saw nothing surprising: it was all so familiar that, a generation later, I hardly needed to look. Evidently this was not, then, just a return to *see* an old flame (Yellowstone had struck me initially as more odd than beautiful). A bit of nostalgia, perhaps, a sentimental journey to awaken memories of our escapades here? Was I, against my better judgment and literary advice, trying to go home again? I didn't think so, yet *something* was pulling at me. Some half-remembered verses of Wordsworth hovered at the edge of my mind:

a famous passage about special times that keep the power to nourish and repair the spirit for years afterward. My summer here must have been one of them. It wouldn't go away, but went on ramifying, assuming different guises, not least as a Muse, making me write. And now here I was, still trying to trace the echo to its source.

Above Madison Junction some elk were feeding along the Gibbon River, tails flicking white in the shadows. That too ran back along the mental pathways, was more valuable than itself. Interest on my principal! Yes, certain periods (and spaces) stand out in our lives. They may seem extraordinary at the time, or keep bobbing to the surface later, or both; may be funny or serious, or both. Call them "spots of time" or what you will, a special magic charmed or cursed them, and we keep returning to them however we may. Steering north through the meadows to Kingman Pass, I kept wondering how such times are created. What is the recipe? Why do they mean so much that we "wouldn't give anything" for them? And when do they end? Of all these questions I could answer only the last. They don't.

4   Trading Notes

Morley welcomed me cordially enough, though his manner seemed a shade less warm than his letters. He had the air of someone determined to be civil to a suspect character. Well, my articles hadn't spared the YPCC, and I had sent him an outline of the book I was planning. To them I probably looked like a scandalmonger. When the polite preliminaries were over - how well we both looked, how smart the new office was, how my trip had been - I asked if he had had a chance to look over the outline. Morley nodded and opened a thick folder on his desk. "I see you have a file on me."

"It goes back almost twenty years, to those stories of yours," he chuckled. "You can imagine how they shook up some folks around here. 'Course some of the things you came down on have changed. Still, the notion of your doing a *book* now has the worriers worried. They think it could be bad for the Corporation."

"I appreciate your candor! What do *you* think?"

"Oh, the Corporation can take it...by which I mean, take care of itself."

"Good. Any comments on what I sent you?"

Morley pursed his lips. "Well, what can you tell from an outline, really...all depends on how it's done, right? Could be funny, could be informative. Anyway, it's all water over the dam, so it shouldn't do any harm."

"Certainly hope not: don't intend any. Look, I know you must be busy. Shall we tackle the list of names?"

"Okay." He pulled from my folder several sheets of yellow legal paper written over in his neat hand. "How do you want to proceed?"

"Can we just go down the list I sent you and compare findings? We may be able to update one another."

Morley frowned. "Don't expect much from me: all I have are YPCC employment records, a few Christmas cards, things like that. Though you got me curious, and I have asked around. Can't help you with the Ham's people or the YPS, though, and that's all the ladies."

"Right, I'm checking with them, but their records seem sketchier than yours. Most of the girls can't be traced, I'm afraid. So: anything on the one I call Beatty?"

Shuffling the papers, Morley settled his specs on his nose and his rear in the swivel chair. "Nothing. Left early to attend ROTC, as per contract. Never heard of him again."

"I have a bit more. He graduated from the University of Tennessee, class of '61, and went into the army. But I can't trace him farther: my letter was returned; his parents had moved. I hope he was out before Vietnam. Sure played a sweet trumpet. Probably a good bugler too."

Morley nodded. "Can't help you with Clay, either. A late arrival, not much paper. Left on schedule. End of trail."

"We were at Debrew together for another year, so I saw more of him until he graduated in '58. He was Air Force ROTC, went to a base in the South Pacific, then to Thailand, I think. Not sure what he did: maybe intelligence. Trueblood saw him once in San Francisco; Clay said he'd "looked up" one of Cal's ex-girlfriends on Hawaii. Then his father died and Clay left the Air Force. Lost track of him for a while, then last year he checked in from New York, working as an investment banker. Married with kids."

Morley smiled. "Doing well, probably. Lou rated him very high, but said he wouldn't be interested in us." He moved his finger down the yellow page. "There's not much on 'Creeper,' as you call him. He did come back with us in '58, then disappeared. Likewise 'Cyril': no information."

"I drew a blank on Creeper, too, but found Cyril. He has science degrees from three colleges and universities, including a doctorate in radiation biology, has taught at several institutions, and now works as a radiation biologist in a Louisiana hospital. He and Will Harkness exchanged visits in West Virginia and New Jersey while Cyril was in Salem and Will was at Princeton around 1960."

"That's good to hear," said Morley. "I like it when these Yellowstone connections last beyond the Park."

"Yes - *and* I can trace them! What about Lou?"

Morley brightened. "Ah, now *him* I can talk about! Worked for us until '61, went as high as Operations Manager. Graduated from Auburn and was hired by Case Foods. Selling, of course! They moved him around to various southern and midwestern cities, but he stuck with them. An area sales manager now, lives near New Orleans. Wife and two kids, named Lee and Grant! Do you s'pose that was inspired by Mason Dixon?" His eyes twinkled. "I still hear from him almost every Christmas."

"Nobody around Thumb ever doubted that Lou would do all right. Do you know if it was Shelley that he married?"

"The girl who came out here? No…as I recall, her family was rich and in high society and didn't go for Lou - at least that was his view of it. I believe he met his wife on the job."

"It figures. Shelley was gorgeous and a real classy lady. She *looked* expensive. Anything on Gair? I have nothing."

"Ditto. I seem to remember Lou saying he was in real estate around St. Louis. Or maybe it was banking…I'm not sure. Nothing on Will Harkness, either. Seemed a very able fellow: Lou gave him high recs and wanted him for assistant manager. I wrote to him, but he wasn't interested. End of *that* trail."

"Ah, he had his sights trained elsewhere, Morley. B.A. in English from Princeton in '61, law degree from Stanford in '64, called to the bar. Served three years in the Marines, including a tour in Vietnam, and came out a Captain. Became a public defender in California, then tried journalism school for a year, but came back to law. He went into private practice and has his own firm in San Jose now. Also a wife and three kids. To my mind the most talented and interesting of our bunch."

Morley nodded. "So Lou was right about him. You seem way ahead of me on most of these." He glanced at his watch. "And now comes a string of blanks: Hayward, Henderson, Hole, Horn. You probably knew that Lou fired Hayward for theft, so he was finished with YPCC. Horn was with

212

us again in '58. We offered him a management position, but he turned it down and disappears after that."

I made a note. "All I know is that he left the reservation and went out to the coast, the Bay area, maybe to go back to school. Probably grad school: he was older. What?"

Morley had started."Left the reservation? Our address of record is in Berkeley."

"Berkeley! Well, he used to mention 'the reservation' and Chickasa, Oklahoma, but it always sounded like a joke. Maybe he was pulling our legs the whole time?"

"He could have had family there," Morley suggested. "Maybe kept a foot in each place."

Seeing that we were in Speculationland, I said, "Let's move on. I had no luck with Hayward. Henderson did start Debrew in the fall of '57: I saw him there a few times before I graduated, but we didn't keep in touch. Hole took a year off, came back and finished Debrew in 1960, then went home to Daytona Beach and worked in real estate or insurance for awhile. But I lost him: no more Christmas cards. I guess he moved."

"People still remember that climbing accident of his."

"Yes, in fact I met an older gentleman, a driver and factotum at the Jackson Lake Lodge, who recalled it clearly - even the name of the guy who was with him and died."

"Ray Jacobs. Yes, people hang onto things like that."

"They surely do. Okay, anything on LaBouche, 'The Mouth'?" Morley shook his head. "Me either. What about 'Owl Brain' then? Will thinks he became a dentist."

"Ah." Morley gave me a quick, sober glance. "I happen to be slightly acquainted with the family of your 'Owl Brain'. He completed college and dental school in California, had a private practice out there and got married. But he committed suicide several years ago."

"My God." I stopped writing. "How strange. He was so loud and brash and extroverted, and I would have said self-confident. I recall thinking that his skull looked like a death's head, but…. Could you have predicted that?"

He nodded. "They're often just the ones you need to watch. Ask Dr. Vine when you see him."

"That's a shock, Morley. Will felt that Owl improved that summer, that we had a hand in civilizing him. You don't have any other surprises of that order, do you?"

"No. In fact I have very little else, period. Nothing on 'Schlitz' or Trueblood."

"Schlitz was a dead end for me, too, but Peter and I keep in touch. His career might surprise that summer of '57 crew. After Debrew and a stint in the Navy, he did an MA in history at Colorado, then started a history PhD in Florida. Won a fellowship and lived in Chile for a year, doing research, learning Spanish. Taught college for a while in Texas, but got disillusioned with academe and abandoned his dissertation and his doctorate. He kept up his church ties, though, working for a church relief program that sends food into famine areas. Married with children."

"Interesting," said Morley, who had been listening closely. "You just can't tell *what* people will do with themselves from who they are at nineteen or twenty, can you?" He looked down at his notes. "Lou gave him good words, and recommended him for assistant manager."

I wrote that down. "Okay. How about Woo?"

Morley chuckled. "He's done better than some folks might have predicted in your time. Worked for YPCC until 1961, got to be manager at Fishing Bridge. Stockbroker for a while in North Carolina, but when he came through here with his bride a couple of years ago he had moved to California and was working for a bank, maybe Wells Fargo. I have his current address here."

"I'll want that, thanks. Finance, then: I guess pre-med didn't work out. Did he ever finish college?"

"I don't know for sure: seems likely with those jobs, though." Morley flipped through his sheets. "Ah, we've left out Bill, that fellow Lou hired on his own."

"Right. He and his wife were Debrew people. I'd been in a singing group with her, and they had Peter and me over for dinner that fall, so I've kept up with them. Bill's a lawyer on Long Island, and Jacky teaches music in a public school. She was a Ham's girl that summer. Okay, that takes care of West Thumb. What about...?"

But Morley shook his head and wagged a finger. "Whoa, you forgot the Canadian. Bastille."

"Well, he was so different I put him in a category of his own. And I didn't think you'd have anything on him."

"He may be the strangest hire I ever had. His editor in Vancouver paid half his salary so he could move around from station to station, which gave us a half-cost employee - someplace!"

"That's why he was at Thumb so seldom. Did you ever see anything he wrote about the park?"

"No, I think it was just stuff for his editor in Vancouver." Morley smiled. "That doesn't bother us."

"Ever hear from him afterwards?"

"Yes, he wrote me a thank-you letter not long after he left, from Los Angeles, thanking me for 'cutting him so much slack.' Is that a Canadian expression?"

"Oh, California, probably. It's popular with the younger generation. L.A. makes sense: he left suddenly one day with his girlfriend, who was a *chicana* from there."

"And once I had a postcard from South America, Buenos Aires, I think. He said he was traveling around, stopping to play sports and earn some money. Did you know that?"

"Yes. Paul checks in from time to time. Paquita had family in South America and wanted to do a 'roots' thing. She invited him to come along, and he did. It turned into years, and he learned Spanish and Portuguese along the way."

"Years!" exclaimed Morley, leaning forward. "And he's been able to make a living? Doing what?"

"Oh, various things. Journalism, for one: that's a portable trade! He writes for papers and magazines down there and up here. And sports: he was quite a good athlete - we saw that on Lou's basketball court. He played basketball and baseball semi-professionally in Brazil and Argentina. *And* finished his B.A. - at a military college, I think."

"Well, that's the most exotic biography I've heard yet!" laughed Morley. "Is he still down there?"

"I think he's back, either in Quebec or Vancouver. I'm hoping to see him this summer. May be getting a bit old to earn his bread from athletics! But with all the experience he's had there, I expect he'll go back. Listen, maybe we'd better finish up with the ordinary guys so I can get out of your hair. What about my list of non-Thumbies?"

Morley turned to a new page, shaking his head. "Not much. Nothing on 'Cal'."

"He graduated from Debrew with high honors. Cleve says he teaches college physics in Tennessee, but I haven't been able to confirm that."

Morley raised his eyebrows. "So you're in touch with Cleve. How's he done?"

"Oh, very well. B.S. from Debrew, three years at Oxford - as a Rhodes Scholar, I think - M.D. with medical training in some very good places. Has a private practice in Tennessee now. He was always a whiz."

Morley nodded. "You probably know he broke his contract and left early. Manager said he'd been fine until then, but not to rehire. Not that he ever asked."

"His sister was a waitress at Faithful that summer, but it was her first time away from home and she got homesick. Didn't know anybody up there. Too bad she couldn't have been closer to Cleve - or some of his friends! And there was a romance that may have gone wrong somehow. So perhaps he jumped ship to take her home sooner."

"I'm glad to know that side of it. It puts Cleve in a better light: the dutiful brother."

"Yes, belatedly, after having neglected her, some said. Though what he could have done…. By the way, he married a girl he met at Canyon that summer. They have four kids."

Morley beamed. "Another post-park connection! That's good to hear. I wonder how many savage romances manage to go on for so long."

"None that I know of. How about Marsh?"

"All I know about your 'Marsh' is that he worked here two summers, '56 and '57, and…"

"No, wait, Morley, that can't be right. He told me that '57 was his first year."

Morley tapped the sheet with an admonishing forefinger. "Our records say otherwise. And his manager described him as a 'gadabout' and a playboy."

"Marsh?!" I stared at him. "This must be mistaken identity! Anyway, I have nothing after his graduation from Debrew. Wonder if he stayed in touch with that fine waitress from Mammoth he dated…now *that* was a connection worth keeping up post-park!"

For the second time Morley checked his watch. "Tech was with us just that one summer." He smiled. "His manager said that he had only two gears, stop and reverse, but that he was lots of fun. And Virg you know about. That's it." He tossed his bulky sheaf onto the desk.

"Clay says that Tech works for his father in Atlanta because he doesn't have the push to make it on his own. And yes, I've been corresponding with Virg. I plan to stop in and see him on my way north."

216

"Virg got hooked on this country early. We stay in touch. Get him to show you his cabin in the Absorkies."

"Right, he's mentioned that. Morley, I know I've taken a lot of your time. Could we just run quickly through the few adults who were at Thumb?"

"Sure, but the only ones I can help you with are right up here." He tapped his head. "Those were mostly Ham's people, and of course I just have YPCC records. Still, some of them were friends. Gray retired to Florida in the early '60s. In fact, most of the folks you mention are in trailer parks or rest homes along the Gulf Coast or in Arizona."

"The Sun Belt."

"Right. Jack, the Ham's manager at Thumb, lives in Sun City. Bud, who drove our gas truck, left us a few years ago, to go back to Canada, I believe. There might be people over in West who'd know where he is. Otherwise...no, that's about it for your concessionaire staff."

"There was an attractive middle-aged woman, a widow or divorcee from Florida. We called her "Florida Lady," but I think her name was Elizabeth. Never heard her last name. Any knowledge of her?"

"No." Morley seemed to be looking at me narrowly - giving me the fish-eye, I might have said, had he been anyone else - but perhaps that was my imagination. "Any reason why you ask about her particularly?"

"Oh...she was very nice to me, that's all, and then I never saw her again. Life leaves some gaps that you'd like to close. Anyway...I was sorry to hear that Judge Evans died."

"Yes, a couple of years ago. But Andy was getting on in his eighties, you know, and he had cancer. There's not much doubt he was ready to go."

"He died of cancer, then?"

"No." Morley looked down, then up. "He was cleaning his rifle. You don't need to stare. The coroner looked into it. Officially it was a 'firearm-related accident'."

"Ah well, if it's official...."

"Right. We understand that these things happen. Now, you wanted to know about some rangers. 'Course you realize that I have no records on them, either."

"I know, but the rangers here either don't have or aren't willing to share personnel records from that era, and I would *hate* to have to start digging in Washington." Morley smiled at the idea. "Don't folks around here remember them?"

"Sure we remember," he chuckled, "some of them. Who could forget Ranger Simmons? Stony stayed in the Park for a few years after '57, some of that time here in Gardiner. Eventually he was transferred, I don't know where, or why. People I asked think he's still with the NPS, maybe in Washington. He'd be pretty high up by now. Now Ranger Curtis is another matter." Morley shook his head. "Folks *don't* remember him. But he's not around here any more."

"A quiet, basically decent man: I guess I expected to lose him. Maybe he quit rather than serve under Stony Simmons. What about Dan McLeod, then? He's the one I'm really interested in. Big fellow, keen botanist, played the banjo? All the Park Service can tell me is that he resigned in 1960. I've lost the trail."

"You've been looking in the wrong places." Morley broke into a wide smile. "Dan resigned to go back and finish law school. Worked up here as a seasonal ranger for awhile to pay his way, actually - the NPS ought to have known *that*. Became a lawyer, then a judge. And married a fine girl along the way. He's done real well."

"Judge McLeod! Do you know where he is now?"

Morley looked at his watch again. "Either at the courthouse in Mammoth, or at his place up in Clematis Gulch, or off flower-hunting."

"You're kidding! You're not kidding. He's *here?*"

Morley shook his head, then nodded, beaming jovially. "I've been saving this one."

"As well you might! That's my idea of good news - and the end of my list. Lists." I looked at *my* watch. "Morley, I've taken too much of your time! I'll get out of your way now. I should try to see Dan while I'm here, and Virg is expecting me tonight."

"I didn't think I'd keep you long after you heard about our new judge! But it's been interesting. Here, you'll want these." Morley pushed his sheaf of addresses and notes toward me. "You know, the 1957 savage *I* want to hear more about is Mason Dixon. All this curiosity about other people, and you've said very little about yourself. Where did *you* go, what did you do?"

"Oh, I've bounced around, Morley. I started law school, switched to a theological seminary, gave *that* up to start an ecology degree, then went off to teach in Africa."

"I see." Morley looked concerned, and seemed to choose his words carefully. "Would it be unkind, or incorrect, to describe that as a period of floundering, of drifting?"

I managed a laugh. "Well, my father would agree with you. I call it my 'searching period'. Anyway, it has a surprise ending, a twist. When I came back from Africa I finished law school, and now practice in Boston."

"I see," said Morley again, more confidently this time, and with apparent relief. "It's interesting how many of your generation - including several of your 1957 friends - go far afield, but circle back and come home in the end. Your father must be pleased."

"Well, not entirely. I didn't settle in with his firm as he wanted. Instead, I got together with some other young lawyers and set up a People's Law Firm in South Boston. Not quite what Dad had in mind! He calls it a "storefront" firm in a "rundown" neighborhood, which is technically accurate, but that's where we're needed."

Morley shook his head and chuckled ruefully. "Well, he's not the only father who's had to swallow that pill. So, and are you married?"

"No, no I'm not."

He raised his eyebrows. "Haven't found the right girl?"

"Oh, I've found her several times - hooked up with someone else!" We both laughed. "I'm not averse to the idea even now, though I'd be hard pressed to support a family on what I make at our 'storefront'. The people who most need a lawyer often can't pay him much. And here I am working on a book about Yellowstone that won't make money or enhance my professional reputation. But I must go!"

This time Morley rose. "I suppose we all do what we have to do in the end. Good luck with the book. Do you think you'll use any of what we talked about today?"

"Right now I'm not sure how, but I'll try to work it in." To my surprise he came with me down the hallway, through the main office and out the front door, which stood open to a heady mix of rangeland aromas. Beyond the parking lot, the valley of the Yellowstone, mile upon mile of sagebrush, and beyond that the rugged contours of Electric Peak, basked in the hot sunshine.

"You could put it in a sort of appendix," said Morley reflectively, getting into the authorial spirit. "Like 'Where Are They Now?' or *American Graffiti.*"

"Not a bad idea! I didn't realize you were a moviegoer."

"Oh, long winters in Livingston, you know."

When we reached the car I stopped, turned to him and extended my hand. "Thanks for everything, Morley. I'm more indebted to you for all your time and trouble than I can repay. You won't be worrying about my book, will you?"

He smiled placidly. "Oh, I generally leave the worrying to others. I think I can trust you to be fair. Just remember, 'Speak of me as I am' - not only me, but everybody. Once something is said, or written, it's hard for people to forgive and forget. So, 'Nothing extenuate, nor aught set down in malice'." He actually wagged his forefinger at me.

"Why Morley, you remember your Shakespeare!"

"People look down on small-town western educations," he mused, "but we had some dedicated teachers who loved good literature and made us memorize the best speeches - at an age when we could do it!"

"Morley, I wasn't looking down on anything! They say the miners in the gold camps knew and loved the Bard. I said 'you *remember* your Shakespeare'."

"So you did," he laughed. "And that's the trick now, I guess."

"Well, I'll take your advice," I promised, "though I also live by another famous phrase: 'The truth shall set you free'."

"That's a different truth," he said firmly.

"And so it is," I conceded as we shook hands for the last time.

*

The Mammoth courthouse had closed, and it was late afternoon by the time I found the log cabin in Clematis Gulch and knocked on the door: a tactless hour to arrive unannounced, but that was not the main reason for my nervousness. Of all the old familiarities I was renewing or trying to renew, here and in this project, *this* was the one I would have wanted to work up to with an exchange of letters, or a phone call. This way was like being dropped suddenly, after many years, with no opportunity to prepare, back into some exotic culture - Sikkim, or Senegal - where you had lived briefly as a child.

The place was very quiet, possibly empty. Maybe he was off on a botanical excursion or an errand. If so, I might have to explain myself to a stranger. That would be awkward. Dan with a family! Dan as the new Old Timer! It boggled the mind, required adjustments. I wondered if this had been Andy Evans's cabin, passed on from judge to judge. Of course they might all be out and I would make no contact. Well, then I could leave a note in the mailbox and still make it to Virg's tonight.

There was a slight noise within the house, a stirring, and the front door opened. Standing there was a young woman who took my breath away and left me stunned. A tall, straight girl with clear eyes and a brown ponytail: what memory was trying to struggle into the light? She regarded me frankly, 'with neither fear nor favor,' and said, "Hello." Except for the height she could have been....

"Julia?" I said - foolishly, for she could not have been more than sixteen or seventeen, but at the moment it was the only word I could utter, the only thought I could pursue. "It's Mason. Hole's friend?"

She smiled. "My name is Lily, but you've come to the right house."

"Glacier Lily?"

Still smiling, she turned gracefully and called, "Mother? There's a gentleman asking for you."

CPSIA information can be obtained at www.ICGtesting.com
Printed in the USA
LVOW092334171111

255479LV00001B/40/P